Something was wrong.

The store was a mess. The glass teapot, the one he had noticed the day before, was on the floor, shattered into several pieces. Beside it on the floor was a bloody handprint.

It felt like the world was collapsing around him. He glanced back at Gwen. She didn't need to see this, but he couldn't keep her from the truth…or what they could possibly find if they went into the shop.

"Gwen," he said, turning around slowly to face her.

"What's wrong?" she asked, all the playfulness that she had been exuding disappearing.

He shrugged. "I can't be sure until I look."

"What do you want me to do?"

He could make her wait in the car, but whoever was gunning for her had to be someone they both knew, someone close to them, and it was likely it was someone who could lure her out of the car… and do whatever they deemed necessary.

He couldn't risk it.

MS. CALCULATION

BY
DANICA WINTERS

First Published in Great Britain 2017
By Mills & Boon, an imprint of HarperCollins*Publishers*
1 London Bridge Street, London, SE1 9GF

© 2017 Danica Winters

ISBN 978-0-263-92916-4

46-0917

Our policy is to use papers that are natural, renewable and recyclable products and made from wood grown in sustainable forests. The logging and manufacturing processes conform to the legal environmental regulations of the country of origin.

Printed and bound in Spain
by CPI, Barcelona

Danica Winters is a multiple-award-winning, bestselling author who writes books that grip readers with their ability to drive emotion through suspense and occasionally a touch of magic. When she's not working, she can be found in the wilds of Montana, testing her patience while she tries to hone her skills at various crafts—quilting, pottery and painting are not her areas of expertise. She believes the cup is neither half-full nor half-empty, but it better be filled with wine. Visit her website at www.danicawinters.net.

To Mom
You show me what it means to be empowered.
I couldn't have done any of this without you.

Prologue

There was nothing that could make a woman go crazy more quickly or more profoundly than a man. The same went for mares and studs, and the proof was the lame horse that had brought Bianca to Dunrovin Ranch in the little town of Mystery, Montana.

The paint had her rear end backed into the corner of her stall, an instinct to protect herself from predators who, if she'd been in the wild, would have already taken advantage of her injury and moved in for the kill.

Bianca snorted slightly at how the instincts between animals and people were the same. When everything was stripped away—the names, the relationships, the social frameworks and the money—humans were nothing more than animals.

According to Mrs. Fitz, the paint mare had been in heat and had gotten into a fight with another mare when they'd turned the paint out. Normally the two mares had gotten along, their hierarchy and roles within their social group well established, but due to the proximity of a buckskin stallion, things had taken a turn for the worse and the mare had injured her foot in the fight.

Bianca wasn't sure if the animal's leg was sprained or broken; she'd have to get her hands on the horse before she'd know.

"Hey, baby," Bianca cooed as she slowly opened the stall's door and moved in closer to the mare.

The horse gave a long huff as it looked over at her. It had the wide eyes of an animal in pain and it was breathing hard. Her left front leg was swollen and angry-looking, and from the state of it, it was easy to see why Mrs. Fitz had been upset when she'd called. If a horse broke a leg, which appeared to be the case here, it sadly often ended with the animal being euthanized.

It was the worst part of her job—making the choice between life and death.

In preparation for the worst, she'd already drawn up the syringe of Beuthanasia and left it in her bag just outside the stall in an attempt to keep from spooking the animal more than necessary. Though the recommended dose was two milliliters for every ten pounds, she'd doubled it. It was always better to have too much of the powerful anesthetic—it was more humane. One little prick of a needle and a squeeze and the numbness would wrap the animal's world in a shroud of darkness.

The mare moved to paw the ground in agitation, but as she shifted her weight, she stumbled and squealed in pain. The sound made the hairs on Bianca's arms rise. She personally knew all about pain—though hers was of the emotional kind. The kind no one noticed, until they looked deep in her eyes and then—fearing what they saw would catch—they turned away.

The whites of the mare's eyes were showing, her

chest was flecked with saliva and sweat rolled down her coat. These were just more signs that what Bianca feared doing most may be just the thing she would be forced to do. She already hated herself for the choices she had made in her private life. This would only make her feel worse.

She watched the horse carefully as she approached with metered caution. A hurt animal was a dangerous thing.

"It's okay, girl," she whispered.

The mare threw her head and staggered as the motion forced her to catch her body weight on the injured leg.

"No, sweetheart, no, calm down." Bianca moved closer and gently ran her hand down the mare's leg. From touch alone, she couldn't feel a definite break.

Maybe she could save the animal after all. Some of the dread she'd been feeling drifted from her. Perhaps today, instead of taking a life, she could save one.

Bianca stood up and traced her fingers over the star on the mare's forehead. The horse's ears flicked to the right, like a finger pointing to something just over her shoulder.

Bianca turned to see what the animal was looking at. The person was small, but they moved fast.

The needle plunged into Bianca's neck. The anesthetic burned as they forced the syringe's contents into her.

Bianca's scream echoed through the stable as she grasped at the empty syringe that protruded from her skin. She fumbled with it, pulling it out and watching in horror as the needle fell onto the hay strewn at their feet.

Red boots… She recognized those horrible boots.

The darkness flooded in from all sides as the anesthetic pumped through her body.

She'd been right. More Beuthanasia *had* been better. Death came quick.

Chapter One

Everyone in law enforcement would admit the worst aspect of the job was notifying the next of kin when a loved one died. Today that job fell on Wyatt Fitzgerald's shoulders… Well, not *fell* exactly, so much as it was a weight he'd offered to bear. The fact that they were only a few weeks away from Christmas only made it that much harder.

He parked his patrol unit at the end of the Johansens' driveway, as far from the front door as possible so he would have plenty of time before he would have to face them—and his former high school girlfriend, Gwen. The last time they had spoken, almost a decade ago, she'd made it clear she hated him. What he was about to do would only make her hatred for him worse, and he wouldn't be able to hold those feelings against her.

Though it was early in December, he was surprised they hadn't started to decorate for the holidays. When he'd been younger, they'd always had the Widow Maker Ranch decked out, complete with handmade pine-bough wreaths and thousands of lights. From the look of the derelict place, with its shabby siding and in-need-of-new-shingles roof, it was like the Johansens were just waiting for someone to arrive with news like his.

This moment, his coming to the door with the news of the death of their beloved sister and daughter, would be etched in their memories forever. And he would always be remembered as the catalyst for this tragic change in their lives. Without a doubt, they would always blame him for the hurt they were about to experience. In a way, he felt almost responsible for Bianca's mysterious death.

The snow crunched under his boots as he made the long march up the driveway to the ranch house's door. Maybe he should have brought along the other officer. They'd always been taught to go in pairs. It made it easier to face what had to be done. But this time, under all the extenuating circumstances, he felt this was one journey he had to make on his own—that was, right up until the door was within his line of sight.

He would make it quick. Like a Band-Aid. One rip and it would all be over—at least for him. Then the real pain would begin for them. He cringed at the thought of how Bianca and Gwen's mother, Carla, would take the news. Ever since her husband's accident with the hay tedder at Dunrovin Ranch, she'd never been the same and she'd never forgiven his family or the crew that helped run the place. To her, everything about the accident had been Dunrovin's fault, and therefore its owners—Wyatt's parents—were to blame.

His stomach clenched as he realized this moment, his coming to the door with tragic news, was something Carla had gone through once before. Their shared past would amplify everything. He hated having to be a part of her pain once again.

He took a long breath in a failed attempt to calm his anxiety and knocked on the front door. The glass rattled as he tapped, loose thanks to the years of neglect since Mr. Johansen's death.

The last time Wyatt knocked on this door had been the night of their senior prom. If only he could go back in time to the days when his biggest worries were centered on how much playtime he would get in the Friday-night football game, and whether or not Gwen would be free to watch.

The curtain was drawn back and Carla's face appeared in the window. Her nose was red and purple and covered with the spider veins indicative of a long-term alcoholic—not that he could blame her after the life she had led. Her wind-burned skin, the mark of all serious ranchers, had more lines than he remembered and her hair had turned gray, but she still had the same dark eyes of a haunted woman.

"What the hell do you want? I'm fresh out of dough-nuts," she said through the glass, her words slowed by booze even though it was early in the day.

"Mom, seriously?"

He recognized Gwen's voice and his heart picked up pace as she stepped into view. Some feelings really didn't change over ten years, no matter how much they should have.

Unlike her mother, Gwen was even more beautiful. Her long blond hair was haloed around her face, as wild as the woman it belonged to. She looked at him and her mouth opened in surprise, her hands moved to her hair and she tried to force it to submit. Pulling it back, her blue eyes picked up the bits of the morning sun, making them glow with life. Her eyes were just like Bianca's, reminding him of the death that had brought him here.

Gwen opened the door and stood in silence for a moment as she stared at him in his full uniform. Without saying hello, she turned to her mother. "What did you do last night?"

He shifted his weight, uncomfortable that she was chastising her mother in front of him like he wasn't even there.

Carla rubbed her nose drunkenly, like she was trying to process her daughter's accusation. "I wasn't doin' nothing."

"Then why is Deputy Fitzgerald standing on our doorstep?"

So they weren't on a first-name basis anymore. Apparently she wasn't feeling the effects of nostalgia like he was. He forced his feelings down. It didn't matter what she thought of him; that wasn't why he was here.

Carla looked at him and frowned as though replaying the events of last night through her mind. As he looked at her, he couldn't help but wonder if she was still drunk from the night before, or if the alcohol on her breath was just this morning's continuation of last night's party.

"I don't think I was driving." She leaned around him, looking out into the driveway for a car that wasn't there. "Bubba drove me home. I kinda remember…"

Gwen crossed her arms over her chest as she glared

at her mother. "Are you kidding me? You don't even remember how you got home last night? This has to stop. It's only a matter of time until you're going to get into real trouble—" Her glare shifted to him as if she remembered exactly who he was. "So what did she do this time? How bad is it?"

The look on her face made him want to be standing anywhere but in her bull's-eye.

"Actually, I was here for—"

"Where's Bianca?" Carla interrupted, glancing behind her for her other daughter—a daughter who wasn't going to come.

"Mom, be quiet. Bianca will be along," Gwen said, moving between her mother and the door as if she was so embarrassed by her mother's ramblings she wanted to hide her from his view.

He cleared his throat, wishing he had loosened the top button of his uniform before he'd made his way to the door. Even his body armor felt tight, and he gave it a slight tug in an effort to dispel some of the discomfort he was aware wasn't really physical.

"Actually, I'm here about Bianca." As soon as the name fell from his lips, Gwen's scowl disappeared, replaced by a wide-eyed look of fear.

"She's upstairs," Gwen said, absently motioning toward the wooden staircase that led to the second floor of the ranch house. "Do you want me to go get her up?" There was an edge to her voice, a sharpness that came with panic.

He moved to touch her, but stopped and gripped his

hands together in front of him to keep his body and emotions under control.

"I'm afraid to tell you this, Ms. Johansen," he said, moving slightly so he could look the older woman in the face as well. "Mrs. Johansen. I'm sorry, but in the early morning hours, we found Bianca's body. She is… deceased."

He knew he should have just said *dead*, but he couldn't get the word past his lips. It was too harsh for Bianca, the veterinarian who'd been a regular at Dunrovin. He'd seen her so many times over the years, and they had a friendship based on their mutual attachment to animals—and her sister. In fact, Bianca had been kind to him, offering him tidbits about Gwen's life and her dating status, and once in a while pushing him to make his move to get her back. But he'd always brushed away Bianca's urging. He and Gwen had already had their chance—he couldn't go through that kind of heartbreak. It nearly broke him once. He couldn't risk something that raw again.

"Deceased?" Gwen said the word as though she tasted its full, bitter flavor and spat it out.

He wanted to look down at the ground, to escape that gaze of hers that made every part of him charge to life. "Yes. I'm so very sorry for your loss."

Carla stared at him and blinked, the action slow and deliberate. "No."

Gwen's hand slid down the door with a loud squeak, like nails on a chalkboard…but he knew what the sound really was—it was the sound of a heart breaking.

She collapsed on the floor, her head hitting the wood

with a thump so loud he rushed to her side to make sure she was still conscious.

"Gwen… Gwen, are you okay?" He touched her face and looked into her eyes. They were filled with tears, tears that wet his hand as they dripped over his skin and fell to the floor. There wasn't blood or a bruise where her head had hit the ground, but she wasn't okay. She wasn't going to be okay for a long time.

He stroked away her tears as she lay on the floor and cried. Her body was riddled with sobs, hard and heavy.

He wanted to tell her everything was going to be all right. That she would get through this. Yet he couldn't bring himself to lie.

Some people held the belief that time healed all pain, but he knew all too well it wasn't true. All time did was push it further from the mind, but just like a deep flesh wound, any time he brushed the area the pain was just as all-consuming and powerful as when the blow first struck. That cliché about the healing power of time was for the weak—for the ones who couldn't face the reality of a future filled with wounds that wouldn't heal.

Regardless of the state Gwen was in, he knew how strong she was. How much it took to bring her to this point. And he'd been the one to break her.

He hated himself.

"Shh…" he said, trying to calm her and help her in the only way he knew how.

Carla opened the door wider and stepped by him and out into the crisp morning air. "Not again…"

Gwen looked at her mother and, moving his hand aside, she rubbed the tears from her face and took a series of long breaths. "I'm fine… I'm fine…" she said, as though she was trying to convince herself. She sat up and smoothed back her hair.

Wyatt stepped out of her way and tried to ignore his feelings of rejection at her pushing him away. "Currently, Bianca's body is at the crime lab. As her death was unattended, she will need to undergo an autopsy in order for us to generate a full report."

Carla hugged herself as she rocked back and forth. Gwen stood up, and, brushing off her red plaid nightgown, she stepped to her mother's side and wrapped her arm around Carla's shoulders. "It's okay, Mom. It'll be okay."

At least one of them had the strength to feed Carla the lines she needed to hear.

Gwen looked at him, her eyes red and thick with restrained tears. "A full report? What does that mean? You don't know how she died?"

He shook his head. "The coroner was unable to make a determination as to the cause of death. It will need to be fully investigated by the medical examiner."

She frowned and her gaze flicked to the right as though she was remembering something. She opened her mouth to speak, but stopped, and then after a moment started again. "Where did you find her?"

The discomfort he had been feeling amplified. "She was found in the stables of the Dunrovin Ranch."

"Your family's place? Again?" Gwen asked, like she was calling him out for somehow being party to her sister's death.

He nodded, guilt rising in him as her poorly veiled

accusation struck. "One of my mother's mares had come up lame. Last night, Bianca came to assess the animal and determine a course of treatment. We found Bianca's body at about 1:00 a.m. From our estimates she had been dead for at least an hour."

"No one found her until then?" Gwen's voice rang with disgust. "How is that possible? You have more hands and staff than most working ranches. Someone had to have found her before then."

He heard the slam at the fact that his family's place was merely a guest ranch and not a working cattle ranch like theirs. Her words were flecked with pain, anger and denial—whatever she said now couldn't be held against her.

"I don't know the ranch's current schedule. I've been out of that world, or at least a casual bystander, ever since I went to work for the department." He realized he was answering her and defending himself against her allegations when all he should have been doing was being compassionate and taking the verbal hits she chose to let fly.

"You're a bastard," Carla spat out. "You and your dang family. You're a scourge on the valley. You are the reason…you're the reason my daughter's gone. And now you tell me you don't know how she died. You're about as good at police work as your family is at ranching."

Gwen sucked in an audible breath at the sting of her mother's lashes. "Mother, stop." She let go of her mother's shoulders, repulsed.

Carla pointed at him with an unsteady finger. "You can't tell me I'm wrong. He is doing a piss-poor job.

How dare he come here without answers. If he was a real cop, he'd be able to tell us what we need to know. He'd be able to tell us about Bianca."

It was as though her mother's words had pulled Gwen back from the platform of anger she'd been standing on a moment before, a platform that had been targeted at him.

She looked at him with a mix of pity and pain. "Don't say that, Mom. Just go inside. Go to bed and sleep off the booze."

Carla shook her head, but staggered inside and toward her bedroom at the back of the house.

Gwen leaned against the porch's white railing. "Did she commit suicide?" she asked, the question coming out of nowhere…almost as though she knew something he didn't.

"Right now we believe that may be so, but we are unsure as to the cause of death—we'll have to wait on the results of her autopsy. But may I ask if you believe Bianca had motive to kill herself?" he asked, wondering if Gwen knew something that would help him make sense of Bianca's death.

She shrugged. "Vets have high rates of suicide—more than a lot of other professions." She said it like it was just another fact from a book she read and had nothing to do with her reality.

"Was she having some mental health issues? Issues you believe would have led to her taking her own life?"

Gwen sighed. "She's been unhappy, and with the holidays coming up… But I don't think she'd have the power to do something like that. She wouldn't." She shook her head, like she could shake the idea from her mind.

But now the cat was out of the bag and there was no going back. His investigation had just moved from what some had assumed was a natural death to something else entirely. Why would a woman like Bianca, who had a family who loved her and a mother who clearly needed her, be that unhappy—was it her mother's drinking, or something more? What had been going on in her life?

His gut twisted with a nagging feeling that everything wasn't as it seemed—and that his life, as well as Gwen's, was about to get turned upside down.

Chapter Two

She couldn't even look Wyatt in the eyes. Why did *he* have to be involved with the investigation of her sister's death? There had to be at least a dozen other guys on the force who could have stepped in on this one—at least to notify Gwen and her mother of the death. Yet, there he stood…with his broad shoulders, honey-colored skin, scruffy jaw and those cheekbones, all of which often found their way into her dreams. It only made the news worse.

Regardless of what he said, there was no way Bianca could be dead. Gwen had just seen her yesterday at the dinner table. They'd had grilled steaks and Bianca had cooked the potatoes—if Gwen looked, she was sure the knife Bianca had touched was probably still sitting unwashed in the sink. How could it be possible that the woman she'd talked to, and shared a bottle of wine with, was gone this morning? No.

She dabbed her eyes. It wasn't real. A fresh tear twisted down her cheek.

It was stupid, but as she cried, she couldn't handle the thought that Wyatt had seen her turn into a blubbering mess. When he saw her after the last time, she was supposed to be at her best—maybe down a size or two, hair perfectly colored and flung in symmetrical curls over her shoulders like one of those models from the pages of *Country Living*. But no…he had to break her heart—though admittedly, the last time she'd seen him, she may have been the one doing the breaking.

Was that why he had agreed to take on the assignment of telling them about Bianca's death? She wiped the rest of the wetness from her face and stomped down the steps of the porch and into the driveway.

She just needed fresh air—anything to pull her into a different reality, where none of this was really happening.

"Gwen?" Wyatt called after her.

She stopped but she didn't turn around. She couldn't look at him and his ridiculously sexy features. Not right now. Right now she'd like to look at anything but him… the oh-so-confusing him.

"What, Wyatt? What do you want? You gave me the news you came here to give. Now I've got to go to work. This ranch and the cows on it are all we have— if I don't turn a profit this year, it's over." Her knees felt weak, but she refused to let herself to succumb to the feeling. She had to be strong. She had to fake it… at least until he was gone, and then she could turn into a big mess for as long as she needed.

If there was any silver lining to what was happening, it was that her mother had drunk enough whiskey to pass out for at least the rest of the day. The last thing she needed was to have to deal with that train wreck before she had everything figured out—she could only handle one major catastrophe at a time.

"Don't run off, Gwen. I need to ask you a few more questions." He rushed to walk by her side, so she sped up.

"Ask away, but you're going to have to walk because I've got to feed the horses." She motioned toward the red barn that sat in the distance.

"In your nightgown?" he asked, motioning toward the red plaid thing she'd forgotten she was wearing. "And you do know you're wearing slippers, right?"

She stopped and spun to face him, but carefully pulled her nightgown over her moccasins. He was wearing a stupid, charming grin—a grin she wanted to slap right off his face. How dare he, at a time like this?

"What do you want to know?" As she thought about the things he'd want to ask—Bianca's favorite restaurant, where she'd liked to spend her time, her love life—she choked up and had to take a long breath. She couldn't cry again.

He reached up, so slowly that she watched his motion and thought about moving out of the radius of his touch, but she stayed put. He took her shoulder gently and stroked her arm with his thumb. It made her think of her favorite mare, Dancer. The mustang was fifteen, yet anytime she was stressed or acting out, all Gwen had to do to calm her was rub her hands down her flanks and make those same circles with her thumbs.

No matter how much Wyatt might have liked her to be, she wasn't a damned horse that would turn soft under his touch and bend to his wants. He should have known better. It hadn't worked in the two years they had dated in high school either. In fact, it only infuriated her.

She pulled away from his touch. The place his hand had been chilled and she covered it with her own hand, trapping some of the leftover heat.

"Gwen, it's okay to be upset about this. If you want, I can take care of the livestock. Why don't you go inside and lie down? I can come back and talk to you another time if you'd like."

Some of her anger at the world slipped with the kindness in his voice. He wasn't here to hurt her. He was here to do his job. And maybe, just maybe, he was here because he was still her friend and he could look past how she had treated him when they were younger—not that it had been unjustified, her anger toward him, but she should have been kinder. His heart had been just as much on the line as her own.

She ran her hand down her nightgown and started to move back toward the house. Maybe she should lie down, take a break, have a cup of coffee and collect her thoughts. She thought about sending him away, but it made her heart shift in her chest.

"The last thing I want is to be alone right now." She was surprised by her blunt honesty. It was unlike her, but, then again, nothing about this morning was in the realm of normal. "If you don't have anywhere else to be, maybe you can wait while I get dressed and then take care of the animals. Then we can head up to Bianca's cabin."

Wyatt frowned. "She had a cabin?"

Gwen sighed as she walked back into the house and

motioned to her mother's bedroom door as a loud snore escaped from under the door. "We each adopted one of the hands' cabins at the edge of the property. Having a place of your own comes in handy when *she* gets a little too out of hand."

"How often does that kind of thing happen?" His face twisted with concern but not judgment, and it softened some of the hard edges of her feelings toward him.

Most of the time, when people talked to her about her mother's problem, it was with a mixture of pity and judgment. Then again, few people wanted to bring it up. It was like the worst-kept secret of Mystery, Montana, that her mother and her family were one hot mess. In fact, it would probably be only a matter of time before the news of her sister's death would hit the airwaves. She would know as soon as it did because within the hour casseroles would start showing up on their doorstep.

She looked toward her mother's bedroom. At least it was unlikely Carla would get up to answer the door in the condition she was in. Gwen glanced up at the clock. On days like this, when her mother had been drinking all night, Carla normally wouldn't get up until it was time to go to the bar again. Tonight, she'd probably be in hog heaven—getting free drinks from the other lushes and lechers who frequented the bar, all in honor of her daughter's death.

Hate reverberated through her—but the hate wasn't just for her mother, or their situation, or even her sister's death. It was hate for everything.

Her life was such a disaster. And there was nothing

she could do about it. No way to control all the emotions that flooded through her. All she could do was
feel. She glanced back at Wyatt, staring at him for a
moment too long.

"Do you want me to get you something?" he asked,
motioning toward her upstairs bedroom. "You can just
sit down. I'll grab your gear." His face turned slightly
red, as though he'd suddenly realized that "gear" may
involve her panties.

She shook her head and walked to the stairs, his embarrassment pulling her back to reality. "I'll be right
back."

When she reached her room, it took all her strength
not to collapse onto the bed and bury her face into the
pillows and scream—yell at the world, tell it of her
hate, tell it of her pain, tell it about the injustices that
filled her life.

BEING ALONE IN the Johansens' house felt surreal, like
somehow he was reliving moments of his past—moments he had fought hard to forget. He walked to the
fireplace and looked at the collection of pictures that
rested on the mantel. All were covered with a thick
layer of dust, forgotten or perhaps intentionally ignored
by the women of the house. He rubbed the dust off the
closest one. The picture was of a man, whom he recognized as Mr. Johansen, wearing a Hypercolor shirt and
drinking a Miller Lite beside a small, white, inflatable
kiddie pool. A young blonde girl was splashing water
and laughing. The man wasn't smiling, rather he was
looking off into the distance as a cigarette trembled on

his lip, almost as if he were looking into a future where only tragedy waited.

Carla's snoring sounded from the other room, reminding him of why he'd always hated coming into this house.

He glanced at all the other pictures. None were from any time within the last fifteen years. It was like life had stopped the moment that Mr. Johansen died. He could only imagine what would happen to their lives now that Bianca was gone as well.

Wyatt had to get out. He couldn't let himself get sucked back into this world. Not when it was clear that Gwen could barely tolerate him. He couldn't carry her through this like he used to carry her through the nights her mother had left her alone when Gwen was younger. He couldn't save her—he'd already tried.

He rushed outside to the barn. Horses he could understand. Women, on the other hand… Women were an entirely different issue.

One of the barn cats sauntered over to him as he made his way inside. It wrapped itself around his legs, rubbing against him. He picked it up and scratched under its chin as it purred and kneaded the front of his shirt. As he stood there stroking the long gray hair of the cat, he glanced up at the hayloft. They had spent so many hours up there, just him and Gwen. They had been able to talk for hours; it had always seemed like they would never run out of things to discuss. They'd had this wonderful bond with each other that, no matter how many women he'd dated since, he was never able to re-create. Maybe it was the one thing he missed most about her—their deep bond, so strong that he could feel it even when no words were spoken.

Putting the cat down, he moved over to the bales of hay. He pulled off flakes and dropped them into the stalls for each of the horses. Though it was cold, in an effort to keep the hay from digging into his uniform, he stripped off his uniform shirt and his ballistics vest, leaving only his tank top. It felt good, the chill of the winter air, the scratching of the hay against his arms and the smell of horses on his skin.

He wasn't involved with the business of his family's ranch enough anymore to really help in the everyday comings and goings, and sometimes, when he caught a whiff of fresh hay or the heady fragrance of sweet oats, he missed being more available.

There was a thin cough, and he turned around. Gwen stood in the barn's doorway, looking at him in a way that made him wonder if it was attraction or revulsion. He moved to grab his shirt and vest, but she stopped him with a wave of the hand.

"It's fine. Just be comfortable. There's not going to be anyone up at the cabin who's going to care if you're wearing your uniform. At least not since…" She trailed off, as though she couldn't bring herself to talk about Bianca.

He grabbed his shirt and slipped it over his tank top anyway. It felt strange to be standing in front of her even semi undressed. In all their time together, they hadn't taken things to a deeply physical level.

He stared at her for a moment, wondering if she was still the same girl he had known before, or if she had given up on her quest to wait until marriage. He'd always appreciated, or at least respected, the effort it took to restrict oneself from pleasures of the flesh, but it wasn't a dogma that he had been able to follow.

She looked disappointed when he put on the shirt—or was she relieved? It would have been so much easier if he could just read minds.

The drive to the cabin was short, but the entire time he had been glancing over at her, wondering what she was thinking and trying to hold back from asking her the million questions running through his mind. Most were stupid, insipid… Whether or not she liked her job at the ranch, what it was like to still be living with her mother or, for that matter, why she was still choosing to live with Carla. No matter if Gwen stayed or went, her mother would continue her self-destructive behavior. It was only a matter of time…

He pulled to a stop in front of the cabin that Gwen had directed them to. There was a small chicken coop outside it, and there was a bevy of hens clucking inside, waiting to be fed.

Gwen nearly jumped out of the patrol unit and ran to the chickens. She grabbed the bucket out of the galvanized can beside the coop and poured the cracked corn into the trough. The hens came running in a flurry of feathers and clucks.

He stood and watched her, taking in the sight of her body flexing as she moved around the coop. She seemed nervous, but he could have her all wrong. Most people he could read at a glance. The ability to tell whether someone was lying, hiding something or telling the truth came with the job. Yet he didn't have the same innate gift when it came to Gwen. She was his enigma.

"I'm going to go inside. Feel free to take your time out here, okay?" he asked.

"Yeah. That's fine. I'll be out here if you need me." She didn't bother to look back at him, fully consumed with opening the henhouse to collect this morning's eggs. This late in the year, without a light in the henhouse, they both knew that there wouldn't be many, if any, eggs, but he didn't say anything.

He walked to the front of the cabin. Its walls were made of the aged, gray logs like those from the pioneering days when the town had been founded. The wooden door sat crooked in the frame, listing like Bianca's drunk mother. For a moment, he wondered if Bianca had left it like that on purpose as a reminder of what she had to move past in order to live her own life.

He pushed the door open. His breath caught in his throat. Papers were strewn around the room, every drawer was open and the couch cushions had been thrown from their places, one precariously close to the woodstove. Either Bianca was the kind who never cleaned, or someone had turned the place over.

In an effort to avoid causing Gwen any more emotional trauma, he walked inside and closed the door. He pulled out his camera and clicked a few pictures. It was odd how, in just a few short hours, his assignment had led him from thinking this was a natural death to a possible suicide to now something much more sinister.

He couldn't say if Bianca's death was a murder. Nothing about Bianca's body or presentation at the scene had pointed toward a struggle or malevolent act, but his instincts told him to push the investigation deeper.

Unfortunately, he was leaving in a few days for a prisoner transfer in Alaska. If he followed his instincts, he could be wrapped up in this investigation for weeks—and he had been wrong before. Just a year ago, he'd wasted time investigating a case similar to this. Maybe it had been his bravado, or his need to follow every lead, but he'd spent two weeks tracking down every thread just to find out from the medical examiner that their victim had died of a methadone overdose. The guy had been seeking euphoria—and all he'd found was the grave.

Wyatt walked through the cabin, careful not to disturb things in case he needed to call in his team of investigators—and what a team it was, two of the least-trained CSI guys anyone had ever met. In fact, he wasn't sure if Lyle and Steve had ever gone to college, or if their certification had come from some online university where they never had to actually set foot on a crime scene to graduate.

There was a squeak from behind him. Gwen stood there, her hands over her mouth as she stared at the mess of papers, clothes and overturned chairs.

"Do you know who would have done this?" he asked, staring at her.

Her eyes were wide and she dropped her balled fists to her sides. She glanced at him and shook her head.

He'd been wrong about Gwen. He'd thought he couldn't read her. Yet when she looked at him, he could see she was lying.

Chapter Three

They'd gone through everything. Or at least it felt like it. Gwen closed her sister's dresser drawer with a thump.

"Anything?" Wyatt asked, motioning toward the drawer that had been filled with her sister's bras.

From an objective point of view, it struck her as a bit funny and maybe a touch endearing that Wyatt, the type-A man who seemed most at home in his squad car, was squeamish about riffling through her sister's underwear drawer. In high school he had seen just about every pair of panties that Gwen had owned, though things had always stopped there.

She glanced over at him. He had been good-looking back in the day, but he was nothing then compared to the man he had become—the man she had just watched throwing bales of hay around like they were pillows rather than seventy-five pounds of dead weight. If things had been different, if she could have ignored the pull of reality, she could have stood there all day and watched him sweat.

He brushed past her, leaving the room, and he still carried the sweet scent of hay, horses and leather. The heady aroma made her lift her head as she drew in a long whiff of the man she had once loved.

It wasn't that she hadn't been in relationships, it had only been a few months—wait, a year—since her last thing. It hadn't quite been a Facebook-official relationship. No, it had been more of a burger-and-a-beer/Netflix-and-chill kind of thing. No real feelings beyond lust and the occasional need for a back rub. It had been great until he had suddenly disappeared, and two months later she had seen the guy's engagement to another woman splashed across their tiny paper, the *Mystery Daily*.

The news hadn't hurt so much as caused her the emotional whiplash that came with being so quickly replaced. A month after the engagement announcement, she still hadn't gotten an invite to the wedding that nearly the entire population of the small town had received. She had always resigned herself to the belief that everyone knew everyone's business in Mystery—yet a few had still asked her why she hadn't gone and she had been forced to tactfully remove herself from the conversation.

"You okay?" Wyatt surprised her as he touched her shoulder ever so lightly.

How long had he been standing there?

She nodded, thankful he'd pulled her from her thoughts. "What do you think they were looking for in here?" She motioned around her sister's cabin.

"First, we don't know if this was a *they* kind of situation. Maybe your sister did this. There's no proof that her death was anything unnatural, or more than a—"

Suicide.

He didn't need to finish the sentence to inflict the pain that came with the word.

"My sister wouldn't kill herself. You knew her. You saw her almost every week. Do you really think that she could do something like that—or like this?" She waved at the strewn couch cushions. "No one turns over their own place."

He looked away, but she could see in the way his eyes darkened that he was already thinking the same thing.

The desk where her sister's laptop normally sat was conspicuously empty. But the printer was still there, and there was a wastebasket on the ground, its contents strewn across the floor like everything else in the cabin. She pulled away from Wyatt's touch and picked up one of the balled-up pieces of paper. Uncurling the wad, she found an email. It was dated November 27—one week earlier. She didn't recognize the email address or the long bits of code that her sister included in the printout. It looked like it had been pulled from the printer before it was done, and long dabs of ink were smudged down the paper's length.

"What's that?" Wyatt asked, sidestepping her as though he was trying his best not to touch her again.

"I dunno… It looks odd, though," she said, flipping the page so he could see.

It was probably nothing. She crumpled the paper in her hands and, picking up the garbage can, dropped it in. Maybe she was looking too hard and trying to see things that were not really there—she glanced at Wyatt—especially when it came to him.

He bent down and picked up another of the papers. He sucked in a breath as he looked over the page.

"What is it?"

He held the paper and didn't move, almost as though if he stood still she wouldn't have asked the question.

She stepped closer and looked over his shoulder.

The email was almost identical to the one she had picked up, but instead of black smudges of ink, the message was there in its entirety:

RUN AND LIVE.
STAY AND DIE.
CHOICE IS YOURS.

Why hadn't Bianca told anyone about the threat? And why, oh, why, had she chosen to stay?

HE SENT A picture of the email to the head of the IT department, Max, along with a promise that if Max got back to Wyatt within a day, Wyatt would personally take him on a ride-along. He hated ride-alongs, especially when it entailed taking a person who would ask more questions than a kid on Mountain Dew. Yet without a doubt, it would expedite the process—and he needed answers as soon as possible.

He was having one heck of a time focusing on anything other than the way he wanted to take Gwen into his arms and hold her. She looked so broken. Every time she stopped moving, she zoned out, almost as though she couldn't find the strength to start moving again.

He knew the feeling all too well. It was why he never

stopped—the moment you started bringing up the pain was the moment the world collapsed around you. In his line of work, it was best to just bury the past…along with anything else that kept him up at night. Bianca's death was definitely going to fall in that category.

Bianca had looked nearly pristine when he'd arrived on scene. Her hair was pulled back into her signature ponytail and her scrubs were still clean, like she'd just pulled them out of the dryer before she had come out to the ranch.

His heart sank at the thought of the ranch. No wonder Gwen was so lost. She had so many reasons to be angry. So many people she could point a finger at, and no one more than him. Even in the event of Bianca's death he could be held responsible—at least tangentially. He had likely been home, resting comfortably after a long day on shift. If he'd been more involved in the comings and goings of Dunrovin, if he had agreed to feed the horses, or been around at all, maybe she would still be alive. Not that Gwen knew that—but her being unaware didn't relieve any of his guilt.

Gwen was doing it again, staring at the floor like it was the exact spot where Bianca had been found. His hands twitched with the need to feel her in them.

"Let's go. I'll run you back home."

She jerked as though she had forgotten where they were.

He took care to lock the door to the cabin to stop anyone from coming back in, and then he held her hand on the way back to the car. Her fingers were limp in his. She was a ghost of what she used to be—strong and hot, as wild and free as the Montana mountains and wilderness that surrounded them. He wished he could pull her from her stupor, pull her back to the land of the living instead of falling deeper into the pit of the despondent.

It wasn't long before they were bumping down the Widow Maker Ranch's long, snowy driveway, laden with potholes and ruts left over from hard use in summer and fall. As Wyatt twisted and turned, trying to avoid the worst of the bumps and the largest snowdrifts, he was reminded of how life was just like a road—full of obstacles and dangers.

Something hit the car and he tapped on the brakes as he tried to identify the source of the sound. There was another thump and he pulled to a stop.

"What was that?" Gwen asked, looking around.

Pastures lined both sides of the drive, grasses so tall that even in the snow it looked like they were in a sea of brown reeds—making it nearly impossible to see who or what could have been responsible for the sound.

"Stay inside," he said as he stepped out of the car.

He walked to the front of the patrol unit. On its fender were the scattered, oozing remnants of two eggs. He turned just in time to see Carla holding a carton and pulling her arm back to take aim.

"Stop, Carla!" he ordered, his voice hard-edged and full of authority.

The egg flew through the air, missing him by just a few inches and smacking against the car's windshield.

Gwen stepped out of the car and slammed the door. "Mother, what in the hell do you think you're doing?"

Her mother smeared her forearm under her nose and

dropped the carton of eggs, its contents rolling on the ground at her feet. "He's a bastard…" She motioned to Wyatt as though he couldn't hear her. "It's his damned fault." She reached behind her back.

His fine-tuned senses kicked into full gear. "Hands where I can see them!" he yelled.

Carla laughed, her sound high and malicious. "You don't get to order me around. I've known you since you were born. You loved my daughter. You knew Jimmy. Yet you did nothing…nothing to protect my Bianca. You let your family's demons take her."

There were any number of demons she could have been talking about when it came to his family, but in this moment it didn't matter—all that mattered was what she was holding behind her back and what she planned on doing with it.

"Put your hands where I can see them." He slowly reached down for the Taser on his utility belt.

The last thing he wanted to do was to tase Gwen's mother. Things were already tense enough, but no matter what his feelings toward Gwen and her family were, his job and their safety came first.

"I don't want to hurt you… I don't…" Carla said as she moved toward him, her motions jerky as though her body and her mind were in disagreement. "But you and your family… You all keep ruining my life. You want to take everything from me."

"We didn't take anything from you." He knew he shouldn't argue with the grief-crazed woman, but he couldn't hear her drag his family through the mud anymore. She needed to be pulled back to reality.

She dropped her hand to her side. In her grip was a snub-nosed revolver.

Either she was going to shoot him or herself—either way, he couldn't allow her to keep that gun in her possession.

"Drop the gun, Carla," he said.

She looked at him, and a tear slipped down her cheek. As the wind kicked up, he could smell the strong scent of whiskey wafting from her—even stronger than before.

She shook her head, the action slow and deliberate.

"Mother. No. Don't do this," Gwen said. "You can't play at this. Not again. Wyatt is a deputy. He has every right to shoot you if you lift that gun. Drop. It. Now."

Not again? Was Carla's threat something she did on a regular basis?

He thought his family had the corner on putting the *fun* in dysfunctional.

Gwen stepped around the car and moved toward her mother.

"No," he ordered, putting his arm out and trying to stop her without actually losing sight of the gun. "Stay back, Gwen." He tried to hedge his tone between the hard edge of work and the softness of the feelings he still carried for her, but it came out much sharper than he intended.

Gwen looked at him like he had struck her.

He chastised himself, he'd screwed that all up, but now wasn't the time to fully explain himself. "I don't want her to hurt you."

"She's my mother," she spat out. "She's not dangerous. Really. You need to trust me."

He felt the slice of her words as she cut away at his flaw—trust had never been his strong suit and she knew it. Why did she have to call him out at a time like this?

If something happened, if Carla pulled that trigger, he would have to answer to those above him. They would never understand if he went against procedure— even for a woman he used to know and her daughter, whom he wanted to get to know again.

"Your mother or not, Gwen, she can't do this." He raised his Taser. "This is the last time I ask, Carla," he said, moving into range. "If you don't put the gun down, I will be forced to tase you. Your choice."

Carla lifted the gun.

"Wyatt, no!" Gwen yelled.

He pulled the trigger.

Carla hit the ground, convulsing as the electricity pulsed through her.

He ran to her side and kicked the gun from her hand before picking it up and opening the cylinder to look for rounds. The gun was empty.

Chapter Four

The next morning, Wyatt puttered around his trailer on the edge of the Dunrovin Ranch. Sleep had been elusive, and as he waited for the coffee to fill his cup, his mind wandered to Gwen and Carla. He shouldn't have taken Carla down. Then again, what choice had she given him? He'd warned her—repeatedly. Did she think he was bluffing? That he wouldn't pull the trigger?

If he was good at anything it was falling back onto his training—and he was a better officer for it, though it didn't always make him a better person. There was a certain safety and comfort that came with being in-flexible.

He couldn't be like Gwen—she seemed to have her emotions and well-being dictated by the people in her life all the time. For as long as he had known her, she had been living her life in accordance with her moth-er's ever-changing needs. In a way, he pitied her for her role as caregiver. No wonder she hadn't wanted to be in a major relationship when they were younger—her life was already overtaken by the emotional needs of her mother. Were things any different now, or was she still emotionally unavailable?

He grabbed his coffee, slipped on his utility belt and moved toward the front door. Work waited. He needed to figure out exactly what happened to Bianca before things could get any more confusing with Gwen.

His phone pinged with an email. It was IT. He sipped the hot black coffee as he opened the message.

Fitz—

Took a look at the printout of the email you sent me. Looks like it was originally sent from a computer at the Mystery County Public Library from a one-use email account. Hope that helps. Let me know if you got any more questions.

Can't wait for the ride-along. Next week?

—Max

That was one ride-along that wouldn't really be worth it. Max was a great guy, but the information he'd sent was nearly useless. The only thing Wyatt could pull from it was that whoever had made the threat was probably a local.

The library was completely outdated; its desktop computers were still the same ones used during the advent of dial-up. No one went there to use the computers. The beasts were so slow that most people avoided them. Maybe he could run with that—the librarians might remember someone who had used them to send Bianca the threatening email. If everything went smoothly, he could get to the bottom of the email by the end of the day, Gwen could once again move to the back of his mind and things could return to his habitual, inflexible normal.

He opened the door.

Leaning against the fence was Gwen. Her long blond hair was pulled back into a ponytail as high and tight as her expression. She was looking out into the field, watching as two of his mother's mares nibbled at the bits of grass sticking out of the snow.

"How long have you been out here?"

She turned slightly to face him, but she didn't greet him with a smile. "Long enough to know that you slept in."

He glanced down at his phone. It was 8:00 a.m. Most ranchers were up at five in order to get the daily chores taken care of. When he'd been working on the ranch in high school he'd followed that schedule, but now that he was on his own, he rarely forced himself to get out of bed that early. Yet Gwen undoubtedly still thought he was the kid he had once been— what would he have to do to prove that he'd changed?

"Long night," he said, but the moment he said it, he wished he hadn't brought it up. The last thing he wanted to do was talk about why and who had kept him awake—or the guilt he felt about his action with Carla. Nothing good would come of bringing up the events of yesterday.

Gwen lifted her chin, but thankfully didn't say anything.

Maybe she didn't want to talk about it either.

He was tempted to apologize, but he couldn't say he

was sorry for doing what had to be done, and he didn't want to start a fight, so he just kept his mouth shut. He clicked the door shut behind him and made his way out to her. He leaned against the fence beside her.

She smelled like a fresh shower and the sweet fragrance of roses. It was the same shampoo she had been using since they were young, and the smell made him remember the nights they had spent making out in the bed of his truck. He'd loved those nights under the stars, flirting with the boundaries of their relationship. His fingers twitched as he recalled running them up the soft skin of her belly, his touch only to be trailed with his languishing, hungry kiss. He'd wanted to make love to her so badly.

He moved, readjusting his body, which was responding to his memories. That was all they were—memories. They were as the seasons, the heat of summer all too soon replaced by the chill of the fall.

She stepped away from him, reached down and scooped a bit of the snow together, balling it. She laughed as she pitched it at him. Most of it disintegrated in the air before a tiny bit splattered on his jacket.

"Hey, now, what was that?" he asked with a laugh. He reached down and made a snowball and gently lofted it toward her.

She ducked with a laugh and it breezed past her. "Missed me," she teased, sticking her tongue out at him.

It reminded him of when they were younger, full of life and joy. It was as if they were innocent again, and it made him long for what they had once been.

She wiped the bits of snow off her hands. "I stopped

by hoping you would show me where you found Bianca." Her voice was tinged with sadness, and it made him wish she would just go back to throwing snowballs.

He glanced in the direction of the main house that, from where they were standing, was completely out of view thanks to a large stand of cottonwoods. The barns were behind the house, but he could have drawn them in complete detail from memory, down to the tiny carving in the hayloft of *W+G 4Ever* he'd cut into the soft wood when they were kids.

"There's nothing there. It wasn't much of a crime scene."

"You didn't think it was a murder either, remember?"

Ouch. He thought about arguing with her about what exactly he was and wasn't allowed to do with his investigations, and what he'd been presented with on scene, but he bit his tongue. Apparently she was still in the anger stage of her grief. Next came depression, at least for most people, but knowing Gwen as well as he did, he doubted that she would let him see her like that again.

He rubbed his fingers together as he recalled brushing her tears from her cheeks when she'd collapsed on the floor. It probably wasn't normal for him to feel this way, but he appreciated that moment of weakness when he'd told her about Bianca's death. For once, he'd gotten a real reaction—a response not muted by her strength or her desire to veil the truth. Getting to have the real her was another thing he missed about their dating.

It was a rare thing in this world to know the essence of a person—especially in a small town where everyone feared the jaw-jacking of the neighbors. Any little thing could be a full-blown phone-tree emergency. It was like living in a game of telephone. What may have started out as something innocent enough would be a prison-worthy offense in under twenty-four hours—and that fear kept everything muted, even emotions.

It was maybe the thing he hated the most about living in a small town.

He pushed off the fence and walked toward his patrol unit. Gwen had parked her father's old beat-up Ford in front of his one-car garage.

She followed close behind him. "Are you going to take me over there? Or do I just need to go and figure it out?"

Yep, definitely still in the anger phase.

"In the car," he said, answering her with the same level of shortness.

It wasn't really a distance worth driving, but he immersed himself in the silence between them—letting it remind him of exactly all the reasons he should cap any of his nostalgic feelings for the girl he'd once known. The Gwen beside him, while she had many of the old habits he had once loved her for, was not the same.

He would give almost anything to see that smile he'd fallen in love with, the one he'd caught a glimpse of when she pitched the snowball at him. He'd always remember that girl.

He parked in front of the stables. A little girl was standing by the front door; her hands were red from the cold but she still had her thumb planted in her mouth. He smiled as he got out of the car and gave an acknowledging nod to his former sister-in-law Alli Fitzgerald's daughter. He'd never really cared for Alli—especially after she had cheated on Waylon—but he'd always had a soft spot for her daughter and was glad that she had chosen to raise her child on the ranch.

The little munchkin, Winnie, had curly brown hair and a smile complete with all of her baby teeth in their gapped and crooked glory. And when she smiled at him, everyone on the entire ranch knew that he was mush. Whatever the girl wanted…it was hers.

He walked around to open the door for Gwen.

"How's it goin', Win?" he asked, sending the little girl a playful grin.

The two-year-old bounded over to him, throwing her arms around his knees. "Wy-ant!" she cried, saying his name with two distinct syllables. "You bring candy?"

He reached into the breast pocket of his uniform where he always carried fun-sized banana taffies for Winnie. "Oh, no," he teased. "I'm all out!"

Her plump cheeks fell and her smile disappeared as she looked up at him. "Wy-ant… Don't tease da poor girl," she said it with all seriousness, but he couldn't help but laugh as her high-pitched voice mimicked her mother's words.

"Oh, well, if you say so." He pulled the candy from his pocket and handed it to Winnie, who took it and ran toward the barn and out of the vicinity of anywhere her mother might see her gobble the treat.

Winnie turned back as she moved to slip through the barn door. "Thank you, Wy-ant."

Gwen stood next to him. "Looks like you have a fan."

He looked at her and smiled. "She is something special," he said, wanting to add that the girl wasn't the only special one in his life, but he stopped.

Gwen looked at him and moved to speak, but stopped and then walked to the barn where Winnie had disappeared. "Where did it happen?"

He motioned forward, opened the door for her and followed her inside. The lights were on, illuminating the darkened stalls. It was quiet since the horses had already been fed and turned out for the day. The place smelled like hay and horses, a smell that always reminded him of home.

"We found her in the back pen, just there," he said, motioning to the stall.

Gwen stood still, staring in the direction he had pointed. Aside from it being the place where they'd found Bianca's body, it was like every other barn— stacks of hay, the tack room, stalls and a door leading to the pasture. Yet Gwen was holding her arm around her body like this was the first time they'd ever been inside, even though there was evidence in the hayloft to the contrary.

Her gaze moved to the ladder that led up to the hayloft, and for a moment, he swore he saw a smile flicker over her lips. Was she thinking about the last time they had stepped up those rungs as well?

He walked around her, hoping she was envisioning all the possibilities of giving him one more shot in the hayloft. Moving to the stall, he looked to the spot where they had found Bianca. For a moment, he could see her there again. At the time, there had been talk about calling her family in, but he was glad now, looking back, that they hadn't. Some things couldn't be unseen. It would be hard enough for Gwen to see Bianca in the casket—the last thing she needed was to see her sister sitting in the middle of the horse stall surrounded by dirty hay, water buckets and the hooves of a hurt and scared mare.

The horse was gone and the stall had been recently cleaned so well that he could smell the strong, suspicious scent of bleach. That was unlike his mother or the staff—normally they never used bleach out here. Some things weren't going to get completely clean no matter how much scrubbing they did, and a horse stall was one of them.

"What happened to the horse—is she okay?" Gwen asked.

The wood of the door was rounded and smoothed by the years of horses chewing it, but as he took his hand away it still scraped at his skin.

"My mother had another vet come in and take a look at her. Luckily, the horse's leg wasn't broken, just a sprain."

"I'm glad the horse is going to be okay." She said it like it carried some measure of comfort that only one of the beings in this stall had lost its life. "Bianca would have liked to have known the horse was okay, I'm sure."

"I'm sure she's watching down." As he spoke, he knew it was a platitude.

Gwen glanced over at him and put her hand on top of his. "Thanks. I know you don't mean it, but thanks."

Seriously, it was like she could read his mind sometimes and it scared the bejeezus out of him. As it was, however, with her warm hand on his, he would take whatever he could get. It was better than having her angry.

He took her hand in his. "I do mean it. Sort of."

"You don't believe in that stuff, remember?"

He shrugged. "What I believe doesn't matter. What matters is that your sister was a good person. If there is any justice in this world, her soul will rest in peace, maybe where she can watch down on you and help keep you from finding yourself in too much trouble." He smiled, trying to lighten the mood. He hated talk of death.

"If there was any justice in this world, Wyatt, she wouldn't have been killed. And I wouldn't be standing in the middle of the crime scene."

"Actually," a woman said, her voice cutting through the tension, "you aren't really standing in the middle of the crime scene. Bianca died inside the stall."

He turned to see Alli standing there, Winnie in hand, staring at them. Gwen pulled her fingers from his, and as much as he loved Winnie, he silently wished they hadn't been interrupted.

"Heya, Alli. You're right, but this is still part of the scene," he said. "Come here, Winnie-girl."

Winnie let go of her mother's hand and scampered over, and he picked her up. She was heavy in his arms in a way that made him wish, for half a second, that he had a child of his own.

Gwen looked over at him and smiled, but the action was short-lived.

"You know, Wyatt, you don't have to give Winnie

a treat every time you see her," Alli grumbled. "She's getting spoiled. Soon she's going to be a brat if you keep it up."

He lifted Winnie so he could look up into her face. He turned her from right to left as though he was inspecting her. "Yep. Nope. Don't see a brat here. Just see a few bats in the cave."

Winnie giggled, the sound was infectious and he caught himself laughing with her.

"What, don't you ever pick those boogies?" he teased.

Winnie reached up and stuck her finger in her nose. She lifted her finger for him to see. "Look, I get them boogies!" she answered excitedly.

"You're just like your brother," Alli said, her tone heavy with dislike. She reached over and grabbed Winnie and set her back on the ground. "Go wash your hands, girl."

Winnie gave him a backward wave as she escaped the confines of the barn and the castigation of her mother.

"The gardens looked good this year," he said, trying to make small talk with Alli.

She shrugged. "I'll do better next year. It was just too dry a summer."

He'd tried to work in the gardens one year, as his family sold their vegetables and fruits at the local farmer's market every Saturday in the warm months, but he'd found in a single month that he had a brown thumb rather than a green one. Though, admittedly, he had been working there with their old gardener, Bernard, who'd had even less of an amicable nature than Alli.

Not all professional gardeners he'd met were light on personality, but it seemed like the last couple his mother had employed were no Bob Hopes.

Then again, his mother hadn't really hired Alli so much as been forced to bring her into the fold when Waylon had eloped with her. Now Wyatt's brother had been gone for almost three years, but here they were stuck with the only part of him that he'd left behind.

Alli hadn't always been rough to be around, but the day Waylon left everything likable about Alli had gone with him.

"How were the tomatoes this year?" Gwen asked, in what he assumed was some kind of olive branch.

"Not as good as I woulda liked, but I did pretty good at the market. The people in Kalispell ate them up. Get it?" She laughed at her own pun.

Gwen gave a light, polite laugh.

"That's great." He tried not to sound too dismissive, but with everything going on he wanted to get moving instead of getting stuck making small talk with the woman who betrayed his brother. "Do you know who cleaned up the stall? I'd like to talk to them." He dipped his chin in the direction of the bleach jug that sat in the corner near the front door.

She looked in the direction and frowned. "I dunno. People have been coming and going ever since your crew came through and took the body out." She turned to Gwen. "I'm sorry for your loss. It's always hard losing someone you love."

Gwen nodded in acknowledgment. "By chance, did

anyone see a bag around here?" She stuck out her hands in measurement. "It was black, about yea big?"

"I didn't see nothing. I ain't been around here too much. Just saw your car out front and Winnie was munching on the candy. Put two and two together and thought I'd come say hi." She shrugged. "If you're looking for something specific, you might want to ask your mom, Wyatt. She's been poking around in here."

It didn't surprise him that his mom would have been spending her time in here after everything had gone down—of all the folks at Dunrovin, she'd taken Bianca's death the hardest. She had a soft spot for the vet.

"I'll chat with her," he said, all too aware that in the next conversation he had with his family he would have to tell them what direction the investigation had headed.

The news wouldn't come without blowback. And that was to say nothing about what the death would do to the tourism that kept the ranch afloat. If anyone caught wind that this was a possible murder case, it would undoubtedly hurt his parents' bottom line.

"Do you know where they dumped the hay from the stall?" Gwen asked, pulling him from thoughts of his family.

"Oh, yeah," Alli said, her sullen frown returning. "They always take that out to the gardens. It's high in nitrogen so I'm always making it into compost for the beds. Why?"

Gwen gave him a look, a look that told him that no matter how crappy he thought some of his investigations had been, they were going to be heading to entirely new levels.

"No, Gwen." He shook his head. "The team already went through the stall before. They didn't find anything. There's no point going through...anything."

"If you don't want to get your hands dirty, Wyatt, that's fine," she said, but her tone told him there would be worse things than horse manure to deal with if he didn't play along. "But this wasn't their sister. I need to do everything in my power to figure out what exactly happened to Bianca. You loved her once too. I know. We both owe her to try our damnedest to solve her murder."

Alli visibly twitched. "Murder?"

No. He hadn't been ready for the rest of the world to learn what they had started to uncover.

He shook his head violently...almost too hard to be convincing. "No, not murder. Bianca wasn't murdered."

Alli raised an eyebrow. "Then what happened to her?"

He took Gwen by the hand and led her toward the back door of the barn and the gardens. "I don't know yet, Alli...but that's what we're hoping to find out." Even if it meant getting his hands dirty.

They grabbed a couple of pitchforks from the wall of tools and made their way from the barn.

"Good luck," Alli called from behind them.

He couldn't blame her for not joining them. Right now, he wished he was anywhere—even the prisoner transfer in Alaska—rather than here and having to do what needed to be done.

As they approached the mound of compost, Gwen pulled a bandanna out of her pocket and tied it over her face in what Wyatt assumed was an effort to save herself from breathing in the scent of manure for the next hour.

"Are you sure that you really want to do this?" he asked, sticking in his pitchfork and flipping through a frozen pile of the detritus. He could think of a thousand things he would rather being doing than going through a pile of compost for evidence they weren't going to find.

She gave him a glance and her face was pinched tight, as though she was as disgusted by this as he was. "Just look." She scraped at the pile.

He followed her lead, but all he could think of was how close they were and how much he'd rather be anywhere else with her.

He worked his way through the hay as diligently as he could, given the circumstances. After ten minutes, the cold had started to nibble at his fingertips. They were never going to find anything.

"Look…" she said, leaning down and pointing at something from her side of the mound.

He moved closer to see what she was looking at. There, lying in the heap of refuse, was what looked like a small white pen. Bits of frozen hay were stuck to its sides.

"What is it?" he asked, moving so he could take a closer look.

"It's a used needle," she said. "And I bet you we just found the thing that killed my sister. Now we just need to find out who was holding it—her, or someone who wanted her dead."

Chapter Five

Wyatt took the syringe and headed to Kalispell to hand deliver it to the crime lab. In truth, the last thing Gwen had expected was to find anything in the compost pile—it had been done on a whim, a dare she thought he wouldn't accept. He had surprised her with his willingness to go along with her.

Was it possible he was trying to impress her, or was he just trying to do whatever was necessary to keep her happy and quiet?

She glanced down at her phone and pulled up his picture from when they were kids. He still had the same wide jaw and caramel-colored eyes of the boy she had once loved, but now there was something different—something that seemed to haunt him.

Then again, she was the one with the most ghosts.

She flipped to the next picture, the one of Bianca holding a handful of purple and yellow wildflowers. In the photo, Bianca was laughing, her mouth open with glee and her eyes full of life. She looked beautiful. It was one of those perfect moments when everything was going her way, and all the best of life was coming together.

How quickly those moments faded and reality closed in, and the ghosts that floated through their lives returned. Gwen had her own secrets, but none were quite like Bianca's. Gwen's sister had a penchant for living life with one foot in the world of danger.

Gwen slipped her phone back in her pocket as she thought about what she had to do. Her gut ached. Some of the secrets between her and her sister weren't things she wanted to explore. Yet she needed to talk to her sister's darkest secret, William Poe—no matter how badly she hated the man and the role he'd forced her sister to play.

She glanced at her watch. The roads were a bit icy, but if she hurried she could catch him before he went to work and avoid Wyatt finding out what she feared telling him. Wyatt had always been kind to her sister and given her the benefit of the doubt about her choices, but if he found out what she'd really been doing, all of his good opinions of her would probably fly out the window. And if he wasn't on her and Bianca's side, it was unlikely that he'd put everything behind this investigation. He needed to be emotionally connected and remember Bianca as the person she really was—instead of the warped version that William had required her to become.

If Gwen was going to protect her sister's honor, she couldn't let anyone else—not even Wyatt—find out the truth.

She started the old Ford, letting it smoke and sputter

to life. It rumbled as though even the truck questioned her plan, but instead of listening she pushed it in gear and drove toward the one place she said she was never going to return to.

As she made her way down the frontage road that led to William's house, she thought of the last time she'd seen the man. He and Bianca had gotten into a fight, and Bianca had called her—it was how Gwen had found out about their illicit affair. When Gwen had arrived at the man's house, William had been standing on his porch half naked, screaming at Bianca and calling her every foul name Gwen could have imagined. Bianca had scurried from the house, wrapped in nothing more than his hundred-dollar sheet. Tears had been streaming down Bianca's face as she threw herself onto the truck's bench seat.

Gwen glanced over at the truck's seat. It had been just over six months ago, and though she had told Bianca to kick the man to the curb, as far as she knew, Bianca had gone back to him whenever his wife was out of town.

Hopefully William's wife wasn't out of town now. There would be nothing better than confronting William about his mistress, and what he knew about her death, in front of his wife. In so many ways, Bianca's life reminded Gwen of one of the many soap operas they had grown up watching in the days when they had only three channels—and the only thing on television when they got home from school was *Days of Our Lives*.

She smiled at the thought of them balled up on the couch watching as the show revealed the latest secret baby. It was one of the reasons she had been hooked on reading romance novels. Even now her bedside table was covered with this month's latest releases. It was her favorite vice.

It wasn't far from Dunrovin to the Poes', but then again, nothing in this town was really that far. In fact, with a pair of binoculars and a high vantage, she was almost certain that she could see most of the town and its goings-on. The lack of privacy made the hair on the back of her neck stand up. She hated the thought of how easy it was for her life to be tracked—who knew who all was watching.

The Poes' garage was separate from the house. A long, covered walkway was the only thing connecting them. As Gwen drove up the driveway, she noticed William standing in the walkway like he was waiting for her. He looked out of place standing there surrounded by the pine garlands with pretty white lights and the Santa Claus decoration in his front yard—it was almost like he was normal.

It gave her chills. He wasn't giving her a look that was particularly dangerous. It seemed more as though her presence, while not a surprise, was a nuisance. Had he had some clue she would be on her way to see him? Maybe he heard about Bianca's death and was just waiting for her to arrive. Either way, the dislike she felt for him intensified.

He ran his fingers through his waxed hair, making sure everything was in place, and readjusted his suit jacket before hurrying toward her truck. He motioned for her to stay put. She rushed to turn off the truck and slip out its door. She wanted to make him as uncomfortable as possible. He deserved to feel pressured by her being there.

"Gwen, why are you here?" It sounded more like an accusation than a question.

"You don't know?" She tried to read his reaction, but as a semi-politician his face remained placid. It made her hatred toward the county tax appraiser tick upward.

"Gwen, I don't have time for you or your sister's games. She needs to just accept that we are over. I'm tired of her trying to manipulate me and you can tell her I said that."

So they weren't together. Or was he just playing some kind of game with her?

"You should tell her that yourself." She felt the weight of the unspoken truth on her tongue, but she wasn't ready to tell him about Bianca's death. He didn't deserve anything…no measure of kindness or pity.

He turned to walk away, but she grabbed his arm and forced him to turn and face her again.

"Gwen, I have to get to work. Seriously, just tell Bianca this has to stop. I'm not taking her back."

She hated the fact that she had no idea what William was talking about. Clearly he and Bianca had broken up, but when and why? Not for the first time, she wished she had talked to her sister more. Yet neither of them had really wanted to bring up the issue of William because Gwen hated the man, and she assumed Bianca was ashamed of her decision to be with such a shady person.

William glanced toward his house, where the kitchen window looked out toward the driveway.

"Is your wife inside?" she asked, taking some small measure of comfort that Monica might bear witness to some of her husband's secrets.

His eyes widened with what she assumed was fear. For a moment, she considered going in there and telling Monica exactly what kind of man William was. The poor woman needed to know the things he did when she was out of sight. Then again, some secrets didn't need to see the light of day—especially when it involved her sister's memory.

Regardless of her desire to reveal the truth, he needed to fear her and what chaos she could bring to his life. She felt a bit ruthless, but she didn't care. The man was one of the reasons she feared dating again. If all men were like him, with questionable morals and sharp, cutting tongues, she could live without them.

Wyatt's face flashed in her mind, but she pushed the thought of him aside. He wasn't like William, but he also wasn't interested in her. Wyatt didn't seem interested in anything beyond getting her out of his hair so he could avoid her family's drama.

He'd always hated her family and their twisted dynamics—not that *his* upbringing was without its problems. Yet he hardly ever spoke of his time in the foster care system or the few years he'd spent with his real parents. In fact, in all the time they had spent dating, he'd only spoken to her once about it—and it was merely that he was thankful for what Mrs. and Mr. Fitz had done for him. It was just one of those things they skirted around, each of them fearing what the other would say or the memories it would bring to the surface. Some wounds just didn't need to be exposed.

If only she could say the same of having to deal with William Poe.

William glanced back at her and had a scowl on his face. "Don't bring my wife into this, any of this. She doesn't deserve to be hurt just because your sister is angry."

"My sister isn't angry. And there are worse things that would hurt her far more than my sister's feelings. How about the fact that you screw anything that walks?"

"You don't know what you're talking about, Gwen." He said her name like it left a bitter aftertaste.

She didn't care.

"When was the last time you saw Bianca?"

"What?" He looked confused. "Why?"

"Don't worry about it." She smiled, the motion dangerous. "When was the last time you saw her?"

He shrugged. "I don't know. Last week sometime?"

"Where?"

He stared at her as though he was the one trying to read her now. "At her clinic. Why? What are you trying to get at? Is she missing or something?"

She stood in silence, not ready to say the words and acknowledge the reality of where Bianca currently rested.

The back door opened and William's wife, Monica, walked out with a dishtowel in her hand. Her dark hair was pulled back in a small, stylish chignon that made her look every bit the high-end antiques shop owner that she was. Over the years Gwen had gone into Monica's shop, picking up odds and ends, pieces for the ranch, and once in a while even selling things her family didn't need. Before everything with Bianca, she had thought the woman a friend, but thanks to her sister and her sister's secrets, she had let their friendship dissolve out of fear she would be caught in the middle.

Gwen sucked in a breath as she realized how, in this moment, that was exactly where she was.

"Hi, Gwen. How're you doing?" Monica asked, sending her a smile that made guilt roil within her.

Gwen smiled. She could tell her right now.

"Hi, Monica. I'm okay. You?" she asked, trying to sound as though she didn't have a war raging within her.

"Good," Monica said, with a look that spoke of her confusion at why exactly Gwen was standing in her driveway and talking to her husband. "Do you want to come in and have a cup of coffee?" She glanced at Gwen's clothes and added, "If you want you could come in and get cleaned up? What have you been up to?"

Gwen looked down at herself and realized why the woman was offering. Her shirt was sprinkled with bits of hay and her shoes were covered in the filth of the compost pile. She must have looked like a mess to them, but no matter how bad she looked on the outside it was nothing to the mess she was within.

"No. No, I'm fine," she said, trying to keep her embarrassment from seeping into her voice. "I was just going."

"Is there something I can help you with?" Monica

asked, looking to William as though she were trying to get a clearer picture.

"No, honey, she's fine. Just had a question about the Widow Maker's taxes, isn't that right, Gwen?" he said, leading her into the answers he wanted.

As much as she wanted to tell him to pound sand, and tell Monica why she was really here, she bit her tongue. She hadn't gotten the answers she needed from William—and if she started a war between him and his wife, she doubted she ever would. But his day was coming. William would pay for the way he treated women—and her sister.

Gwen nodded. "I'll stop by your office sometime soon. I still have a few more questions."

William gave Monica a quick peck on her cheek, like he hadn't been kissing Gwen's sister all that long ago. It made a feeling of sickness rise within her.

Gwen turned away, unable to stomach watching the vile man any longer.

"Have a great day, Gwen," Monica called from behind her. "And stop by the shop sometime. I have some new things I think you'd love!"

Monica sounded excited, and it made the hatred Gwen felt for William even more palpable. Monica didn't deserve to be treated the way William treated her—even if she didn't know it.

Gwen got into the truck and reversed down the driveway. As she stopped near the bottom, in the distance she could make out the profile of Wyatt's squad car returning from Kalispell. He approached her truck, then slowed down and pulled to a stop beside her. He frowned as he looked at her.

"What are you doing at the Poes'?" he asked, glancing up toward the house. His face contorted with disgust as though he held the same opinion of William Poe she did—but then again, William had a reputation. "You know William? How well?" He gave her a questioning look.

Wait. Did he think she was here to see William for *that*? She blanched at the thought.

"No. I came here…" she started, but if she told him why she was here she would have to tell him about Bianca's relationship with William. If she didn't he would assume she was the one sleeping with William. Both options made her want to turn and run.

She stopped. There was no right answer here. "I was just about to run to take a shower."

The disgusted look on Wyatt's face disappeared and she caught a glimpse of a naughty smile. Was he thinking of her in the shower? No. She must have had it all wrong. He was probably just glad she was leaving the Poes'.

"Are you going home?" he asked.

She glanced down at her pants and realized that if she went home, her mother would likely be waiting to barrage her with a litany of questions about Bianca and what she and Wyatt were working on. Gwen didn't know if she was ready to face her mother. Not yet anyway.

"I…uh…" she stammered. "My mother is probably up."

"It's almost noon." He glanced toward his dashboard, where there must have been a clock.

"She hit the bars again last night. Didn't come home at closing time. Nights like that, she normally comes rolling in about the time the man she went home with wakes up and finds her in his bed."

Wyatt's face turned to stone. In fact, that stoic look was the one he always had when it came to her family—and she hated it. It was almost as though they embarrassed him, or was it that he pitied her because of them? Either way, it made her want to talk about anything else.

"If you like," he said, "you're welcome to come to my place and get cleaned up. I have a T-shirt or two that might fit you."

His offer came as a shock. Did he really mean to invite her over? She tried not to read too much into his invitation. No doubt he was just trying to be nice and she'd just heard what she wanted to when she picked up the hint of something more in his voice.

Wait. Did she want him to come on to her?

She chuckled. Of course she did. Who didn't want to be thought of as beautiful?

She'd been lonely for so long. Her relationships in recent years had been nothing more than surface-level attractions—nights spent fulfilling her need to be touched and to feel another body against hers. It would have felt good to have him want her, to have him think of her as something more than the girl who'd once broken his heart.

When she'd ended their relationship, she'd felt justified in her decision. Life had been pulling them in dif-

ferent directions. He wanted to leave and go to NYU
to escape the sucking maw of ranch life while she was
restricted by her mother's disapproval. After her father's
death, her mother hated the Fitzgeralds because of their
association with what Gwen had come to realize was
really the end of her mother's life. He had to go and
she had to stay—it wasn't a gap that could be bridged.

Yet when life hadn't turned out to be as glamorous
as Wyatt had planned in the big city, he had returned
home. At the time, Gwen had thought about seeking
him out to see if the old feelings were still there, but
at the last minute she had thought better of it. Some
kinds of pain you could never heal or apologize enough
for—especially when her actions had caused her just
as much agony.

She looked into his soft brown eyes and he smiled.
Or maybe she had been wrong. Maybe it was her fear
of being rejected for the hurt she had caused that was
really holding her back. Maybe he had grown past the
pain she had inflicted when they'd been young and, in
her case, stupid.

"So?" he asked, pulling her from her thoughts. "If
you don't want to come back to my place to clean up,
I totally understand. I was just thinking… Well, I was
hoping to get in touch with the crime lab to see if they
found anything, and then maybe work on the library
lead. Thought it could save us both some time and a
few trips, but it's completely up to you."

He was rambling.

The realization made her chest ache. Seeing him like

that made some of the feelings she thought she'd buried rise to the surface.

He had always been a good man, and nothing if not a gentleman. Of course his offer had come from a place of sincerity and not some player's attempt at getting her to land in his bed.

"All right," she said with a nod. "I'll follow you back."

He moved to speak, but stopped and instead dipped his head and motioned for her to follow him home.

She pressed down on the pickup's gas pedal and made it rumble with life. Though she should have been thinking of nothing but Bianca and their investigation, as she pushed the truck forward, all she could think of was how glad she was to find Wyatt back in her life.

Chapter Six

Some of the snow had started to melt and dirt patches were showing through as Gwen and Wyatt drove down the winding, bumpy road that led to his trailer at Dunrovin. She could see his place in the distance, a single wreath on the door—a single man's attempt at Christmas cheer.

She was looking forward to going inside and seeing what his life had become, but at the same time she was nervous. If one thing led to another, she didn't know how she would react. Or what it would be like if nothing happened. She wasn't sure which order of possible events disappointed her more.

She ran her finger over her lips, imagining his kiss. He had been a good kisser in high school. She could only imagine what he would be like now, ten years and what was probably dozens of women later. The thought of him with another woman made her skin prickle with jealousy. She tried to ignore the sensation. It was crazy to feel that way about him and what he chose to do. She had no claim on him.

He pulled to a stop in front of his trailer. The little

tan box wasn't anything like the house she had imagined he would end up in—or rather, when she'd been imagining back in high school, the house *they* would have ended up living in together. In her mind's eye, she had once pegged them for living the American dream: two kids, a dog and a white picket fence.

She chuckled as she got out of the truck. How naive she had once been. Life wasn't some dream. She had been stupid to think it could be. Life was simply a constant battle between wants and needs. And here in Montana, in a world where winter and Mother Nature seemed to constantly reign, needs were all that mattered.

"What are you laughing about?" he asked, waiting for her by the front of the truck.

She hadn't even realized she had been laughing at the thought, and his calling her out caught her off guard. "What?"

"You were laughing at something."

"Oh," she said, closing the door. "It was nothing."

"Huh," he said, sounding slightly disappointed that she refused to let him in on the joke. "I'll grab you a towel and some clean clothes. Maybe I have something that won't hang on you too much."

She followed him up the rickety wooden steps and into the trailer. She wasn't sure what she had expected, but the place was a bit of a shock. Everything was in order. When he took her coat, she noticed that even the coat closet was organized: on one side were all his black work jackets and from there everything was arranged by color. She walked into his living room. The room was simple: a flat screen on the wall above an electric stove and a leather couch at the room's heart.

There wasn't a single forgotten sock or speck of dust. In fact, it was almost a little too clean—which made her wonder if he was the kind who was so concentrated on his house that he forgot to leave it. Perhaps he had gone from the boy who wanted to escape the confines and trappings of ranch life to a man who wanted nothing more than to bask in the comfort of the ranching lifestyle. It struck her how much he may have changed from the boy she had once known.

He made his way through the dining room off the kitchen and into what must have been the master bedroom. She followed him to the door of the room but stopped, unsure of whether or not he wanted her to be in his domain. His bedroom was just as clean as the rest of the place, and his bed was made with a pink floral quilt that she had no doubt was handmade by his mother.

"I like the quilt," she said, leaning against the door frame as she motioned to the blanket.

"Huh?" He looked surprised by her talking, or maybe it was that he was just as uncomfortable as she was. "Oh, that? It's just a hand-me-down. My mother had it forever and then made herself a new one." He chuckled. "It may be pink, but I'm enough of a man not to be afraid to rock it. Until now, no one ever really saw it anyways."

She could have sworn she saw the color rise in his cheeks when he mentioned his bedroom activities, or lack thereof.

"It's okay, I'm pretty sure I still have *Star Wars*

sheets from when I was a kid. Heck, I still use my twin-size bed." She laughed as she tried to make him feel better.

His face lit up. "Oh, I remember that old thing. That bed was a bit creaky when we were together. I can't believe you still have it." He laughed, but then stopped abruptly as though he had realized exactly what they were talking about. "I mean, I would have thought you'd have gotten rid of it by now."

"Why get rid of a good thing?" As the words left her, she realized the other meaning they held and she wished she could reel them back in. Yet, there was no coming back from putting her foot that deeply into her mouth.

"That's… I didn't mean…" she said, struggling to stop the light from going completely out of his eyes. She had liked seeing him smile, seeing him light up when they were talking about the past. She hated herself for what she had done to him, regardless of her reasons at the time—everything going on with her family, their loss and the hatred her mother carried toward him had seemed like things they would never be able to overcome if they wanted to make a life together. Even then, she had known that true love meant sometimes sacrificing the things she held dearest—even if that meant stopping the relationship so that neither of them would have to go through a lifetime of pain. He had deserved to have a life filled with happiness—and he still did.

He waved her off. "It's fine. I'm sure you were just talking about that old mattress."

She could hear the hurt in his tone.

"I really was. I… I'm sorry about the past, Wyatt.

About what happened. You know…when we were younger. I was stupid. I just thought the divide between our families was too big and I was trying to protect us both. Who knows, maybe I just watched too much *Romeo and Juliet* or something."

"You weren't stupid," he said, his voice quiet with what she assumed was discomfort at having this conversation. "You did what you thought you had to do. I get it. You don't need to explain yourself to me. What happened, happened. There's no going back." There was a finality in the way he said the words, and it made the air thick between them.

"You're right. There's no going back," she said, trying to make it sound soft and repentant, and she hoped that he could hear the apology in her words. "But there is always moving forward."

"I'm truly sorry about Bianca," he said.

He was right to assume she had been talking about the investigation and her sister. Bianca should have been who she was talking about. Her sister's death should have been consuming all her thoughts and actions. Yet, standing here by Wyatt's bedroom and looking at his warm bed, her mind moved to the wants she had been repressing for so long.

"Thanks, I appreciate it. I do." She stepped into his bedroom and moved close to him, so close she could feel the warmth radiating off his body. "But I wasn't talking about Bianca."

He took in a long breath as he stared at her. She had no idea what he could possibly be thinking. All she could think about was how weightless she felt as she looked into his eyes and the way her chest clenched with want. She hadn't been this nervous around a man in long time.

She stepped closer, until she brushed against the thick brown polyester of his uniform shirt and her belly bumped against his utility belt. He was just a bit taller than she had remembered. She looked down at his pants, the action of looking at him feeling even naughtier when she thought about it, and heat rose in her cheeks.

Instead of laughing at her embarrassment, he put his hands on her shoulders. His thumbs made those familiar circles she had thought she hated, but now she leaned into his touch, wanting more. It felt good to be touched by him…so good.

She looked up. There was nothing but him. His eyes. The fine crow's-feet that sat at their corners. The smooth skin of his freshly shaven face. His pink, full lips were damp. He must have just licked them.

The thought made her body quiver to life. Her center grew heavy with want and the desire for his hands to move from her shoulders. For him to rub those little circles he liked so much in darker, more forbidden places.

She wanted to speak, to tell him how badly she wanted him. Yet the words caught in her throat, and before she had the chance, he dropped his hands from her and turned away.

No. He couldn't.

Was he rejecting her? Didn't he want her? *This?*

She moved to reach for him, but stopped. If he didn't want her, it was his choice. He had every right to refuse her.

Reality and the disappointment that came with it poured in from all sides as he walked across the bedroom and, opening the linen closet, grabbed a towel.

"Here," he said, handing the towel to her.

Her hands shook as she took it. She didn't know what to say or how to cover her embarrassment and graciously accept the fact that he no longer wanted her in the same way she wanted him.

"I…er… Thanks," she said, but as soon as the words were out of her, she turned and nearly sprinted for the bathroom that was connected to the room.

She closed the door behind her harder than she intended, and the harsh sound reverberated through the room, echoing the pain in her chest.

She was such an idiot. Of course he didn't want her like she wanted him. They'd only been speaking to each other for a day. Up until then, they had treated each other like they were invisible. What had happened in the past, and the feelings it had generated, couldn't vanish overnight.

Then again, she'd never forgotten him. More nights than she could count, he was the last person on her mind before she slipped away to sleep. And during long days on the ranch baling hay or moving the cattle, she would let her thoughts wander…always to him and the what-ifs. What if she hadn't let him go? What if they had stayed together? Would they have stayed in Mystery, or would they have run away from this place? He'd run, but if she had gone with him, how different would their lives have been?

She thought of the way he had just looked at her. His

look hadn't been indifferent, he hadn't seemed put off by her or her move toward him, but it hadn't been the look of a man who loved her either.

She sighed.

Not for the first time, she was letting her emotions run away with her. She couldn't move this fast.

She tried to stop chastising herself. She couldn't regret the action she had taken. It was brave to follow her heart, even if it had been foolish. If she hadn't tried, she wouldn't have known his true feelings—or that he wasn't interested.

She flipped on the faucet in the shower and let the water run until steam poured from behind the glass. She was fine. It would be fine. It wasn't like she had completely thrown herself at him. If she was careful, she could make it seem like nothing. She could bounce back from this. She had to. She had to face him again.

They had work to do.

With a renewed sense of spirit, she stepped into the shower. It was so hot that it made the skin of her back tingle and burn, but she didn't turn down the heat. She wanted—no, needed—to feel the pain. The stinging needles reminded her that things could be so much worse. She was alive. Unlike Bianca.

She put her hands on the tile of the shower wall. It was cold against her hot hands. In here, away from the prying eyes of the world, she let the tears come as the crazy mixture of emotions she'd been trying to hold back finally bubbled to the surface. Here, she didn't have to hide.

Heaving sobs rattled through her body and she sank

to the warmed floor. The water swirled down the drain as it mixed with her tears.

Screw being strong. Screw the world for what it had done to her sister—and screw it for continuing to break her down.

She shouldn't have felt sorry for herself, but she couldn't help it. Every time she turned around, it was as if the world was throwing another curveball her way. Just as soon as she had dealt with one thing, it was always like there was another thing coming.

She was just so dang tired.

Leaning against the tile, she let her tears fall.

"Gwen?" Wyatt called from behind the door. "Are you okay?"

She wasn't, but she wasn't about to tell him. "Fine. I'm fine." She turned off the water and stepped out of the shower, wrapping herself in the oversize towel he'd given her.

There was a long pause. "I, uh, got you some clean clothes. Do you want me to set them outside the door here?"

She opened the bathroom door, carefully holding her towel in place. "I'll take them," she said, as a drip of water slipped down her leg and pooled on the floor.

Wyatt looked at her and his eyes widened. His gaze moved down her body to the puddle on his floor.

"You're dripping." He moved toward her, so close that they were nearly touching. Instead of continuing past her, he stopped and their eyes met.

Her breath hitched. Maybe she had gotten it wrong.

Maybe he did want her. Maybe he'd been acting the gentleman by turning her away before.

He leaned in and his lips met hers. He smelled like the compost pile and hay, but she didn't care as he pulled her into his arms. She let go of her towel, letting it be held by their bodies as she wrapped her arms around his neck and ran her fingers through his hair.

His lips moved over hers, then she sucked and ran the tip of her tongue over his skin. He tasted like peppermint gum and sweat, just as he had when they were younger. Yet his kiss was not the same. It was the kiss of a man—a man who knew exactly what he wanted.

He pushed her body against the wall and lifted her hands over her head. The radio on his utility belt pressed hard against her and, as he noticed her discomfort, he unclasped the belt and let it fall to the floor at their feet.

He traced the line of her jaw, kissing the places where his fingers had touched. Each time his fingers slipped lower on her skin, down her neck and onto her collarbone. He licked and sucked the beads of water from her skin, and for a second she wondered if he could taste the salt from her tears.

She pulled her hands down and took hold of the buttons on his uniform, stopping him from going any lower. She wanted him. His touch. His lips upon her skin. But she'd envisioned this moment so many times, so many nights when she'd been lying alone in her bed and thinking about what could have been, that she wanted to savor this moment and make it last.

"You need a shower," she said with a coy grin.

As though she had reeled him back to reality, he

stopped and looked down at his shirt. He chuckled as he must have realized the state he was in.

"Sorry," he said, pulling back from her.

Her towel slipped and she moved to grab it, but stopped and let it fall to the floor atop his utility belt.

"There's nothing to be sorry for," she said, her voice high and airy with lust.

She slipped the buttons free as he stared at her body. Under her fingertips, she could feel the erratic beating of his heart and his short, choppy breaths as her hands worked lower. She pulled his shirt from him and dropped it to the floor away from her towel.

Bits of hay were still stuck to his tank top from his digging through the compost pile. She pulled a piece from his shirt. He was such a good man. How could she have ever let him go?

She had regretted her decision in the past, but never more than right now. If she had just followed her heart and not her head or the pressures of the people around her, she could have been with him all these years. They had missed so much time together all because she had made a major miscalculation.

There was only moving forward.

She reached down and unbuttoned his pants. He took her hand and lifted them to his lips and kissed them.

"Are you sure?" he asked, kissing the inside of her palm. "Are you positive that you want to take things down this road again?"

"I am sure, but are you?" She wrapped her free hand around his neck and leaned back against the wall, letting him glimpse her in full glory.

She wasn't playing fair and she knew it, but she didn't care. All was fair in love and war. Not that she loved him.

No. Definitely not love.

Probably.

She pushed the thought from her mind as she led him to the shower and stripped off his shirt. There was a piece of hay in the sparse hair that adorned the center of his chest. She liked a man with a little brown sugar. As she pulled the hay off him, she ran her fingers through the little patch and giggled.

"What's so funny?" he asked, a grin on his sexy face.

"Nothing. It's just a little thicker than the last time I saw it." She pulled at the single gray hair that was mixed in the patch. "And it looks like you are starting to get a little salt in the pepper."

"It's not gray," he said, looking down at his chest and pulling at the hair. "That is summer blond, baby."

She laughed, the sound warming her from the inside out.

How she had missed him.

She turned the water on in the shower as he slipped his pants off. He stood there in his boxer briefs, looking at her as she turned back around.

"Did anyone ever tell you how beautiful you are?"

She waved him off. As much as she loved hearing the compliment, she didn't quite know how to respond.

"No, really. And if you turn around again…" He leaned around, trying to catch another glimpse of her behind.

"What?" she said, playfully turning away from him.

He gave her an impish grin. "Do you really want to find out?"

She giggled and stepped into the shower, pulling the curtain just far enough closed that it covered her body, but she could see out. "Only if you meet me in here."

Just when she thought he couldn't get any hotter, his impish grin grew into a full smile, making a dimple appear in his right cheek. He reached down and slipped his fingers under the edge of his underwear and wiggled his hips.

It felt so good to see him being playful.

"I like it. Dance for me, baby," she teased.

He laughed as he swung his hips in a full circle and lowered his underwear, exposing the edge of his pubic hair.

"Lower…"

"How low?" he said, continuing to swing his hips.

"All the way."

He raised his brow and stopped dancing. He paused for a minute, then pulled the boxers down his legs and stepped out of them.

She sucked in a breath as she looked at all of him. She had felt him against her, but she hadn't quite expected what faced her.

He stepped into the shower and pulled her back into his arms. The water splashed on him, creating rivulets that streamed down his body. It was strange, but she couldn't help but think that being in his arms was the one place where she truly belonged.

They let the water run over their bodies as he pushed

her against the water-warmed tile of the shower wall and kissed her. He tasted savory in all the right ways.

He traced her curves with his fingers until he found his way to her backside. He cupped it, and his kiss moved deeper, harder with want. His hunger for her made every inch of her body scream to be touched, to be felt and tasted. She opened her legs and pulled him closer to her, so close she could feel all of him against her.

The sensation of him against her wet skin made her prickle to life. Every dream she had envisioned and every thought she'd had about this time with him was nothing in comparison to the reality of feeling him between her thighs.

He leaned down, pulling her nipple into his mouth and making a sucking noise. She loved that noise, the pop of his mouth on her sensitive nub. She moaned his name and his kiss hardened on her.

She could live in this moment forever.

There was the sound of the phone ringing somewhere from beneath the pile of clothes just outside the shower. She tried to ignore it, but the Gary Allan song "Get Off on the Pain" continued to sound, and it pulled her from her euphoria.

"Is…is that your phone?" she said, drunk with want.

"Huh?" He stopped kissing her and she immediately regretted having spoken.

"Your phone."

It stopped ringing. For a moment they stood there in silence, just letting the water rush over them. Then the phone started ringing again, persistent with its need to be answered.

"Son of a—"

"What?"

"It's probably the medical examiner. He promised he would call." He gave her a look that said he had to take the call.

She was immediately brought back to reality. Their stolen moment was over… No matter how badly she wanted to fall into the daydream, the nightmare of the real world waited.

Chapter Seven

He wasn't sure how he'd gotten so lucky to find himself alone with her in the shower, but he would give just about anything to get back in and not have his phone ring. He'd never thought of himself as unlucky, but when he'd been forced to step away from her, he couldn't help but think the universe had it out for him.

He pulled the device from his utility belt as it sounded again. "Deputy Fitzgerald," he answered, irritation filling in his voice.

"Fitz, how goes it?" the medical examiner asked, either ignoring or completely oblivious to his tone.

Wyatt looked at Gwen, who had already turned off the shower and wrapped her body back in the towel he had watched hit the floor only minutes before. He walked to the rack and grabbed his own towel, wrapping it around his waist as modesty dictated, though his body wanted something entirely different.

He could have sworn a look of disappointment swept over her face, but he couldn't be sure. Then again, she had been the one who had tried to seduce him—though admittedly she didn't have to try too hard. It had taken all of his willpower to turn her away the first time because he had thought her too raw from grief to make a good decision about their being together. But the second time, when she dropped that towel…well, he couldn't say no. A man could only resist and listen to his head so much before his body and its desires took over.

"Fitz?" the woman asked.

"Yeah, so… Find anything?" He forced himself to look away from Gwen and the perfect curves of her body. With a body like that, round and soft in all the right places, there was no way he could pay attention to the woman on the other end of the phone.

Though he tried to look away, he could still see her in the mirror, bending over and running the edge of her towel down her legs.

Dang, she was so flipping sexy.

He left the bathroom and gently pulled the door shut behind him so he wouldn't be tempted to look back. He had to focus.

"The syringe you brought us was quite helpful. Upon closer inspection, we did manage to find a small mark on her neck that was consistent with the mark that would be made by a large gauge needle."

"Did you test the syringe's contents?"

"That's really why I was calling." The woman paused. "We found something interesting. Something that I didn't even know we tested for, to be honest. Have you ever heard of the drug Beuthanasia?"

"What?" he asked, struggling to imagine what exactly the woman was talking about.

"Beuthanasia, it's used on animals…to put them to down."

"Are you kidding me?"

The woman clicked her tongue against her teeth. "Once my techs learned about the syringe and the victim's job, it was one of the next chemical compounds that they tested for. If it wasn't for them and their ability to put two and two together, I can't say we would have figured out exactly what killed her. With the amount of phenytoin and pentobarbital in her system, I can say that without a doubt it was what killed her."

"Who has access to it?" Wyatt asked.

"Well," the medical examiner started, "anyone who is registered with the DEA has access. They can order the drug, but they have to have a good record-keeping system. Actually, most veterinarians keep the drug on hand—especially the large-animal vets who may be called to a scene in which they can't transport a hurt animal and have to humanely end its life."

"So it could have been *Bianca's* medication?"

"Certainly… She was a vet, correct?"

"Is there any way to track where the drug could have come from? You know, which vial or something?" Wyatt asked.

The woman snorted into the phone. "No. We aren't some crime show. It's not something that's DNA based. The solution from one company is pretty much the same as the solution from another company. And truthfully, not knowing much about veterinarian medicine, I would assume there isn't a whole lot of diversity as far as who would carry and distribute the medicine."

"Huh. Okay. Did you manage to pull any prints from the syringe?"

He could almost imagine the lady shaking her head. "Unfortunately, due to its condition, we couldn't pull any full prints that would be usable. However, the partial prints appeared to have a ridge pattern that wasn't that of your vic—ruling out any possibility that she may have killed herself."

"You are sure that it was the implement used in her death?"

"You're the one who would have to prove it in court, but thanks to the size of the needle and the size of the mark on your vic's neck, added to the fact that it was filled with the same chemical that killed her, I'd say you'd be more than likely to prove that it was what killed her beyond a reasonable doubt."

There had to be something he could use here. Maybe even something that could point him in the direction of who wanted Bianca dead—and why.

"Thanks for the information. I appreciate it. And, hey, if you find out anything else about this med, or about her death, please let me know. I'm at a bit of a loss with this one. Few known enemies and she was pretty well liked within the community."

"You're welcome. I'll let you know if I run across anything more," the medical examiner said.

He hung up the phone. From inside the bathroom, he could hear Gwen's footsteps as she moved around the room.

He set the phone down on his dresser and moved toward the door, but stopped at taking the handle. Undoubtedly, she would want to know what the examiner had found, but he wasn't sure that he wanted to tell her. Not yet. Not when they could finish what they started.

The handle turned in his hand and he let go.

Gwen opened the door. She was wearing the Yankees T-shirt that he had kept from his very limited days attending NYU. That shirt was about the only thing, besides maybe the baseball games and the food, that he'd really enjoyed in the monstrously huge city.

"You look cute," he said, putting his hands on the top of her hips and leaning back to take her in completely.

She stepped out of his hands, but the movement wasn't out of rejection. Rather, thanks to the faint pinkness in her cheeks, he assumed it was out of embarrassment. Was she upset about the choice she had made in the bathroom?

For him, what had just happened would probably go down in the books. He had loved it. It had been the first *real* thing that had happened in a long time. He was always working and moving. It was just an endless, habitual cycle that he had come to accept was his life—until yesterday and the moment he had seen her standing in the doorway in her red flannel nightgown.

That was the moment he'd sparked back to life. And he would forever be thankful for having her back in his world—it was just too bad it had to come under some terrible circumstances. If only he had listened to Bianca one of the million times she had tried to tell him to go after her sister, he could have come back to life a long time ago.

Or maybe he wouldn't have fallen into the trap of complacency.

"Who was that?" she asked, looking at him with the raise of her brow.

"Just some girl," he said, almost teasing as he tried to put off having to tell her what he'd found out.

"Oh, yeah?" From her tone, it wasn't just an innocent question; there was almost a fleck of jealousy.

He had to have been wrong. There was nothing for her to be jealous about.

He must have misread her. He was making something out of nothing, he'd probably heard something in her voice that wasn't even there. Regardless, their moment was over. He moved to his closet and pulled out a fresh uniform shirt and pants.

"That," he said, motioning to the cell phone on his dresser, "was the medical examiner. She was calling about your sister."

Her jaw went slack and her questioning expression disappeared. "What did she say?"

"You were right about the syringe and its tie to the case. It was filled with a compound they use for euthanizing animals. Someone ended up using it on your sister." He tried to say the words slowly, so each syllable wouldn't come as a slap to the face, but there was little he could do to lessen the fact that her sister really had been murdered.

Her gaze fell. Thankfully, unlike when he'd first told her of Bianca's death at the Widow Maker, she didn't sink to the floor.

"What does it mean for the case?" she asked, the

words coming so slow it was like each was its own sentence.

"It means that this just became an official homicide investigation."

She leaned against the wall, trying to regain her balance.

"Are you okay?" he asked, throwing his clothes over his arm as he moved toward her. When he got close she turned away, hiding her face.

"I'm fine," she said, but she walked out the door of his bedroom, closing it in her wake before he could say anything else.

He grumbled. Women were so complicated. He loved them, but, man, sometimes they were like a giant puzzle. Just when he thought he had gotten something figured out, another piece went missing.

He threw on his clothes and utility belt and slipped his phone into his pocket. Gwen was sitting at the island in his kitchen. She'd poured herself a glass of water and, as he approached, she was running her finger around its edges.

The sight of her there, looking brokenhearted, pulled at him. The first time he'd seen her looking like that had been the day she had learned about her father's death. Why did he always seem to come to her in moments of disaster? Was he her personal angel of death?

If he was, it was no wonder she was always pushing him away—that is, until they had been in his bathroom. His body tingled with unreleased desire, but he forced himself to ignore the sensation.

That had been a onetime thing. Heck. It had barely

even been a thing. They had only seen each other naked. Though, it had been very, very naked and a bit more than simply just seeing. He thought of her pulling him between her thighs. At the thought, he could almost feel the heat of her again. She'd been hot, so hot. At sixteen, he had dreamed of being there—both of them naked and her body begging for him.

He snorted as he thought of how, no matter how old they were, or their situations, life always got in the way.

He stepped around the island and stood in front of her. "I know you said you're doing fine, but you know, you can talk to me about this…about *anything*." He motioned toward the bedroom. Not that he was exactly sure that he wanted to talk about what had happened in there, but he didn't want to let it go either—not if there was a way he could somehow make sense of what she wanted.

She didn't look where he motioned, almost as if she was purposefully ignoring his reference. "I…" She sighed, taking a moment. "Look, I'm sorry. For…*that*. You know, in the bathroom. I just… I don't know. If you have a girlfriend or something… I didn't have any business acting like that. Not that I didn't like it, but…" She stumbled over her words.

So that had been her problem? She thought he was dating someone? The thought made him laugh out loud. Sure, he'd dated, but none of them had ever compared to the memory of her.

He raised his hands from the counter, an action almost like that of a person surrendering. "Whoa. Stop. Babe." As he said the pet name, he wished he could have pulled it back. In the light of the kitchen, and with them both dressed, it just sounded out of place and awkward. "Gwen, I don't know why you'd think I have a girlfriend. I haven't had one in a long time." Her face brightened and some of the light seemed to return to her eyes.

"No girlfriend. That's *good*." She said the word as if she wasn't sure if it really was a good or bad thing. "But why…"

"I get it. I should have just said it was the medical examiner," he said, trying to stop the hatchet from falling before he had a chance to escape its blade. "Teasing you was a bad idea."

The brightness in her eyes once again disappeared.

"Yeah, it was," she said, standing up and making the kitchen stool squeak against the floor. "Look, let's just go. We got a much-needed piece of the puzzle. I knew she wouldn't hurt herself. But now we need to find out who was behind her death."

He was thankful that she had changed the subject, but with the change he could also feel the emotional distance between them shift and widen.

"Let's go to the library," she continued. "Let's look more into the email and see if they have anything that could point us in the direction of who wrote it."

The library was a great next step, especially when she had been teasing him in the shower.

"About what happened in there—" He again motioned toward the bathroom, but she turned around and stopped him with a wave of her hand.

"What happened back there… It was great. I wanted it. You wanted it. But it can't be. Bianca and this investigation need to come first. I don't have the emotional space to have anything more in my life."

He opened his mouth to speak, but she interrupted him. "Do you remember when you once told me a dead-end road only needs to be driven once? Well, we both know this thing between us is a dead end. Let's just stop it before we have the chance to make the same mistake twice. Let's save us both the heartbreak."

GWEN LOOKED OUT the car window as they made their way down Main Street past the late-1800s brick build-ings that lined both sides. The library was just up the road, a couple of storefronts down from Monica Poe's antiques shop, Secret Secondhand. It hadn't been a long car ride, but the silence between Gwen and Wyatt had made it seem like a marathon drive.

She hadn't meant to confront him about the phone call when he'd said it was a woman—she wasn't un-hinged or possessive. He could talk to whomever, when-ever he wanted. She held no claim, and what claim she had once had she'd willingly given up a long time ago.

Then again, maybe if she played her cards right she could get back in his good graces—but being jealous wasn't a good start.

Yet he had ended their time so abruptly and left the bathroom, and then the way he had teased her... He had made it seem like something more than just the medical examiner. So what else was she supposed to think? Men only acted like that when they were try-ing to hide something. That was something she knew all too much about, thanks to a handful of relationships that always ended with secrets and lies—not that she had really cared. If anything, she had always been called cold thanks to her general state of indifference toward men and the choices they made—at least men who weren't Wyatt.

Was it possible that she didn't care about what other men did because the only man she really wanted was Wyatt?

She glanced over at him as he stared out at the road. He had on a pair of aviators that perfectly accented his uniform. Everything about him was all business—and was one heck of a turn-on.

Yet she'd made her choice and pushed him away. It was just so much easier not to care—emotions were messy and she already had enough of that kind of thing on her hands. If she opened herself up, and listened to the desires that whispered through her, she would only get hurt. Her life and her heart had already been shattered with Bianca's death—if he hurt her, there would be nothing left.

He pulled the squad car into a parking spot. Coming around to her side, he opened the door without a word and waited for her to step out.

"Thanks," she said as he closed the door behind her.

He grumbled something unintelligible as he turned away and made his way up to the front doors of the library. She followed behind him, slowly picking her way through patches of ice in an attempt to give him his space.

If this was what it was going to be like, working with him and his hurt ego, she wasn't sure it was something she could handle. Then again, she didn't have any other options. He was the only one investigating her sister's death. Because Mystery was so small, even though it was now a homicide investigation, there was no one else to turn to and no one else who could have possibly cared as much as he did.

He would just have to get over it. They had both made the mistake of falling into each other's arms. Sure, she had been the one to push it forward, but it had been done in a moment of weakness. All she had wanted was to feel again. It had been spontaneous and poorly thought out. There were so many reasons they shouldn't be anything more than friends—or rather, colleagues. Right now, they needed to concentrate on the investigation. Then maybe they could try again, or at least work on creating a friendship.

He opened the front door and waited for her to catch up. Even slightly annoyed with him, and trying to ignore her feelings, she couldn't help appreciating the fact that, regardless of his mood or the events of the day, he was always a gentleman. It was a lost art, and something she had assumed would have been taken from him after his days in the city. Yet, if anything, he was even more of a gentleman than she had remembered.

She wished she could just ask him all the questions she had, but she couldn't—not now. There was no question of whether or not she liked him, everyone who knew Wyatt as anything more than a sheriff's deputy liked him. He was a good man. A man who was built on strong morals and principles, a man's man—actually, he checked every box on the husband-material list.

She pushed the thought from her mind as she glanced up into his face, but he looked away as she moved past him and into the library. She couldn't think about him like this, there was no point to it. She needed to focus. She needed to find justice for Bianca—not a bedroom partner.

As the library's door slid shut behind them, the scent of old books wafted toward her. She loved that smell— the odor of wood pulp, ink, glue and dreams of both authors and readers. This one small building, this little brick outcrop in a town of shadowy secrets, had always been her mecca.

They made their way to the front desk, where the librarian was nose-deep in a book. She didn't look up until Wyatt cleared his throat.

The woman jerked, glancing up from behind her reading glasses. "Oh, hi, sorry," she said, lifting the book like it was more than enough of an excuse for her obliviousness.

"Completely understand, Frannie," Wyatt said, with an appreciative nod to her love of reading.

Dang it. Did the man have to be perfect all the time? Didn't he know that Gwen was trying to find reasons *not* to like him?

"I didn't see you standing there, Wyatt," Frannie said with a smile as she gave them both an acknowledging tip of the head. "'You can never get a cup of tea large enough or a book long enough to suit me.'"

"C. S. Lewis quote?" Gwen asked.

Frannie's smile widened. "A fellow bibliophile, I love it. I can't say that I've ever been able to understand why

more people don't love books." The librarian slipped
a bookmark between the pages and laid the book on
the counter.

"They're worlds where we can escape. We can live
a thousand lives in the pages, or we can live merely
the one we are given—I'll take a thousand lives every
time," Wyatt said with a light chuckle.

Gwen could have sworn she had seen Frannie swoon.

"I…uh… Yes." The woman just stopped short of fan-
ning herself. "Was there something I could help you
two with?"

Gwen had seen Frannie at least a hundred times over
the last few years, when Gwen would come to escape
the confines of the ranch and find a book that could get
her mind off whichever of her mother's antics she had
been dealing with, but she'd never seen Frannie smile
the way she did when she looked up at Wyatt.

"Actually, we were alerted to the fact that one of your
computers may have been used in a crime. Would you
mind if we asked you a few questions?" Wyatt leaned
against the counter, taking a passive stance instead of
his normal straight, shoulders back, no-nonsense officer stance. It was like he was trying to put the woman
at ease, but Frannie kept looking back and forth between Gwen and Wyatt, so much so that Gwen felt out
of place.

"If you don't mind," Gwen said, taking the woman's
hint, "I'll excuse myself and go check out the computer
bank. Is that okay?"

The woman nodded, almost a bit too fervently. "Help
yourself. You know where the computers are, Gwen."

It came as a bit of a shock that the woman knew her name—it was certainly the first time that she had ever bothered to use it. Did her sudden friendliness have something to do with the fact that handsome Wyatt was there, or was it due to the fact that he was there in an official capacity as a deputy?

It was funny, but over the last day she had almost forgotten what and who Wyatt was to everyone else. He wasn't the silly boy from high school who had loved nothing more than AC/DC and laying in the back of his pickup on hot summer nights. No. To others he was the voice of authority, the man who came to their rescue in their moments of terror. He was their hero.

What would it have been like if she'd allowed him to be hers?

Ha. No. She could save herself.

The bank of computers was down a long set of stairs that creaked as she followed them into the belly of the building. The air grew a bit dank and earthy as she made her way into the basement. There was something about the smell that always made the hair on the back of her neck stand at attention. She was too old to be afraid of a smell, but there was just something about it that made it seem dangerous and foreboding.

She was tough, but for a moment she considered turning around and moving back up into the main library and the safety of the book stacks.

Whatever. Whoever had sent Bianca the threatening emails from this room wasn't still there waiting for her like some kind of bogeyman. They were definitely a monster, but it was possible they weren't responsible for killing Bianca. Maybe her sister had been a victim of merely being in the wrong place at the wrong time. *Or not*.

She sighed. She wished they had more to work with. Right now it just seemed like there were so many more questions than answers, and she didn't see it changing at any point in the near future.

The computer lab was full of computers from the 1990s, complete with heavy-looking monitors and keyboards so ignored that several of them were thick with dust and she couldn't see their letters. The place was warm from the heat put off by the ancient machines and it hummed as the beasts struggled in what she was sure was their death throes.

There were only four computers up and running and, for a moment, she wondered which one the possible murderer had sat at. What had they had been thinking when they'd written Bianca the threat? Had they really meant to follow through with their plan? Was this the first time they'd threatened someone? Was it even the first time they had threatened her sister?

The room was nearly empty, except for the hanging industrial lights that buzzed as they looked down on her and the six desks that were lined against the dark, nearly black walls. She walked around the room, looking for anything that could possibly point in their suspect's direction, but there were no loose papers or notes scratched into the wooden desks.

The place was industrial. Whoever came down here, into what was a modern-day dungeon, had to have had a plan to kill her sister.

There was the sound of footsteps and the creak of the stairs. The eerie sound made her heart race and she looked up. Thankfully, it was just Wyatt.

"Did you find anything?" he asked as he walked into the hot room.

She shook her head. "What did the librarian know?"

Other than that she wanted to be in your pants? She snorted at the thought.

"What?" he asked, frowning.

"Oh, nothing. What did she tell you?"

He continued to stare at her like he was trying to read her, but she turned away, pretending to look around one of the desks. Just like the keyboards, it was covered in a thick layer of dust.

"She said there have been a lot of people in and out of the library lately, but she couldn't recall anyone asking to use the computers or seeing anyone come down here in the last few weeks."

The staircase that led to the basement was out of view of the librarian's desk and, given the way she was buried in a book when they'd arrived, it didn't come as a surprise that the woman wouldn't have noticed someone coming or going from the depths. But Gwen was disappointed.

"What are we going to do, Wyatt?"

"It wasn't a completely wasted trip," Wyatt said as he ran his finger over one of the desks. He wiped the dirt from his finger on the leg of his pants, leaving a streak. "According to Frannie, she ran into Monica Poe when she was opening up her store this morning."

"And?"

"She was sporting a fresh black eye." He looked at Gwen with a raise of the brow. "Did you slug her when you were at her house?"

"What?" she asked, completely affronted by the question. "What are you talking about?"

"So *you* didn't hit her?" he asked.

"Absolutely not. Did she say I did?"

She and William's wife had barely spoken to each other before she'd left. And Monica most certainly hadn't had a black eye when Gwen left. If anything, they'd been more than cordial with each other.

Wyatt shook his head. "I was just wondering, why exactly were you up at the Poes' this morning? Did it have something to do with Monica? Or did it have something to do with William?"

Her stomach clenched. "I don't know what you're implying, Wyatt."

He glanced down at his pants and, noticing the streak of dirt he'd left, dusted it off. "I'm not implying anything, Gwen. You may or may not know this, but William Poe has a bit of a reputation when it comes to women. He has been with most of the single women in this town—and several who weren't single. At least that's the word on the street. No judgment, but I need want to know if you are or aren't sleeping with William Poe."

Her face turned hot with embarrassment. "I am aware of his reputation and I can barely stand being in the same town as him. I can't believe you think I'd have anything *like that* to do with a man like him."

"Look, you won't tell me why you were at the Poes'

house this morning, and now Monica has a black eye… I have every right to question you." Wyatt leaned against a support beam near the room's center. "If you're into men like William, I think you were right in assuming we wouldn't be a good fit."

Her hand balled into a fist as she thought of what he was implying and the kind of girl he thought she was.

"I don't have anything going on with that pig William Poe. I'd rather spend the rest of my life in a nunnery than have to spend one single second more with him. So you have nothing to worry about." She flexed her hands as she tried to control her temper. Wyatt wasn't wrong for reacting as he was. When she'd learned about Bianca and William, her reaction had been far more volatile…and filled with several expletives that she hadn't unleashed in years.

"And about Monica," she continued. "That woman deserves a medal, not a slug to the face, for putting up with a man like her husband."

"So you weren't, and have never, slept with him. Good." Some of the tightness in his features seemed to slip away. "But you still didn't answer my question about why you were there."

She sighed. "If I tell you, you have to promise to keep the information between us. Got it?"

He pushed away from the wall and looked over his shoulder like he was checking to make sure they were alone and out of the librarian's hearing distance. "I promise."

"*I* didn't sleep with him. But he and Bianca… They were having an affair."

Chapter Eight

That changed everything. Wyatt wasn't sure if he should be relieved or angry with Gwen. How could she have kept a secret of that magnitude from him for this long? She had to have known what implications it could have in their investigations.

"Why didn't you tell me this before?" he asked.

She dug the toe of her shoe into the concrete floor. "I don't think he had anything to do with her death. That's why I went to their house, to see exactly what he knew—and just to see his reaction. I had to."

"Did it ever occur to you that you could have compromised everything? If he's behind your sister's death, then you just showed our enemy our cards."

She looked up at him with wide eyes. "No. That's not it. That's not what I did. I swear."

"Then what were you thinking, Gwen?"

"Don't come at me like that," she said, anger filling her voice. "I didn't want to tell you about their affair because you were Bianca's friend. You can't tell me that something like this—her relationship with a married, piggish man—doesn't change your opinion of her. And if word of it got out…" She paused. "Now that she's gone, her reputation and our memories of her… That's all we have left."

He stood in silence, unsure of what to say. He wanted to make her feel better. He wanted to take her in his arms and tell her there were so many important things that mattered more than her sister's reputation in this small town. But then again, he could understand why she was so protective of her sister's honor.

He loved his brothers, Waylon, Rainier and Colter. He would protect them just like she protected her sister. Heck, once in the fifth grade, right after Rainier and Colter had been adopted, Wyatt had gotten in a fistfight on the school's playground. One close-minded little jerk had made the mistake of thinking he could make fun of them for being a different color.

He had taken the boy down, splitting his lip with one well-placed punch. But even though he had won the fight, it had done little to help the war he and his brothers had to face in the small town after word had spread that the two new Fitz boys were of Native American descent. In a rural town like Mystery, there would always be those people who hated those who were different.

And if word got out about how different, or immoral, Bianca's behavior had been in having an affair with a married man, it wouldn't just be Bianca's memory that could be impacted. Without a doubt, Gwen hadn't yet realized that the revelation could hurt her reputation as well. And it was more than possible that some self-righteous slob would think some kind of justice would need to be paid for Bianca's sinful actions—and that was where things could get dangerous for Gwen and her mother.

"Does your mom know about Bianca's relationship?"

Gwen shook her head.

At least they had one thing going for them. If Carla knew about it, it was more than likely she would spill the beans to the other barflies, and that would be a recipe for danger.

"You need to make sure she doesn't find out. No matter what," he continued. "I will keep this to myself. But you know we're going to have to look into him—and Monica. Do you think his wife knows about the relationship?"

"No," Gwen said with a long exhale. "When I stopped by, William was in a hurry for me to get back on the road."

"Do you think it was because she may have a clue about his dealings with other women? Or do you think that he was trying to cover up something about Bianca's murder?"

She nibbled at her lip. "I'm not the cop here, but my gut's telling me he didn't have anything to do with Bianca's murder. I don't think he was the one in your family's barn. He's not the kind of guy who would get his hands dirty. At least not like that. As for Monica, I don't think he does anything in front of her. Before the thing with Bianca, she and I used to be friends. She never whispered a word about him or his affairs to me."

"Did you know he was having affairs back then?"

"Honestly, I didn't know him that well. I just saw him between the normal comings and goings of things.

I never liked him. He always treated Monica like she was an employee rather than his wife."

"What do you mean?"

She shrugged. "Once when I was waiting for her to finish getting ready, he came in and told her that he needed a new printer for his home office. Instead of recognizing that we had plans, he made us go pick out a new one and bring it back and set it up for him. He wasn't that busy. He could have done it himself, but no. It's just stupid little things like that. Like his life is so much more important than hers. It made me sick every time I was around them."

"Well, it's no wonder he cheats on her. He doesn't appreciate her."

"Just shoot me if you ever see me in a relationship like that," she said flippantly, then as though she realized that she was talking to him about a relationship, her face turned red and she started to stammer. "I mean... I don't want... You know. I just don't want to be with a man who treats me like that."

There were so many endearing things about her. No matter what happened between them, he could still like her for the person she had once been, and the wonderful, albeit confusing, woman she had become.

"What do you want, Gwen?" he asked, unable to help himself or the desire that started to fill him as she stammered over her words like she had when they were young. Yet, as he asked the question, he wasn't entirely sure he wanted to know the answer.

She bit at the side of her cheek as their eyes met. What was she trying to tell him with that look?

"I… I don't know, Wyatt," she said, her voice soft. "But I don't think crazy is a good look on me." She motioned toward the world outside the library. "I mean, like what happened at your place. I'm sorry. I don't know what happened back there, but I can't… I don't know. I guess I just want to be able to just *be* with you… or someone. I don't want to have to worry about other girls calling them. Or their wives. Or if they mean what they say. I'm just no good at the dating thing—I've been burned so much in the past. I mean, my ex was engaged *two months* after we broke up. I don't have it in me to play games again. It doesn't bring out the best in me. I'm so sorry."

"You did let a little bit of your crazy show," he said, with what he hoped was a comforting and dismissive laugh. "The good news is that I always liked your kind of crazy."

She tilted her head and gave him a smile that made his heart shift in his chest. "You say that, but I doubt you mean it. I'm a lot of work. And I'm a hard woman to date."

Was that her way of saying she would date him?

Is that what he wanted?

He liked her. He always had. And as understanding as he could be about what had happened back in his bathroom, he hadn't really thought she was open to anything. It was amazing how she continued to surprise him.

"And I'm probably even harder," he said in an attempt to be real. "I'm not around a lot. I'm always working, either at the department or helping out on the ranch. I don't know if I could make you happy, Gwen. I mean… I already tried once. Sure, we were young, but that doesn't change the fact that we failed." He stepped back from her, and for the first time he noticed how hot the room was. "You were right about what you said back at my place. Maybe it's not a good idea to go driving back down a dead-end road… We both know how it's gonna end. And, as much as you don't want your heart broken, I don't want mine to be torn to pieces either. Not again."

"I'm so sorry it has to be this way, Wyatt." Her face fell and she stared down at the floor as she scuffed her shoe over the rough concrete.

"It's okay. I guess it's good that we're on the same page, at least." Even if he wasn't sure it was the page he wanted them to be on, he had to protect himself and her from being hurt again.

He took her by the hand. Her fingers were stiff and unyielding in his, and though he should have let her go, he couldn't force his body to do as his mind told. He thought about all the things he wanted to tell her— that he wanted her back in his life, that he didn't want to get hurt and that the thing he feared the most was falling in love.

He led her up the stairs and past the librarian.

"Thanks for everything," he said, giving the librarian a warm smile and a tip of his head.

She gave him a sour look, surely noticing him holding Gwen's hand, but he didn't care. Not waiting for her to answer, they walked through the front door.

As they stepped out onto the sidewalk he turned back

to Gwen, unable to handle the tense silence between them any longer. "Let's just get through this. Then we can talk about things when I get back from Alaska."

She pulled her hand from his and frowned. "What are you talking about, *when you get back from Alaska*?"

Had he forgotten to tell her?

He stopped and turned toward her in an effort to deflect some of the blow. "Yeah… I have a prisoner transfer in a couple of days. I have to go up there, then bring him back to the county for his trial."

"When were you going to tell me that you were just going to leave me high and dry with Bianca's case? You just yelled at me about keeping secrets, yet here you are not telling me something like that. Don't you think I deserved to know you were going to push me and the case on someone else?" Her words came hard and fast, and each was like a fist.

"You have it all wrong, Gwen. I wasn't keeping anything from you. It just slipped my mind."

"Don't tell me that."

"No, really," he said, raising his hands in surrender. "I've had other things on my mind besides going." He gave her a soft grin; the grin he knew she loved.

She sighed, taking a second to collect herself. "So, you're not going to go on the trip?"

He grimaced. "That's not possible. Everything's set up for me to go. I have to. It's my job, Gwen."

As he looked at her, he couldn't help the feeling that he had been right. He was never going to be the kind of guy who could make her happy. There were just so many things standing in their way.

Even knowing that, he couldn't help the desire that filled him every time he looked into her lake-blue eyes. The wind kicked up and blew her scent toward him. He drew the aroma of flowers and sweet grass deep into his lungs. Why did everything have to be so alluring when it came to her? Everything but the torture they seemed to always inflict upon each other.

Gwen started walking down the sidewalk. Was she just going to leave him and walk back to the ranch? Was she that mad?

"What are you doing, Gwen? I'm sorry," he called out, catching up to her. "I didn't mean to hurt your feelings. It's just that there are just some things I can't change. My job is one of them."

Gwen turned on her heel. "I don't care about your damn job, Wyatt. I get it. I was stupid to let what happened happen this morning. If anyone is sorry here, it's me."

How could he tell her that, even now when they were fighting, he wanted to be with her? That some feelings never went away?

"Wait, Gwen," he said, reaching for her hand, but she jerked away.

"Don't. No. Let's not put ourselves through this. Let's just get to the bottom of the case and each of us can go back to our own lives. We don't need to talk about it. We don't need to bring up old hurts—or new ones. Let's just let each other be. We're no good together."

He couldn't disagree with her more. Things weren't easy between them. There was too much history for things to be simple. But what they didn't have in ease, they made up for in passion. If they could just let go of some things, they could be like they were in the shower—laughing and truly letting each other see who they were at their core.

He loved her for the woman she was inside—if she would ever let him see that person again.

She started walking, making her way past the Pretties and Pastries café, and he trailed behind, unsure of how to proceed. No matter how he felt, he couldn't make her feel something too. And he'd already apologized for making the mistake of not telling her about Alaska. What more could she want?

Gwen stopped in front of Secret Secondhand. He glanced in the window. Monica was talking to a customer, but, as she noticed them, her face pinched and she gave a tight wave. Just as Frannie had told them, Monica had a large fresh bruise on her left eye. She turned away, covering her face in shadows.

Whatever had happened after Gwen had left had been something that Monica obviously wouldn't want to talk about. Had William hit her? Wyatt wanted to walk in and ask her about it, but from her body language, it was clear that she didn't want to see them.

All of his deputy spidey senses tingled. William was guilty of something. And, if Wyatt had to bet, William had something to do with Bianca's death. If Wyatt had learned one thing, it was that the type of men who used violence to control were often the same ones who ended up becoming murderers. Usually it wasn't intentional. Or at least that was what they loved to say in court—

that they didn't mean to, or that things had just gotten out of hand.

He hated that kind of man—the kind who thought hitting was okay. No woman—heck, *no one*—deserved to live in a constant fear of physical violence. PFMA, partner or family member assault, were among his least favorite calls to take, and one of the most common. It seemed like most days he had at least one, if not two, calls in which he had to break up a family's fight.

Unfortunately, in the case of abuse, the woman was very unlikely to go against the husband. In the state of Montana, the court systems were starting to toe a harder line against perpetrators of domestic violence, but there still wasn't much they could do to protect the victims. There were hundreds of cases in which a woman finally got the strength, or hit rock bottom, and turned in the abuser—only to have the abuser get out of jail and murder the woman they felt was responsible for putting them behind bars.

It was a no-win system.

Gwen pulled on his hand. "Are we going in or what?"

He motioned toward Monica. "She didn't call the police and report anything. I bet you a hundred bucks that William hit her, but if you asked her what happened she'll have some stupid excuse—she ran into something, fell down the stairs…something."

"I know Monica. She'll open up to me."

"You said she hasn't in the past. Why do you think it would be different with me, a deputy, at your side?" He gave a cynical laugh. "The more you hang out with me, the more you'll see that this uniform tends to make everyone tighten up. We aren't going to get anywhere with Monica. I think it's better if we look into other things first. Namely, William. He's a hell of a good place to start as far as our list of suspects."

"Sure. If you think it's best, but…" She turned away from the window, but glanced back at Monica as if she was thinking about exactly how good their friendship was…and if what he was saying was true.

"Trust me about Monica. Before we can go to her, we need to figure out what motivates her. And what it will take to make her flip against her husband—that is, *if* her husband is the murderer. He may be nothing more than a piece of—"

"Oh, I can guarantee he's *that*," Gwen said, finishing his thought. "So, if we're not going to talk to Monica, what did you have in mind for your next step?"

He started walking back to the car, Gwen following. In truth, he didn't have much to go on, so he went with the first thing that came to mind. "The medical examiner was talking about Beuthanasia, but what I've been wondering is where it came from. Did she have it with her? Or did someone else have it? Does she have a partner in her vet practice? Or does she have an employee who would have access to the drug and had a problem with her?"

Gwen tapped on her lip. "There's always something going on at the clinic. You know, small-town stuff. But there's not been anything going on recently, at least nothing that she'd mentioned to me."

"Let's head over there." He glanced down at his watch. "They have to be up and running. Maybe we can talk to someone who has been working closely with Bianca—maybe they can tell us a little more about her affair with William."

He was grasping for straws, but that was exactly what an investigation normally was—following tiny leads, most that led nowhere... But once in a while, in a moment of intuition, of following that little wiggle in his gut, they led him to the answers he needed.

SHE WAS ACTING like a lunatic and she knew it. She wanted him, all of him, but the fear of being close to someone was nearly overwhelming. She had so much on her hands with her mother, her sister and the needs of the ranch. That, mixed with all the apprehension she was feeling... It was all so confusing.

All she could do was move through this one moment at a time, then one day, then one week. If he was the man she thought he was, he would understand and forgive her for the way she was feeling.

She glanced over at Wyatt. He turned toward Bianca's vet clinic. His caramel-colored eyes were hidden behind his aviators and he seemed focused on the road—maybe a little too focused. Was he avoiding talking to her? Was he trying to stop them from having another disagreement? Or was he just waiting for her to say something?

"How long are you going to be in Alaska?" she asked, hoping he was just waiting.

He sucked in a long breath that told her she may have been wrong.

"I know you have to go," she said, trying to take the

edge off her question. "I know what your job entails. I guess I want to know more about the man you are—as my friend. That's all."

"As your *friend*?" He gave her a look she wasn't able to read—but the best she could guess was that it was halfway between questioning and confused.

"Yeah. The truth is, Wyatt, I've missed you." She sighed. "You were my whole life for so long. It was hard when I… I ended things. You helped me through so much, with my dad and all…and my mom. When you weren't around, it was like I had lost myself and who I was. I was a ghost of the person I had been. I lost everything. I never want to feel that way again."

"You couldn't, Gwen. You know who you are now. Who knows? Maybe it wasn't a bad thing that we broke up… You got to know who you are and I got to know who I am. We each got to go out in the world and experience things we wouldn't have if we'd stayed together."

She wasn't sure she agreed with him. If they'd stayed together, maybe they would have simply experienced the world together instead of apart—and maybe they both would have been better for it. Or maybe they both would have been so pulled to this town they would never have left. That had certainly been the case for her, and without a doubt, if she would have allowed their relationship to continue, he would have given up the world for her.

Now, rightly, he wouldn't even give up a trip to Alaska. Not that she blamed him, or didn't understand that he had to go. Plus, they'd only been speaking again for a couple of days. She couldn't expect anything from him.

She sighed. *Stop.* She had to stop. She couldn't pick apart everything he said, every choice he made and every feeling she had—it wasn't healthy. For either of them. For once, she just needed to go with the moment and let life happen. She couldn't micromanage this. She couldn't plan the unexpected.

Then again, some questions needed answering. "So you're not mad at me for the past? For breaking things off?"

His fingers gripped the steering wheel tight, but after a moment they loosened and he glanced over at her. "At first, I was like you—you were the only thing I knew. I loved you with all my heart. I didn't understand why you did what you did. I still don't. For being so young, we really were good together."

"We were." She nodded.

"Do you remember the barn?" he asked with a light laugh.

She thought back to the dozens of nights they had found themselves meeting up in his family's main barn at Dunrovin. They would sneak up into the hayloft and make out. He never pressured her for more, even though she had known exactly how badly she left him aching.

Her gentleman.

"What about the barn?" she asked with a wiggle of her brow.

He chuckled, and the sound made some of the heaviness in her disappear.

Yes, she just needed to let things be. What would happen would happen and she would have to accept their connection for what it was, not what she wanted it to be. If she didn't, she would be lucky if they even ended this investigation as friends.

Wyatt shifted slightly in the seat. "You remember the night we carved our initials in the post?"

She smiled. "That was the night of the Sadie Hawkins dance, right?"

He nodded. "Bianca went with us. Wasn't that when she was going after Rainier?"

She laughed as she thought back to the days when she and her sister had dreamed of marrying the brothers. "How life changes…"

"It was too bad they didn't work out."

Those had been the days before her father's death. The days they had still been innocent and untouched by tragedy. The days when her mother had still been functional.

"But she and Rainier…" he continued. "If you want to talk about two people who were completely different."

She laughed at the thought of her preppy sister dating their county's infamous bad boy. As soon as her parents had found out about their relationship, her father had put an end to it.

"Their relationship had some fireworks."

His eyebrow quirked as he looked over at her and smiled. "You mean like ours as of late?"

"I wouldn't consider this a relationship." She gave him a coy glance.

Wait. Did *he*?

"True, but…seeing you in that towel… You definitely brought out the animal in me."

She tried to restrain her grin. "Really?"

His smile widened. "I haven't been that turned on in a long time. You have no idea what you do to me."

She reached over and sat her hand between them under the police-issued computer on the console. He let go of the steering wheel and slipped his fingers between hers.

They weren't anything beyond friends, but within her there was a glimmer of hope. Regardless of what she did to him, he had no idea what he did to her—or her heart.

Chapter Nine

The clinic was locked and someone had taped a closed sign to the door in between two plastic Santa decals. Wyatt was surprised at the lack of activity. He would have thought that, even with Bianca's death, the show would have needed to go on at her clinic. Animals always needed tending and phones would always ring. Yet the place was eerily quiet.

"Is this how the place normally is?" Wyatt asked as Gwen stopped beside him.

She shook her head. "No, but with everything that's been happening…someone must have let the employees know they weren't to come in." She walked around the side of the building toward the barn that normally housed the large animals that her sister couldn't see in the small clinic. "Even the barn's empty. That's strange."

"She had been working, right?"

Gwen shrugged. "As far as I know, but lately Bianca had been off. And the more and more I see, I guess I can understand why."

"You think it's possible someone just came in and

cleared out the animals after they found out what happened?"

"For sure, but I don't know where they would have taken the animals that were in more serious condition. But maybe she didn't have any super serious cases or something."

Wyatt nodded. There was something wrong about the place. If some well-meaning person had taken the animals, he would have thought they would have left a note or something, but there was nothing besides the sign on the front door to let anyone know what was going on.

"I think you should wait in the car," he said, motioning toward his patrol unit. "Let me clear the building, then I'll come get you."

"There's no way I'm going to let you go in there alone. Besides, there's nothing to worry about." She peered in the front picture window with her hand over her eyes in an attempt to shield the evening sun from her eyes.

"Anything?" he asked as she turned back to him.

"I can't see." She shook her head. "Hold on," she said, reaching down into her pocket and drawing out a key ring that was chock-full of a variety of brass and aluminum keys. "I think she gave me a key in case I ever needed it. I don't think this is what she had in mind at the time, but…" She flipped through the keys and stopped at a brass one the same color as the doorknob.

She slipped the key into the lock and clicked it open. The door opened with a long, shrill squeak. For a moment, Gwen stood there just staring. Wyatt moved closer to her, trying to see what she was looking at.

"Holy…" he said, looking in.

There was dog food strewn across the floor, and all the papers that normally sat on the counter were thrown around the room. Every picture was crooked or had been taken off the wall and tossed on the floor. The receptionist's computer screen was cracked and the keyboard was hanging over the edge of the desk by its cord—it made the shrill tone of a phone that had been off the hook for too long. Even the waiting room chairs were overturned and pulled away from the walls.

Whoever had come into this place wasn't there just to steal; they had been there to destroy. They must have hated Bianca and her work. Was it possible that whoever was behind this had been a jilted customer or someone who had felt that she had done them wrong?

Monica came to his mind. Could she have found out about Bianca's affair with William? Perhaps she went to Bianca's cabin, then here to take her down? Maybe when she didn't find Bianca she had gone to the ranch. Or maybe she had come here first and had stolen the Beuthanasia and then gone to Bianca's cabin.

Gwen walked toward the back of the clinic, pushing past the half door that led to the back.

"Don't touch anything," he called. "I want to get my team in. Maybe they can pull some prints."

Gwen stopped and turned around. "Oh, I'm sure they can pull hundreds of prints. There are normally at least a hundred people in and out of this building in a single working day. You could probably pull most of the people's prints from this town—everyone comes to my sister for their livestock."

Whoever had done this had put thought behind what they wanted to do and how they wanted to do it. This was a crime of anger and perhaps revenge, but it wasn't one done carelessly.

Regardless, he had to get his people in here and give it a shot. He couldn't call the game until it had been played.

"Don't go back there alone, Gwen," he said, motioning for her to stay put. "I need to clear the place before we go poking around. We don't want to surprise anyone if they are still here."

Even as he spoke, he knew he was being overly protective. It was unlikely anyone else was in the building, but he had to keep Gwen safe and, if they got their hands on the perpetrator, he would have to have all his ducks in a row for the prosecuting attorney. He wouldn't be able to look himself in the mirror if whoever was behind all this got to walk on a technicality—something every defense attorney loved.

He moved after her down the hall and took the lead. The front had been a mess, but the back of the clinic was even worse. Every cupboard was opened and a medley of supplies from gauze to bottles of Betadine were torn off the shelves and scattered through the hallways and rooms. There was a room filled with cages, for what he assumed was for the small animals that came through the clinic, but the pens were empty and half of them stood open.

Bianca's office sat next to that small room. Every drawer of her black metal desk was open and the one on the right bottom sat crooked, like someone had pulled on it just a little too hard. Broken glass littered the top of her desk and an empty, bent frame was thrown on top of her nameplate.

"Do you know what picture she had on her desk?" he asked, pointing toward the frame.

"Sure, that was one from this year's Fourth of July. We had a big barbecue at the ranch. Everyone was there and we got a photo. It was one of the best parties we've ever had."

"Could you name some of the people from the picture?"

She tapped on her lip and looked toward the ceiling like she could pull the faces out of the air. "Well... We were there, Mom, Bianca and me. Then there were some people from around town—a lot of my mom's friends from the bar. There was the staff from here. And your brother's ex-wife, Alli, with her sister, Christina, and Winnie. Just about everyone we knew came." Her mouth went into an O shape. "And the Poes were there... William and Monica."

"Were they in the picture?"

She nodded. "I'm sure."

He sighed. Everything came back to the Poes. There was no question they were involved in this, but it was up to him to figure out exactly how deep their connections lay.

"Did everyone at the party get a picture? Or did your sister post it to Facebook or anything?"

"I don't think so. And Bianca doesn't do the whole social media thing."

He didn't either. And to be honest, he didn't mind

it. Many of the PFMAs he was called on seemed to involve one or more of the social media sites. It was a testament to the times that so many feelings could be hurt with just a few mistyped words or an inferred slight that originated on a screen.

Was it possible that this case had something to do with a slight? Maybe someone besides Monica had found out about William and Bianca's affair and had grown jealous.

It seemed like a stretch. Monica and William seemed like the most likely suspects. In cases like these, most often the wife had found out and and had come after the girlfriend. And usually deaths perpetrated by women were just like Bianca's—passive kills—murders that involved a poison or some kind of implement that wasn't as brutal, and one where the killer didn't have to actually watch the person die.

The signs were beginning to point more and more in the direction of a woman as the killer, but that didn't take William off the suspect list. He was just the kind of guy who would also commit a passive murder. He didn't want to get his hands dirty, but maybe he would if the conditions were right—like if Bianca was blackmailing him.

There were still so many missing elements keeping Wyatt from fully understanding this case, but as he walked out of Bianca's office, for the first time since they started, he knew he was getting closer to pinning the perpetrator down.

In the back of the clinic there was a refrigerator. Its door was ajar, and medications had spilled out of it. He moved closer. In the open cupboard next to the fridge, there was a lockbox.

"Is this where your sister would have kept the scheduled medications?" he asked, pointing toward the box.

"What's that?" Gwen asked, stopping beside him.

"Those are the drugs that the DEA deems dangerous and addictive if not used properly—you know, like the Beuthanasia."

"Oh, you mean is that where she keeps—er, *kept*—her narcs?" she asked.

"Not all scheduled meds are narcs, but yeah. Is that where she kept them?"

Gwen nodded. "I think so. Why?"

He knelt down by the box. "It's still locked, which means one of two things. Either the perp took the drugs from the cabinet while it was still open, which means they wouldn't have had to turn the place over. Or, what I believe, is that they took the drugs from Bianca's bag at Dunrovin. But if I'm right, we're going to have to prove it."

"Let's say you're right. Let's say they took the drugs from her bag in the barn. What does that change?"

He smiled as he felt another piece of his investigation fall into place. "If they didn't take the drugs while they were here, maybe it means they weren't really planning on killing her. Maybe they were following her, watching her work. When she went to see the mare, a mare that she may have been prepared to put to sleep, the perp saw an opportunity to make the kill—and they took it."

"I'm not following," Gwen said with a frown.

"If they hadn't been planning to kill her, maybe they

were a little less prepared. Maybe they made a mistake in their haste. Maybe they forgot to wear gloves when they went through her bag. And Bianca was probably the only other one to touch it, which means maybe we can get the prints we need."

Gwen sucked in a breath.

"We need to find your sister's vet bag."

"Alli said your mother had been in the barn after your team had been through. Maybe she found it some-where, or can at least tell us whether or not she saw it."

He pulled his phone out of his pocket and dialed his mom. He walked back to his car, took out the camera he kept in the trunk and made his way back into the building.

His mom answered on the second ring. "How's it going, sweetie?"

No matter how old he got, his foster mother would always call him "sweetie," and as much as it probably would have bothered other men, it was one of the many things he loved about her. She was the kind who al-ways put everyone else ahead of herself, sometimes to a fault. She had a habit of bringing on employees who had dark pasts—pasts that usually came back to bite her in the butt.

Once, Eloise Fitzgerald had hired a felon—the man had worked in the guest quarters, cleaning and taking care of the rooms. Two weeks after he'd been brought on, he'd broken into one of the rooms, stolen the guest's keys and made off with their car. The ranch's insurance had taken a hit, and the car had later been found aban-doned at the Canadian border. They didn't talk about it and she hadn't hired another known felon since, but she was still a sucker for sob stories.

"Good." He started to take pictures of the scene. "I was calling because Alli mentioned that you had been in the barn after Lyle and Steve went over the scene. By chance did you see Bianca's bag lying around anywhere? They didn't report finding a bag, but there should have been one on scene."

"Didn't you look when you were there?"

He hadn't come in until later, and when he'd arrived on scene it had been busy thanks to the coming and going of Lyle and Steve. It was only because he'd volunteered to notify the next of kin that he had even gotten the case. "I did, but Lyle and Steve took point."

"Lyle and Steve are lucky they found the barn. You do know that, right?" his mother said with a sharp laugh. "I mean those two men... How are they working at the same department as you? I can't believe you aren't just flying up the ranks over there."

She wasn't wrong about Steve and Lyle, but he couldn't control the only men who were his department's acting forensics team. The only things he could control were what he did with this case and how he could help the woman whose life it impacted the most.

"Mom, the bag. Did you see it?" he asked, trying to avoid falling into the chatting trap with his mother.

It had been a while since he'd seen or spoken to her, and no doubt she was chomping at the bit to hear about the case and how it was playing out. She was kind and smart, but she was also probably worrying about the impact the case would have on her business—not that she would bring it up to him.

"What did the bag look like?" she asked in a way that he couldn't decide if she was being coy or if she really had no idea what he was talking about.

"Don't play, Mom. You know. It's black. Kind of like a doctor's bag. Likely full of vet supplies." He looked over at Gwen, who was mimicking the shape with her hands.

"Oh, that?" his mom said. "I assumed you all must have been done with it, so I dropped it off at the Widow Maker a couple of hours ago."

"Widow Maker?" He thought of Carla and her penchant for tossing raw eggs. He could only imagine how she would treat his mother—a woman Carla hadn't spoken to since the day of her husband's funeral. "*You* went to the Widow Maker? Why didn't you just leave it for me?"

Gwen's mouth opened with surprise. "She did what?"

There was a slight pause on the other end of the phone. "Sometimes the most honorable thing isn't the easiest, Wyatt."

It was a lesson his mother had drilled into him a long time ago, but he never grew above hearing it.

"This isn't about being honorable, Mom—"

"Besides, Carla was quite nice," his mother continued, cutting him off. "She even invited me in for a cup of joe. I think she's very lonely and hurt with Bianca's death and… Well, *you know*."

She didn't have to remind him of their battered pasts.

"Are you sure she didn't invite you in so she could poison your coffee? Or was she drunk again?"

"She's still a drunk?" his mother asked.

He glanced over at Gwen. She was shaking her head as she pinched the bridge of her nose. "It doesn't matter. Did you go in the house?"

"I chatted with her a bit on the porch, but there was work that needed tending to at the ranch. With that mare down and everything up in the air with…*things*, well, I just didn't feel good being gone for too long. She seemed to understand. But it might be nice if you stopped by and visited with her for a bit. She wanted to talk about you."

The woman who had pelted his patrol unit yesterday wanted to talk about him? Either she was slobbering drunk, or she had sobered up and forgotten her earlier egg warfare and the gun she'd pulled on him.

He sighed. The last thing he wanted to do was have another run-in with that woman, but if she had the bag, her place was his next stop.

He dropped his hand down on the counter and papers slipped to the floor. It was about right. This day had seemed not only to have started with manure, but was seemingly destined to end with it as well.

Gwen ran her hands through her blond hair, and it caught the light that was streaming through the windows of the back room.

What he would give to be back in the shower and escaping from reality.

Chapter Ten

As she trudged up to the front door of the ranch house and kicked the snow off her boots, Gwen couldn't help but feel like she was headed to the gallows. After her mother's scene in the driveway and the Taser, regardless of the show she had put on for Eloise Fitzgerald, this wasn't going to go well.

The door was unlocked, but before she stepped inside, she turned back to Wyatt.

His eyes were stormy. No matter how much she felt like she was going to the gallows, he was the one who *looked* it. His shoulders were rounded and his hands were opening and closing into tight fists as he stared in the front window.

The living room's curtains were drawn shut, blocking the last of the evening light from seeping through and illuminating the mess that was their lives.

She hated this place. Every time she came to the door it felt like she was entering her own personal hell. It was a reaction that had been learned over years of coming to this door and not knowing what she would find inside.

Once, when she'd been about twenty, she'd come

home to find her mother smearing peanut butter on herself. She had tried to have her mother see a therapist afterward, but her mother had sworn the incident was because she had been cleaning up a downed pine and needed to get the sap off her skin. It was a story she could have bought had her mother not been buck naked. And drunk.

She glanced back to the man on death row. He stared at the door as he sucked in a long breath.

"Are you sure that you want to go inside? I can just run in, get the bag and get out. You don't have to put yourself through this," she said, motioning toward the chipped door.

Wyatt shook his head. "It's fine," he said, but there was a hardness to his voice she hadn't heard him use before.

Was that his officer voice? If it was, she could see why he was good at his job. He could probably scare the wits out of any criminal if he came at them with that kind of edge during an arrest or interrogation. As it was, the sound made her core tighten and a strange, unwelcome surge of apprehension moved through her. This wasn't a good idea. She should have just called her mother.

But it was too late to turn back now.

Hopefully her mother wasn't even home. She looked down at her watch. It was more than possible that Carla would be at the bar by now. And if she was, all the unpleasantness could be avoided. And heck, maybe if things continued on between her and Wyatt in the same way—with their constant failure to find a balance between their past, present and future—well, maybe he would never have to see her mother again.

The thought of them not working out coated her in a layer of heavy sadness.

Whatever they were or had been, it didn't really matter. What mattered was the longing she had felt when she'd been standing outside his trailer and the thrill when she'd been in his arms.

She pushed open the door and walked in ahead of Wyatt. Every part of her begged that her mother would be anywhere but here. Yet as she walked into the living room, she heard the familiar banging of the cabinets as her mother moved around in the kitchen.

Sometimes it was like she had no luck at all.

She looked over at Wyatt, and even in the near darkness of the room she could still see flashes of the tempest in his eyes.

"Why don't you wait here? I'll go in and find out where she put the bag. No need to start a *thing*." She held up her hand, checking him as though he was some kind of animal that she could control.

She should have known better.

"Gwen, I'm not letting you walk back there alone. What if whoever is behind your sister's death broke into your house? What if it's not your mother in there? Or what if she's being held captive?" He motioned to the door that led to the farm-style kitchen. "I'm not letting you walk into trouble."

"I hate to mention this, but…" She gave a nervous laugh. "Regardless of who's standing in that kitchen, there's going to be some amount of fireworks."

He motioned her forward, not taking her polite no as an answer. Sometimes he was so pushy and controlling, but at the same time his concern for her safety made him all that much more lovable.

"You know I'm looking forward to seeing your mother about as much as I'd look forward to getting a root canal. Actually, I'd take the root canal."

She chuckled. "Mom, you in there?" she called, afraid to let her thoughts go any further.

There was an unintelligible grumble from her mother inside the kitchen.

"Seriously," she said, motioning to Wyatt. "Wait for a minute. Let me make sure she's at least wearing clothing. If anything goes wrong, or if you are concerned in any way, you are welcome to come in. But you know my mother. I have no idea what kind of state she's going to be in."

Wyatt nodded. "Okay, but if I think anything's going haywire, I'm coming in."

Before she had time to think about what she was doing, she leaned in and gave him a quick peck on his stubbled cheek. Wyatt looked at her with wide eyes and she smiled. He was such a good man.

"Thanks." She turned and entered the kitchen, ignoring the desire she had to turn and tell Wyatt exactly what she thought of him—and how sorry she was for their misunderstanding back at his place.

How differently the day would have gone if she hadn't let her stupid emotions and insecurities get in the way.

In the kitchen, her mother was standing by the fridge.

Her face was a shade of red Gwen recognized from her mother's many nights of drinking.

"How much have you had?"

Her mother looked up. There was a glass of vodka in her hand and, as she noticed Gwen looking, she pushed it behind her back like she was a kid caught in some guilty act.

"I don't know whatcher talking about," Carla said, her words slurred with drunkenness. But as she spoke she forgot about hiding the drink in her hand and brought it back around where Gwen could see it.

Gwen gave a resigned sigh. "Mrs. Fitzgerald said she stopped by here today and talked to you. Is that right?"

Her mother took a long drink, her need to hide outweighed by her desire for more. "I played all nicey-nicey, but she's still a piece of work. She thinks she's all high and mighty. Like her life don't stink…" She took another drink.

"Did she drop anything off?" Gwen couldn't help but feel like she was talking to a two-year-old.

Her mother shrugged, but her gaze moved to the back door where Bianca's vet bag sat on the counter. Gwen moved toward it, but her mother stepped in her way.

"Are you shacking up with that boy Wyatt?"

Gwen looked back at the door, praying Wyatt couldn't hear their conversation. He didn't need to hear her mother's smear campaign or anything else she probably had to say right now.

"Do I need to remind you of what he done to me? He had no right to tase me." Her mother picked up the nearly empty bottle of vodka that sat on the kitchen table and refilled her glass.

"You're lucky he didn't arrest you. He could have. And think about how badly you'd be detoxing if he had."

"He didn't have nothing on me. I'm gonna sue him and the county. They're gonna have a real mess on their hands."

The only mess here was her.

"I shoulda sued them all for more. Do you remember the pissy little settlement his family's insurance gave us?"

Her mother had made it a nearly daily habit of complaining about how they had only gotten forty thousand dollars from the Dunrovin's insurance company. That, added to her father's life insurance, had covered his burial and about six months of the ranch's overhead costs. Six months in which her mother had fallen deeper and deeper into her depression—a depression that seemed to never end thanks to the constant numb of alcohol.

Gwen walked over and pried the glass from her fingers. "Aren't you tired of acting like this? Of feeling this way? It's been long enough. And now with Bianca gone… This isn't going to help you or me get through this."

Her mother reached after her as she walked to the sink and poured the drink down the drain.

"No!" her mother called, running to the sink. She grabbed the glass out of Gwen's hand and swirled her finger around the rim. "Who do you think you are? That was mine. I paid for it. I pay for everything in this dang place. You got no right to come in here and take anything of mine—especially in a week like this."

"I'm the one who runs this ranch, Mother. Do I need to remind you how little you do?"

She knew now was a poor time to pick a fight, but she couldn't stand idly by and let her mother try to slowly kill her with the lashes lain by her words. Not anymore.

"How dare you, Gwyneth Marie Johansen." Her mother tried to take on an air of authority by using her full name, but it came out as a slow, slurry mess of syllables that made her sound even drunker than before.

Wyatt stepped into the kitchen. "Mrs. Johansen," he said, greeting her with a dip of the head. "I hope you're feeling better."

"What the hell are you doing here?" She motioned her glass toward Wyatt, then turned and lifted her shirt. There, on the side of her waist, was an angry black-and-blue mark where the Taser's prongs had bitten into her skin. "Look what you did to me, you bastard. I hope you feel real good about taking down an old woman. What else are you gonna do to me? Get Gwen killed—just like you did with Bianca and my husband? You want to kill my whole damned family. Admit it."

She staggered as she moved toward Wyatt. The glass slipped in her hand and fell to the floor, shattering. The shards of glass spewed across the linoleum, landing on the tips of Gwen's boots.

Her mother kept moving, seemingly unaware of the glass and the scene she was causing.

"Carla, don't move," Wyatt ordered, motioning at

her mother's bare feet. "There's glass all over the floor. If you step, you're going to cut yourself up. Just stay where you are and we'll clean this up."

Her mother hiccupped, and she listed to the left so hard she was forced to grab the counter. The glass crunched under her and dots of blood oozed out from beneath the soles of her feet.

"Carla." Wyatt rushed to her side, wrapping his arm around her. "I told you to stay put. Are you okay?"

She tried to push his arms away, but the movement was feeble and weak. Normally her mother was so strong when she was drunk that she could nearly take down a full-grown moose.

"I… I got…this," her mother said, her words suddenly even more slurred and gummed together than before.

She fell into Wyatt's arms.

Something was very wrong.

"What…did ya do to me?" her mother asked, looking at Wyatt like he had slipped her a roofie.

"How much did you drink, Mrs. Johansen? Really. It's important you tell me."

Carla slipped down, forcing him to hold her as she gently slid to the floor and her body rested along the bits of glass. Her eyes started to close.

"Mrs. Johansen! Don't go to sleep. Stay awake." Wyatt reached down to his handset and, speaking in codes, called an ambulance. "Does your mother normally drink to this point?"

"She drinks a lot. You saw how she can be." Gwen motioned toward the driveway. "That's how she usually is. Sometimes she's so good at this that she can even seem sober. This isn't like her."

Her mother started to convulse and white foam poured from her lips. Wyatt rolled her over on her side and held her head so she wouldn't choke.

He looked up at Gwen and there was a look of panic in his eyes.

She dropped to her knees, taking her mother's hand. "Mom. Mom!" she called as Carla's eyes rolled back into her head so only the whites showed. "Stay with us! I'm so sorry… No… Mom, don't leave."

Chapter Eleven

The St. James Hospital emergency room was a flurry of motion as the doctor jogged past them toward Carla's room. The EMTs stood outside, watching as the nurses took her vitals and asked questions about the scene.

Wyatt wanted to be angry at Carla for what she had done, but he couldn't feel anything except a deep pooling sadness for Gwen. She had such a tough life. It was like bad luck was constantly flying right over her and just waiting for the next moment it could swoop in and scavenge away another piece of what she loved.

No wonder she was so resistant to moving their relationship into anything serious—or toward anything at all.

Then again, she had kissed his cheek back at her mother's place, before everything had hit the fan. That had to have meant something, didn't it? Or had it simply been her way of thanking him for trying to take care of her?

He wished she came with a set of written instructions, or maybe a procedure manual—anything that could help him make sense of all the emotions and questions that swirled through him.

He glanced over at her. There were dark circles under her eyes and her hair was disheveled. Reaching over, he smoothed her hair. She looked up at him and their eyes met, and he was reminded of how scared she had been when she had watched her mother have the seizure. No matter how much she must hate her mother sometimes, and regardless of how mad or embarrassed the woman made her, Carla would always be her mom.

He could understand that kind of forgiveness and love. He hated to think or talk about it, but his mind went back to the pool of blackness that was his past before he'd come to the Fitzgeralds. His mother, a drug addict, had sold herself in order to support her drug habit, until one day she was arrested.

She hadn't bothered to tell the police she'd left a child, him, at home. He had been five at the time; just old enough to remember the feeling of being all alone in the middle of the night, listening to the sounds that came with living in a cheap motel.

Some nights he could still remember the smell of her, the thick vanilla perfume mixed with the pungent odor of cigarettes.

He hated her now, but he could still remember on the day the police had come to take him away and he'd been placed into the foster care system, being scared and telling them how much he missed and loved his mommy.

Oh, those wounds that would never heal.

For some, those like him and Gwen, these were

wounds they would carry with them for their entire lifetime.

He reached down and laced his fingers between hers. Perhaps together they could both heal, if only she would let them try.

"Do you think she's going to be okay?" Gwen asked, squeezing his fingers.

He nodded as he rubbed a small circle on the back of her hand with his thumb. "I think she'll be fine, really…"

Gwen lifted their entwined hands. "Do you know that I've always hated those little circles you make with your thumb? It used to drive me crazy when we were younger."

He stopped moving his thumb. "Oh," he said, trying not to be embarrassed. "Why didn't you tell me? I would have stopped."

She pulled their hands to her face and brushed the back of his hand against her cheek. "Don't stop. I don't want you to stop."

Her face was soft and warm against his skin and he made a slow, meticulous circle over the back of her hand.

"Are you sure?" He wasn't quite sure if they were talking about the circles or something else.

"Sometimes what we think drives us crazy are the things we end up missing the most."

"I'm glad you missed me," he said with a small, playful smile.

Some of the darkness lifted from her eyes. "I missed

you more than you can know. I'm so sorry, Wyatt. I just thought…"

He leaned in and kissed the back of her hand. As much as he wanted to hear what she had to say, he didn't want her to regret her decision when she was better rested and not under the stresses of the day.

"It's okay, Gwen. I know. And I'm sorry, too, but…"

She gave him a weak smile. "*But* is right. And for now, *but* is good enough."

Dr. Richards walked out of the hospital room, toweling off his hands. He looked around the ER and, spotting them, he made his way over. "I've got good news."

Gwen shifted as though her knees were going to give out, and Wyatt wrapped his arm around her in an effort to keep her from falling.

"What is it? What happened?" Her words came in a flurry.

Dr. Richards motioned to the bank of chairs that sat against the far wall. "Do you wish to sit down?"

Gwen shook her head. She was usually so strong— sometimes almost to a fault. At least this time, she was just letting Wyatt support and comfort her.

Wyatt nodded for Dr. Richards to continue.

"While she isn't out of the woods, your mother should pull through this."

"What is *this*? What happened to her?" Gwen asked, her voice high with stress.

The doctor looked back toward the nurses' station and the stack of charts like he wanted to go grab one, but he stopped himself and turned back. "We received the results of the toxicology screen. It looks as though your mother may have overdosed on Tramadol."

"Tramadol?" Gwen repeated.

"Yes, it's a pain med. We prescribe it frequently. Do you know where your mother may have gotten the drug?"

She shook her head. "My mother hasn't seen a doctor in at least ten years. There's no way she could have had access to a medication like that."

There was a sick feeling in the pit of Wyatt's stomach. "Isn't Tramadol frequently used by veterinarians?"

Gwen jerked in his arms.

Dr. Richards nodded. "Sure, I think it's actually utilized quite often in their line of work."

"Is it something that could have been in your sister's bag?" Wyatt asked, looking at Gwen.

She was staring off into space as though she were struggling to understand everything that was happening around her. "Yeah... I know Bianca used it all the time. She kept it around for the dogs on the ranch."

"So your mother had some sort of access?"

"Sure," she said, looking at him. "But whatever she may do as far as drinking, she's never been suicidal. She too ornery to have done this to herself."

"You mean, before Bianca's death." Wyatt squeezed her hand tighter. "Do you think she would have done it now?"

Gwen shook her head. "No. Think about it. She acted like she didn't know what was going on. If she had been trying to kill herself, don't you think she would have had more of a clue?"

"Do you think it's possible she was just trying to smooth off some of the rough edges, and somehow it got out of hand?" the doctor asked.

Gwen looked over at him. "My mother didn't take an ibuprofen. I'm not kidding. For her, alcohol could cure anything. She wasn't trying to commit suicide."

"Was anyone around her or at the house before the time of the incident?" Dr. Richards asked.

The sick feeling in Wyatt's stomach worsened and he glanced over at Gwen. "My mother…my mom was there. She's the one who dropped off the bag. But she'd never drug Carla. She didn't have a bad thing to say about your mom. Ever. Not even with everything that's happened between our families. She's a saint."

Gwen chewed on her lip as she continued to stare into space. "No. It couldn't have been her. But it had to have been someone who had access to the bag and my mother's booze."

Wyatt looked at his phone to check the status of the forensics team. He lifted it so she could see the email they'd sent him. "My team is just wrapping up at the vet clinic," he said, slipping the phone back into his pocket. "I'll have them stop by your mom's for the bag. Hopefully then we can figure out exactly what's going on."

Gwen nodded, but he could have sworn she hadn't blinked in at least a minute.

A thought struck him. It was possible that whoever had killed Bianca may have been trying to kill Carla as well. Maybe they were targeting the women of Widow Maker Ranch. If that was the case, it was only a matter of time until they came after Gwen.

"Please keep Carla under the close watch of hospital staff and security, okay?" Wyatt said with a nod to Dr. Richards. "And please let me know if Carla's condition takes a turn." He pointed to his phone. "I'll be available anytime."

"No problem. I'll be in contact," Dr. Richards said with a serious look. "I'll make her our unit's number one priority. She won't be left alone."

Wyatt turned to Gwen. "Now, let's get you home so you can get some much-needed rest."

She didn't bat an eye as she nodded.

He was still holding her, so instead of letting go, he pulled her up into his arms and carried her. She laid her head on his shoulder and looped her arms around his neck. He'd never felt anything better.

Tonight, he wouldn't leave her side. No matter what, he would be there to keep her safe.

THE PAIN IN Gwen's chest, the one that always seemed to be there, was suddenly all-consuming, and for the first time in her life, she realized it wasn't the pain of loss. No. It was the pain that came with living. Of being tired of the constant beating life gave her. Of being perpetually confused as she sorted through the feelings in her heart and the thoughts in her head. More than anything, it was the pain of being pulled between the dreams she had for her life and the reality of it.

Nothing was ever going to change. She would forever be taking care of her mother and the mess she had become.

She was crazy to hope for anything different.

As much as she had begged for her mother to stay and fight for her life, in a deep, dark place in Gwen's heart she secretly wished her mother could have simply fallen to the floor and slipped away. And Gwen hated herself for it.

She looked out from under her eyelashes. Wyatt was asleep in the recliner beside his bed.

He had kept his promise to stay by her side for the night. He hadn't even acted like he wanted the bed, nor had she pushed it. Instead she had simply let him carry her in and lay her in the bed, clothing and all, and tuck her in as if she were a child—a child in desperate need of tenderness and care.

She stared at his sleeping face. It was a face she had looked at thousands of times over the years, but for once she felt like she was truly seeing him for the man he was. At times he was imperfect, but those imperfections—the need to protect at all costs, his stoicism, the fear he seemed to have about opening up—only made him seem hotter.

And admittedly, she couldn't blame him for his fear of opening up. She was part of the reason he felt the way he did. It was an injury that she would never forgive herself for. He hadn't deserved to have his dreams crushed by her—even if she had thought it had been for all the right reasons.

Beyond his endearingly beautiful imperfections there were so many other reasons to fall. She knew him. She could close her eyes and see his face in perfect detail. She knew his smile when he was truly, sublimely happy versus the smile he shared with the world. And she knew the sound he made when he slipped into the comfort of sleep.

Part of her wanted to reach out, to wake him up and pull him into her arms, to feel him around her and bask in his warmth. Yet seeing him there, resting peacefully, she didn't want to disturb him. He'd had just as hard a day as she had. And maybe that self-sacrifice and compromise was the real mark of true, undying love—even if it was a love she may never get to fully realize.

Chapter Twelve

Sometimes there just wasn't enough coffee in the world. Wyatt felt like he had been hit by a Mack truck. Wyatt's neck ached after the night sleeping in the chair, but it was worth it—especially when he'd come in after morning chores and sat and watched as Gwen opened her eyes to the morning light.

She was so beautiful. He could have sat there all day, watching her breathe as the sun cascaded in through the curtains, flooding the sweet lines of her face. She had always been his dream. All of her. Yet some dreams just weren't meant to be realized.

Or maybe it was some cosmic joke, and he was still in the middle of learning something he hadn't quite yet grasped.

He pulled a long drink from his steaming cup and set it back in the car's cup holder.

"You okay?" Gwen asked as she clicked her seat belt into place. "Are you sure you want to run to the neighbor's? We can wait a bit."

"No, I'm fine. I already fed the horses, and it's just the west pasture with the cattle, right?"

She nodded. "You fed them all? Wow, I'm impressed. Thanks."

"You're welcome. Thought you needed to sleep in."

"I thought it was my turn," she teased, with a wink.

He laughed. "By the way," he continued, "I talked to the doctor this morning. Your mom's doing well. They're going to keep her for a bit, monitor her vitals until they're sure she's out of the woods with this. They're worried, however, that she'll start going through detox if they keep her too long."

The smile on her face disappeared, and he wished he hadn't brought up her mother. It was always one topic that he should avoid, but with things being what they were it was nearly impossible. Yet he would have done anything to bring the smile back to her lips.

"Did they ask her if she took the pills?" Gwen sighed.

"She didn't remember anything. And she said she couldn't remember where she had gotten the vodka. She made it sound like you had left it for her."

"I never buy her alcohol. She's full of crap." Gwen sighed and she looked out the window as he started the car. "She's trying to stir the pot and make it sound like I enable her. I hope you told the doctor what kind of woman my mother can be."

"I didn't have that kind of time, but I happen to know that Dr. Richards knows a person can't be weighed and measured by their kin."

"Well, at least that's something." Gwen laughed. "Did he learn anything about her mental state? You know, whether or not he thought she could have wanted to end things?"

"From what he said, he didn't think she had made any conscious choice. They aren't going to seek psych for her."

"I don't think it would be a bad thing. She needs help. Maybe this can be her rock bottom."

He hated to tell her, but most rock bottoms—the moment when an addict decides to turn their life around—were myths. It took near death to make an addict realize they had a problem, and sometimes even that wouldn't work—and death was the only way to end their addiction.

For his biological mother, prostitution and jail were the norm, not the exception. And, in the case of Carla, she was probably just as desensitized as his mother had been. It was probably not the first time she found herself on the floor after a day spent drinking—for her, it was probably just another day she didn't remember.

He glanced over at Gwen. Her mother needed help to step out of her addiction, but if she did seek rehabilitation, Gwen would have to remodel her life into something completely new and foreign—it would be a life for just her—and he couldn't have been happier for her and the idea of her freedom.

He took another drink of his coffee and started down the road to the neighbor's house. The caffeine was kicking in. Maybe there was hope for the day after all.

They bumped down the driveway toward the Widow Maker and a house that used to be part of the ranch, but had been sold off in order for the Johansen women to make ends meet. Now an older couple who had retired and moved to Montana from Chicago lived in it. The place was well kept. Fake bunches of red poinsettias filled the flower baskets on each side of the porch. As they parked and made their way to the door, a Border collie bounded around from the backyard to greet them.

"Hiya, pup," Wyatt said, squatting down to give the dog a good scratch behind the ears. He'd always loved animals.

"His name's Rufio. You know, like the boy from the movie *Hook*." A woman in her midfifties stepped out from the side of the house from which the dog had come.

"Great movie," Wyatt said. "I loved watching it when I was a kid." He gave a slight wave in greeting as the woman stepped up onto the porch. "Name's Deputy Fitzgerald. I was just hoping I could ask you a few questions if you wouldn't mind."

"Oh, I know who you are. Who wouldn't in this town? I'm Dorothy Donaldson," the woman said with a knowing smile. "Your mother and I play cribbage down at the Fraternal Order of Eagles clubhouse about every other Saturday. She tells me all about you and your brothers. She's proud of you boys."

The thought of his mother expounding on him to strangers made him uncomfortable. "I don't know what she could've told you about. I just get up and go to work every morning."

"That's a heck of a lot more than what some kids do these days." Dorothy rubbed her gloved hands together and sent bits of snow to the ground. She glanced over at Gwen. "And how are you doing today? It's nice to see you. How's your mother doing?"

Gwen gave a polite smile, the one that masked all the pain she was feeling inside—he knew it all too well. "Actually we're here about her."

"Is that right?" Dorothy said, looking at Wyatt. "What can I help you with? Has she gone missing?"

He thought back to the moment he had first seen Gwen again, before he'd told her about Bianca's death, to the reaction she'd had at seeing him on their doorstep. She had been so angry with her mother for some mistake she had assumed she'd made, but now it made more sense. It seemed as though Carla had a bigger reputation as the town mischief maker than he had realized.

"Not missing," Gwen continued. "Not this time. Actually, she was drugged last night."

Wyatt nodded. "And we were wondering if you, by chance, happened to see anyone coming or going yesterday?"

"Well, there was your mother, Wyatt." Dorothy motioned toward the road. "She stopped by here on her way over. She said she had to drop something off."

"Did you see anybody else?"

The woman puckered her lips as she thought, and the action made him wonder if she was a recovering smoker.

"After your mother left... I think there was another car. I couldn't tell you the model."

"But it was a car? Not a truck or an SUV?" Wyatt asked, pressing her to get the best description he could get.

"No, it was definitely a car. Not one that I'd seen before. I think it was black."

"Did you manage to catch a glimpse of whoever was driving?"

"Yeah. It was a woman, but I didn't get a good look at her face."

"Young or old? Blonde, brunette?" he pressed.

Dorothy shrugged. "I really couldn't tell you. You're lucky I remember the car at all."

"What made you remember it?"

"You mean besides the fact that there are only about three cars that go to the Widow Maker with any consistency?" She laughed.

He chuckled. It was one of those realities of country living that he equally hated and loved—especially when it came to his investigations. He could always go to the neighbors in a remote rural place. Someone usually saw something.

"I guess what drew my attention," Dorothy continued, "was that the woman had a pair of red Ariats in the window."

"Ariats?" he asked.

"You know," she said, motioning to her feet. "Cowboy boots. I think they were Fatbabies. I've been wanting a pair. They have a blue pair down at the ranch-supply store I think I may have to go pick up."

"Oh, they are cute," Gwen added. "They're the ones with the thick soles, right?"

"Yep. And the ones in the car window were very nice. You know, if you're into red boots." Dorothy gave a raise of the brow as she glanced over at Gwen, like the color of the boots made them obscene.

"Oh, I like red boots. Sometimes," Gwen said with a little laugh and a dismissive wave.

"Do either of you know anyone who would wear those kind of boots?"

Dorothy shrugged. "No one comes to my mind, but then again, I don't get out of my house much. You know how it is."

Wyatt smiled. "I appreciate your help, and hey." He reached into his pocket and pulled out a business card and handed it to her. "If you think of anything else, or if you see the car again, please don't hesitate to give me a call."

She took the card and, giving it a quick glance, stuffed it into her back pocket. No doubt if Dorothy wanted to tell him something, he would probably hear it from his mother long before he would hear it from her. In fact, it was more than likely that his mother would get a call from her friend before he was even out and onto the main road.

He gave Dorothy an appreciative nod as he got into the patrol unit.

"What was going on with the whole red boots thing?" he asked, easing the car out of the driveway and toward the road that led into the small town.

"My mother used to have red boots." Gwen smiled. "And that neighbor and I… Let's just say that if she never saw my mug again she wouldn't miss it. I've had to rescue her from my screaming mother, wearing those damned red boots, more than once."

"From your mother?"

"Sometimes, on real bad nights, she forgets we've

sold the place." Gwen shifted in the seat as she reached down and took out a lipstick from her purse and applied it without looking in the mirror. "Once," she said, "she thought that the woman living there was seeing my father."

"She thought your dead father was having an affair?"

She nodded. "Our neighbor really didn't appreciate getting woken up at 2:00 a.m. when my mother accused her of being a slut."

The pink color of her lipstick made her face brighten with color, and for a second he wondered if she'd put it on in an effort to look even more beautiful for him. He pushed the thought aside. She wouldn't be trying to impress him. Not after everything they'd been through. Yet as he looked at her, she smiled, and there was a new softness in her eyes.

She sighed. "I'm not sure, but I think toward the end, my father may have been going behind my mother's back. She had been drinking before he died, but it didn't take a dark turn until he was gone. And I can't take my mother's word on this kind of thing… Half of it is real and half of it… Well, it's just whatever she's imagined."

"It must be so hard," Wyatt said, reaching over to put his hand on her thigh.

She looked down at his hand, but she didn't move away. Instead she put her hand on his. She started making small circles with her fingers on the back of his hand. "Is this how you do it?"

He smiled. She was doing it right and had to have known it, but he couldn't miss this chance.

He pulled the car to the side of the road, just around

a bend and out of view from the nosy neighbor. "Here, let me show you."

He unbuckled his seat belt and, leaning over, reached up and cupped her face in his hands. In a slow, meticulous move he ran his thumbs over her cheekbones, rounding the motion into a smooth, small circle. Then he let his right thumb move down lower…toward those pink lips he hoped were just for him.

She leaned into his touch and pulled the thumb into her mouth, sucking on the tip in a way that told him that she was just the kind of woman he wanted in his life.

He moaned as she nibbled on the tip of his finger, and at the sound she leaned back, releasing him from her seductive hold. His body quaked to life and he tried to ignore the lust that pulsed through his veins.

Was it possible that she wanted him as badly as he wanted her? Was it a direction he wanted to go in? She had rejected him yesterday, and everything had gone askew. If they took things down this kind of road, would it be as disastrous as they had both assumed? Or did it have a chance of not being as dead-ended as they thought?

Maybe together they could build something off the connection they had once had, and both seemed to continue to feel. They could take this in a new direction, a direction leading to something far more real and meaningful than what they'd had in high school.

But it was so risky. There were so many roadblocks. None of which was more real than the fact that if he went with this, there was more than a good chance he would get his heart broken again.

She smiled, her lip brushing against his thumb. He traced the line of her lips and dropped his hand from her face.

He wanted her. He wanted this. But now wasn't the time or the place for them to make those kinds of choices. They still had to work together, and if everything went wrong again, he didn't know if he could handle the tension that would come with their attempts at having a relationship.

Besides, he was leaving. He'd be gone for about a week. A lot could happen in that time. She could remember something about him that she hated, or she could think of a new reason not to be with him. Or maybe she wouldn't like the way he communicated when he was gone. They could make a relationship in the car work, but he wasn't sure it would have a real chance when it was tested by the outside world.

He let go of her and leaned back into his seat. She looked at him, her eyes full of a familiar heat…a heat and want that he had seen those many nights in the barn. He forced himself to look away or he knew he'd fall victim to those eyes and that face. And there would be no shielding his heart from the things that he wasn't sure he was ready to feel.

"Wyatt…" She said his name in a voice barely above a whisper, and the sound made his pulse quicken.

He cleared his throat and gripped the steering wheel. He didn't want to talk about what had just happened. He didn't hold the answers. All he had was questions. And, maybe more than anything, he didn't want to screw this up.

She started to say something, but closed her mouth as if she had thought better of it. She wiped at the corners of her lips, fixing an invisible smear, then turned to him like she was ready to come back to reality—a reality in which their feelings for each other weren't the priority.

He didn't know what to say, so he said the first thing that came to mind that didn't involve her or them or the things he wanted to do to her. "You know what? I just had an idea. You know who drives a black Audi?"

"Who?"

The name rolled around in his mouth like a foul-tasting morsel. "Monica Poe."

"You're kidding me." The tightness in Gwen's features that had come with his changing of the subject disappeared. "Everything seems to point at her. Doesn't it?"

"And sometimes, when the signs all point in one direction, it's the answer we're looking for." There was a wiggle in his gut that told him he wasn't sure if they were on the right track, but he ignored the feeling. Even if Monica wasn't the one who had drugged Carla and been responsible for Bianca's death, she had to have been involved.

He pulled the car back onto the road. They weren't far from the antiques shop. He glanced down at the clock. It was a little early, but it was possible Monica's shop could be open.

Even though he wasn't sure about opening his heart, he reached over and opened his hand. Gwen held back for a moment, just looking at his open palm, but she finally laced her fingers with his. It wasn't that he had wanted to reject her—far from it. Maybe she understood, or maybe she was even experiencing the same confusing rush of feelings.

This time, she didn't move her fingers in those sweet little circles he now loved so much, and he didn't either.

The closed sign was still up in the little antiques shop, but the lights were on inside as they parked out front.

"Don't say anything about our investigation or what happened to your mother. Let me see if I can feel her out a little bit first. Sound good?"

Gwen nodded but didn't say anything, and he couldn't decide if he was in trouble with her again. Thankfully, as he came around her side of the car and opened the door, she looked up at him and gave him a soft smile, making some of his fears drift away.

Maybe she did understand.

As they made their way up to the front door of the shop they each kept their distance from one other.

He tapped on the cold glass of the door, the hollow sound echoing down the empty Main Street.

At the sound, Monica poked her head out from the back room of the shop and, seeing them, waved. "I'll be right there, hold on a minute!"

The nervous tone of her voice made him wonder if she was trying to hide something. He tried to control his need to just null his way inside uninvited. Sure, some of the clues in the case pointed toward her, but there wasn't much that they could actually use to prove she was behind the murder.

After a minute, Monica came out from the back

room, carrying a towel as she dried her hands. She tossed the towel over her shoulder as she gave them a stiff nod and opened the door.

"How's it going, guys? I'm surprised to see you again so soon." She looked between him and Gwen, searching their faces for clues.

Her black eye was looking a bit better. Some of the swelling had subsided and now there were places on her cheek where the bruise had started to turn a lighter shade of purple. She waved for them to come in and locked the door behind them.

The shop was full of ranching knickknacks, the kinds of things that always seemed to fill the area above his mother's kitchen cabinets—baskets and rolling pins, antique teapots and little dainty cups and saucers. In fact, he was sure his mother had a water pitcher and bowl with little blue flowers that matched the set on display in the front window.

"Is there something I can help you with?" Monica asked, making him aware he hadn't really returned her greeting.

He hadn't done it on purpose, but now she seemed almost nervous with their presence.

"Sorry, just browsing…" He motioned to the blue flowered tea set in the front window. "I think Gwen's mom has something similar to that." He looked at Gwen. "Doesn't your mom have something like that?"

Gwen frowned at him. "She has some china, but I couldn't tell you what pattern it is. I think it has some pink flowers. Maybe it's Noritake or something."

"Oh, Noritake china is very nice. I have several

pieces here," Monica said, walking across to the other side of the room and picking up a white teacup with dainty white flowers and a silver trim. "This is from the Lorelei collection, one of my favorites. Just the teapot in this pattern goes for around two hundred."

He had been baiting Monica for a reaction to talking openly about Carla, but instead of growing more upset, it was almost as if the conversation about dishes brought her back into her comfort zone. And if Monica was okay with talking about Gwen's mother this soon after someone had drugged her, it was more than possible Monica didn't have anything to do with the event—or she was a dang good liar.

If she was like her husband, they could be dealing with the latter.

Monica set the teacup back on the shelf and turned back to face them. As she moved, he noticed a hint of makeup masking her black eye. Maybe it hadn't really gotten better, and she had just done her best to hide what had happened.

"How's your eye doing?" he asked.

Monica reached up. "Oh, it's fine. No big thing."

"What happened?" Gwen asked, her voice soft and full of concern.

"Oh, it was nothing, just klutzy ol' me." Monica waved them off.

He'd heard that one before. "Fall down the stairs or something?"

Her eyes widened in mock surprise. "How did you know?"

Monica was never going to tell them the truth. And

she was never going to give them William as the guy who had placed the punch. She was the kind of woman who would consider it her fault if a man hit her. The thought made him hate William Poe even more.

"Where's William today?" he asked as he moved around the shop, careful never to take his eyes off her face as he searched it for tells.

She stiffened at the sound of her husband's name. "He had to head to Spokane for a few days for a conference. Why?"

"Where was he on the evening of December third?"

She looked from him to Gwen. "What does this have to do with?"

"It's nothing you have to worry about. Yet," he said. "But it would be incredibly helpful if you could give me a better idea of where you and your husband have been over the last few days," he said, his tone so sweet that he could almost taste it on his tongue.

"You weren't really talking to William about the Widow Maker's taxes, were you?" Monica said, glaring at Gwen. "Does this have something to do with your sister? About her death?"

Excitement coursed through Wyatt. They were getting somewhere.

"How do you know about Bianca's death?" Wyatt pressed.

Monica's eyes were full of anger and fear—a dangerous combination. "Everyone in the town knows about Bianca."

Did Monica fish around for information because she

knew what kind of man her husband was? How much did she know about him, about what he was capable of?

"And whatever you are thinking, you can stop now," Monica continued. "William's been out of town. He was only home for a couple of hours yesterday to get some clean clothes. He'd been in Bozeman, stopped in, and left for Spokane."

"What about you? Where were you on that evening?" Wyatt asked.

"Me?" Her voice was high, so much so that it came out like a mousy squeak. "I… I was at your family's ranch."

Wyatt tried to control his excitement at her revelation. "So let me get this right… You were at the site of Bianca's murder…the night it took place?"

Things just got a whole lot more interesting.

Her gaze moved to the door, like she was thinking about running. He stepped in front of her.

"I don't know anything about your sister's murder, Gwen. I swear," she said, her voice edged on pleading.

Wyatt stared at her. "If that's right, Monica, then why do I have the feeling you're not telling us the truth?"

Chapter Thirteen

Monica was in a stage-four meltdown by the time Wyatt pulled into the parking spot in front of his mother's office at Dunrovin. She was sobbing in the back seat, the sound muted by the thick layer of Plexiglas that kept him from being hit, kicked and spit on by his normal class of back seat passengers. Though he had heard his fair share of crying—usually by men—from back there as well. Yet this time, he felt a touch of empathy.

Though Monica was his prime suspect in Bianca's murder, something about the whole thing didn't fit. Most of the time, when someone was truly guilty of a crime, they either acted completely indifferent or they started rambling—and that chatter usually led to some type of admission. But this time, he had a feeling an admission of guilt wouldn't be coming. Not from the hot mess that was currently Monica Poe.

"I swear. When I was at the ranch, I was with Christina Bell the whole time," Monica said between heaving sobs. "She and I… We were playing with Winnie. I wouldn't. I'd never. I barely even knew Bianca."

Gwen turned around in the seat to look at Monica. "What's your take on red boots?"

Monica's inhaled and wiped away a tear that had slipped down her cheek. "Red boots? What are you talking about?" Her voice was hoarse from her ugly crying.

"Do you own a pair?" Gwen asked, making Wyatt proud as she passively interrogated the woman. That was his girl.

Monica shook her head. "No, I don't wear boots."

"At all?"

"No. They hurt my feet, I have high arches." She lifted her foot for them to see her shoes. They were high heels, black with a red sole, and they looked expensive, but they definitely were about as different from a pair of cowboy boots as a person could get.

"Christian Louboutins? Wow." Gwen stared at the shoes like they were made of gold. "I've only seen those on the internet. They're beautiful."

Monica put her foot down and sat up a bit in the plastic hard-shell seat as she regained a bit of her composure.

Gwen pointed to the back. "Those are at least a thousand dollars," she whispered.

"Thirteen hundred, but I got them on sale when I was in Vegas," Monica said, reaching for her purse and taking out a small makeup compact. She dabbed at the last bit of wetness on her face before reapplying her makeup.

Something about her sudden shift in demeanor struck Wyatt as strange, but then again, nothing about the woman or her husband was completely normal. Here she was, sitting in the back of his patrol unit, wearing a pair of shoes that cost more than his first beater pickup and reapplying her makeup like she was on a trip to the mall instead of being questioned for her involvement in a murder.

Maybe she wasn't as innocent as he had begun to think. She was just as much of an enigma as Gwen, but in an entirely different way.

He got out of the car and made his way over to Gwen's door, then Monica's to let her out. As Monica stepped out of the car and into the snow, she had to carefully maneuver around some horse droppings. He chuckled, enjoying the juxtaposition between the high-end woman's ideals and the Montana reality.

They walked into Dunrovin's main office. His mother wasn't there, and the phone was ringing. Hopefully it was for reservations, and not for someone wanting to cancel after they heard about this week's events.

Christina came out from the back of the office, chewing on an apple as she walked toward the phone. She didn't notice them. "Dunrovin Guest Ranch. This is Christina, how may I help you?"

He stood there in the door, watching as the dark-haired woman put something in the computer and, after a couple of minutes, hung up the phone. Normally this kind of thing was their receptionist's job, but Whitney was nowhere to be seen.

Christina turned around and nearly jumped as she finally saw them standing there. "Holy crap!" She clutched at her chest, apple still in hand. "Where did you guys come from?"

Monica stepped between her and Wyatt. "I need you

to tell Wyatt we were together the *whole* night when Bianca was murdered."

Christina frowned at him. "Are you kidding me, Wyatt? Are you seriously coming down on my Monica?" She dumped her apple in the trash and came over and wrapped her arms around Monica, as though she were shielding her from any of his accusations.

"I'm not saying or assuming Monica had anything to do with Bianca's death," he lied. "I just need to make sure I go down the list and clear everyone who could have been involved with this."

Christina let go of Monica and motioned for her to take a seat on the other side of his mother's desk. Monica sat down, gracefully crossing her legs at the ankle.

"Monica wouldn't hurt a fly." Christina waved toward her friend like she was completely affronted by the fact that he would question her.

"What about William?" Gwen asked as she leaned against the doorjamb.

Christina passed a look to Monica that told him Christina had a clue about William's reputation.

"William wasn't here. I don't know anything about him or his dealings," Christina said, still staring at Monica. "He was out of town on the night they found Bianca's body, wasn't he?"

"Could anyone account for him at that time?" Wyatt pressed.

Monica turned to him. "Look, if you think it's him, do whatever you need to do. Track his phone… Whatever. But I'm telling you he was out of town. He wasn't behind this." Anger coursed through her voice.

"How are you so sure?" Wyatt asked.

"Because…" Some of Monica's self-assurance seemed to slip away and her shoulders and back relaxed. "Look…" She sighed. "I'm tired of playing the dance-around-it game. Let's all acknowledge the elephant in the room. I know about William and Bianca. I'm not stupid. I know he *likes* other women."

Wyatt tried to keep his jaw from falling open.

"Did he do that to your face?" Gwen asked, motioning to her eye.

"It's why he's gone. After you left the other day… I confronted him about Bianca. And about *you*."

"Me? He and I? No," Gwen scoffed.

"If you knew my husband as well as I do, you wouldn't put it past him. No offense, but he'll screw anything that walks."

"Is he going to be coming back anytime soon?" Wyatt asked.

Monica shrugged. "I have no idea. The last time something like this happened—when I found out about one of his mistresses—he stayed on the road for a couple of weeks. But with his name and reputation somewhat tied to Bianca's murder, he may come back sooner."

At least the man was smart enough to know when his butt was on the line—and that running made him look even more suspicious.

"Why did you stay with him, Monica? If you knew what he was doing with Bianca?" Gwen asked, pity flecking her voice.

Monica sighed and rested her chin on her hand. She sat in silence for a moment as if she was trying to find exactly the right answers to such a hard question. "I knew from the day I said yes at the altar that he was the kind of man who was going to seek the company of other women."

"And you still said yes?" Gwen pushed.

Wyatt wanted to make her stop prying into the woman's private life, but in truth he was just as curious about what would possess a woman to make what must have been a terribly painful compromise.

"When I met him, I was a bit lost. I didn't know what I wanted in life. I didn't know where I wanted to go. And everyone around me was getting married. It may sound shallow, but he offered so much—thanks to his family's wealth and his job. I knew I would have a life where I would never have to worry about money, I'd never want for anything…at least not anything material. If I want to travel, I book my flight. I have my independence. And I have a man who doesn't stand in my way. Ever. He appreciates his independence—and what he can do with it."

"And you aren't jealous?" Wyatt asked.

She looked over at him, her eyes tired, and he could tell she hated that she had been forced to admit the reality of her situation to them. "I signed up for this. I don't like it. But I did this to myself. It wasn't Bianca's fault she fell for him. He can be quite charming when he wants to be."

Wyatt didn't understand it at all. To him, it seemed like an impossible lie to live. He could barely even imagine the dance they must have had to do to avoid talking about the truths of their lifestyle.

Then again, he wasn't like some men. He didn't want a million women. He didn't care about a one-night stand, or the need to have a woman validate him or fulfill his physical needs. He wanted a woman who just loved him for him. One woman...the *right* woman, and he would be endlessly satisfied.

He glanced over at Gwen.

Maybe it wasn't that he wasn't like other men. Maybe it was just that he had a taste of the woman he'd really wanted and had been waiting for her to come back to him ever since.

A thought popped into his head. "Do you think any of William's *other* women would have had a problem with Bianca?"

Monica shrugged.

"How did you know he was seeing Bianca?" Gwen asked.

Monica's gaze flickered to Christina, who was looking everywhere but at Gwen.

"Did you tell her about it, Christina?" Wyatt asked.

"I just... I put it together and—" Christina started.

Monica interrupted her. "She was just being a good friend. It's a tough spot to be in, to know someone's spouse is cheating. It's a terrible position. And I appreciate her telling me and, Gwen, I understand why you didn't—especially since it was Bianca. You were in an impossible position."

"Do you know if he was seeing anyone else?" Wyatt asked.

Monica shook her head. "I don't think so. After Christina told me about the relationship, I was tuned in to his comings and goings. To be honest, I think they were in love. Every minute he wasn't working or with me, it seemed like he was with her."

"But you're not upset? That doesn't seem right," Wyatt said, trying to make sense of it all.

"I was upset, but not with her. It wasn't Bianca's fault. Like I said, I could only be mad at myself."

He wasn't sure if she was simply more emotionally evolved than he was, or if she was just a bit dead inside because of the emotional roller coaster she had been experiencing over the years. Either way, he pitied her.

"Are you done here?" Christina asked, once again coming to bat for her friend, and it made him like her even more.

He nodded. "Sure. Thanks for taking the time out of your day to answer my questions. Would you like us to drive you back to your place, Monica?"

Monica shook her head. "I'm not getting back in a police car if I can help it. Christina, would you mind taking me back to the shop? I need to get back to work." She stood up and, as she was about to walk out, she turned back to him. "I know my life probably doesn't make any sense to you, but I promise… I had nothing to do with Bianca's death. And, as much as I sometimes hate my husband and he hates me, he's not the kind who would do something like this. Like I said, I think he loved her. And when he's in love, he can be a magnificent man."

She and Christina walked out, not bothering to look back.

He turned to Gwen. "I need to call my team and check to see if they've found anything at your place, or if they were able to pull any fingerprints. Is there anything you need to do?"

She smiled. "I could use some food. You have a terrible habit of keeping me hungry."

He laughed. "I got some… I mean, I *have* some food back at my place," he said, nearly tripping over his words with the smooth form of a teenager.

Gwen laughed, and the sound resonated through him. It felt good to hear that sound. "Okay. Unless it's bologna. I may not be Monica with her Louboutins," she said, motioning toward the women in the ranch truck as they pulled out of the parking area, "but I do have some standards. Conglomerated pig meat is where I draw the line."

He wasn't sure, but he could have sworn there was something more in the way she looked at him. Was it that their talk about William made her remember what kind of man Wyatt *wasn't*?

When they left the office, Alli was standing outside, holding Winnie's hand.

"Wy-ant! Where you been?" Winnie threw herself around his legs.

It made his chest tighten as he was reminded how much he loved that little girl…and how badly he wanted his own.

"Hey, Winnie-girl. How goes it, dollface?" He lifted her up and gave her a hug, then dropped her back down to her feet.

"You got candy?" Winnie asked, reaching up toward his pocket with her pudgy toddler fingers.

He reached into his pocket. When he went back

to his place, he'd need a refill, but luckily he had one more piece for his best bud on the ranch. "Here you go, sweetie."

Gwen sent him a warm smile as Winnie took the piece of candy from his hand.

"Thanks you, Wy-ant!" Winnie turned to her mom and lifted the candy for her to see. "Look, Mama, he gave me this." Before her mother could take it away, Winnie unwrapped the candy, popped it in her mouth and ran toward the barn.

"No running with food in your mouth, Winnie!" Alli called after her, before turning back to them. "What were you doing in there? Why was Monica here?"

It surprised him that she would care. On the other hand, his brother's ex-wife was nothing if not nosy. No doubt, within the next few hours she would have the news that Monica had arrived at the ranch in the back of his squad car spread far and wide.

"We just had to ask everyone a few questions. No big thing. Why?" Wyatt tried to remain impassive so he could read her response.

Alli shrugged, but the motion looked forced. "Do you think Monica has something to do with Bianca's death?" She looked toward the barn. "It wouldn't surprise me if she did it. She's a vile woman. I don't know how my sister likes her. She barely speaks to me any time she comes here. It's almost like she thinks she's too good for the rest of us. But if you ask me, she stinks just as much as the rest of us."

He thought about Monica's expensive appearance. She was the kind who liked to keep up her looks. No doubt, to the dirt-covered gardener in front of him, Monica was a perfect target for Alli's hate.

He didn't understand how sweet little Winnie could have come from a woman who seemed to be solely focused on her own bitterness. At least Winnie had his family—he had no idea what he would do if she ever was forced to leave because of her disaster of a mother.

"Thanks for your opinion, Alli, but Monica has been more than helpful."

"Then she's full of crap. You shouldn't trust her farther than you can throw her." Alli looked toward the parking lot.

He'd had enough. Whatever her opinions, his dislike for her erased any objectivity he should have had in listening to her. Without bothering to say goodbye, he took Gwen's hand and led her back to his patrol unit. Sometimes it was just easier to walk away from a fight in which idiocy and close-mindedness were the only things really up for debate.

Chapter Fourteen

It was a short drive to Wyatt's place, and Gwen was glad. Her stomach grumbled with hunger as she walked to Wyatt's refrigerator and opened the door. Stale air poured out at her, making her wonder exactly how much he ate at home. She smiled as she looked in at the fridge's contents. He had an old loaf of bread, a wrinkled tomato and a block of cheese sitting on the shelf. Tucked into the far corner was a stick of salami and a pint-size jar of mayonnaise.

It wasn't pretty, but she could do something with the man-ish contents of his fridge.

Wyatt walked out of the bedroom. He was still on the phone with what she assumed was the crime lab. "We could really use a rush on those fingerprints. We have a lead on a couple of suspects, but I can't make any arrests until we have conclusive results. I'd love to have everything in order before I leave." He paused. "Yep, Alaska." Another pause. "You know it. I am one lucky son of a gun. Gonna take the fishing pole! Maybe I'll bring you back some fish since we both know you can't catch any on your own." He laughed and the sound was warm and full of life.

Normally that sound would have made her body tingle, but all she could think about was Alaska. Two more days and he would be leaving for a week.

Standing there in his kitchen, she wondered what it would have been like if they hadn't ended things when they were younger. To have let things between them naturally progress instead of her cutting them down? Sure, there was no going back and changing what had already happened, but there was no harm in dreaming.

Or was it *hoping*?

She laughed, brushing back a hair from her forehead, taking out the contents of the fridge and setting about making them sandwiches.

Maybe if she ignored reality, she could pretend this is what life would have been like if they had gotten married—her puttering around their place, him working and making plans while she was taking care of them. Or if they had stayed together, maybe she could have dreamed of something bigger than being a domestic goddess.

She'd been thrust into the role of caregiver for her mother, and now that Bianca was gone, everything about the ranch would also fall into her lap. They had put the bulls out to pasture with the cows, so in the spring she would at least have a hundred new calves—and then hopefully they could sell them for enough to keep the ranch going for another year. But without Bianca here, Gwen would have to take on extra hands.

She sighed as she glanced over at Wyatt, who stood by the window looking out at his family's spread.

In all truth, she hated ranching. Most thought of it as this romantic thing, early mornings spent around a campfire drinking coffee and nights in the arms of a cowboy, but her reality was nothing like that. Her mornings were usually taken up with feedings and moving animals, her afternoons were spent cleaning and then, when an animal was sick, Bianca had stepped in. The ranch had captured her sister just as much as it had trapped her, and now that Bianca was gone, it would be so much harder.

There was no way she could do it all by herself.

Wyatt hung up the phone and walked over to the counter to stand beside her. When he didn't wrap her in his arms she was surprised by the faint wave of disappointment that filled her.

Her daydream was definitely not the same as her reality. Then again, when had her dreams ever come true?

"Would you ever want to go back into ranching?" she asked, in hope that somehow their stars would align.

"I don't mind ranching. But I like what I do. Why?" He pulled open a drawer and, taking out a knife, set to spreading mayonnaise on the bread.

She could hardly tell him that she was feeling him out, or that she was praying he would help her make sense of her life and what she hoped was their future.

"That's great that you like your job," she said, in an attempt to maneuver around her fears.

"Do you like ranching?" he asked with a quirk of his brow.

She took a long breath as she sliced the salami and set it on the bread he'd prepared. "It's a lot. There's so much I should be doing right now, especially now that it's winter. We're close, but I want to get one more pass on the fences before more snow falls."

"If you need help now that, you know, everything's changed." He was careful about not saying what they were both thinking—that she was lost without Bianca.

She chewed on the inside of her cheek as she stared at the counter. "I might need to bring on another hand. We'll have to see. Right now, with just me, it's tough and it's only going to get harder. Then again, we can't really afford anything. Things are tight."

As soon as she admitted the truth, she wished she could take it back. He wasn't anything more than a friend. He didn't need to add her struggles to his plate. He needed to stay at surface level when it came to the real things going on in her life.

"Why are you keeping the ranch?" He reached over and took a piece of the meat and popped it into his mouth.

She had given thought to that question a thousand times, each time she and Bianca had been forced to sell bits of their ranch in an effort to keep everything afloat. Each time, she'd come back to the same conclusion— she didn't want to be the generation that let it crumble. The Widow Maker had been in her family for four generations. Each generation had their own obstacles— both financial and personal—that had made it nearly impossible to keep the ranch, but no matter how bad things got, they had always managed to make it work.

She couldn't be the one to fail.

"There's no shame in selling it," Wyatt continued, thankfully not waiting for her to answer.

He didn't know how weak she felt, or how out of control. And how, if she put her thoughts of possibly failing out into the world, she feared they would be what came to be.

"There is shame in it, Wyatt." She handed him his sandwich and took a bite of her own.

He watched her as she took another bite. "How are you going to run that place on your own? I mean, it's a huge job. You never even really seemed to like this kind of life. Isn't there something you'd rather be doing? Something that you *really* want?"

She set the sandwich down. The one thing she *really* wanted was him. She wanted to be his everything. She wanted for them to get married. To travel around the world and be as free as the wind. Then, when they were ready, she would love to have kids—to see him light up like he did whenever he saw Winnie. She would love to be wholly consumed by their reality.

Maybe what she wanted most was to be truly, completely happy. No matter what job she did or where life placed her, she didn't care. She could be satisfied. But she had a sinking feeling that the only way to have true happiness was to find it with the man standing beside her.

"You know what I really want?" Her voice was soft and sultry and she moved toward him. "I want you…" She reached up and ran her fingers through his hair.

The sandwich in his hand came to full a stop at his

lips. He smiled and swallowed the bite in his mouth. He stared at her like he was trying to figure her out, but there was really no need. She had said what she had meant.

She took the sandwich from him and sat it on the counter beside hers. Wiping the crumbs from the corners of his lips, he turned toward her and pulled her into his arms. His kiss was hard, and she grabbed his hair with both of her hands, pressing him against her lips even harder, until all they had was each other, their breaths on each other's skin and the taste of salt on their tongues.

He growled as his hands slipped down and he cupped her ass. He squeezed, and she pulled back as she giggled. His brown eyes were full of heady lust.

Maybe he wasn't as unsure about this as he had seemed before. He probably was still at the "it would be great, but" stage, yet right now she didn't care. Not when she could have him like she had wanted to for so long.

He reached down and lifted her up, wrapping her legs around him. She kissed his neck, taking in the flavor of his skin and the aroma of fresh air he always seemed to exude.

"Where are you taking me?" She hugged his neck.

"Where would you like to go, my lady?" he said with a sexy half smirk.

"Hey now, who said I was a lady?" She gave him a sexy quirk of the brow.

"You are one, but for the sake of argument, if you're not a lady…" He sat her down on the counter and pushed all the sandwich-making supplies to the floor with a one-armed swipe.

"Someone is going to have to clean that up," she said with a laugh.

"Don't worry about it. I've been on my own for a long time. I'm more than capable of cleaning up," he said, pulling her close so that she could feel his body's response against her.

His heat mixed with hers, making the desire she had been feeling seem that much more raw and urgent. She reached down. At least this time he wasn't wearing his utility belt like he had before the shower—it would be a little less work to get what she wanted, and it would give them each less time to think of the hundred reasons they shouldn't be doing what they were.

He took hold of her hand and she stopped moving. "Are you sure?" he asked, leaning in so his hot breath caressed her earlobe.

She looked up at him and their eyes met. "We should have done this a long time ago. I can't believe all the time we wasted." She took his lips, kissing him as her fingers went back to work opening his fly.

He was rock hard in her hand, and for a moment she considered just playing with him and stroking him until he couldn't stand it any longer. She moved her hand over him. He felt so good that she could only imagine how he would feel in other, more forbidden places.

She couldn't stand the thought of waiting a minute longer.

He pulled back slightly, almost as if they were of one mind. He reached down, unbuttoned her pants and, in one smooth motion, pulled them from her and let them fall to the floor. He ran his fingers up her thighs, making her moan as his fingers trailed over the outside of her panties.

He moved to her hip and, taking the panties, he ripped them. "I hope you weren't fond of this pair."

She shook her head. All that she could think about was the way he moved the fabric against her, making her think of all the things she wanted him to do and all the places she wanted him to explore.

There was the crinkle of a wrapper as he pulled a condom from his pants pocket and ripped it open, and then slipped it on.

She didn't let him take the time to pull off her shirt; instead, reaching down, she pulled him to her. Some things just couldn't wait. Her body was one of them.

As he moved into her, he groaned, making the feeling all that much more pleasurable. There had never been a sweeter sound. He moved slowly, letting her body grow accustomed to the full feeling of him inside her. She wasn't one who was fast to completion…usually. Yet, he felt so good—far better than she had ever imagined.

There were so many times when their communication had failed, but apparently their bodies didn't have the same problem. It was as if, before he even moved, she knew what he was going to do, and she moved her body in a way that drove him deeper, harder and into places that promised a quick end.

She ran her fingers through his hair, pulling his short locks. He moaned as he grew impossibly harder inside her. He kissed her neck. His hot breath came in the same cadence as the movement of his body.

It was all too much.

This reality was much better than any daydream.

HE COULDN'T BELIEVE it had happened. Twice.

He'd spent so many nights thinking about what it would feel like to have her wrap her body around him, to feel her warm, naked skin on his. Every imagining he'd ever had paled in comparison to the real thing. She had been perfect. Everything about her, even when he'd lifted her from the counter to find a piece of bread stuck to her back.

They'd both laughed as he pulled it off and threw it into the sink before carrying her to the bedroom.

They had been at it for so long that somewhere along the way it had turned to night and the cool air caught his cheap curtains and made them flutter in the breeze. He traced his fingers down her arm; her skin was cold under his touch, so he pulled his quilt over her. There was no way he would disturb her slumber just to get up and close the window. Not in a moment as perfect as this.

He played with the ends of her hair, lifting the strands and twisting them between his fingers, then letting them fall softly back down to her skin. She had always had the same hairstyle, the same long and flowing locks pulled half up and out of her face. Only the color had changed, growing darker over the years from a nearly white-blond to the honey color it was now. As he rolled another strand around his finger, he thought about all the other things that had changed about her as well, and what would change now that their relationship had grown.

Hopefully when she woke up and thought about what they had done, she wouldn't regret it.

He thought back to when he'd been a kid. Now he understood that his mother's addiction and the problems she had faced weren't his fault. Yet as a child, he'd always tried to be perfect, to protect the people who needed it and to make himself worthy of their love. Most of the time, he had fallen short—and with his mother, it had ended with her losing him. She had never come to look for him, and he'd never felt really worthy of being loved. Not when there were so many things that were broken within him—and not when he'd always continue to make mistakes.

Hopefully over time Gwen could just learn to love his imperfections instead of hating him for them. Maybe someday he could show her how worthy he was of her love. There would always be mistakes, but if they were supposed to be with each other they would make it work.

His mind went to their investigation and the list of mistakes he could be making there, and the things he feared he had missed.

He couldn't get the thoughts of Monica and her possible role in his investigation out of his mind. She was guilty of something—well, something more than just putting up with a less-than-ideal spouse. She was hiding something. Just because she didn't own red boots, that didn't mean she was innocent. Maybe she had them in the window of her car for someone else. Or who knew, maybe the neighbor had been wrong and there weren't even boots in the window. Witnesses had been wrong before.

Monica had sworn her innocence and given a testimony about not having feelings of ill will toward Bianca…but she had been at the right place at the right time and she had the right motive. All she had to do was tell Christina she was going to the restroom or something, then slip out and jab the needle in Bianca's neck. It wouldn't have been hard. Hell, she could have done it on a whim, just as he had assumed.

He thought of Carla. Who knew why Monica would have gone after the woman. Maybe she simply hated her. Or maybe Carla had found out about Bianca and William and had threatened to blackmail the Poes. There were a thousand possible reasons that Monica could have for wanting Carla dead.

Just because she had paid him a little bit of lip service didn't mean she was actually innocent. He needed the results from those damned forensics idiots. Or he was going to have to find something else to definitively pin the crime to her.

Gwen sighed in her sleep.

If anything, she was proof there were angels out there. She fought and tried so hard. Maybe things could start going her way.

He closed his eyes, willing himself to go to sleep. He would need all his faculties tomorrow if he was going to get this all figured out. Time was ticking away.

He lay there in the dark, listening to the sound of

her breath and feeling her heartbeat against his side as she lay curled up beside him. He basked in the feeling of her against him as he slipped in and out of sleep.

Just outside the open window, there was the crunch of snow and the sound of footsteps. They stopped suddenly.

Wyatt stiffened as he listened for the sound again. There were only the comforting sounds of Gwen and the echo of his heartbeat in his ears.

There was something, or *someone*, outside. He would swear on it.

He tried to control his breathing. In and out. Slow.

Then, in the window, profiled by the moon, was a person. As Wyatt jumped to his feet and ran toward the window, the petite shadow disappeared.

Chapter Fifteen

Who would have been spying on them, and why?

Gwen stared out at the spot where Wyatt had said the person had escaped into the shadows. He'd sworn the person had only looked in at them for a moment, but who knew how long they had been watching or what they had seen. The thought made her skin crawl.

Wyatt walked into the bedroom. He was already dressed in his full uniform, belt and all, and he carried two cups of coffee. He handed her one. The cream swirled in the mug, and for a second she wondered where it could have possibly come from as she recalled the woefully lacking contents of his fridge.

"Why didn't you wake me up?" she asked, motioning toward the window. "We could have gone after them."

"Whoever it was, they were quick. And who knows, maybe I was just seeing things. Maybe I was just tired."

She could hear the lie in his voice.

Taking a sip of the hot coffee, she let the lie disappear into the waves of silence between them. The coffee was sweet, with a touch of almond, and she loved the fact that she had found a man who knew his way around a coffeepot. There was a lot to be said for a guy who could make a decent cup of joe.

"Who do you think it could have been?" she asked, moving around his attempt to protect her once again. "Do you think it was the murderer? Or do you think it was just someone from the ranch being nosy?"

He snorted. "I thought of that. If anyone saw you come home with me last night, they might have wanted to know where things had ended up. But I don't think there's anyone here crazy or desperate enough to stand outside my window to find out."

She realized exactly how much of what had happened seemed to be tied to Dunrovin. Even the drugging of her mother had been after Mrs. Fitz's appearance at their house.

Then again, it was all circumstantial. Plenty of other things had happened: Bianca's hate mail from the library, her cabin and clinic being turned over and the picture being stolen… Maybe Gwen was just tuned in to the ranch right now, and the connection meant nothing.

She didn't understand how Wyatt could want to do a job that required thoughts like this all day, every day. It felt as though she was going through a special kind of emotional and mental torture. Everyone was a possible suspect, and everywhere she turned, she feared what she would find. This was his reality.

"For all I know, it was just a deer. I don't think it's anything you should worry about," he said.

"Huh. Okay," she said, setting down the mug on his dresser before grabbing her pants, which he had neatly folded over the chair in the corner. She slipped them on.

They felt strange against her nakedness, but she liked the way it reminded her of what they had done.

Wyatt watched as she slipped on her clothes, but said nothing, only amplifying the awkwardness she felt.

"You know…" she started, then paused. "You don't have to protect me all the time. You don't have to keep the truth from me. I'm a tough girl."

She glanced over at him, there was a slight look of shock and hurt on his face.

"I'm… I know you're strong," he stammered. "But here's the thing," he tried again with a sigh. "You are one of the strongest women I know. But with everything going on, I'm not going to let anything happen to you. For all we know, the person who came here last night came with the intention to hurt you."

"So you *admit* there was someone outside the window?" She motioned to the glass. "What did you find?"

He gave a resigned sigh. He reached down and pulled his phone from his utility belt. He clicked a few times and then lifted the screen so she could see it.

There, in the photo, was a set of footprints in the thin layer of snow. He enlarged the photo so she could see it more clearly.

"That," he said, "is a set of boot prints. If you look right here at the center of the boot—" he pointed to the spot "—that is the symbol for the Ariat brand."

The killer *had* been outside the window. The realization hit her like a fist to the gut. Wyatt was right. Whoever had come after her mother and killed her sister had come for her too.

What had she ever done to deserve being hunted down like an animal?

"Do you…do you really think they were here to hurt me?"

Wyatt stuffed the phone back on his belt. "I don't know. And we can't know for sure, Gwen, but what I do know is that I'm not going to leave you alone. Not until this bastard is behind bars."

She didn't want to ask him about Alaska. What would happen when he went north? What if they didn't get whoever was behind this? Would she be killed next?

He took a long drink of his coffee. "I was hoping we could look into Monica a little more today and see if we can get any further with our investigation. Her shop should be open. If we get over there, maybe we can talk to her before customers start showing up."

"But I thought you had already cleared her? She had an alibi."

"She did, but she and Christina were two of only a few who might have known you were at my place last night." Wyatt walked out of the bedroom toward the kitchen.

"That doesn't mean it was her at the window." Gwen grabbed her coffee and followed him, guzzling down the rest of the creamy goodness. She would need as much coffee as she could get to handle the rest of the day.

"No, but maybe she called someone…or maybe she hired someone to take you all down." He set his coffee cup in the kitchen sink and turned back to her. "She knows something more than she is telling us. And I intend to figure out what she's holding back, and why."

Gwen wasn't sure why he was so adamant. When they'd seen Monica, it had gone better than she had expected—though she was still surprised by Monica's admission about her knowledge of William's affairs.

She could never live a life where she would compromise her principles like that just to keep her social life in working order. Nothing was more important than being happy—no amount of money, number of friends or material goods could make up for the constant pain that came with a broken heart.

Gwen set her cup in the sink beside his and took one last look around his place before she followed him outside. It was a terrible thought, but as she closed the door, she couldn't help but wonder if this would be the last time she would be in Wyatt's house…if she had just reached the pinnacle of her life and everything now was going downhill.

HE HAD TO get to the bottom of this murder, and fast. He had called his sergeant, but things hadn't gone as he'd hoped. Wyatt had tried to convince him to send another officer to handle the prisoner transfer in Alaska, but his sergeant was having none of it. In fact, he'd made it more than clear that not following his orders would only end with Wyatt getting kicked off the force. Would it be worth it? Losing everything to protect the woman he had always loved?

He had twenty-four hours to find the person they were looking for.

He pulled into a parking spot down the street from the door of the antiques shop. Gwen's face was tight, but her fingers were loose in his hand. What he would give to go back to last night when everything in life had been forgotten and they had just lived in the bliss of one another's bodies.

He walked to her side of the car and stood there for a moment, looking in at her and at the soft, full contours of her lips. He had kissed that spot last night, and he wished he could kiss that spot again. But in the middle of the morning traffic moving down Main Street and people rushing toward their jobs, it just didn't seem like a good time to start kissing the woman in the front seat of his patrol unit.

He opened her door. "You look beautiful," he said in an attempt to make the tautness around her lips disappear.

She smiled and it made some of the aching in his chest fade.

Even if he didn't have a clue what his next move should be, at least the rest of his steps today would be made with her at his side. If only the same could be said for the rest of his life. He loved his job, but if he could just have her, nothing else really mattered.

Yet he was sure if he told her about the decision he was poised to make about his job, she'd never let him give up what he had worked so hard to achieve. No matter how forlorn she seemed any time they'd spoken about his going to Alaska, he was certain she'd never want him to do anything to put his career in jeopardy.

On the other hand, he wasn't prepared to put her life in jeopardy by leaving either.

He helped her out of the car and watched her walk in front of him to the antiques shop. He should have been thinking about the questions he needed to ask Monica, but all he could concentrate on was the way Gwen looked in her jeans. She no longer had the high and tight behind that she'd had at sixteen, but she had become perfect in her soft curves. Curves he had loved running his hands over when she was on top of him. He stopped moving and just stood there, staring as she walked ahead with a quiet grace of a woman confident with her body. As she shifted her hips, he wondered if she was doing it on purpose just in case he was watching.

He smiled and looked up just as she stopped to wait for him.

"What are you doing?" she asked with a coy smile.

She *had* played it up for him.

"Nothing," he said with a quirk of his brow. "I was just taking a sec to enjoy the view. Feel free to keep walking."

She giggled as she sauntered back to him and took him by the hand. He looked around. A few of the older women were looking over at him, and he wondered how long it would take for word to spread that he and Gwen were officially an item. He smiled and gave the woman closest to them a quick, acknowledging wave. The woman nodded but quickly turned away.

He didn't care if the world knew. He'd waited so long for this, so long to be with the one woman who had filled his thoughts during the day and his dreams in the night.

Gwen stroked his fingers and gave them a quick kiss as they turned toward the store. As her lips left his fingers, he finally looked up. The lights of the store were off, and even though Secret Secondhand should have been open, the closed sign was still flipped in the window of the front door.

Wyatt glanced down at his watch. It was nearly 10:00 a.m. Monica wasn't the kind to be late. Ever. She was entirely too perfect to be an hour late opening the store.

Something was wrong.

He stepped up and pressed his face against the cold glass of the front door, shielding the morning sun from his eyes. The store was a mess. The glass teapot, the one he had noticed the day before, was on the floor, shattered into pieces. Beside it was a bloody handprint. Next to the counter was a large pool of blood.

It felt like the world was collapsing around him. He glanced back at Gwen. She didn't need to see this, but he couldn't keep her from the truth…or what they might find if they went into the shop. He needed to get in, clear the building and get help if there was someone hurt inside. And yet, he had promised himself he wouldn't let her be alone again.

"Gwen…" he said, turning around to face her.

"What's wrong?" she asked. All the playfulness she had been exuding disappeared.

"I need to go in there. Something's happened."

"To Monica?"

He shrugged. "I can't be sure until I look."

"What do you want me to do?"

He could make her wait in the car, but just because she was in his car didn't mean she'd be entirely safe. Whoever was gunning for her had to be someone they both knew, someone close to them, and it was likely someone who could lure her out.

He couldn't risk it.

Though he had a feeling that it was unlikely they had arrived in time to help whomever the blood belonged to, he notified dispatch and requested that they send an ambulance.

He twisted the shop's doorknob, but it was locked.

"Follow me," he said, taking Gwen by the hand and leading her around to the back of the building.

Her hand was sweaty in his, but he couldn't tell if it was her sweat or his. Normally he would have been fine in this situation, he would have easily gone into work mode, but he couldn't let his emotions go. Not when he was holding the hand of the person he cared about most in this world. If something happened to her, he would never forgive himself.

The back door was wide-open. The alley behind the store was empty except for a large blue Dumpster and an orange tabby cat that quickly scurried out of sight. The alley muffled the sounds from the street and the muted effect made chills run down his spine.

"No matter what happens, you need to stay back. Got it?" He couldn't help the darkness that flecked his tone.

He squeezed her fingers and then let her go. Drawing his gun, he made his way up the steps. He charged the door, stopping with his gun drawn as he flagged the room. The back of the shop was empty except for shelf after shelf of dust-covered knickknacks. He looked back at Gwen and waved for her to follow him.

Her eyes were wide with fear as she stared at him, but he couldn't let her fear get to him any more than it already had. He had to keep them safe and he had to do it by being prepared and taking the lead.

"Lake County sheriff's deputy! Come out with your hands up!" he ordered.

They were met with a sickening silence.

"Monica Poe, are you in here?" he called again.

There was no answer.

The hair rose on the back of his neck.

He silently prayed that his intuition was wrong and that Monica was okay.

He lowered his Glock as he moved forward and toward the main area of the store.

Next to the doorway was a smashed clock in the shape of a black-and-white cat. The jovial cat's face looked up at him, and right between the eyes was a droplet of blood.

There was another spatter of blood as he stepped inside the room. A cabinet full of glass ornaments had been pushed over and he stepped around it, the glass crunching under his shoes.

There was a smear of blood on the floor, where it looked as though someone had crawled toward the front desk.

"Wait here," he said, motioning for Gwen to stop and stay out of the crime scene as much as possible.

He moved toward the front desk. A pair of feet with black high heels poked out from behind it. The shoes had red bottoms. Christian Louboutins.

"Monica?" he asked, but he knew it was too late.

She wouldn't respond to her name.

She wouldn't answer to anything ever again.

He stepped around the desk. Her hair was wrapped around her face, almost obscuring her open, sightless eyes. Blood pooled around her. So much blood.

Her neck had been cut so deep that he could see the white viscera of her severed windpipe. Whoever had wielded the weapon had been vicious. It was the kind of savage attack that came from a place of deep-seated hate.

He'd seen death at least a hundred times, but this was the first time he'd ever been forced to turn away.

Out of the corner of his eye, he spotted a print. One solitary boot print, each groove and line perfectly preserved and captured, thanks to Monica's blood.

Chapter Sixteen

There was a crowd of people outside the store and everyone was trying to get to Gwen to ask her their questions. Wyatt was standing next to a reporter who was holding up a microphone so close to his face that Wyatt had to remind himself to breathe.

He hated this part of his job, when he had to play to the media. They wanted to know every detail, and in cases like this, details were in high demand and short supply.

It wasn't every day something like this happened in Mystery.

He really felt worse for Gwen. She wasn't used to this kind of thing, and as the reporters descended on her, she looked like a shivering puppy. He tried to get closer to her, but the reporter stepped between them and raised the microphone higher.

"Deputy Fitzgerald, it has come to our attention that you are the lead investigator on the Bianca Johansen murder case. Do you believe your involvement is a conflict of interest since the murder happened on your family's ranch?"

It was low, but as Wyatt ignored the annoying reporter and moved past him, he did his best to step on the toe of the man's well-polished leather loafers.

Who did he think he was? He didn't tell the reporter how to do his job. What gave the reporter the gumption to come at him like he had no business taking this case?

"Out of the way," Wyatt said, elbowing the man as he grabbed Gwen by the hand and led her out of the crowd.

Another officer pushed the reporter back as the guy tried to move after them and cast another net of questions. "Everyone back!" the officer ordered. "This is an active crime scene! We would appreciate your keeping your distance until we have finished our investigation. At that time you are welcome to reach out to our public information officer and they will provide an official statement. Until then, go on about your day!"

A few of the people turned away, but they didn't move off the sidewalk.

Wyatt was filled with disgust. Normally he didn't mind living in a small town, where everything was fair game for the rumor mill, but right now he just wished the crowd would leave him alone.

An officer walked toward them as he finally helped Gwen out of the melee. "Fitz, I think you may want to step inside," the officer said, motioning toward the shop. "We found something."

Gwen glanced at him with a look begging him not to leave her.

"Gwen's coming with us," he said to the officer. He turned toward her. "You don't have to stay out here with the vultures."

She relaxed. He was glad he could be there for her, that she needed him…and truth be told, he liked it.

The officer led them up the steps, through the creaking door and into the front area of the store, carefully avoiding the body that was now being photographed and documented. He was glad Gwen didn't have to look at her friend's body. She hadn't taken it well, and he didn't want to put her back in that kind of position again.

He turned to her. "Do you want to wait here?"

She stared over in the direction of the front desk, where Monica's body lay just out of view. She didn't say anything, but gave him a slow, stiff nod.

"We haven't called Monica's husband yet," the other officer said, walking with him toward the desk. "I know that you're acquainted with the family…"

They were trying to pass the buck. Not that he could blame them. He glanced back over at Gwen. She had her arms pulled tight around her body. The memory of her lying on the floor, crying after he had told her of Bianca's death, came to mind. William Poe wasn't Gwen, but Wyatt had had more than his fair share of notifying the next of kin for a while.

Besides, he cringed at the thought of what William would say when he found out about his wife. Though, would it come as a surprise? It was possible that William had a hand in this.

"I'll get someone to take care of it," Wyatt said. "Now, what did you guys find?"

The officer walked over to him. Lyle was standing beside the cash register, his round belly pressing against his shirt and pulling the buttons open. He hitched up his pants, giving a break to his struggling suspenders. "How's it going, man?"

"It's going. Heard you found something?" Wyatt couldn't help the little bit of surprise that filled his tone.

Lyle raised a brow, like he'd heard the unintentional jab as well.

Wyatt started to open his mouth to apologize, but Lyle turned around before he had the chance to speak.

"By the way, I'm real sorry about missing the syringe…but you know what they say about a needle in a haystack," Lyle said with a laugh. "And we did manage to pull some fingerprints from that vet bag, but they ain't comin' up in the database. We'll keep tryin', though. However, look what I just found…" Lyle lifted the cash register. Underneath was a white envelope. He pulled it out and handed it over to Wyatt. "There's some interesting stuff in there. In fact, I'd like to think it might just break your case wide-open."

He wasn't sure he believed the guy.

Wyatt flipped open the envelope and a series of pictures slid out. On the top was a photo of Bianca. She was standing in her cabin, wearing only a black lace teddy. Wyatt instinctively looked away. It felt so wrong seeing her like that, in a private moment meant only for the person she was with. Without looking too closely, he flipped to the next picture. It was of a brunette woman, her head down in William Poe's lap and her face completely out of view. Even from behind, he could tell by the hair color it wasn't Bianca. Picture after picture was William Poe with a different woman.

"What do you think? Gonna help your case?" Lyle asked.

Wyatt looked up from the pictures. "Why would Monica have these?"

Lyle shrugged. "If I had to guess I'd say she's been keeping an eye on her husband's bedroom activities. From the pics it looks like there's been plenty of 'em." The man chuckled.

He wasn't wrong about that. Wyatt wasn't even a third of the way through the pictures. There had to be at least forty of them. His thoughts went back to what Monica had told him about William's relationship with Bianca—and how William had slowed down when it came to dating other women. Seeing these, it was no wonder she knew exactly what had been going on as far as his affairs.

He flipped to the next picture. There, standing in front of William, bent over, was a woman in red boots. Red. Ariat. Boots. The woman's face was down, but she was small. Just like the person he'd seen in his window.

He tried to see anything that would give away the woman's identity, but there was nothing beside the boots and her naked body for reference. There were no visible tattoos, no birthmarks or piercings. He lifted the photo for Lyle to see. "You know who this woman may be?"

Lyle shook his head. "No, but William had good taste." He chuckled, but Wyatt didn't think there was anything funny about the picture, or the woman in it.

The woman in the photo had to be the killer.

He flipped to the next picture.

She was there again. This time she was standing in

the middle of a hotel room wearing nothing but those damned red boots. She was smiling, almost as if she knew there was someone right outside the window taking the picture.

It was the smile of someone who knew they were guilty—and didn't care.

It was the smile of Alli Fitzgerald.

Chapter Seventeen

The parking lot at Dunrovin was full of guests' cars.
They ranged from old beat-up trucks like hers to high-
end sports cars. As they got out of Wyatt's squad car,
for the first time since she'd been working with him,
he didn't come around to open her door. He was a man
on a mission.

How could they not have seen Alli was behind this?
It all made sense. She had been at the ranch. It would
have been all too easy for her to get the drop on Bianca.
Bianca would have trusted her. She probably wouldn't
have thought anything of the woman coming into the
barn. If anything, maybe Bianca had thought she had
come to help.

Deep, burning hate filled Gwen. Bianca hadn't done
anything to Alli, and yet Alli had come after her. All
because of a man and what Gwen had to assume was
jealousy. Alli must have wanted him all to herself.

A lump grew in Gwen's throat as she tried to keep
her anger and tears in check.

Her sister had fallen in love with the wrong man, but
who hadn't made a mistake when it came to love? Love

wasn't an emotion that made sense. It wasn't something that could be controlled or put in a vacuum.

She glanced over at Wyatt as he strode through the parking lot, and she rushed to keep up.

Once someone had told her that there was no such thing as a selfless act. She couldn't disagree more. Being in love was the most selfless act anyone could ever undertake. Just like with Bianca. She had given up who she was and what she believed in in order to be with a man. In the end, that love, that need to be with the person her heart yearned for, had cost her everything—even her life.

Winnie ran out of the barn toward them. "Wy-ant!" she called, waving wildly.

Wyatt rushed over to the little girl and pulled her into his arms, the action so protective that it made Gwen wonder if he feared for the girl's safety. Alli wouldn't do anything to put her daughter at harm. Then again, she already had—she had murdered. Twice. And she'd tried to kill Gwen's mother.

Gwen stopped and just stared as Winnie hugged Wyatt's neck. The girl reached into his shirt pocket without asking and pulled out her beloved banana taffy.

Why *had* Alli tried to kill Gwen's mother? There was no way William Poe would go after her. She wasn't his type. The attack couldn't have been motivated by jealousy. So why?

It didn't make sense.

"Where's your mama, Ms. Winnie?" Wyatt asked.

"Which one?" Winnie asked, ripping open the candy's wrapper and popping the little morsel into her mouth.

"Huh?" Wyatt asked, walking with her in his arms toward the main office. "What do you mean by 'which one,' sweetheart?"

"Mama say she not my mommy no more. Mommy gone. Christina's mommy now." Winnie was surprisingly nonchalant about her mother's sudden disappearance.

When Gwen had been a young child, if her mother would have disappeared, she would have been distraught. Then again, those had been the days when her mother was sober and almost normal. And maybe Winnie's age, added to the fact that she had no concept of time, was the reason she didn't understand the ramifications. Maybe to her, as young as she was, she thought of her mother's disappearance as if it was nothing more than her mother going to the grocery store.

Gwen was going to be without a sister forever, but she wasn't the only one who had lost someone.

"Have you seen your grandmother?" Wyatt asked, bouncing Winnie gently in his arms.

Winnie shrugged, sucking the stickiness off her fingers.

What Gwen would give to go back to those days, when life was easy, things were simpler and she had spent her days ranking which candy was best. Even with everything going on, the thought made her smile. She loved Winnie. She couldn't understand how her mother would just leave her behind.

Maybe it was just another example of love—maybe

Alli knew her life was a mess and giving her daughter to her sister was the one selfless thing she could do to make things right for the girl.

The lights in the office were off, so they made their way to the main house. The wooden steps that led to the front door creaked as they walked up—the sound was disquieting and it made the hair stand to attention on Gwen's arms.

Before they could even get to the door, Mrs. Fitzgerald opened it. "We heard about Monica. Are you guys okay?"

Gwen nodded as Wyatt stepped inside with Winnie. He set the girl down. "Stay close. Okay, sweetheart?"

Winnie nodded, but she turned toward the kitchen before the words were even completely out of his mouth.

"There are homemade cinnamon rolls on the stove. Your auntie is in there and can help you," Eloise called after the girl.

"So, what did you hear?" he asked, turning to his mother.

"About Monica? Just that she was found dead in her store. Why? What happened?"

"Have you seen Alli?"

Eloise shook her head. "Why?"

"Do you know what kind of car she drives?" Wyatt asked, motioning toward the parking lot.

"She just bought a new little black Genesis, why?"

Wyatt's face fell. "Son of a… When did she buy it?"

"I don't know. She and I aren't that close. Maybe a week or two ago?"

Gwen turned to him. "Can we put out a BOLO on her?"

Wyatt nodded. "We can try, but I have a feeling that with all the roads around here…" He looked down at his watch. "If she's smart, she's already in Canada by now."

Wyatt's phone rang. His face tightened as he looked at it. It was his sergeant.

"Sir?" he answered.

Even from where she stood, she could hear the husky voice of Wyatt's superior. "Did you find the woman yet?"

Wyatt rubbed his hand over his face. "Not yet. She and her car are missing. I need to put out a BOLO on a new black Hyundai Genesis. Temporary tags."

"I'll handle it," the sergeant said. "But are you sure she is the one behind this? What exactly do you have that ties her to the case?"

Gwen's stomach sank. She didn't know much about police procedures. Everything pointed to Alli—even the woman's sketchy behavior made her seem guilty—but the only real evidence they had was a pair of red boots and a few compromising pictures.

"We're pretty sure it's her. She was in the pictures. There were boot prints outside my window. It had to be her. She had the motivation and the opportunity to have been behind all these deaths."

"But you don't have a witness. The DA is going to have a field day when they run us through the ringer on this one—even if we do find Alli. And if we don't…"

A witness. They needed a witness.

Gwen gasped, the sound so sharp that Wyatt stared at her.

"What about my mother?"

"What about her?"

"What if she saw something? What if that's the reason Alli came after her?"

Wyatt gave her a sexy half grin and lifted the phone higher on his ear. "You send the guys after Alli."

CARLA WAS SITTING up in her bed, pale and sweaty, jittery from the effects of detox and coming down off the ample supply of drugs that had been filtered through her system over the last few days.

"How are you feeling?" Gwen asked, walking into the hospital room with Wyatt at her side.

They stopped beside her mother's bed, and Wyatt shifted his weight from one foot to the other, antsy with the need for answers.

"I feel like I got bucked," Carla said, her voice hoarse and dry. "I haven't felt like this since…" She trailed off, not bothering to finish her sentence.

Gwen moved closer and lifted her mother's hand. "We'll get through this. We always do."

Her mother's smile was drawn and tired, but it was perfect in its authenticity. For the first time in years, the love Gwen held for her mother grew. Maybe it wasn't wrong to hope for better days.

"How are you doing?" her mother asked.

Gwen smiled. "Better. We're close to finding the person who tried to hurt you, but we need to ask you some questions. Okay?" She motioned to Wyatt.

Carla nodded, her motion stiff. "I don't know how much help I'll be."

Gwen tried to ignore the way her stomach clenched.

Everything depended on this. Wyatt took her hand and made the little circles on her skin she now loved so much. The simple action made some of her nervousness disappear.

He leaned in close so his lips nearly brushed against her ear. "It'll be okay." His warm breath cascaded down her skin and, surprisingly, considering their situation, she believed him.

Even if this didn't work and her mother was of no use, they would spend every last minute going after the person responsible for Bianca's and Monica's deaths.

"Mrs. Johansen, do you know Alli Fitzgerald?" Wyatt asked.

"Alli? As in your brother's ex-wife? Sure. She came to our ranch's Fourth of July party. Why?"

"Wait." Wyatt paused. "Don't be offended…but you've made it clear that you don't like my family. Why would my brother's ex-wife be invited to your party?"

Carla sighed and she readjusted the pink hospital blanket that was arranged around her. "I don't *hate* you, or your family."

Gwen snorted with derision. "Mom, you don't have to lie to him. It's not like you hide the fact very well."

"I don't hate them, or *you*," Carla said, looking at Wyatt. "And I certainly don't hate Alli. She wasn't even around when everything happened. It's just that, sometimes when I'm drinking…"

"Your true feelings come out?" Wyatt asked with a raised brow.

"Your family, you took the only man I ever loved from me. Your family left me alone to raise two girls and run a ranch. It was all too much. And now with Bianca gone…" A tear slipped down her mother's face. "I… I just can't get through this all by myself. It's why Alli and I became friends. She just *listened*. You know?"

"You're friends with Alli?" Wyatt's voice was filled with surprise.

"Sure. We see each other at the bars all the time."

Gwen looked over at Wyatt. She'd never heard about her mother's relationship with Alli, or anyone from the bar, before. Though, admittedly, she hadn't ever bothered to ask about her mother's nightlife.

"You hang out with her? How often?" Gwen asked.

Her mother shrugged. "I dunno. I haven't been seeing her around as much lately."

"Why not?"

"Well, ever since your sister shacked up with that Poe guy… Alli didn't take it real well."

"Alli was seeing Poe for a while," Gwen said. "Did you know?"

"Yeah, though I was one of the few. I just happened to walk in on them *making things happen* in the Dog House Bar bathroom one night. She begged me not to tell anyone."

"You saw them *together*?" Wyatt asked.

"Oh, yeah, but I ain't ever told anyone. Alli was real nice. She even gave me a bottle of vodka the other night as a thank-you for staying quiet."

"A bottle of vodka?" Wyatt's voice took on a dangerous edge. "You mean the vodka you were drinking the night you were drugged?"

Her mother's face went slack. "She...she wouldn't do something like that."

"No one else touched that bottle of vodka besides you and her," Gwen said, as a wave of exhilaration coursed through her.

They had the evidence they needed. Together, she and Wyatt could bring Alli down.

Chapter Eighteen

The next morning, the police station was nearly empty as they arrived at Wyatt's sergeant's office. It had been a surprise when Sergeant Hubbard had called and woken them up, requesting that they come see him. It had been hard to find the willpower to get out of bed after Wyatt had held Gwen in his arms all night. And thanks to everything that had been happening, as they drew nearer to his superior, Wyatt couldn't help feeling that he may have been a dead man walking.

Hubbard was sitting with his back to them, talking on the phone as they arrived.

"Thanks for coming down." Hubbard hung up the phone. "Heya, Gwen. How goes it, Wyatt?"

"I don't know. You tell us," Wyatt said.

Hubbard looked at Gwen and gave her the soft smile he reserved for people dealing with trauma. "By the way, I'm sorry for your loss. Your sister was a real nice gal. I always liked her," Sergeant Hubbard said, motioning for them to each take a seat in front of his desk.

"Thank you," Gwen said. "It will be better once we

get Alli behind bars. At least then I can rest easy, knowing she will pay for what she's done."

Hubbard looked down at the files on his desk and fiddled around with the corner of one of his manila folders. "Actually, that's why I called you to my office. I got some news."

Unless it was that they had Alli in custody deep in the bowels of the county jail, Wyatt wasn't sure he was ready for anything the man had to say.

"First, Wyatt," he said, bumping the folders into a neat pile. "I have taken you off the Alaska trip. With everything going on, now isn't a good time for you to be leaving the area."

Wyatt couldn't say he was disappointed about staying. Gwen still needed him. Yet he wasn't sure he followed Hubbard's reasoning. "What's that supposed to mean, Sarge?"

Hubbard sighed. "We found Alli's car. It was parked about an hour north. It looks like she dropped it and made her way over the Canadian border. She's gone."

Wyatt slammed his fist down on Hubbard's desk, sending his neat pile of files scattering over the surface. "Are you kidding me? She just disappeared?"

"We notified the Feds. They're going to be on the lookout for her. For now, you need to look to your family and stay close. With Christmas just around the corner and everything else going on, Sheriff Stone and I just thought it best. She may try to contact you—especially since her daughter is still in the care of your family. In the meantime, I want you both to go back to your routines. If you can, try to keep your minds off Alli."

"How am I supposed to do that?" Gwen pressed. "She's at large. And we're in danger. What if she comes back?"

Hubbard gave Gwen a soft smile. "Why would she try to come after you now? You aren't her enemy. Now she's going to be after only one thing—flying under the radar of law enforcement."

The thought didn't comfort Wyatt, but Hubbard was right. They could only concentrate on moving forward.

Without Alli, the only closure she could have would be her budding relationship with Wyatt—and all the possibilities it held. As long as they were together, they would always be safe.

Epilogue

There were moments in life when Gwen would always look back and wonder why she had made the choices she had, and how she had ended up where she was. But right now, lying in the hayloft in Wyatt's arms, she didn't regret a single thing. Even in the cool chill of the December night, it felt good. He was hers and she was his…down to the very beating of her heart.

She looked up at the beam where their names were carved into the wood. Time had worn away the harsh, jagged edges, and the scars had faded to marks that were just as much a part of the wood as the grain itself.

Wyatt ran his fingers down the length of her naked body. Reaching her hip, he pulled a piece of hay from her and let it fall from his fingers to the ground.

"Are you okay?"

She wouldn't get over her loss for a long time, but at least something positive had come out of it—her mother had agreed to go into a rehab facility. And with things heating up with Wyatt she had something to look forward to again.

He motioned between them. "I mean, with all of *this*?"

She laughed. Not at the question, but at the thought that he would ask if she was okay lying naked in his arms. There were few places she felt at home, where everything was right in the world, but with him there was no question—she was where she was meant to be.

"I'm fine. Just thinking about everything," she said, rolling onto her back. The hay was scratchy, and she wished they had grabbed a blanket to lie down on before they had fallen into the haystack just like they used to when they were younger.

It was almost surreal to be back in the same place she had been a decade before. "What are you thinking about?" he asked.

She traced her fingertips over the little line of hair that rested just below his navel. It felt good to feel all of him, to take the time to get to know his body. He had all of her heart, and she had his; it was only right that she would have all of his body too.

"I don't know," she lied. "I guess I was just thinking about…" She struggled to come up with a plausible thing that didn't involve his naked body or the love she felt. "I guess I was thinking about the holidays."

"You were thinking about Christmas? Really?" He cocked his head and gave her a playful grin.

In truth, she hadn't really been thinking about Christmas. All she could think about was the way it felt to be with him—and how much she loved him.

She nodded. "Sure."

"Well, you're coming here," he said it like it was a statement rather than a request.

"Is that right?" she teased. "If you weren't aware, I have plans on Christmas."

He sat up and grabbed his pants, pulling them on over his nakedness. "You can come to my parents'. My brothers will all be there. It will be amazing. You'll love it. Besides…you'll have to show everyone the present I got you."

"The present?" she asked, perching up on her arms. "What present?"

He reached into the pocket of his pants. "This one," he said, extending his hand. In the center of his palm was a simple gold band. He picked it up and lifted it for her to see. "Gwen Johansen, I've loved you since I was sixteen years old. I've always loved you. Nothing has ever changed. I don't want to spend another single day without you. Will you marry me?"

She sat up and wrapped her hands around his neck so violently that he had to grip the ring in his hand to keep from dropping it.

"Yes. I love you too. Yes." She buried her face in his neck, nearly forgetting about the ring in his hand.

As lovely as the band was, it was nothing compared to the beautiful feeling of being loved by him—the man who had always filled her dreams and who would now become her reality.

No matter what the future would bring, or what would happen with Alli, they would always have each other.

From this Christmas on, she would have the one gift that she'd always wanted—his love.

* * * * *

Leaning down, Spence kissed her forehead.

The light touch of his lips set off a chain reaction of shivers that had more to do with her internal engine than with the snow and cold. Her inner machinery had definitely come back to life. She exhaled on a soft moan.

"What else?" he murmured.

Resisting him wasn't going to be easy. "Nothing much."

"It's okay. You can tell me."

But maybe she'd better not. Though his tone was gentle and cajoling, she knew he was digging, probing, interrogating. If he discovered the gaps in her memory, what would he do? He said he was a federal agent, but that didn't mean he was innocent.

She turned the tables with a question of her own. "What do you do for the FBI?"

FROZEN MEMORIES

BY
CASSIE MILES

MILLS & BOON

First Published in Great Britain 2017
By Mills & Boon, an imprint of HarperCollins*Publishers*
1 London Bridge Street, London, SE1 9GF

© 2017 Kay Bergstrom

ISBN: 978-0-263-92916-4

46-0917

Cassie Miles, a *USA TODAY* bestselling author, lives in Colorado. After raising two daughters and cooking tons of macaroni and cheese for her family, Cassie is trying to be more adventurous in her culinary efforts. She's discovered that almost anything tastes better with wine. When she's not plotting Mills & Boon Intrigue books, Cassie likes to hang out at the Denver Botanical Gardens near her high-rise home.

A salute to the geniuses who work at NORAD and still manage to run the Santa Tracker every Christmas. And, as always, to Rick.

Chapter One

Jagged branches clawed the arms of her sweatshirt and tangled with her bare hands as she fought her way to the edge of a clearing in the mountain forest. Falling snow blanketed the open space. Spears of afternoon light cut through the snow and clouds, but she still couldn't see all the way across, to the wall of pines on the opposite side. She shivered violently. If she tromped straight through the clearing, she'd leave tracks. They'd find her.

Who were they, those men with guns? What did they want from her? She peeked over her shoulder but didn't see them following. Her ears prickled, but she didn't hear them coming after her.

They'd left her on the floor in the back of the van. She hadn't moved, hadn't opened her eyes. They must have thought she was unconscious. One of them had nudged her with his steel-toed boot, but she hadn't given any sign of wakefulness. They'd talked about whether or not they should take her into the cabin with them. And they had decided not. They hadn't wanted to carry her. If she froze in the van, they didn't care.

Glad that they were so stupid, she'd waited until they'd gone inside. Then she ran. Without a parka. Without mittens. Without boots. Wearing only sneakers and a hooded sweatshirt over a flimsy pair of hospital scrubs, she'd staggered into the storm. The cold should have awakened her, but she'd felt lethargic. Her legs were heavy; her feet weighed her down like cement boots. She lurched through the trees, uncoordinated, unable to keep her balance.

As she'd gone farther, her physical abilities had improved. But that didn't mean she was out of the woods—literally out of the woods. *Making an unfunny joke, I messed up the punch line.* Still, she chuckled. When she stretched her mouth, her lips cracked. *I always wanted to die laughing.*

My God, what was wrong with her? She ought to be terrified. Instead, she felt oddly giddy and confused.

The gusting wind threw icy flakes into her teeth. Her clothes were cold and wet. Her shoes soaked through. She'd seen photos of people who were frostbitten, with their fingers and toes turning black and falling off. But she'd also heard that dying of hypothermia was supposed to be peaceful, like drifting into a gentle sleep.

Sleep would be good, maybe just for a minute. Her eyelids closed. She imagined a boat pulled by snow geese with a glittering snow god at the helm. All she needed to do was climb aboard. Looking down, she smoothed the white feathers of her gown. Sleep was so very good. *Or not!* Delusions were a symptom of hypothermia. Her mind was going. She needed to find warmth as soon as possible. Leaving a track across the clearing was a small price.

She charged forward with the storm beating at her head and shoulders. The accumulated snow was almost up to her knees. When had it started? When would it shut and clenched her jaw against the flaring pain. Everything burned—her arms, her thighs, her hands and feet, her nose, even her earlobes. She would have passed out, but gentle hands guided her into a tiled bathroom. Trudy shouted directions to her husband while she seated her on the closed toilet. Together, she and Trudy peeled off her wet clothing and shoes.

"Dry off with the towel," Trudy instructed while she grabbed fresh clothing from the pastor, who stuck only his hand into the bathroom. "These jammies ought to fit. They belong to my granddaughter, and she's your size. How tall are you?"

"Five feet nine inches."

"I used to be tall." Trudy glanced into the mirror above the sink, gave herself a smile and adjusted her long silver braid. "Lately, I've been shrinking."

"Still beautiful," she said, and she meant it.

"Later, we'll get you into a bath. For now, we need to warm you up slowly and get your blood circulating. You're not frostbitten but close. Hurts, doesn't it? You're very brave."

She appreciated the compliment. Though running away from those thugs didn't seem particularly courageous, she'd survived what was clearly a bad situation. What if the bad guys came this way? "Danger," she mumbled, "dangerous men...they're after me."

"You're safe now. Clarence doesn't look like a tiger, but he's a very good protector."

She fastened the last button on the warm, dry pajamas and stumbled to her feet so she wouldn't fall asleep on the toilet. Though her skin still stung like fire, she felt stronger as she hobbled into the front room. After sinking onto the sofa, she pulled up the wool socks on her poor, frozen feet and tucked a fuzzy yellow blanket around her shoulders.

Pastor Clarence placed a mug of fragrant lemon tea on the coffee table. "Don't drink too fast," he warned.

"But you need to rehydrate," Trudy said.

She nodded and took a sip. "I want…to thank you."

"You're doing much better." Trudy handed her a tube of lip balm. "Are you well enough to recall your name?"

Carefully, she applied the salve to her cracked, chapped lips. Her mind was blank. "Maybe…in a minute."

Trudy sat in the overstuffed chair nearest to the sofa and tucked her robe snugly around her. "You said there was danger."

"Yes."

"Let's ease into your memories gradually," Trudy said. "What's the last thing you remember?"

"A van…there was a van…men with guns."

Trudy shot a nervous glance toward her husband, but her voice stayed calm. "What color was the van?"

She took another sip of tea. The liquid soothed her throat. "I think it was black…or dark blue."

"I want you to concentrate," Trudy said. "Tell me about the men. How many of them? Did they say each other's names?"

"Four of them. One had an accent… Southern, I think."

The pastor scowled. He went to a window at the front of the house and peered into the storm, on the lookout for danger.

"Where was the van parked?" Trudy asked.

"At a cabin…a log cabin."

"And what did this cabin look like?"

"I think the door was painted green."

"One story or two?"

She cleared her throat. The words came more easily if she whispered. "Don't know… I couldn't see it very well through the trees and the snow. Those men…they might come after me. I didn't cover my tracks very well. I'm sorry."

"You did the right thing, getting out of the storm, and I appreciate the warning." Clarence opened the door to the front closet and reached up to a high shelf. "If we've got wild-eyed criminals running around in my forest, I sure as heck want to be ready for them. What else can you tell me?"

"Their weapons were HK417 assault rifles."

"That's mighty specific, little lady. How come you know so much about guns?"

She shrugged.

"You might be in the military." He took a hunting rifle down from the shelf and set it by the door. Then he removed a long wooden box from the closet and carried it to the table.

A sign flashed in her mind. "Peterson Air Force Base."

"That's not too far from here. Is that where you're stationed?"

"I don't know. I don't think so."

Another image replaced the first. She was staring into the maw of a tunnel large enough to drive a couple of semitrucks through. This huge half circle abutted the mountain, Cheyenne Mountain. It was the entrance to the underground NORAD complex, and she wasn't supposed to talk about it—not even with nice people like Trudy and the pastor.

She'd said too much already, should never have given her trust so freely. What did she really know about Pastor Clarence and his wife? Nothing! The pastor unloaded a SIG Sauer and two Colt revolvers from his wooden box. Plus there was the rifle by the front door. These two definitely weren't helpless woodland creatures.

"Honestly, Clarence." Trudy rolled her eyes. "If you're going to play with your guns, put down some towels so you don't scratch my table."

He put the revolvers away in the box and tucked the SIG into his waistband beside his suspenders. "I'm going upstairs. The windows up there make better vantage points."

"Before you go," Trudy said, "would you please call 911? I'd like to get the sheriff up here. And an ambulance."

"Not for me," she said.

"I'm afraid it's necessary, dear."

She didn't want to go to the hospital. Turning herself in would violate her mission. *Her mission? What mission?* "I'm already feeling a lot better."

"Except you can't remember your name." Trudy leaned forward to pour. "More tea?"

"Yes, please." She studied the older woman. Trudy's movements were disjointed, her right arm seemed stiff, and her hands were twisted in a knot. Under her flannel gown and robe, she was very thin, possibly sickly. "If I can borrow a coat, I'll be on my way."

"Don't be silly." Trudy's voice was sharp edged. "In this weather, you won't make it a mile. I didn't haul myself out of bed and help you get warm only to have you go running outside to freeze again."

"You're right." She sank back against the sofa. "I'm sorry…for waking you up."

"I wasn't sleeping, just lying down. It's too early for bed."

"She has rheumatism and a nerve disorder," Clarence explained as he picked up his cell phone. "There's only so much we can do to alleviate the pain. The one thing that relaxes her is music."

"I used to be a music teacher," Trudy said with a wistful smile. "And I'm still the choir director at our church."

When she'd first entered the cabin, she'd heard a symphony from upstairs. "You didn't have to turn off your CDs because of me. I adore classical music."

"You're sweet to say so," Trudy said.

She sat up straighter on the sofa, roused by a vivid memory. "I play the violin."

"Do you?" Trudy lightly applauded. "I'd love to hear you play."

If it would keep them from sending her to the hospital, she could play all the Mozart concertos with Beethoven thrown in on the side. She'd do whatever was necessary to evade the danger that encroached on all sides. From the thugs in the van to the vicious storm to her unnamed fear of being hospitalized, everything appeared to be against her. She felt as doomed as a skier racing downhill, trying to escape a churning, roaring avalanche. Her chance of survival was slim.

Chapter Two

Through the ragged curtain of falling snow, FBI Special Agent Spence Malone spotted headlights approaching. "About time," he muttered.

Spence wasn't running this operation, but his directions had summoned two vans—one for the local SWAT team and another from the FBI—to this isolated mountain cabin with a dark blue van parked in front. It had been twenty-seven minutes since he called for immediate emergency backup.

His tension was epic. When it came to making sharp, street-smart decisions, he trusted the instincts he'd learned at an early age in foster care. But this assignment was different. Not only was he dealing with a global situation, but his partner was the woman he loved.

Spence feared that he'd made the wrong decision by not going after her when he found the van. He could easily have followed her tracks into the forest. But he'd wanted to make sure these four thugs were apprehended and secured. Backup was required.

He bolted from his rented SUV and charged toward the vans. The SWAT commander and an agent in an

FBI jacket joined him on the road. A wall of pine trees separated them from the cabin.

After introductions, Spence filled them in. "My partner is missing, and I think these men grabbed her."

"Her?" Ramirez, the agent, yanked off his FBI watch cap and combed his fingers through his thick black hair.

"Agent Angelica Thorne is NSA, not FBI. We're partners for the duration of this assignment." And the assignment was top secret. They didn't need details about Angelica. "I followed her tracking signal to the van and checked inside, where I found evidence."

"Evidence?" Ramirez questioned.

"Her prints and hairs," Spence said dismissively. "Trust me, she was in that van."

"But not anymore," Ramirez said.

"As far as I can tell, she's in the wind. But she left these four goons behind. I've been observing them with a heat sensor. They're all in the kitchen."

The SWAT commander gave a quick nod. "Armed and dangerous?"

"Yes," Spence said. "I've got questions for them and would appreciate if you keep them alive."

"Consider it done," the commander said. "I'll deploy two snipers in the trees, just in case. And we'll storm the house from the front and side."

"Go for it," Spence said. "I'm sitting this one out."

He and Ramirez returned to his SUV, where he picked up his rifle, infrared goggles and a backpack. He needed to hurry. Dusk had fallen. Soon, it would be dark.

"Should I come with you?" Ramirez asked.

"Not necessary." If Spence couldn't find Angelica, he might as well throw himself off the nearest cliff. He wouldn't be able to live with the guilt if he lost her. "I need you here to take those four into custody."

"No problem. We've got a cage at headquarters that's just the right size."

Ramirez chewed on his lower lip. Spence guessed the other agent was fighting to suppress his excitement. There probably wasn't much action at the FBI offices outside Colorado Springs. Spence held up his cell phone. "Call me when they're in custody."

Ramirez exchanged numbers with him. "Tell me about the NSA agent. How did she get grabbed?"

"This is the first time Agent Thorne has been in the field."

"Inexperienced," Ramirez said with a disgusted shake of his head. "Am I right? The chick is a typical rookie."

"Don't say *chick*." Spence retrieved his phone. "And there's nothing typical about her."

"Sorry, man." Ramirez raised both hands, placating. "I'll call when we've got these guys."

Spence took off at a jog, heading into the forest in the direction he had already tracked. It wasn't her fault that she was missing. It was his. He shouldn't have left her alone, not even for a minute. If his brain had been working, he would have refused to be her partner in the first place. This assignment wasn't the type of thing she was accustomed to handling.

Angelica worked in the Cyber Security branch of NSA. She'd been there for three years and had a reputation as an outstanding hacker. Though she usually stayed behind her desk, she was chosen for this assignment because her dad was a retired general in the air force who lived in the area. People around here knew her family, and the gates of the North American Aerospace Defense Command, or NORAD, complex were more likely to open for somebody familiar and friendly. As soon as they'd arrived, she'd proved useful in cutting through military red tape. He wasn't sure if that was due to her high-ranking contacts or her dynamite body.

He saw her footprints in the snow. Branches had been broken on the pine trees. She'd come this way. He dug into his pocket for his GPS device. The blip from her implanted tracker was loud and clear. She was close, less than a mile away. He dared to hope that she'd be all right as he moved quickly through the trees.

She'd charmed him six months ago, on the first day they'd met at Quantico, where she'd come to do a consultation. If he'd been a movie producer looking for a woman to play the part of a secret agent, Angelica would have been number one on his list. She was five feet nine inches tall with long, slender legs and classic curves. Her black hair fell straight and sleek to her shoulders. And she was stylish in high-heeled boots, tailored clothes and expert makeup that showed off her mysterious green eyes. One thing was for damn sure, Angelica didn't look at all like a computer geek—which was exactly what she was, an NSA expert called in to advise on an FBI hack.

To say that he and Angelica got along well together would be an understatement. From their first kiss, he'd known that she was special. They'd started dating after that first case was closed, which shouldn't have been a dating-in-the-workplace problem because he never expected to work with her again.

Behind his back, he heard the sounds of the SWAT team assault on the cabin. His shoulders tensed as he listened for gunfire. First, there had been three loud explosions from flash bangs. Then there were loud shouts. He counted gunshots. One. Two. A spray from an automatic, two more, then there was silence. The whole thing had taken less than five minutes, a good sign. Quick operations were usually successful.

He hoped that his and Angelica's mission would also be swift and effective. They were investigating an attempted hack at the supposedly impregnable NORAD complex. With Angelica's technical expertise and his experience in undercover ops, their collaboration should have gone smoothly, except that she'd been abducted within twelve hours of their arrival.

At a clearing in the forest, he paused. Obvious tracks went straight across the middle. The fact that she hadn't taken time to disguise her route told him that she must be desperate. He charged across the snow and up the hill on the opposite side.

Spencer saw the lights of a cabin beside a church, an obvious safe haven against the storm. The wind had erased most of her tracks, but he still saw indentations as he rushed toward the two-story cabin. The lights were less than ten yards away. He could smell the smoke that rose from the chimney.

The gentle strains of a violin wafted through the air as he pulled off his glove and rapped on the door. There was no answer. He hammered more loudly and shouted, "Open up. FBI."

The door opened, just a crack, and a voice commanded, "Step back."

When Spence saw the barrel of a rifle, he decided to cooperate. An elderly, bearded man came out onto the wide, covered porch and pulled the door closed.

There was a Santa Claus thing going on with the white beard and the red suspenders, but this old guy wasn't jolly and smiling. He aimed his Remington at Spence's chest. *Bad Santa.*

"I'll need some ID," the man growled.

Spence reached inside his parka pocket and took out his badge. "I'm looking for someone."

"What for?"

"She might be in danger."

"I'm going to let you inside. But if you make one false move, you'll be sorry."

As soon as the door opened, Spence saw her. With perfect posture, she perched on a wooden chair, wearing flannel jammies and playing a violin.

He called out, "Angelica."

Abruptly, she lowered the bow and stared at him.

An elderly lady, who seemed to be the mate of the man who opened the door, chuckled. "Angelica is a perfect name for you, dear. You play like an angel."

"A snow angel," her husband said.

Unable to keep his distance, Spence strode across the room toward her. He needed to gather her in his arms, to stroke her hair and whisper reassurances that he would never leave her unprotected again.

"Stay back." She stood and faced him. "How do you know my name?"

ANGELICA, MY NAME is Angelica. She thrust and parried with her violin bow, fighting to keep the guy in the huge parka away from her. *Angelica!* The word echoed inside her skull, and she liked the sound. It felt right. She remembered a rowboat with that name written in fanciful letters across the stern. *And so, Angelica, what are you going to do now?*

"He claims to be with the FBI," Clarence said.

"We'll see about that." Her first priority was to deal with Parka Guy. "Give your rifle and backpack to Pastor Clarence."

He spread his hands. "I'm not going to hurt you."

She touched the tip of her bow to the center of his chest. The slender, fiberglass stick looked ridiculously delicate and flimsy against his girth and strength. His shoulders were as wide as the Frankenstein monster. He could snap that bow in half and use the horsehair strings as a garrote if he felt like it. For that matter, he could snap her in half, too. If she had any sense at all, she'd be shaking in her socks.

More forcefully, she said, "The rifle. Do it."

In a few swift moves, he unfastened the rifle. He also removed the backpack, which he held toward her. When she didn't take it, he growled and dropped the pack on the floor next to his gloves.

He unzipped the front of his parka and flipped back the fur-lined hood. His complexion was ruddy from being out in the snow, and he had a tiny scar on his chin that she somehow knew he'd gotten in a barroom brawl. Everything else about him was perfection. Square jaw, wide mouth, high cheekbones and the most intense, ice-blue eyes she'd ever seen. His gaze was mesmerizing and predatory like a wolf.

"Now," he said as he thumped his very solid chest. "You recognize me now, right?"

Though there was something familiar about his towering height, the pattern of stubble on his chin and the blond streaks in his hair, she couldn't say for sure that she knew him. And she really wanted to. It'd be a shame to beat this handsome man to death with her violin bow.

"On your knees," she snapped. "Hands behind your head."

"Oh, my," Trudy said with a gasp. "Sounds like you've done this before."

Had she? Where were these commands coming from? How did she know what to do when threatened? Classes… She remembered the exercises; she'd taken training. Every agent in her division was required to learn the basics of law enforcement and firearms. "Quantico," she whispered.

"That's right," he said. "You trained at the FBI facilities."

The FBI? She was an agent? It hardly seemed possible that a real federal agent would attempt to subdue an attacker with a violin bow. "I don't think I'm in the FBI."

"You're in the NSA, in the Cyber Security division."

Sure, why not? She turned away from Gorgeous Parka Guy, flipped the violin onto her shoulder and played the opening notes of "Blackbird" to show there were no hard feelings. Perhaps a silly, delusional thing to do, but it seemed like a positive gesture.

Angelica asked Pastor Clarence, "Would you please reach inside his jacket and disarm him?"

"Wait," Parka Guy said. "I can save us a lot of time if I take off my own weapons."

"Fine." Angelica perched on the edge of her hard-back chair and continued to play the classic Beatles song. She segued to "Yesterday."

Concern about Gorgeous lingered in the back of her mind, but she wasn't scared of him. The opposite, in fact. She felt safe, ridiculously safe considering that she'd just escaped from four thugs and she was some kind of agent who had special training. She really ought to worry, especially since he was carrying two Glocks, an eight-inch serrated hunting knife and a small-caliber pistol in an ankle holster strapped above his heavy-duty boots.

Stripped of his weapons and his parka, he approached her, stood and waited for her to finish her violin solo. Gently, he took the instrument and the bow from her hands and laid them on the long, wooden dining table. He came back to her, leaned down and gazed directly into her eyes. "Say my name."

Her breath caught in her throat. The whirlwind of confusion buffeting inside her head went still, and she was suspended, floating in midair. She felt neither cold nor hot, neither right nor wrong, neither safe nor terrified. She was simply there.

"Spencer," she said. "Spence Malone."

And then she was in his arms. The cold from outdoors still clung to his Irish fisherman's sweater, but the internal heat from his body raised the temperature. She snuggled against him, inhaling the natural scent of lamb's wool and warm man.

He whispered in her ear, "You couldn't forget me."

Apparently, she'd guessed correctly.

Chapter Three

Now she knew his name was Spence Malone, but Angelica had no idea what that meant to her. He was incredibly good-looking, just exactly her type. She glided her hand across his rock-hard chest and down his arm. Even through his thick sweater, she felt the ridges of his biceps. Were they lovers?

He tilted her chin so she was gazing up at him. His blue eyes flicked from left to right, reading her expression. "Seems like you've forgotten a few things," he said.

"A few." She shrugged.

"What do you recall?"

"There were four men, big guys, dumb as dirt." His penetrating gaze was like a truth-seeking missile, and she wasn't sure how much she should reveal. She turned toward Trudy and said, "Remember? I told you about them. One had a Texas accent. They were armed with HK417 assault rifles. They took me to a cabin."

"And she mentioned a van," Trudy said helpfully, "a dark blue or black van."

Leaning down, Spence kissed her forehead. The light touch of his lips set off a chain reaction of shivers that had more to do with her internal engine than with the snow and cold. Her inner machinery had definitely come back to life. She exhaled a soft moan.

"What else?" he murmured.

Resisting him wasn't going to be easy. "Nothing much."

"It's okay. You can tell me."

But maybe she'd better not. Though his tone was gentle and cajoling, she knew he was digging, probing, interrogating. If he discovered the gaps in her memory, what would he do? He said he was a federal agent, but that didn't mean he was innocent.

She turned the tables with a question of her own. "What do you do for the FBI?"

"Mostly administrative stuff," he said in a silky voice. "Do you remember where we are?"

"Near Peterson Air Force Base." Luckily, the pastor had provided her with that much info.

"Do you know why we're here?"

"For one thing, my parents live near here." Before she could think twice, she said their names. "Peter and Lana Thorne."

"General Thorne?" Pastor Clarence straightened his posture, almost as though he was snapping to attention. "You're their daughter?"

"One of their daughters," she corrected.

Her memories came fast and furious as a mental family portrait formed. There were two girls and two boys. Angelica was second or third oldest depending on who was doing the counting. She and her sister, Selena, were identical twins, and they always argued about who was born first. The youngest—a boy who chose the marine corps over the air force, much to his father's chagrin—had moved out last year. Though Dad was mostly retired, her parents kept their six-bedroom house in the hills above Manitou Springs.

She was looking forward to visiting them and having them meet Spence, which meant he must be important to her. Since it wasn't her habit to introduce casual lovers to the parents, Spencer Malone must have a different significance. Maybe she worked with him. He was a born leader, similar to her high-ranking father. Both were tough, competitive and feisty.

She gave him a grin. "You and Dad are going to love each other."

The gleam from his cool blue eyes dimmed. "You introduced me to your father yesterday."

"Indeed." *Couldn't be. That's not something I'd forget.* She treasured every moment with her mom and dad. Family was everything to her.

"We were at their house for dinner. You don't remember?"

"Give me a minute. It'll come back."

He sat her on the hard-back chair. His touch became less sensual and more clinical as he massaged her scalp. "Does your head feel sore? Is there a possibility of concussion?"

"I was afraid of this," Trudy said as she clenched her fingers into a knot. "It's amnesia, isn't it?"

"Maybe," Spence said. "She needs a CT scan. And she ought to be examined by a doctor."

"We put in a 911 call," Trudy said. "It felt like an hour ago."

"I'll call again," Clarence said. "They warned me about slow response time on account of the weather. And there was a pileup accident on I-25. When I told the dispatcher she wasn't bleeding and didn't appear to have broken bones, he suggested I drive her myself if it was possible."

"I'll take care of it," Spence said.

"Wait!" Angelica waved both hands to interrupt the plans that were being made for her. She was wide-awake, sitting right here, and she didn't like having other people take control of her life. "I don't need a hospital. I didn't hit my head."

Spence hunkered down in front of her. He captured her fluttering hands and held them. "Would you remember if you had?"

"Did you find any bumps on my head?" she demanded. "No, you did not. And my skull doesn't feel concussed. There are plenty of other places on my body that are painful, but not my head."

"Where does it hurt?" he asked.

"My lips are chapped and were bleeding." She yanked her hands from his grasp. "My feet are stiff and sore. My throat is scratchy."

"She has bruises," Trudy said. "I noticed them when she was changing clothes."

Shrinking back in the chair, Angelica wrapped her arms protectively around her midsection. She knew very well that she had injuries. Both her knees were scraped. A massive contusion spread from her rib cage to her lower pelvis on her right side. Though she couldn't see her back, she felt an occasional throb of pain.

The physical damage might have come from a hard fall or a car wreck. She might have been beaten but didn't remember, didn't want to remember. She'd been doing her best to ignore these aches and get back to the business at hand—whatever that was.

She glared at Spence. "No way do I have a concussion."

"There are other ways to lose your memory." He placed his hand on her knee, reestablishing contact. "You could have been drugged."

She glanced down. Her eyelids closed. For an instant, she caught a glimpse of what had happened. A brief sliver of memory revealed itself, and she saw things as they had occurred instead of as they were now.

Her wrists were fastened to the arms of a chair with duct tape. She wasn't uncomfortable but firmly secured, immobile. Behind her back, disembodied voices talked about dosage. They mentioned a drug.

She repeated their words, "A derivative mixture of benzodiazepine and propranolol."

When she looked up, she saw Spence nod. "Those are drugs that could be used to induce memory loss."

"I knew that." Oddly enough, that was her first outright lie. She knew zip about drugs and memory loss, but she wanted desperately to speak with some kind of authority.

"If you were drugged," Spence said, "we need to take you to the hospital for tests. Be reasonable, Angelica. I want you to be checked out. I feel responsible."

"Please don't."

"Don't what?"

"Feel responsible."

She bolted to her feet. Even though she couldn't exactly identify her career at the moment, she was dead certain that she was well respected in her field. She'd always been an achiever, proud when her slacker sister teased her for being "daddy's little darling." Ever since Angelica hit her first home run in T-ball, she'd been a winner. Valedictorian and senior prom queen in high school, magna cum laude from college, and she'd received dozens of grants in computer cryptography, science and hacking.

The past was becoming clear to her. She worked at the Cyber Security division of NSA and focused on cryptography and hacking. Her long-term memory was reassembling itself. The short-term still eluded her.

In any case, she didn't want to be tucked away in a hospital. Though she didn't know why, being here—in the field—was an opportunity for her. Going into the hospital meant admitting defeat. She needed to convince Spence that she was okay, and they should get back to work. "I'm fine."

"Do you remember dinner?" he asked.

"Of course, I do."

"Prove it."

Dinner at the home of General and Mrs. Thorne with one outside guest followed a certain ritual. Angelica, along with her brothers and sister, had attended hundreds of Lana's simple but elegant dinners. This one wouldn't be much different.

"The centerpiece on the table was made of pinecones painted orange and blue…" It was football season, and her father was a season ticket holder. "In a salute to the Denver Broncos."

"What did we talk about?"

She knew this one: the primary topic for every true Bronco fan. "We discussed the quarterback. Elway was mentioned."

Spence nodded, and she brightened. *I'm going to get away with this.* She continued, "Mom served Cornish game hens and cheesy potatoes. The pie was pecan."

She could tell by his expression that she'd nailed the menu of her mom's favorite dishes. "Is that accurate?"

He gave another terse nod. "Do you remember why we're here?"

She took a leap of logic. He was FBI; she was NSA. He had come looking for her. "We're on assignment together."

"I still want you checked out," he muttered. Then he looked toward Pastor Clarence. "Can you give me a ride to my car?"

"Sure, but I need to dig out the driveway to the garage. And that might take half an hour or forty-five minutes."

"I'll hike," Spence said as he started loading his weapons back into their holsters. After he slipped into his parka, he picked up the extra-large backpack and dropped it at her feet. "I brought your clothes, boots and a jacket. While I'm finding the car, you can get dressed."

"I'm not going to the hospital," she said firmly. "I'll call my dad. He can pick me up."

"Not a chance." Spence forced his words through a tight-lipped grin. "I want General Thorne to like me. That's sure as hell not going to happen if I tell him how I slacked off on the job and let his daughter get kidnapped. And then, even worse, I have to call him for help."

Though Angelica didn't want to turn to Daddy for help, she considered having Spence rescue her to be equally frustrating. She hefted the pack by one strap and slung it over her shoulder causing a pain that crawled up and down her spine. She held her breath and willed the hurt to stop. She didn't have time to be injured. She refused to be taken out of the game.

Spence said she was kidnapped. *Kidnapped?* That must be why those thugs had her in the van and why he'd been searching for her. "Did they demand a ransom?"

"No."

Well, of course not. Kidnappers wouldn't ask the FBI for money. "What about my father? Did they contact him?"

"This isn't about money," Spence said. "At least, it's not about the piddling amount that a kidnapper could demand."

She didn't understand. If her kidnappers hadn't been after money, why did they take her? "Is it because—"

He stepped up close, interrupting before she said too much. He gave a quick glance over his shoulder at Clarence and spoke to her softly. "We'll talk about this later."

"But I—"

"Later." He took the backpack from her grasp, asked directions from Trudy for someplace private and carried her pack up the staircase and into a guest bedroom. Pillows were stacked at the head of a queen-size bed, and the brightly patterned duvet was neatly made. With the door partially closed so the pastor and his wife couldn't hear, Spence whispered, "I'm guessing that they kidnapped you because of the computer codes you were working on before we left. That's the bad news. The good news is that you must have hit a nerve. You're on the right track."

"Would computer codes be worth more than a ransom?"

"Hell, yeah." He raked his fingers through his sun-streaked hair. "The weapon codes stored at NORAD can be used to activate, launch, deploy and shut down various missile and satellite systems, mostly for ICBMs. Foreign governments would pay a small fortune for that information."

"I got it."

"Do you remember the kidnappers or what you told them?"

"I'm drawing a blank." What if she'd given up the codes? She might have already betrayed their mission. This investigation might have a real unhappy ending. "I'm sorry."

"Once we get back to the hotel, I have a technique that'll help you remember." He took her hand and gave it a squeeze. "Get changed. I'm going to pick up the car."

When he left her alone in the bedroom, Angelica placed the backpack on a cedar chest at the foot of the four-poster bed, which was one of the few surfaces free from knickknacks or photos. She unzipped the main compartment. The soft beige turtleneck, the jeans and the lightweight, superwarm Patagonia jacket were familiar. As she changed into the clothes, she remembered when she'd bought them, remembered trying them on, washing them and taking them out of the dryer. Her memory seemed back to normal, except for recent events.

It was as if a neuroprogrammer had reached into her skull and erased chunks of her brain. Last night and yesterday were totally blank. Until Spence had explained the investigation at NORAD, she didn't know why she was here. What kind of computer hacking did she do? Who taught her? And then, there was Spence. He was the most fascinating puzzle of all. She remembered him but didn't know if they were tangled in a hot-and-heavy relationship or if they were just friends.

When she raised her arms to slip the turtleneck over her head, her torso twisted and she felt a stab of pain from the big, nasty bruise on her side and hip. Unwilling to admit how truly lousy she felt, Angelica forced herself to stand erect. Wearing her own clothing felt good. Even better, she found a makeup kit and toiletries in the backpack.

Confronting the mirror that hung above the dresser was horrific. From her snarled black hair to her chapped cheeks to her hazel-green eyes, which were road-mapped with red squiggles, she was a mess. How could Spence even look at her without gagging? If she ever hoped to find out what kind of relationship she had with him, damage control was necessary.

After she combed her hair, put on lotion and dabbed at the worst parts of her face with makeup, she looked around the guest bedroom. On the top of the dresser was an army of clay figurines that were obviously sculpted in kindergarten classes. And there were tons of framed photos of kids in costumes, playing games, skating and skiing.

Trudy was the opposite of Angelica's mom, who kept tidy scrapbooks and limited her displays to formal pictures, such as wedding photos, graduation pictures and framed diplomas. Angelica figured she was more like Trudy, favoring snapshots of kids with dirty faces and stolen moments caught on film. She liked to think that pictures were a good way to capture memories, her memories.

Eyes closed, she attempted to focus. She visualized

the headquarters where she worked, an attractive space filled with bold artwork, curving corridors, horizontal windows and computer screens with cascading streams of numbers. She imagined her desk in a smallish, orange-and-white office with a window, an ergonomic chair and a white desk that extended the length of one wall. Her gaze zoomed in on a framed photo of her and Spence, laughing and embracing. In another intimate picture, they were holding hands and walking at the edge of a frothy ruffle of surf.

The sound of a ringtone from downstairs pulled her out of her reverie. Spence's ringtone, it played the opening notes to *Camelot*. He'd changed it to that theme after they saw a revival of the musical at the Arena Theater.

Vivid images of what happened after they went back to the hotel after curtain call rushed through her. She tasted the fizz of champagne, smelled the scent of fresh roses, felt his huge hands encircling her waist as she opened her mouth for his kiss. The definitive answer to one of her questions became clear. Their relationship was anything but casual. Deep and intense, they were lovers.

Chapter Four

Spence zipped up his parka and took his cell phone out-side onto the snow-covered porch that stretched across the front of the cabin. The caller ID displayed: "SA RAMI." It had to be Special Agent Ramirez calling to let Spence know that the SWAT takedown was success-ful. But the first words Ramirez said were, "I'm sorry."

"Why?"

"One of the suspects got away."

He launched into an explanation of what had hap-pened at the nearby cabin, but Spence stopped him. "That's enough."

"You need to understand that—"

"You and a trained team of SWAT officers failed to apprehend four mindless goons in a sneak attack." In spite of the cold, Spence was steaming. "Spare me the details."

"It wasn't my fault," Ramirez complained.

Spence hadn't forgotten that SA Ramirez was quick to sneer at Angelica's rookie status. "Is SWAT in pur-suit?"

"They are, but this guy got out of his cuffs, grabbed a weapon and—"

"He's armed?"

"Oh, yeah, he was slick. He took off like a jackrabbit. They aren't going to catch him."

And why aren't you chasing him? Spence had little respect for feds like Ramirez who left the real work of law enforcement to the cops while they stood around posing in their black suits and their FBI windbreakers. Part of Spence's investigation at NORAD would include checking out Ramirez's office, and he wouldn't be surprised to find a mole. Even a half-assed spy wouldn't have much problem outsmarting the likes of Ramirez. His boss, Supervisory Special Agent Raquel Sheeran, was another story. She was as sharp as a stiletto.

Spence ordered, "Arrange for the three in custody to be delivered to the FBI offices."

"I already have."

The escaped thug complicated the situation. Spence couldn't leave Angelica and the elderly couple unprotected while he hiked back to pick up his vehicle. But he wanted to get Angelica checked out by a doctor as soon as possible. Being in two places at one time wasn't an option.

Though he hated relying on Ramirez, he needed help. He leaned against the porch banister and peered toward the church next door. Though the storm was pretty much over, a blanket of snow lay heavy on the unplowed road and the parking lot. Night was starting to fall, but it wasn't totally dark. The glow of starlight filtered through the clouds.

"Ramirez, I want you to drive here. Bring one other man." Spence gave directional driving instructions and used Pastor Clarence's address for Ramirez's GPS. "Do you understand?"

"Got it."

"I'll be waiting."

Pastor Clarence came onto the porch. In spite of his age and potbelly, he moved with the stealth of a hunter. "I can help you find that van at the cabin," he said. "Angelica mentioned a green door. I know exactly where it is."

The old man wore a red knit cap, again making Spence think of Santa. But the pastor's red gloves were clutched around his rifle instead of a bag of toys. The parka that was belted around his ample midsection was black.

"I'm getting picked up," Spence said. "Besides, you need to be here when the ambulance arrives."

"The sheriff can figure it out. He's a real crackerjack."

"Yeah? Well, he's not winning any prizes as a first responder." Spence had to consider the possibility that sweet old Clarence hadn't, in fact, contacted the emergency dispatcher. Santa might be lying. "How long ago did you make that call?"

"A while." He tugged on his beard. "Something's fishy. What was your phone call about?"

"There's a dangerous armed man on the loose. I'll get Angelica to the hospital. An officer from SWAT will be left behind to protect you and your wife."

"I can take care of my family." Clarence puffed out his chest. "I don't want some SWAT punk hanging around."

"You need protection." Spence was fairly sure the old man was hiding something but didn't have time to dig for the truth. "The punk stays, and that's an order."

"Hah!" The pastor threw back his head. "I've been

retired for fourteen years. I don't obey orders unless they come from my sovereign."

"Who's that?"

Clarence pointed skyward. "My Lord in Heaven."

Spence gazed across the snowy crossroads toward the dark, impenetrable forest. A shaft of moonlight illuminated the simple cross above the church's entryway. Clarence was a man of God, but that didn't mean he was without sin. "What does your Lord say about lying?"

"You know the Commandments."

"Do you?"

The pastor fidgeted and sputtered, and Spence could see the truth struggling to get out. If he stood here quietly and waited, Clarence would confess whatever he'd been holding back.

The pearly white landscape spread before him, so ethereal and beautiful that he almost ran inside and grabbed Angelica to show her. Better that he didn't; she might not be enthusiastic about the wonders of snow after being nearly frostbitten to death. The only marks in the unbroken snow were his tracks and Angelica's. Hers were almost erased by the drifting wind.

At the edge of the forest, he saw movement. It could be deer or elk or his own imagination, but he didn't think so. He took his night vision goggles from a parka pocket and held them to his eyes.

He saw a man, staggering from the forest. He disappeared behind the church. A moment passed while Spence waited anxiously for the man to reappear.

Beside him, the pastor cleared his throat. "There's something I ought to tell you, Spence."

"Not now."

"It's important."

A light shone through an arched window at the far end of the church. The man—the fugitive—had found sanctuary. Or so he thought.

Spence grabbed the pastor's arm and spun him around. "I saw the fugitive, the man who escaped custody. He's in the church. When the agent and the SWAT officer get here, send them in that direction."

"What about me? I could be your backup."

"Stay here. Protect Trudy and Angelica."

Spence pivoted and leaped from the porch. His boots hit the snow, and he started running toward the church. The new-fallen snow slipped over the top of his boots and soaked his jeans. He ducked behind a clump of aspen and inhaled a deep, frigid breath. At this elevation, oxygen was scarce.

Between the trees where he was hiding and the front entryway to the church, there wasn't much cover. If he stood upright and ran, he'd be an obvious target. But there wasn't time to dash around to the road and come up from the front.

He kept his repeating rifle slung across his back, choosing instead to arm himself with a handgun for easier mobility. His new Glock 17 fit neatly into his hand. Through the specially woven, nonslip fabric of his glove, he hardly felt the cold of the Glock's handgrip. Keeping his head down and shoulders bent, he tried to make himself small as he rushed toward the front entryway under the cross.

Light continued to shine through the window in the rear part of the building. Was the fugitive standing there, looking out and taking aim? This guy wouldn't be caught napping; he'd managed to get out of his handcuffs and evade a team of trained officers. Ramirez had called him slick, and Spence agreed.

The preferred method for taking a suspect was a straight-on assault, using the element of surprise, yelling to disorient the suspect and being ready to shoot first. But Spence wasn't looking for a lethal shoot-out. This fugitive was low on the totem pole. His greatest value was the information he could give. Somehow, Spence needed to sneak into the church and take the fugitive into custody.

At the entryway, he leaned against the polished oak door with a small diamond-shaped stained glass window at eye level. The church building was a rectangle, with stained glass windows on either side. Spence wasn't sure what he'd find inside. Ruefully, he realized, it would have been useful to have the pastor with him to give him the layout.

The door on the right had a keyed knob. Spence gave it a twist and found it locked. No problem, he'd been picking locks since he was a trouble-making teenager. This was the first time he'd done it at a church.

After turning the knob, he opened the door a crack, slid inside and closed it. The entryway was in darkness. No windows here. In the nave, where the congregation sat, the stained glass windows on either side allowed moonlight to fall across several rows of wooden pews. He edged his way down the wall, expecting—at any moment—to hear the blast of a repeating rifle.

No sound came. And Spence didn't see the fugitive. At the front of the church, there was light from a door at the far right side of the sanctuary. In the entryway, Spence found himself at the foot of a narrow, wooden staircase that hugged the wall. He climbed to a choir loft. Three rows of pews and an upright organ were faintly visible. Quiet as a cat, he crept down to the carved railing, where he squatted and waited.

It was a pretty little church, simple and clean, with a high peaked ceiling and open beams. The carpet in the sanctuary was slate blue and the altar was carved from dark wood. From outside, a fierce wind buffeted the stained glass windows, causing the old structure to creak and moan. *Not a bad thing*, he figured. Those noises had masked the sound of his entry, allowing him to scoot across the back and up the stairs without the fugitive noticing.

A certain amount of skill was required to move with stealth and purpose. But Spence also believed in luck. Being in a church, he wondered if he should shoot off a prayer. He wasn't a religious man, didn't make it to church every week, nor did he quote from the Bible or other sacred texts. But he was spiritual. He believed in a higher power. When he was growing up, two men were instrumental in helping him pull his life together. One was a pastor, the other a priest. Spence had never done a whole lot of praying, but he felt like those church people had done a lot of praying to make sure he stayed on the right path.

A telephone rang. Spence heard the mumbled reply. Was the voice coming all the way from that back room? If so, the acoustics in here were incredible.

The light from the back room went out. The phone call must have tipped off the fugitive. But how? Who made that call? Behind the shadows of the pulpit and a standing candleholder, Spence saw a man dodge across the sanctuary, slam into the side of the altar and then duck behind it.

From his superior vantage point in the choir loft, Spence peered over the banister rail. The element of surprise was gone, but he could still give this guy a chance to make it easy on himself.

"FBI," Spence called out. "I don't want to hurt you. Just put down your weapon and step out from behind the altar."

"What if I don't?"

"I need to take you into custody."

The fugitive laughed. "That doesn't work for me."

Spence heard a voice from behind his back. "Sorry, Spencer. Doesn't work for me, either."

He looked over his shoulder and saw Pastor Clarence, aka Bad Santa, aiming his rifle at a lethal point between his shoulder blades. The old man was working with the bad guys. "This explains a lot."

"What?" Clarence asked.

"You never called 911."

"Nope."

"And I'm guessing that the van hadn't ended up in this area by coincidence. Tell me, Pastor, do you own the cabin with the green door?"

"I do, and three others in this area." He gestured with the rifle. "I want you to stand up real slow and careful."

Seriously? Had Bad Santa forgotten how well armed Spence was? Did this old guy think he could take down a federal agent in his prime?

"Let me remind you," Clarence said, "I've got the drop on you, and it'd be easier to swab up the blood from your dead body than to sand bullet holes out of the pews."

"Were you even a chaplain?"

"I'm retired, but I served."

Something must have happened to turn the old man into a traitor. In other circumstances, Spence might have been willing to delve and probe and put together motivations and answers. But he wasn't in a forgiving mood. This investigation needed to be over so he could return to Virginia with Angelica and repair her memory.

Lowering his rifle and sliding his handgun onto the pew, Spence turned sideways in the choir loft so he'd present a narrow silhouette to the man hiding behind the altar. "Tell me, Clarence, if I hadn't come along, what would you have done to Angelica?"

"What do you mean?"

"She's a loose end. It doesn't seem smart to leave her running free. Would you have shot her?"

Clarence huffed as he adjusted the barrel on his rifle. "You've got this wrong. Just give me a minute and let me explain."

A disembodied voice rose from the altar. "It's not as bad as you think."

How do you know what I think? Spence had never been known for his calm, patient attitude, and he sure as hell didn't need advice from some dumber-than-dirt thug. It was time to take control of this situation.

Disarming Clarence would be a piece of cake; the old guy wasn't exactly in peak condition. The tricky part would be to avoid getting shot by the armed thug. Spence coiled his long legs beneath him. With one well-placed leap, he went into the aisle between the pews. With a pivot, he launched himself off the organ and smashed into the pastor's broad chest.

Clarence went down with a thud. Flat on his back, he didn't bother struggling. As Spence fastened his wrists with a zip tie, Clarence said, "There should have been an easier way to do this."

"Explain."

"First, an introduction," Clarence said. "The dark and scary character who escaped the SWAT team is my nephew, Trevor MacArthur. Help us out, Trev. Turn on the sanctuary lights."

The shadowy figure that had been lurking behind the altar went to the edge of the sanctuary and flipped a couple of switches. Lights blazed in the nave.

A young man with curly brown hair and a beard strolled to the front of the sanctuary. "There's one more thing you ought to know, Spence."

"What's that?"

"I'm FBI, working undercover."

Chapter Five

Trust no one. Her father had always advised her to be suspicious and, as always, Dad was right. Angelica had been fool enough to accept the pastor and Trudy as the kindly, elderly couple they appeared to be. *So wrong!*

Frozen in place, she stood in front of the dresser in the upstairs bedroom of the cabin, where every wall was hung with photos and every flat surface held knick-knacks. Her gaze stuck on a five-by-seven photograph of a young man in a football uniform. His face and his dark, floppy hair appeared in many other photos scattered around the room.

At first glance, he'd looked familiar, and she wondered if they'd gone to the same school. She'd grown up in this area, and he might be somebody she'd met before or had known. Slowly, she'd circled the room, prowling, taking time to study each photo as the man aged from a skinny kid in baggy shorts to full adulthood. His grin was mischievous, with a twist on the left side. A tiny scar bisected his left eyebrow.

Like a lightbulb snapping to life, her inability to remember vanished. The darkness cleared. She knew him.

This young man was one of the thugs in the van—a kidnapper, a traitor or something worse.

Trudy called out from downstairs. "How are you doing, Angelica? Can I help?"

She moved to the top of the staircase. Her throat was still raw and her voice hoarse. "Changing clothes. I'll be down in a minute."

"Would you like more lemon tea?"

"No, thank you," she said politely.

Her thoughts were far less civil. Dear, sweet Trudy might decide to poison her with lemon-scented bleach. Though it seemed impossible that the kindly choir director was involved with thugs and traitors, the dozens of photos were proof. Trudy knew this man, knew him well.

Unfortunately, there was no chance that Angelica was mistaken in her identification. The memory was crystal clear. His face—with the lopsided grin—had peered down at her several times when she was curled up on the floor in the back of the van. He'd rubbed her upper arm as though he wanted to make her warm, but he'd been the one who insisted to the others that they leave her outside, alone in the van, to possibly freeze.

She needed to tell Spence, and he'd have to arrest these two lovely people who had saved her life. Though Angelica had been trained as an agent, she wouldn't be cool about taking Clarence and Trudy into custody.

Fully dressed and wearing her warm boots, she descended the staircase to find Trudy nestled into a corner of the sofa. Though Angelica had said no, two mugs of tea and a small plate of fragrant banana bread rested on the coffee table.

"Where's Spence?" Angelica asked.

"He and Clarence went running off to chase a bad guy."

Angelica gasped. The bad guy was very likely the

man pictured in Trudy's bedroom. And Spence was probably counting on Clarence the Traitor for backup. "I need to find them, right away."

"You shouldn't go out," Trudy said. "We've barely got you warmed up. The last thing you need is to go out in the cold again."

The very thought of snow sent a raft of shivers down her spine, but she couldn't abandon a man she cared about to an uncertain fate. And she'd never been a quitter. This job was important. "I need a gun."

"The men took all of their weapons."

Angelica stalked into the kitchen. Yanking a butcher knife from the chopping block seemed ridiculous. If she managed to get close enough for a knife attack, the bad guy would likely overpower her.

But she couldn't just sit here. At the very least, she needed to warn Spence. Back in the front room, she zipped her Patagonia jacket that appeared lightweight but was surprisingly toasty. "I'm going."

"I'm not strong enough to stop you." Trudy folded her skinny arms below her breasts and sank back on the sofa. "But I wish you'd wait."

"Until the pastor drags Spence back here by his heels like a field-dressed deer?"

"Whatever are you talking about?"

"I think you know."

"What's gotten into you?"

The truth. She pinched her lips together to keep from blurting out accusations. Attacking Trudy wasn't going to do any good. She needed to help Spence.

On the front porch, the cold sliced through her like a blade, and she was tempted to dash back inside to wait. But the danger to Spence might be real. And she cared about him. More than friends, they had a relationship. If she closed her eyes, even for a few seconds, she felt the imprint of his embrace as he held her against his muscular chest. She remembered the deep rumble of his voice and the wood-and-leather scent of his favorite aftershave.

Looking down from the porch, she saw tracks leading from the front of the cabin toward the church next door, where lights blazed through the stained glass windows. Was she too late? Fearing the pastor and the thug had ganged up on Spence, she leaped from the porch. The snow was as deep as her knees, and she hated getting her jeans wet. But she had to warn Spence.

Slogging clumsily forward through the crisp, icy layers that glistened in the moonlight, she made her way across the front of the house to a clump of aspens and evergreens. The snow-covered boughs provided shelter from the brisk wind that swirled the icy flakes like a kaleidoscope. When she inhaled a deep breath, her lungs wheezed. She exhaled a gush of vapor. The pinpricks of frostbite returned to her toes and fingers.

She saw three men walking from the church. The pastor and Spence flanked a tall guy with floppy hair, the thug. Either he'd fooled Spence into thinking he wasn't a danger or Spence was on his side. Could he be working with the bad guys? *Trust no one.* That mantra, that perfect bit of wisdom from her dad, might also apply to Spence.

He'd said they were partners. But did she have proof? Her sensory memories described an exquisite sexual relationship with Spence. But that didn't make him trustworthy. If she'd been able to recall with utter precision,

Angelica was certain that she'd have examples of misunderstandings and mistakes. Every woman did.

Whether Spence was a sleazebag or the straight-and-true man of her dreams, he had come for her. She owed him a rescue. But how? This would have been so much easier if she'd had a gun.

She stepped out from behind the trees and waved her arms over her head. When she called out to Spence, her voice was nothing but a feral growl. When she tried to amp up the volume, her efforts vanished on the wind.

But somehow he heard the harsh sounds she was making. And he responded. Breaking into a jog, he covered the distance between them so quickly that she had to peer around him to see what the pastor and the thug were doing. Just standing there? Neither of the men moved more than a step.

Spence caught hold of her upper arms. "What are you doing outside?"

No time for talk. "Give me your gun."

"I don't think so."

"The guy you're with." She choked out the words. "And the pastor, too. They're traitors. Lock them up."

"I can explain."

"He left me to die." How could she make him understand? "He was one of the men in the van."

"I'll explain everything. For now, you've got to trust me."

"No." Her voice was firm. Her instinct was strong. She didn't owe an automatic bond of trust to him or anyone else.

"His name is Trevor," Spence said. "He's FBI, working undercover. I talked to his handler in Quantico."

"What?"

"Trevor made sure you were left alone in the van so you could escape. He didn't know what their next orders would be, and he wanted you out of danger."

She didn't understand. "Is he part of Trudy's family?"

"Her nephew."

"Why was he with those other men?"

"Undercover," Spence said. "He's working undercover."

He motioned for Clarence and the other man to join them.

Still unsure about whether she should accept this Trevor person as an undercover agent, she narrowed her gaze. It seemed awfully coincidental that Trevor and his bad guy cronies had landed near Aunt Trudy's house.

Trevor reached toward her for a handshake. "I'm sorry, Angelica."

She held back, not ready to be friends, not willing to let bygones be. She forced her voice to an almost-normal level. "Why did you choose the cabin with the green door?"

"You're going to make me work for this apology." He flashed the lopsided grin that some people might call charming. "Can we walk toward the house while I talk?"

"Not yet," she said.

"Okay, here's what happened. I was contacted by one of the bad guys, Lex Heller."

"A computer programmer," Spence said. "He's on our short list of suspects."

"He wanted me and the three other guys—Larry, Moe and Curly Joe—to take care of you." He flashed another smile, clearly his best feature. "When I say 'take care of,' I mean exactly that. We were instructed to keep you from harm. To hold you in a safe place until he contacted us."

So far, he was making sense. "Continue."

"I could see you were waking up and wanted you to have a fair chance to escape. So, I suggested the cabin near Uncle Clarence's place, and I called him to warn him."

"Which is why I never called 911," Clarence said. "I couldn't very well have the sheriff show up and take Trevor into custody."

"You lied to me," she said.

"And I'm sorry."

"What if I'd been more seriously injured?" she asked.

"I would have called an ambulance. I'd never put your life at risk," Clarence said. His blue eyes were intense. His beard puckered around his mouth. "You believe me, don't you?"

She did. "You're not a bad person, Pastor. And I understand why you didn't want to betray your nephew."

"Am I forgiven?" Trevor asked.

She grabbed his glove and gave a firm shake. "For now."

SPENCE SCOOPED ANGELICA off her feet and started to carry her toward the cabin. He liked her nearness, the intimacy and the way she felt in his arms. She was firm but not hard. No six-pack abs. No buns of steel. Her body had a feminine softness, a gift of nature that could never be achieved in a gym.

"Put me down." She lightly punched him on the chin. "What do you think you're doing?"

"Keeping you from getting your feet wet."

She stuck her legs straight out. "I have my good boots, thanks to you."

"We're almost there." He strode forward toward the cabin. Nuzzling her earlobe, he whispered, "I'm just trying to pay you back."

"I missed something." Her lips were inches from his. Her poor, tired eyes were bloodshot. Her skin was reddened and chapped. But she was still beautiful. She croaked, "You owe me?"

"In spite of frostbite, you charged out into the cold to save me."

"I should have been armed."

"I'm glad you weren't."

"Why?"

"If you'd gotten your paws on a gun, Trevor would have paid the consequences."

"Not if he followed my orders."

She didn't look anywhere near as dangerous as she actually was. Angelica qualified as a sharpshooter in pistol and in rifle, which meant her accuracy was over 90 percent. Her hand-to-hand combat skills weren't as good, and Spence was grateful for that. He didn't have to endure a Vulcan death grip every time she got riled.

As they approached the porch at the front of the cabin, she said, "It's hard for me to be authoritative when you're carrying me, but I have a few demands."

He climbed onto the porch and allowed her legs to swing down. "Shoot."

"Whenever possible, I need to be carrying a weapon."

He agreed. "If you'd been armed last night, do you think you could have gotten away from the kidnappers?"

"Don't know," she muttered. "Can't remember what happened."

"I'm with you on this. We'll have to figure out some way for both of us to carry firearms while we're inside the NORAD complex. It's a weapons-free zone."

"You're the superspy. You'll come up with something." She tapped him in the center of his chest with her forefinger. "My next demand is that you treat me like any other partner. No hugging, no carrying, no kissing…unless we're alone…and I give consent."

"That road goes both ways," he said with a grin. "So don't be rubbing up against me or making kissy faces."

"Oh, please, I don't do that."

"We'll see."

Clarence and Trevor clomped onto the porch beside them. Trevor handed her an unexpected gift.

"Your cell phone," he said.

"A thousand thanks. I never thought I'd see this again."

"It was with you when we picked you up. Don't worry, it's untraceable. I've already removed the batteries, sim card and GPS."

Spence suspected the bad guys were still tracking her, using something like his own little implanted device. Modern electronics were too tempting. Sooner or later, everyone would be wearing an array of chips for location and scanners for making payments. They'd all be blips on a giant blue screen, and there would be no need for humans at all.

Clarence opened the front door, and Trudy joyfully greeted her nephew, rushing him toward the kitchen, where she had cookies and muffins. Spence's stomach growled. When was the last time he ate? He closed the door against the cold.

Quietly, Angelica said, "My last demand is the most important. I will go to the hospital with you for tests, but I will not stay. And you're taking me with you when you talk to Lex Heller."

"Why?"

"The obvious reason," she said, "is that Lex is a computer guy. We speak the same language. Also, when he comes face-to-face with me, he'll see that his kidnapping scheme didn't slow me down."

"He might have been the one to give the orders to Trevor and his mates, but I doubt Lex hatched this scheme."

"Why not?"

As soon as he figured out that she'd been abducted, he'd been turning the event around in his head, examining the strategy. The reason for taking her was linear and simple: they wanted to find out how much she knew and to assess her level of expertise.

He wished she could remember what she'd told them or showed them. Though he wanted to believe she was clever enough to point them in a wrong direction, Angelica had been drugged and couldn't help telling the truth.

The big questions came at the end. Why had they bothered with induced amnesia? Why take that risk?

"Spence?" She gave him an adorable scowl. "It worries me when you think so hard. What's on your mind?"

"They erased your memory instead of using the more expedient solution to ensure your silence."

The scowl deepened. "Clarify."

"The best way to make sure you don't talk is to kill you."

She pointed to herself. "Not dead."

"Who's protecting you?"

He had to wonder if Daddy General Thorne was involved.

Chapter Six

This was the first time Angelica had visited this particular clinic on the outskirts of Colorado Springs. Surprising, really. While she was growing up, it felt like she'd spent time in every medical facility in the surrounding five counties. She'd broken her wrist playing on the high school lacrosse team, sprained her ankle twice, had received a total of twenty-three stitches and had sustained a series of other injuries, bumps and bruises. Her mom had always been quick to seek professional medical advice no matter how much her four kids told her they didn't need it.

Secretly, she enjoyed having Mom fuss over her and take care of her when she was hurting. On sick days, the two of them sat in her bed together and read glossy magazines. Her twin hated when Angelica got special attention and sometimes faked an illness so she'd have her turn to cuddle with Mom and talk about clothes and makeup.

Dad was the opposite. He expected his troops and his children to be impervious to pain and injury. Angelica thought of him while she sat on the examination table having her breathing measured, her cheek swabbed and her blood drawn. There would be no tears, not now, not ever.

She owed Dad a call. He'd texted a couple of times during the day, and she needed to respond before it got too late. She hit the speed dial.

Without saying a friendly "hello," he answered, "It's about damn time you return my text messages."

"You know I'm here on business, right?"

"Computer business," he said dismissively. "It only takes a minute to call back unless you were inside NORAD where there's no cell reception. Is that where you were?"

"I can't say."

"You don't have to keep your business secret from me. We're playing for the same team, honey."

"Maybe tomorrow we'll meet for lunch. I'll call."

After she disconnected, she scowled at the phone, then looked over at Spence. "That was weird."

"How so?"

"It's not like my dad to poke into my work. He knows I work at top secret levels. And even if I tried to explain, he wouldn't get it. He's barely mastered the skills needed to use his cellphone."

She met Spence's gaze and, for a moment, got lost in the blue of his eyes. When he cleared his throat, she shook off the mesmerizing effect he had on her and continued, "Dad asked about NORAD. Why would he guess about where I was?"

Gently, he said, "Because he's your father and he cares."

"He's always been a general first." She shrugged. "Maybe retirement is catching up with him. Maybe he's going soft."

"Soft? Not the guy I met yesterday," Spence said. "General Peter Thorne gave me a steely look that said he'd kill me if I didn't treat you right."

She scoffed. "No way."

"Oh, yeah."

When the nurse came into the examination room and told her to change into the hospital gown, Angelica gave Spence a nod. "That's your cue to leave."

"Why?"

He had a point. If her memories about their relationship were correct, this wouldn't be the first time she'd disrobed in his presence. But she didn't want him to see her like this, with an overhead LED highlighting every bruise.

"I want a little privacy," she said.

"Okay, partner." He gave her shoulder a friendly pat. "I'd be looking for bruises that indicate you were hit with a stun gun or head wounds or ligature marks that would show you were forcibly restrained."

Unaccustomed to field investigating, she hadn't thought of all the forensic evidence that could be obtained from her body. She wasn't going to request a rape kit, but she needed to treat herself like a victim, taking scrapings from her fingernails and searching for fibers and potential DNA.

A twinge of embarrassment went through her. "I guess the responsible thing would be to allow a CSI to process me."

"It would be," he agreed. "But I want to play down your abduction. Plus, you've already changed clothes, and you're capable of investigating yourself."

After he left her alone in the room, she started with her fingernails, which she kept manicured, clipped short and shined up with clear polish. Likewise, the skin on her hands was smooth, massaged twice daily with a special cream her mom sent to her. Though nobody else paid much attention to her hands, Angelica liked to treat them right. She found nothing under her nails and no bruises on her knuckles. Apparently, she hadn't fought back.

She'd already had a flash of recall about being duct taped to chair arms, which meant there were no rope burns or ligatures on her wrists or ankles.

The big injury was the bruise on her right side that extended all the way to her hip. Was she slammed into a wall? Dropped from a significant height? Thrown into the trunk of a car?

The car scenario seemed most likely, especially when she discovered a double-pronged bruise typical of a stun gun on her left shoulder. Why couldn't she remember? She imagined herself standing beside the open trunk of a car. All it took to capture her was a zap from the stun gun and a hard shove.

At some point during her abduction, her regular clothing had been changed to the nondescript scrubs and sweatshirt she'd been wearing when she escaped. The conclusion was inescapable: she'd been naked in front of her enemies. Vulnerable. Helpless. She pushed the thought from her mind, not wanting to remember the shame she must have felt.

When the doctor entered, his examination seemed straightforward and simple. He found no head wound; therefore, her memory loss was not due to concussion. Rather, it was drug induced. When she asked how long it would take to get her memory back, the doctor refused to stipulate. Typically, some memories returned within a week. But some were lost forever.

Her other injuries were painful but not serious. No broken bones. No sprains. To find out what was used to drug her, they had to wait for lab tests. In the meantime, the doctor recommended pain medication and eight hours of sleep.

She refused.

Spence would have liked to leave her neatly tucked away in a hospital bed, but she insisted on coming with him to confront and interrogate Lex Heller. Side by side, they strode through the dusting of snow in the clinic's parking lot. At this lower altitude, the weather was mild with swirling flakes that twinkled in the streetlights. She climbed into the passenger seat of the rental SUV and fastened her seat belt.

Spence made one more bid. "Let me take you back to the hotel."

"So I can get kidnapped again?"

His attitude sharpened. "Is that where you were abducted? At the hotel?"

"I don't remember." Frustration weighed heavily upon her, and she exhaled in an angry huff. She couldn't give in, couldn't give up.

"I can arrange for someone to watch you."

"Easier said than done." Who could they trust? Everyone, from the FBI agents to the local cops to the computer nerds, was viewed as suspicious. "This assignment was designed for two people, you and me."

"And we've been compromised." His lips thinned. His brow pulled into a scowl. Spence didn't like losing any more than she did. "We should consider aborting our investigation."

"I vote for trying one more thing. Let's talk to Lex. We know he's involved because he hired Trevor and the goons."

"We might be able to squeeze information from him." Spence considered for a moment. "Even if he's not central to the scheme, he might know something. Maybe he's a black hat."

Doubtful. Breaking into NORAD and stealing codes was high-level, illegal stuff, worthy of the worst, bad-guy hackers that lurked on the dark web. They were called black hats, supercriminals, and she had a hard time imagining Heller in that role. He and his crew of programmers at Peterson AFB were among the first people they met when they arrived. They'd seemed harmless.

In spite of a warrior action figure labeled Sexy Lexy in Heller's cubicle, he was asexual, an androgynous guy with a skinny chest and potbelly and stringy brown hair and greenish teeth that looked like they'd never been brushed.

Why did she remember so many details about him while so much of her mind was blank? When this amnesia wore off, she would never take her memory for granted again. She asked, "Are we going to arrest him?"

"We want him to talk, to tell us who he's working with. And we want him to hand over his computers and his codes."

"Which is why you need me to come along," she pointed out. "I speak his language."

Heller's apartment was in a bland, three-story, blond brick building with wrought iron staircases on the outside. He had the corner apartment on the first floor.

Plain and homely, his place was the closest thing she could imagine to living in his mom's basement.

Spence guided the rental SUV onto the edge of the asphalt parking lot and paused. "Do you remember this place?"

She closed her eyes and concentrated. In the back of her mind, she caught a glimpse of Heller standing in the snow, wearing a faded red parka. "Not here, not this building."

"Where?" he asked. "What do you see?"

"Snow." Heavy snow blanketed the ground. "Other cars. I'm lying in the back of the van."

"What else?"

"Trevor."

Her ragged memory replayed a vision from the back of the van when Trevor met Heller. Behind them, she saw a sign for King Soopers market.

"When Heller left, Trevor got into the van with me," she said, recalling the moment. "And he told me to pretend I was unconscious. He'd help me escape."

"You're doing good," Spence said. "What else did he say?"

The memory tore into pieces and melted away. "Trevor said other stuff. He touched my shoulder. He was clearly the boss with the other guys."

"Do you remember anything before the van?"

She shook her head. "But getting that memory of Trevor is significant, right? The other memories are in there."

"And we'll find them," Spence said. "For now, look out the front windshield. What do you make of the tire tracks in the parking lot snow?"

She unfastened her seat belt and leaned over the

dashboard for a better view. "It looks like somebody pulled into a slot, and then backed out and drove away."

"Sexy Lexy had company," Spence said. "We should approach with caution."

Eagerly, she pulled the weapon he'd given her. "I'm ready."

"Put the Glock away, Quick Draw."

Though she did as he asked, Angelica was ready for payback. Last time, they grabbed her. Now it was vice versa.

Spence backed out of the apartment parking lot, circled the block and found a space on the street. In the rear of the SUV, he had bulletproof vests, which he insisted that they wear. He held out a rifle to her.

"I'm more comfortable with the handgun," she said.

"Suit yourself, princess."

In spite of the princess comment, he wasn't treating her like royalty and not making a big deal about this being her first time in the field. The training exercises at Quantico were different. Because she was a sharpshooter and had good reflexes, her scores on simulations were high. But she'd never faced real danger. Could she actually point her gun at another human being and pull the trigger?

She fell into step behind Spence and crept toward the corner apartment. All the curtains were drawn, even in the kitchen, but light spilled around the edges. She and Spence stood on either side of the dark brown door with a gold number seven attached at eye level. From inside, she heard the chatter of talk radio.

Spence rapped on the door. "FBI, open up."

There was no answer.

After he tried again, he reached down to the door-knob. Unlocked, it turned easily in his hand.

When he glanced at her, his gaze reflected calm and confidence. Though she couldn't recall details of his background, she knew that Spence handled this type of action on a regular basis. He knew what to do. She could trust him.

He shoved the door open and dashed inside. She followed.

Stepping over the threshold, she stumbled. Her steps wobbled. Her arms were weak, and her handgun felt like it weighed twenty pounds. A putrid smell wrapped around her like a filthy, rotting blanket.

Sprawled facedown across a cluttered wooden desk that took up a whole wall of his small apartment, she saw Lex Heller. He'd been shot. The back of his head was a mass of tissue, white skull and matted hair. Blood had spilled down his neck and puddled on the desk under his head. Through the streaks of blood, his un-blinking eye stared at a rotary-dial, mustard-yellow, plastic telephone. Why would a high-tech guy like Lex have a landline, let alone an antiquated rotary phone?

The logical left side of her brain struggled to un-derstand the anomaly of the old-fashioned phone. Did he use it to make untraceable calls to coconspirators? What was he up to? Who was he working with? The more emotional right brain took over as she realized that she was staring at a brutal crime. Lex Heller had been murdered. He was a young man, midtwenties, her age. And he was dead.

She swallowed hard to keep from puking. Angelica wasn't squeamish. Her dad taught her to hunt, and she butchered her own kills. Her gaze stuck on the weird angle of his shoulder blades and the curve of his jaw. She imagined him talking. What had he said to her? He had asked some weird questions about whether she and her twin ever dated the same guy.

Spence stepped in front of her, blocking her view. "We need to call this in."

"I guess we're not undercover anymore."

He took out his cell phone. "I still want to step as far out of the spotlight as possible. It's better if we aren't bogged down with a murder investigation."

"Who are you calling?"

"Ramirez seems to have gotten himself assigned to us."

She didn't like Special Agent Jay Ramirez. He was one of those macho jerks who thought a woman's place in law enforcement was fetching coffee for the men. "I'm going to look around. Don't worry—I won't touch anything."

When she turned her back, she didn't have to see the gore, but the smell followed her down the hall, beyond the tiny bathroom and into the bedroom. Heller's bed was unmade. His clothing was scattered across floor and furniture. The murderer might have been searching for something, but it was hard to tell. When it came to housekeeping, her computer-specialist friends seemed to be two distinct types: slobs or robots.

She leaned toward the robotic, with everything neatly put away in the proper place, but she knew brilliant people who lived in chaos like Lex Heller. Under a stack of papers on the dresser, she found a cell phone.

This was too good a clue to ignore. "Spence, come here."

He responded immediately. His large frame filled the bedroom door. "What is it?"

She pointed. "Can I check and see who he's been calling?"

"Do it quick. Ramirez is on his way with the cops."

In a matter of seconds, she'd bypassed Heller's security codes and passwords. The first text message she saw was a simple Returning your call. The name of the person who sent it turned her blood to ice.

"Professor Morris Fletcher." She stammered, "M-m-my first mentor."

Chapter Seven

In a brief but decisive phone conversation with his supervisor back at Quantico, Spence had been officially warned off the case. There was nothing for him to do but climb into his rental SUV and head back to the hotel. He wasn't happy about the turn of events, not a bit, and he wished there was someone else to blame for the breakdown of their assignment. But it was his fault. Their safety and their cover story had been his responsibility. He should have been more vigilant. He should have proceeded with a strategy instead of poking in dark corners and seeing what crawled out.

He seldom did well when working with a partner. Spence had never gotten high marks in "plays well with others," especially when the partner was as distracting as Angelica. He glanced over at her. She was sitting ramrod straight in the passenger seat and staring through the windshield. Her posture and her refusal to look at him betrayed her tension, but her voice was relaxed, almost cheerful as she chattered nonstop about her old mentor, Professor Morris Fletcher.

He wouldn't have minded hearing a few words of encouragement from her. It wouldn't hurt for her to tell him that he did the best he could. Maybe she could pat him on the cheek and give him a thumbs-up for trying. Instead she launched into another story about how Professor Fletch admired Pythagoras not only for his geometry but also because he believed in reincarnation. As soon as that story ended, she started another, illustrating that Professor Fletch was wise, fun and an all-around cool guy.

Spence figured that anybody who got that much praise had something to hide. "What's his downside?"

"What do you mean?"

"Addictions, womanizing, gambling." He could have listed a dozen more potential problems for the fantastic Fletch. Nobody was perfect. When he got right down to it, Spence was a glass-half-empty guy.

"Why does there have to be a downside?"

"Come on, angel, there's got to be something wrong with the guy. We just learned that Professor Fletch was in communication with a traitor, a man who was murdered."

She turned toward him. The glow from the dashboard highlighted her cheekbones and the wisps of black hair that fell across her forehead. "It almost sounds like you're jealous."

"Of Professor Fletch? A pudgy little guy with a ZZ Top beard?" he scoffed. "Give me a break."

"How do you know about his beard?" she asked suspiciously.

"I looked him up on my phone while we were waiting for the troops to arrive at Heller's place. When you saw his name, you got so…excited."

"And you got jealous," she said with a hint of smugness. "Well, you can relax. Professor Fletch isn't my type. He's gay."

"And he's also a suspect."

"Until you have evidence, I don't believe that." She turned her head and looked out the passenger-side window facing the hotel. "I wish you'd trust my judgment. Maybe I can't read people as well as you, but I trust Professor Fletch."

As far as he could tell, her basis for trust was nothing more than fond memories of an old professor. That wasn't enough to clear Fletch from suspicion. He ought to lecture her about the need for separating emotion from investigation, reminding her that many sociopaths are charming. But he didn't want to make her mad. She was more than a partner. Angelica was his girlfriend, and he meant to treat her that way for the rest of their so-called assignment in Colorado Springs.

"You're staying in my room tonight," he said.

"I have no problem with that. You have a suite, right?"

"And a hot tub. I'm paying for the upgrade."

"Dibs," she said. "I get first soak."

When they checked in, they'd taken separate rooms to keep up the appearance of propriety. No point in continuing that charade. Anybody who didn't know they were a couple would catch on pretty fast.

"You know," he said, "if you'd been sleeping in my bed last night, we might have avoided the whole kidnapping thing."

"I thought of that." She shook her head. "I still don't remember what happened, but it seems likely that I was lured from the hotel."

He'd picked apart the bits of information he had about the kidnapping and put them back together a dozen times. The method used to take her seemed simple. "After we left your parents' house, I had to go to FBI headquarters for a meeting with SSA Sheeran. She picked me up."

"And I drove back to the hotel. That's when I must have been taken from the parking lot."

Though he wasn't a believer in coincidence, he couldn't blame the local branch of the FBI for drawing him out. The meeting with Supervisory Special Agent Raquel Sheeran had been scheduled before he left Quantico. He'd thought she was the only one who knew the real purpose of their investigation, but Sheeran had obviously told Ramirez and another agent named Tapper.

After Angelica had been abducted, Spence's behavior had been so lax that he was embarrassed. Without verifying, he had accepted a phony text saying that she was going to stay at her parents' house. Naive as a schoolboy, he had believed it, decided to give her some space. Then he got another text in the early morning telling him she had a lead, and another saying she was inside NORAD, where cell phone service was pretty much nonexistent. He should have known she wouldn't go inside without him, should have suspected. But he'd been blind. He hadn't started searching for her until after ten in the morning.

In the parking lot outside the six-story, stucco hotel, he drove slowly between the rows of vehicles. Last night, it hadn't been snowing, but the lot looked much the same. He hoped she'd see something that would spark a memory.

"You told me," she said, "that when we got back to the hotel, you had a technique that would help me remember. Were you talking about hypnosis?"

"It's more like relaxation."

"Good. Hypnosis doesn't work for me. I'm too resistant."

He wasn't surprised. She liked to know exactly what was going on at all times, demanded to be in control. These memory lapses had to be driving her crazy. "We can start right now."

"Okay."

"You've got to stop talking. Then, lean back against the seat and open up your mind."

"This is never going to work."

He could tell that she was too tense and restless to allow anything from her subconscious to come through. She wiggled in the seat. Her eyelids flickered. And her fingers twitched. Attempting a relaxation exercise now was useless.

"On second thought, maybe we should wait," he said, "until we're in the room."

"I might do better after I've had a shower. And something to eat."

It was going to take some serious quiet time for her to be in the right mood, but getting her there might be fun. He looked forward to opening her mind and giving her the peace she needed to remember.

IN THE HOTEL, they went directly to his suite on the fourth floor. Angelica had intended to take a shower or soak away the last frigid trace of hypothermia in a hot tub, but she didn't make it that far. Halfway across the bedroom, the king-size bed beckoned, and she succumbed, flopping across the pillows as she kicked off her boots. Sleep might be the best way to reset her memory, similar to rebooting a computer. At least that was what she told herself as her eyelids closed.

When she sank into slumber, she dreamed of fat, white snowflakes tumbling silently through the upper branches of tall pine trees, like confetti in a snow globe. There was no cold, no wind, no chill at all. This was one of those dreams when she was aware of dreaming and watching herself. Snow geese with glistening feathers swooped across the sky, pulling a golden chariot. Had she seen this in a movie? The charioteer was a powerfully built snow god with a halo of unruly blond hair and piercing pale eyes. It was Spence. She took the time to study him as he approached and disembarked.

Of course, she knew that Special Agent Spence Malone had never dressed like this in real life. As if he'd ever wear etched gold cuffs on his muscular wrists? Or a pale toga that flipped open and offered a view of his chest and six-pack abs?

Dream Spence coiled an arm around her waist and pulled her close. Though she couldn't really smell anything in a dream, the odor of afternoon rain and pheromones—whatever those smelled like—scented the air.

"Are you all right?" It was his real voice, not the rumblings of a snow god.

"Fine," she murmured.

"You were making weird noises," he said. "Are you hungry?"

In her dream, she was ready to lock lips, but her hand dropped to her belly. Real-life Angelica wanted food. "Onion rings."

"Good, that's what I ordered, and steak."

"Don't care."

She dived back into her dream, closed her eyes, puckered up and prepared to be ravaged by a brazen snow god. His firm lips brushed across hers and moved away, leaving her craving more. The next taste was deeper. And then his mouth pressed harder, and his tongue plunged into her mouth.

Excitement stirred her blood. An impatient moan rose in her throat, and she realized… *I'm not dreaming.* The real Spence lay beside her on the king-size bed. His expert kisses were driving her wild.

She wanted him, but not now, not yet. There were questions to be answered, memories to be reinstated. Her hands pushed against his chest, holding him at a distance. Like the snow god, he'd stripped off his shirt. The muscles beneath his warm, supple flesh were firm. This wasn't the first time she'd thought of how big and strong he was. That fact didn't count as a regained memory. It was merely an observation.

"Did you mention room service?" she asked.

"I made the call just before the kitchen closed at 1:00 a.m."

She wasn't sure what time they'd gotten to the room. "How long have I been sleeping?"

"A couple of hours." He ran a hand across his bare chest. "I took a shower and made some calls."

"And why did you wake me?"

"Well, there were the weird noises."

She was getting a whole different vibe from him. Not a romantic snow god or a tough undercover agent, he had transformed into Spence the boyfriend. "You thought maybe we should eat before we…you know."

He grinned. "Have mind-blowing sex?"

"You're awfully sure of yourself."

"I have reason to be."

She barked a laugh. Spence might be the hottest, sexiest man she'd ever met, but he was also funny. And she found his sense of humor to be almost as appealing as his gorgeous body.

When he made a grab for her, she jumped off the bed, not wanting to start something they couldn't finish before the food arrived. She announced, "I'm going to clean up."

The hot tub was enticing, but she settled for the extra-large shower with four different heads. Within a few minutes, she had the steam churning inside the glass stall. The soothing heat penetrated all the way to her core.

She wondered if she and Spence had ever bathed together. It seemed likely, but she didn't exactly recall. There were other gaps in her memories of him. Their first meeting was hazy, and their first kiss.

Amnesia had taken a toll, which was not necessarily a negative thing. Without a record of those sensual memories, she could experience them, again, for the first time. It would feel like being a virgin again. As the hot water sluiced between her breasts and down her belly, she imagined his touch. His hands were huge, but she knew he'd be gentle. Why couldn't she remember? Did they sleep with the lights on or off?

She rinsed her hair, turned off the shower jets and grabbed a towel. She recalled their night at the Arena Theater and the aftermath with champagne and roses. That night, they'd made all kinds of passionate love, and she remembered feeling good even though the specifics were hazy.

Did her amnesia reach six months into her past? Or

did that only apply to memories of Spence? There might be a reason she didn't remember him.

She slipped into her blue-and-gray-striped nightgown. All cleaned and combed, she felt like she'd regained some of her self-control. It was time to make sense of her amnesia. Why did she remember some things and forget about others?

It seemed likely that she would block out unpleasant memories. The moment when she was grabbed wasn't clear in her mind, and that fit the pattern. She didn't want to remember her failure in her first field assignment. Her high hopes for becoming more than a desk jockey had crashed when the bad guys lured her and abducted her.

But there were other negative moments that she recalled. She remembered the horrible sense of vulnerability when her abductors had changed her clothing. The thought of that humiliation flushed her cheeks with embarrassment. Being duct taped to a chair was another incident she didn't want to recall, but there it was in her mind.

She'd also like to erase the gruesome image of Lex Heller with the back of his head blown off. But that wasn't under the purview of her amnesia.

Spence was there before she'd been drugged and after. He was central. She hated to think there was a reason she was blanking memories of him from her mind. Was he hiding something?

Using the hotel's gift supply, she applied lotion to her hands and arms. *I'm being ridiculous.* She had to trust Spence. He was her partner.

When she entered the front room, she saw the room service cart parked by the table. The scent of grilled

meat spiked her hunger. When she lifted the round silver cover, she saw a fat, juicy T-bone with tomato and
lettuce and a whole plate of onion rings. Before she
could say anything, Spence signaled for her to be quiet.

Wearing nothing but a pair of sweatpants, he tip-
toed across the room toward the door. In his left hand,
he held a bottle of champagne. His Glock was in his
right. A few feet away from the door, he leaned down
and picked up a thin cord, the type of equipment used
with fiber optics to spy beyond locked doors.

Spence set down the champagne. He coiled the cord
around his hand and gave a sharp yank.

From outside the door, there was a thud.

Spence whipped open the door and aimed his handgun at a plump, bearded man.

"Professor Fletch."

Chapter Eight

If the consequences of the NORAD hack hadn't held the potential for nuclear disaster, if she hadn't been abducted, if Lex Heller hadn't been murdered, Angelica might have laughed. Outside their hotel room door, a perfect nerd tableau had formed. Her favorite mentor, Professor Fletcher, adjusted the ear flaps on his striped, knit cap and twiddled his beard. A skinny young guy with a man bun sat on the carpet and typed frantically into a laptop. In spite of the snow outside, he wore only a thermal long-sleeved turtleneck under a Hawaiian-print shirt decorated with flamingos and macaws. A third nerd, who looked familiar, was on his knees with his butt sticking up in the air and his nose pressed to the reader for the fiber-optic device that he'd tried to slip under their door.

Standing opposite these three was Spence, wearing only a pair of loose-fitting gray sweatpants. In one hand, he held a Glock. A magnum of champagne was in the other fist. His testosterone level more than tripled that of the nerds.

In a strange way, the contrast represented the different sides of her life. She would always be the tomboy who had majored in math and graduated to being a full-fledged computer hacker. But she was also a woman with passions who dedicated herself to solving cyber crime and believed in doing the right thing for herself, her family and her nation. Though not the female version of Spence, she was a capable partner—as long as they were on the same side. The jury was still out on whether or not she could trust him completely.

Clearly out of patience, he glared at the threesome and growled, "Get inside. Shut the door."

They scrambled to do as he said. While two of them alighted on the sofa, Professor Fletch marched toward her with his arms held out for a big hug. He ripped off his cap, releasing a frizzy cloud of steely-gray hair. She thought he was smiling. With the beard, it was hard to tell.

"My, my, my, Angelica, aren't you a sight for these tired old eyes?"

Oh, no, you don't. She wasn't going to let him breeze in here, pretending nothing had happened. "Stop right there, Professor. It would have been easier to see me if you weren't sliding cameras under my door."

"I didn't want to disturb you."

"Don't be ridiculous."

In the past, she'd thought his silliness was charming and amusing—a refreshing change from people who took themselves too seriously. But there was a time to put aside the fun and games. Murder made this the right time to focus.

"Angelica, listen to me." He sounded a pleading note. "I came to help you."

"How?" Was he trying to give her actual evidence? "Do you have information?"

"Nothing you don't already know."

"Are you sure about that? How do you know what I do or don't know?"

"Think for a moment."

The answer was clear. The professor had trained her. He was a talented hacker who sometimes monitored the police radio or cut into their computer systems. As far as she knew, he steered clear of breaking into the FBI computers, but she wouldn't put it past him. "Oh, my God, what do you know?"

"I'm sure your skills surpass anything I might have taught you. I'm here to offer my services," he said with an expansive grin, "and the use of my equipment and technology."

Spence gestured with his gun. "Professor, join your friends on the sofa."

"I'm happy, delighted, thrilled to cooperate."

She'd never before noticed what tiny steps Professor Fletch took. Had he been ill? Was this something new? She had to wonder if he'd been toying with her when he offered his help. He could be trying to use their former mentor-student relationship to direct the investigation. But why? She couldn't imagine Fletch being involved in a plot to hack into missile launch technology. He was opposed to the proliferation of nuclear weaponry.

Her gaze drifted to the room service cart where dinner awaited under silver-covered lids. The smell of deep-fried onion rings was driving her crazy.

Spence slapped his gun in her hand. "Keep an eye on these three while I get zip ties."

Holding them at gunpoint seemed excessive, but she didn't argue. They might look nerdy, but that didn't mean they weren't dangerous. The unwanted vision of Lex Heller's death flashed across her mind, and she forced herself to erase the bad memory of blood and gore. Positioned in front of the sofa, she remained standing with the Glock braced two-handed in front of her.

The guy who had been operating the fiber-optic device unzipped his parka and took it off. His T-shirt said: I Read Your Email.

"You," she snapped, "don't make another move."

"Would you really shoot?"

"Don't push me." Her gaze was hard enough to cut through his thick, horn-rimmed glasses and fierce enough to make him wriggle away from her on the sofa.

"But you know me," he said. "I'm Bo Lambert. I work at the base with Lex Heller."

"That's enough. Please be quiet." *What's wrong with me? I shouldn't have said please.* It wasn't easy to be intimidating while wearing a striped nightgown with a terry-cloth hotel bathrobe hanging from her shoulders. And she'd made herself even less scary by being polite.

"There's no need for the gun," Professor Fletch said.

"Quiet," she muttered.

"Angelica, we're on the same side."

"Quiet!" she said a bit more loudly.

"There's a need for communication." Fletch looked to his two companions. "Am I right?"

"QUIET!" She swept the Glock in an arc. For a nanosecond, she considered shooting them all and sitting down to eat her onion rings before they got cold. "PLEASE. BE. QUIET."

Three sets of eyeballs focused on her, waiting for her to make the next move. Did they already know their friend had been murdered? How would they react? Who could have told them?

Angelica kept her mouth shut. Spence was the expert when it came to interrogation, but she wondered if these three nerds might be an exception. They could identify with her and, therefore, might be more willing to talk to one of their kind.

The guy with the Hawaiian shirt and man bun raised his hand. His scrawny frame pressed tightly against Professor Fletch, and she wondered if they were a couple.

She glared at him. "What?"

"This."

He swiveled his laptop to face her. There was a photograph of Lex Heller, dead at his desk. Startled by the horrific image, she held her breath and tensed her muscles to keep from dropping the gun. This guy with the flamingo shirt was her age, possibly younger, and yet so callous.

"What's your name?" she asked.

"Dunne, Howie Dunne."

Easy to remember; Dunne rhymed with bun. "Where did you get that picture?"

"You should be answering the questions," he said. "How could you let this happen to Lex? He should have been under your protection."

Spence came back into the room. He wore jeans, a black FBI T-shirt and an angry expression. Jaw clenched, he leaned down to stare at the laptop. "What time did you get this picture?"

"I don't have to answer your questions," Dunne said. "I want a lawyer."

"Me, too," said Bo Lambert. "My cousin is a lawyer. He could be here in ten minutes."

"I don't have time for this." Spence took the laptop and handed it to her with a simple instruction. "Get all the info you can off this computer."

She knew the drill. "Consider it done."

Dunne bounced to his feet to protest. Before he could take one single step, Spence shoved him back down onto the sofa. "Give me your hands."

"No." Dunne stuck out his pointy, unshaven chin. "You can't make me. And your girlfriend can't break into my computer."

"I regret," Professor Fletch said, "to inform you that Angelica Thorne was one of my best students. She can do anything she wants with your laptop, maybe teach it to dance and whistle the theme from *Close Encounters of the Third Kind*."

"Thanks for the validation," she said.

Spence stepped between them, ending their moment of mutual admiration. "Now, Professor Fletcher, show me your hands."

The professor complied, and Spence slipped on the zip ties. He did the same with Lambert, and then he turned to Dunne. "You're next."

His righteous anger was fading fast, but he made an effort. "You won't get any fingerprints other than mine from the computer. I wiped it down, even the keys."

"Who are you protecting?" Spence asked.

"None of your business."

Spence growled, "Hands."

"Don't you have to read me my rights?"

"You're not under arrest...not yet, anyway."

"You should cooperate, Dunne. Give him what he wants," Professor Fletch said. "A young man has been killed. I want to know why."

Spence fastened the zip ties on Dunne, took a step back and sat in the overstuffed chair beside the sofa. As he took the Glock from her, he said in a low voice,

"Take the room service cart to the bedroom. I suggest you go in there, close the door, figure out the computer and eat the onion rings while they're still hot."

"And what are you going to do?"

"I already put in a call to SSA Sheeran. She's coming over to take these three into custody for questioning."

"But you have more interrogation experience," she protested. "You could—"

"Until tomorrow, you and I are officially off the case."

As far as she was concerned, that decision amounted to a big, fat pile of bureaucratic baloney. Dropping the cover story about checking systems at NORAD was smart. Nobody had believed them, anyway, which was why she'd been kidnapped.

She'd be glad when they could present themselves as an investigative team with teeth who had come to Colorado Springs to rip into cyber crime. As investigators, they could make demands, have access to forensic information and perform interrogations. They had control—as soon as their bosses at Quantico gave the okay.

Turning on her heel, she set a course for the bedroom. Inside with the door closed, she exhaled a huge sigh and let down her guard. Still tired in spite of her nap, she sank onto the bed, with the room service cart beside her and the laptop on the bedspread in front of her. *Which to do first?* Eating would give her an energy boost, but she was anxious to get started on Dunne's computer.

She lifted the silver lid on the onion rings, snatched one and popped it into her mouth. *Yum, tasty.* With her other hand, she entered codes that would bypass the computer's passwords. Multitasking came easily.

The lightly greasy onion ring made her mouth happy. But that simple pleasure was nothing compared to the electric jolt that charged through her veins when her fingertips touched the keys of the laptop. Working at the computer was something she remembered, 100 percent. Her memory was coming back. A light flashed on in her brain. Neural disconnects were mended and faulty synapses crackled to life.

She closed her eyelids and tried to remember what had happened yesterday. They arrived at Peterson AFB and were escorted to the area where Heller and Lambert worked. Though the gist of their conversation wasn't clear in her mind, she recalled being convinced that their interpretation of the threat was correct: a hacker had broken through firewalls and viral protection to access NORAD's missile data. There hadn't been an actual attempt to launch. The access was worrisome enough.

Eyes still closed, she tried to recall dinner with Mom and Dad. She could almost hear her dad greeting them, could almost feel her mom's embrace and smell her familiar lavender perfume. In her memory, she tilted her head to the left and looked for Spence. Shouldn't he be standing beside her? Shouldn't she be introducing him, carefully phrasing her words to let her parents know he was important? Was he?

Her visions of being in bed with Spence were vivid. But day-to-day life was a blur. How important was he? *I mean, really.* If he was "the one," the man she was supposed to be with, why wasn't she wearing a diamond?

She needed to set her mind right about him and her relationship with him. But first, she needed to decode and decrypt Dunne's computer before SSA Sheeran arrived and confiscated this bit of evidence.

Blindly, she tapped away at the keyboard, following decryption patterns that were so familiar she didn't

need to see the keys. Her sensory memory was returning. Details emerged more clearly. Without thinking,
she typed a series of codes and binary sequences she'd
discovered when initially investigating the hack back
at Quantico.

She opened her eyes, blinked and stared at the screen
in front of her. Most of her work was familiar, but there
was an odd bit that she couldn't explain: Y75110. A license plate number? Digits on an ID badge? An activa-
tion code? If it activated something, what was it?

There was more to learn from this computer. Typing
with one hand and eating with the other, she explored,
delving beyond the mundane emails, processes, tools
and systems. The first—and most obvious—anomaly
she discovered was that the computer didn't belong
to Dunne. It came from Peterson AFB and could be
traced to the department where Heller and Bo Lambert worked.

She reached for another onion ring and realized
there were no more. Without noticing, she'd eaten the
whole plateful. Moving on with her late dinner, she
went for straight protein. She cut off a bite of steak and
chewed while pondering the significance of the computer's provenance. It was only a few months old and
hadn't been activated on a regular basis. Downloads
were what she'd expect for a general office computer.
No other photos were stored. She couldn't tell if this
laptop belonged to one particular person in the office
or was passed from desk to desk.

Had it been at Heller's house when he was killed?
She checked the time stamp of the grisly photo. It had
been taken forty minutes before she and Spence found
the body, which was, according to the local police, ap-

proximately the time of death. Had the murderer taken the photograph? Why? And why did Dunne have the computer?

She sliced off another bite of steak and opened the file for emails. The current file was clear. Only about fifty had been deleted, mostly office memos that were sent to every computer in the department.

While searching the computer's history, she discovered a pattern. Three weeks ago, there'd been a fast and heavy exchange of emails with a sender using the name: C4ICBM. That code was more than a little bit ominous. C4 was a plastic explosive, and ICBM stood for Intercontinental Ballistic Missile. The nightmare scenario for their investigation would be to uncover a plan for launching those missiles and setting off the warheads.

Again, she squeezed her eyes closed and tried to remember what had happened while she'd been abducted. She might have overheard the plan or caught a glimpse of something dangerous. An unauthorized missile launch was unthinkable. Her research on that possibility had concluded that the strategic air defense systems were impregnable and unhackable. Even if they could be hacked, there were fail-safe measures in place to abort the action before the missiles were airborne.

But nothing was impossible. She clicked on one of the mysterious emails to open it. The bland conversation referred to a family reunion that might take place in Dallas or Seattle or Seoul. Why was South Korea mentioned in the same breath with Dallas and Seattle? What was the connection in those far-flung locations? The sixteenth of November—three days from today— was mentioned as the time for the reunion.

She read the sign-off line aloud. "Office1116."

Chapter Nine

Spence credited his effectiveness as an interrogator to a combination of training and instinct. Growing up at the ragged edges of the foster care system, he learned early on that information was power. The more details he had, the better off he was. Knowing who to trust meant the difference between scoring a bottle of gin and getting blamed for stealing cigarettes from the corner liquor store. He developed his instincts. At a glance, he could sense when somebody was lying or hiding something.

Convincing the other kids to spill their hard-won secrets was easier because of his size. By the time he was in sixth grade, he had almost reached his full adult height, big enough that he didn't need to hit anybody to be threatening. He'd loom over another kid, standing in silence and watching until they couldn't wait to give him whatever he wanted.

His FBI training taught him more subtle techniques designed to intimidate, confuse and enrage a suspect. He used every growl, smile and twist on the three miscreants who sat side by side on the sofa. Thus far, his efforts proved futile.

Lambert and Dunne both refused to talk. Bo was scared speechless and just wanted to consult his cousin, the lawyer. Though Dunne had just as much fear, he kept it locked inside a supposedly hard-boiled exterior that didn't fool anybody. It took a special breed of tough guy to pull off a man bun and Hawaiian flamingo shirt. Dunne didn't fit that mold.

The closest Spence came to a conversation was getting Professor Fletch to open up about Angelica's parents. He and the general had always been on the same page about encouraging her work in math and computers. Fletch was also friendly with Pastor Clarence and Trudy, not surprising given that they were close to the same age and social strata. The professor had a little cabin in the mountains and occasionally attended the pastor's church, where his wife directed an excellent choir.

Spence was pinching himself to stay awake when Angelica emerged from the bedroom. Immediately, the room got brighter. There was a bounce in her step. Her green eyes flashed. He knew that she'd discovered useful evidence.

After warning the threesome not to move, he picked up his Glock and guided Angelica toward the small kitchenette at the far end of the suite where he could still keep an eye on his suspects. He placed his gun on the countertop and turned toward her. "What did you find?"

"Number one," she said, "this laptop comes from Peterson AFB, from the decryption unit where Heller and Lambert both worked. The computer wasn't assigned to an individual."

"Either of them could have used the laptop at work."

"Or taken it home."

As could any other person who happened to waltz through their offices where security was low-key. "The real question is, who took the picture of Heller? Was it Lambert?"

"He doesn't seem like the type who goes looking for trouble."

Spence agreed. Bo Lambert was an ostrich not a peacock—or a flamingo like Dunne. When they identified the person who snapped the photo, they'd be close to finding the murderer. "It could be anybody. What do you call that? An infinite number of variables?"

"Close enough."

She tossed her head, and a wing of black hair fell across her forehead. The cedar scent of the hotel's shampoo mingled with her natural intoxicating fragrance.

"Are you sniffing me?" She shot him a grin. "I stink like onion rings, right? And steak?"

"You smell real damn good." He inhaled deeply. "I'm not talking about food."

Her gaze linked with his. They connected for only an instant but the contact was intense. His desire to touch her manifested in gliding his hand along the countertop until his fingertips were only a few centimeters from her arm.

She froze, not moving closer or putting distance between them. "There was only that one photo, taken near the time Heller was murdered."

"How do you know that for sure?"

"Time stamp," she said. "It hasn't been doctored. Nothing else has been erased."

These details were useful but fairly obvious. "What else?"

"Emails." She set the laptop on the counter and clicked a few computer keys to bring up the file. "It's mostly office junk mail, but you can see that a back-and-forth correspondence started about three weeks ago."

"Which is when SSA Sheeran contacted Quantico with her suspicions," he said. She'd been operating on information given to her by the cyber coders who perceived a hack on the weapons systems. "They couldn't track the intruder, couldn't find any changes in the systems or the firewall protections."

"Window-shopping," she said.

That was how she'd explained the hack when first presented with the data. The hacker had slipped inside, checked things out and left without attempting to manipulate the system,

"Tell me about this chatter," he said.

"The methodology is primitive, similar to exchanging coded messages during Cold War spying." She pointed to the screen. "The name of the correspondent is C4ICBM."

"Dynamite," he muttered under his breath.

"No, it's C4."

"Same difference. Not that a nuclear warhead attached to a rocket isn't enough to get my attention."

"The sender has identified him or herself as Office1116. The emails appear to be talking about a family reunion. Three cities are mentioned—Seattle, Dallas and Seoul."

No connection among those locations popped to mind. Seattle and Dallas might be approximately the same distance from Peterson AFB in Colorado Springs. But Seoul, why Seoul? He glanced at the sofa where the three nerds fidgeted nervously. SSA Sheeran would be here at any moment to pick them up. If he was going to get information from them, it had to be now. "I should get back to our suspects."

"Wait." She opened an email and pointed to an odd sequence. "Do you see that? Y75110? Do you know what it stands for?"

"Not a clue."

He pivoted and stalked toward the sofa. Not bothering with the other two, he zeroed in on Lambert, grabbed a chair from the table and swung it around to face the sofa. Unless he swiveled his head all the way to the side, Lambert couldn't avoid seeing Spence. Their knees were almost touching.

"I've got a problem," Spence said in cool, low voice. "You knew about the laptop. It came from your office area."

"I... I... I didn't notice it," he stammered.

"Here's the deal, Lambert, you should want me to be your friend. Supervisory Special Agent Sheeran is on her way. When she takes you into custody, you're looking at a world of hurt."

"What do you mean?" His weasel face twisted into a knot. Using both hands, he pushed his wire-frame glasses up on his nose.

"For starters, you'll lose your job. The FBI will contact every person you know—former instructors like Professor Fletch, other employers, girlfriends and your family."

His eyes filled with tears. "My dad?"

"Mom, Dad and grandparents," Spence said, driving his point home. "If you're lucky, you won't be in prison too long."

"What do I have to do?"

"Cooperate, starting now. Have you seen that laptop before tonight?"

He nodded. "It's been in the department. I've never used it. I stick with my own computer."

"What about Heller?"

Lambert hunched his shoulders. Shivering, he stared down at his fingers and plucked at the zip ties that fastened his wrists. "I can't say."

"You don't have to be afraid."

"I'm not."

"Heller can't hurt you."

After a sidelong glance at the two people who sat beside him, Lambert whispered, "He asked me to help."

"What did Heller ask you to do?"

"He said he'd pay me five thousand bucks for a few hours' work."

"Tell me about this work." Spence felt like reaching down Lambert's throat and dragging the words from him. "Some kind of software or computer coding?"

"Not that." His chin lifted. Through his thick lenses, he scanned the room until he saw Angelica. "Heller said we'd be helping you. That's why I even listened to him for even one minute. I wanted you to notice me, to remember me. I was two years behind you in school. We had classes together. You were one of the first girls I had a crush on."

Moving to stand beside Spence, she masked her reaction well, keeping her expression and her voice calm. "I'm sorry if it seemed like I was ignoring you. You've changed."

"You haven't." A hint of a smile twisted his thin, pale lips. "A beautiful angel."

"Not really, I was more of a devil than an angel. Tell him, Professor."

Fletch cleared his throat. "She hasn't always been a good girl but certainly isn't devilish. That's her twin sister."

She leaned down and gazed directly into Lambert's eyes. "What did Heller want you to do?"

"I looked up to you. And now, you're at NSA investigating cyber crime. You're living the dream."

"Help me, Bo. We need to find the murderer."

He gave a decisive nod. "I got a call from Heller

around midnight last night. He wanted me to come to his apartment and pick him up. That's when he promised the five grand and said I'd be helping you."

"Did you go?"

"I did. It was a lapse in judgment on my part."

Spence would call it more than a lapse. In following Heller's instructions, Lambert had taken a vacation from his conscience and his sense of right and wrong.

"When I got there," Lambert said, "Heller was babbling about conspiracy theories and fortunes to be made. I turned down his offer of money to do something crazy but I agreed to let him use my car. It's an SUV and drives better in the mountains."

Spence was beginning to piece together a narrative. They knew, from what Trevor had told them, that Heller had been responsible for delivering Angelica to the thugs at a mountain location. Heller had been driving Lambert's vehicle, which meant that he not only had an SUV that handled well in snow but Lambert's car would be caught on any surveillance cameras.

"So dumb!" Lambert cursed himself. "I never should have gotten involved."

"Don't blame yourself," Professor Fletcher said. "You were trying to help your friend. And you didn't break any laws."

"Heller was talking crazy, said I shouldn't have called him on my cell, only landlines. We could escape to a nonextradition country, change our identities or fake our deaths."

Fletch nodded sympathetically as he combed his fingers through his beard. "Now and then, we've all considered such fascinating possibilities."

Dunne finally spoke up. "I have."

"Do tell," Fletcher said.

"Someday, if you're real nice, I'll show you my collection of fake IDs."

"That's not me," Lambert said. "I'm just trying to do the right thing."

Spence put him back on track. "How did you get your car back?"

"Heller didn't even have the common courtesy to bring it to my house." He adjusted his glasses. "I don't like speaking ill of the dead, but Lex Heller could be difficult."

"Bo called me," the professor said. "He sounded agitated, disturbed. I sent Dunne to pick him up."

"Yeah, yeah," Dunne said. "I got to Lambert's place at three fifteen, and we drove to Heller's apartment. Bo's car was parked in the lot."

"But Heller's little Honda was gone."

Now that they'd decided to talk, the three suspects were chirping like hungry baby birds. Spence held up his hand for quiet. "Did Heller answer the door?"

"Nope," said Dunne, "and we knew he wasn't home because the curtains were open and we couldn't see anybody inside."

Spence exchanged a glance with Angelica. When they had arrived at the apartment, all the blinds were drawn and curtains closed. He asked Lambert, "Did you check out your car?"

"I most certainly did. Heller went approximately forty-three miles and used a third of a tank of gas, which he did not replace. I can't give you details of his destination because my vehicle isn't equipped with the GPS tracking system."

"Did you speak to Heller again?"

"I was so mad at him."

"We all were," Dunne said.

Lambert frowned, shook his head and looked down. "I can't believe he's dead. I should have done something, tried to convince him to go to the police. Instead, I was worried about my stupid car. After we left the apartment, Dunne and I went to the professor's house and stayed for dinner."

"Hey," Dunne said, "that's our alibi. We had dinner together. We've got nothing to worry about."

"Is that true?" Lambert asked.

Spence didn't reply; these were intelligent men who could figure it out for themselves.

"Sure, it's true," Dunne said. "When we were at Heller's apartment, we looked in the windows, and there were no dead bodies. The rest of the day, we were together."

Lambert exhaled heavily. "I can't believe we need alibis. That doesn't seem right."

"Because it's not," Fletch said. "You're not off the hook quite yet."

"Why not?" Dunne demanded.

"You can't alibi each other," Spence logically explained, "if you're suspected of working together to commit the murder."

Dunne's bubble burst. He slouched backward while Lambert leaned forward, resting his elbows on his thighs.

Spence rose from his chair, went to the kitchenette, picked up the computer and brought it back to the sofa. He placed it on the coffee table. After a brief debate with himself about whether to display the photo, he decided not to. This would be a closed-casket interrogation.

He took a step back. "How did you get this computer?"

"I'll explain." The professor cleared his throat before continuing. "After dinner as Bo was leaving, he found it tucked inside the screen door on my covered porch. The time was a little after eight. When we saw the photo, we panicked."

Spence had only one more question: "Why?"

"I was afraid that someone was trying to frame me," the professor said. "Believe it or not, I have enemies."

"Closed-minded idiots," Dunne muttered.

"You're no genius," Lambert said. "You wiped off all the fingerprints and wanted to pitch the laptop off Pikes Peak."

"Which would have been wrong," Fletch said. "We needed to contact the authorities. That's when I remembered that Angelica was in town. I knew she had an important job with national security and hoped she'd help us."

Spence wasn't sure how much of their story he believed. Some parts were undoubtedly true, but one aspect didn't make sense no matter how he looked at it. *Why had the murderer taken a photo of his victim, and then delivered it to Professor Fletcher?*

The door to their suite crashed open. Supervisory Special Agent Raquel Sheeran charged through and took a shooter's stance, holding her gun in a two-fisted grip. Her long, red mane tumbled halfway down her back. He'd forgotten how dynamic she was.

Behind her were Ramirez and Special Agent Mike Tapper. Almost in unison, they announced their presence. "Federal Agents."

Chapter Ten

Amnesia or not, Angelica knew she'd seen that woman before. In high-heeled boots, SSA Raquel Sheeran stood an inch shy of six feet tall, which made it easy for her to look down her nose at mere mortal females. Her FBI windbreaker had been tailored to show her nipped-in waist and well-rounded bottom while skinny jeans molded lovingly to her superlong legs.

In addition to her intimidating physical attributes, her husky voice resonated with a commanding tone. Most definitely an alpha personality, she was aggressive, tough and competitive. Grudgingly, Angelica had to acknowledge that Sheeran's accomplishments were worthy of applause. Becoming a supervisor in a field dominated by men was impressive. How many individuals had SSA Sheeran had thrown off the ladder to claw her way to the next rung higher?

Raquel approached Angelica for a handshake. "Pleased to meet you."

"It's not the first time." In spite of the residual soreness of near hypothermia, Angelica matched the other woman's overstrong grasp with a hard squeeze of her own. "A few years ago, we were both part of a group that toured inside Cheyenne Mountain."

"Why would you take the tour? You're a local."

"Showing one of my cousins the sights—I never missed an excuse to dive inside the facility. I've been fascinated by NORAD ever since I was a kid and called on Christmas Eve to check Santa's progress."

She'd pointed to the NORAD Santa Tracker as proof when her cynical twin sister quit believing. Angelica recalled the distant past clearly when she'd cited radar images for an unidentified flying sleigh and eight reindeer. And there had been the annual phone call to the jolly old elf, himself.

As a grown-up, she'd volunteered to answer the Santa phones on the twenty-fourth. Pretending to be Mrs. Claus, she'd wish the kids a happy holiday and tell them to get to bed so Santa could visit.

"The Santa Tracker," Sheeran said with disdain. "It might be good public relations but kind of a scam."

"And I suppose you don't believe in unicorns, leprechauns and the tooth fairy."

"I suppose not."

If Sheeran wanted to live in a world without magic, that was her choice. And it wasn't surprising. The way Angelica remembered the tour when they'd first met, Sheeran had been preoccupied with the former astronaut who had been their guide. Before their group left Cheyenne Mountain, she'd been holding his hand. After a bit of checking around, Angelica learned that SSA Sheeran had a reputation for high maintenance and low morals.

Sheeran tossed her long red hair. "It's your first time in the field. Are you having fun yet?"

Apart from being abducted, she was doing okay. "I'm learning."

"I told Spence that he needed to chip you. For once, he listened to me."

To chip me? What was that about? A vague recollection of something about Raquel and Spence teased the edge of her memory, but that wasn't Angelica's focus. She needed to get down to business. "Has there been recent online chatter about NORAD or Cheyenne Mountain?"

"We're not authorized to share."

"What's that supposed to mean?"

Sheeran glanced over her shoulder at the sofa where Spence and the other two agents were fielding objections from Professor Fletcher and his two protégés. With a smug grin, she turned back to Angelica. "I received notification from Quantico that Spence was off this investigation."

So that's the way you want to play this game? Angelica wasn't afraid to dish it out. She squared off, toe-to-toe and wishing she'd been wearing her own high-heeled boots instead of socks. "You weren't contacted by my bosses at NSA."

"Not necessary."

"Are you saying the FBI has jurisdiction over NSA?"

"I don't make those distinctions. All I know is that Spence messed up, and I'm taking over."

Not if I have anything to say about it. "Before I call the director of the NSA—whose number is on my speed dial—let's try to come to an agreement."

"I don't need your cooperation."

"Are you sure about that? You're aware that I was abducted by the perpetrators and escaped. I was with them for hours."

"But you have amnesia."

"I'm remembering more and more all the time—names, dates, passwords, coding numbers."

"You don't scare me."

"Back at you, SSA."

Angelica strolled to the coffee table, picked up the computer and tucked it under her arm. Before she could return to her conversation with Sheeran, the other agent stepped in front of her. The first thing she noticed about him was his shaved head. When he shook her hand, his grasp was reptilian and cold. In spite of his smile, he looked angry.

"Big fan," he said.

She wasn't following. "Okay."

"I'm Special Agent Mike Tapper. We spoke on the phone."

"Right." His name filtered through her memory, and she came up with an answer. He was her direct contact with this field office.

"I appreciate your work in cyber security. That's the future."

"Thanks, Mike."

"I just did a quick sweep of your suite. No bugs."

"I'm looking forward to consulting with you."

"Not so fast." SSA Sheeran stomped toward them. The heels of her boots clunked loudly with each step. "I'll make the decisions about consulting. It's my call."

"Fine." Angelica wrapped both arms around the laptop. "This piece of evidence is in my possession, which makes it part of the NSA investigation."

When Spence joined their little group, he physically dominated it and towered over everyone else. His rumbling tone of voice betrayed his anger. "Agent Thorne, is SSA Sheeran giving you a hard time?"

"Nothing I can't handle, SA Malone." Angelica gave him a tight-lipped but confident smile. "I was explaining to her that if our two agencies aren't working on a joint basis, sharing information, I'm under no obligation to show her all the delicious clues on this computer."

"You're trying to con me," Sheeran said darkly. She planted her fists on her hips, showing off her hourglass figure. "Why should I believe you?"

Though feeling severely underdressed in her nightgown and robe, Angelica angled a glance toward Spence. "Should I give her a taste?"

"You might as well show her what she's throwing away."

Without looking at the screen, Angelica pulled up the photo of the murdered man and spun it around so Sheeran could see.

Tapper caught a glimpse and let out a shocked gasp. "Whoa."

Angelica closed the laptop. "And there's more. I'm willing to work together if you are."

"The situation is out of my hands." But her statement was tinged with regret. Maybe Sheeran had finally realized that cooperation was to her benefit. "I'm guessing that you've already copied the content of that computer onto a thumb drive. Am I right?"

Angelica neither confirmed nor denied. "Continue."

"If you give me that thumb drive, I'll tell you the most salient points of recent chatter."

Looking to Spence for confirmation, Angelica asked, "Do you think I should?"

"Do it."

She fished the flash drive out of her bathrobe pocket. "We have a deal."

As soon as she placed the drive onto Sheeran's out-stretched palm, the SSA dug into the pocket of her skinny jeans and produced a thumb drive of her own. "This is our recent reading, including stuff from a new clandestine site called Office1116."

That was the same name as the sender on the computer. "We need to compare notes."

"Tomorrow," Sheeran said.

The fact that she'd come prepared with her thumb drive tucked into her pocket told Angelica that the SSA had planned to cooperate from the start. Her objections and hostility reminded her of some kind of hazing ceremony. Angelica couldn't be accepted into the sorority of kickass field agents until she proved herself worthy. "When did you decide to trust me?"

"Maybe I have a soft spot for the tooth fairy." She grinned with half her mouth. "Or maybe I knew we'd work together when I came through the door. You've got a big reputation, Agent Thorne. I'd be a fool not to use you."

Before Sheeran herded her two agents and the three suspects from the room, Angelica stepped close to Fletcher and whispered, "Sorry this happened, Professor."

"Things like this keep life interesting."

"Next time you want to talk to me, just call."

He bobbed his head. "I meant what I said about helping. If you need to use my computers, you have my permission."

She patted his furry cheek and watched as he and the others left. In their absence, the hotel room filled with quiet. Neither she nor Spence moved. They stood on opposite sides of the sofa as frozen as her memories.

A hazy recollection began to form in the back of her mind. Not too long ago, they'd talked about the fiery red-haired agent.

"What's the date?" Angelica asked.

"Since it's after midnight, it's November fourteenth."

"When did you first hear from Sheeran?"

"She contacted my supervisor," he said. "About three weeks ago, she reported unusual cyber activity that indicated a possible hack into NORAD."

Her memory became more distinct. She spun around and faced him. His jeans and T-shirt fit so well that they might have been designed especially for him. He had the kind of body that made any outfit—from a tuxedo to sweatpants—look good. He was a catch. She knew it and so did a lot of other women, including Sheeran.

"She wanted you for the investigation," Angelica said. "She asked for you."

His jaw tensed. "We've had this conversation before."

"I forgot."

"Let's hear it for amnesia!" He strode across the room and gathered her into an embrace. "Finally, I catch a break."

"Hold on." Though leaning her head against his shoulder felt incredibly comfortable, she reared back and stared up at him. "I need to remember. Amnesia is the enemy."

"But there are a hundred things more important for you to recall than an old argument."

He kissed her forehead and went into the bedroom where he grabbed the room service cart and wheeled it back into the central room of the suite to the table.

As he arranged his place setting, he said, "I've got a couple of memory techniques I want to use with you."

He gave a brief explanation of relaxation and meditation that she barely listened to. Her attention was still fixated on Sheeran. The date November sixteenth rose up in her mind. One-one-one-six was, for some reason, important. When Spence picked up the champagne and prepared to pop the cork, she wondered if drinking was such a good idea when they should be concentrating.

"Don't worry," he said, reading her mind. "This is nonalcoholic. I wouldn't give you booze when we're not sure what kind of drugs are in your system."

"Thoughtful." Actually, it was doubly thoughtful. First, he was being considerate about her physical condition. Second, he'd remembered that champagne was her favorite.

The cork exploded from the bottle. A few drops spilled before Spence captured the fizzy liquid in a long-stemmed glass from room service. He handed it to her before pouring one of his own. Gazing at her over the rim, he proposed a toast. "Here's to my sweet angel who's a lot tougher than she looks."

She took a sip. The bubbles tickled her nose. "Do I look fragile? I mean, if it came to a showdown between me and Sheeran, do you think I could take her down?"

"You just did," he said as he sat at the table. "I don't want to talk about her anymore."

She sat beside him at the table, sipping the phony champagne that tasted as good as the real stuff. Though not hungry, she picked bits of lettuce and soggy croutons from the salad. The flash drive Sheeran had given her weighed heavily in the pocket of her robe. She couldn't wait to plug it in. The Office1116 reference gave her hope that there was other useful evidence.

"What if it's a date," she said.

He chewed slowly and swallowed. "You're talking about the one-one-one-six. I thought of that when I first saw the email name. One of my accounts is Spence421."

"No way." How did she ever get hooked up with this guy who was so unsavvy about computers? "You used your first name and your birthday?"

"Not very original."

"No, you Luddite, not very clever at all."

"If the date is eleven-sixteen, we're talking about two days from right now. A mere forty-eight hours."

With very little time to decipher the threat and stop it, she and Spence needed to be smart and lucky. If they failed, the result might be nuclear catastrophe.

Chapter Eleven

"This is never going to work," Angelica said as she stormed into the bedroom of their hotel suite.

Though Spence would have preferred to have her stretched out in bed and naked, he directed her to a contemporary-style chaise longue. "It's important for you to remember. You were inside NORAD."

"I've gotten a lot of my memory back."

"Sit on the chaise and get comfortable. If you need pillows or an extra blanket, tell me."

"We're wasting time. We could be going over the data on the FBI flash drive."

"Later." If any of the information Sheeran had compiled included vital or actionable evidence, he was damn sure she wouldn't wait around for them to discover it. How had he ever dated that woman? She insisted on being the boss, which was probably why they never got seriously intimate.

"I hate this," she muttered.

"I'm aware."

"Don't take it personally. It's not you. It's me, my problem." She stood at the end of the chaise with her arms folded around her middle in a classic posture of resistance. "I'm not a good candidate for hypnosis. Other people have tried…and failed. It's just not my thing."

"Sit," he said.

"Ordering me around won't help." But she plunked down on the edge of the chaise.

Stiff as a stick, her rigid spine and clenched jaw were a textbook definition of *tense*. His job was to get her to relax enough to open her mind and let the memories flow. "You don't look comfortable."

"I'm just fine."

He told himself that he, too, was just fine. Not true. Spence suffered from his own distractions. Three paces to his left was a king-size bed with the covers already pulled down and the smooth white sheets waiting for them. A powerful urge tore through him as he imagined making an imprint on those sheets. He cherished those moments when his body pressed down on her and she arched her back and fused with him. They became one.

How could she sit there, so prim and proper, when all he wanted was to shred her clothes and claim her sweet mouth with kisses? It had only been five days since they were in bed together. Had the amnesia made her forget how good it was? Even when they argued, their sexual chemistry surpassed anything he'd experienced before.

In a hoarse voice, he said, "Let's get this over with."

"What do you want me to do?"

"Loosen up, scoot back on the chaise. Open up your arms."

Giving her the time and space to cooperate, he dimmed the lights in the bedroom and selected a classical playlist on his computer. He'd thought far enough ahead to order a candle from room service when they brought the meal. He lit the votive and placed it on the small table beside the chaise.

Still, she hadn't relaxed. Her arms thrust straight down at her side, her knees rubbed together and she stared straight ahead.

Fighting his natural arousal, he took action. As gently as possible, he bent her elbows. When he rested his hands on either side of her slim waist, he asked, "Does this hurt? I don't want to press against your bruise."

"You aren't touching it," she said. "But what are you doing?"

"Forcing you to relax."

"Oxymoron."

"I don't care."

He lifted her and adjusted her position so that her back rested against the chaise. After straightening her nightgown and robe, he stretched her legs straight out in front. Now at least she didn't look like an ice sculpture.

Touching her was having a predictable effect on him. The blood surged like lava through his veins. The opposite of Angelica, he was so damn hot that he was sweating under his T-shirt.

He pulled up a smaller chair and sat beside her. "Close your eyes."

"Is this when you work your magic and hypnotize me?"

"If I had to call this exercise anything, I'd say guided meditation."

"Well, now you sound like a guru." She smirked. "I'd rather have you be a magician, waving a shiny object back and forth in front of my face and telling me that I'm getting sleepy, sleepy, sleepy."

He'd about had it with her attitude. "We don't have to do this. To tell the truth, I'd rather not."

"What would you rather do?"

"I'd rather kiss you. Would rather tear off your clothes and lick every inch of your body."

Her eyes narrowed to emerald slits. "I remember what that's like."

"So do I."

"Sex was one of my first real memories to return," she said. "At the pastor's house, I remembered making love after we saw *Camelot*."

In a desperate effort, he clutched the tattered shreds of his willpower, keeping his bottom in the chair instead of diving on top of her. More to himself than to her, he said, "This is my job."

"Mine, too. I'm your partner."

"We're a team, and I need for you to remember. You spent hours with the bad guys, and there must have been something you saw or heard. The stuff locked up inside your pretty little head is some of our best evidence."

"Okay, I'll try."

A shudder rocked her shoulders as she reined herself into control. He felt her putting distance between them. Though he'd said that was what he wanted, Spence nearly wept when she looked away from him. "Angelica, are you okay?"

"What do I have to do?"

Jumping into peaceful meditation probably wouldn't work until they had both settled down. "We should talk for a while, get back on track."

"There's only one thing on my mind," she said. "All those really juicy, really good memories you've given me."

He deserved a medal for staying on course. "You

mentioned not being a good subject. Have you been hypnotized before?"

"Once," she said. "On a family vacation when I was sixteen, we went to a magic show. We had great seats near the front, and when the magician asked for volunteers, my sister raised her hand. He took both of us. The identical twin thing appeals to a lot of people."

"What was the magician's name?"

"The act was a man and woman, Nightshade and Belladonna. Actually, they were pretty good at mind reading, which is only a matter of codes and numbers."

"The hypnosis," he said, pulling her back from a digression.

"He did his relax-and-sleep thing, and my sister went right under. Not me. He tried again. I was still wide-awake."

"A performer's nightmare."

"Mr. Nightshade whispered in my ear that if I played along, he'd give me fifty bucks after the show." She shrugged. "I faked it. Squawked like a chicken and did a hula dance. My sister upstaged me by acting out a death scene for a chicken. She loves an audience."

"Did he pay you?"

"Yeah, and he gave me some free advice. He told me that people who can't get hypnotized have trust issues."

Spence had noticed that tendency in her. Others might consider her natural mistrust to be a character flaw, but he appreciated her caution. He, too, had been burned enough times to be initially suspicious. "Was Nightshade right?"

"Probably," she said with a shrug. "A shrink told me the same thing after several hours of therapy and a boatload of cash."

Never before had she mentioned going to a shrink. He wanted to hear more but not right now. "Let's get started."

"Can I ask a question first?"

"Shoot."

"Why did the FBI wait so long to start investigating? Evidence of hacking showed up three weeks ago, which was when Sheeran reported a problem. Nothing was done."

"The data passed from desk to desk and there were meetings, but nobody took it seriously. That's why they sent the two of us—a small reconnaissance team to poke around." He'd already had this conversation with her, but hesitated to point it out. "Is any of this ringing a bell?"

"I just can't understand. We're talking about nuclear missiles, bombs that can devastate an entire city. Why wouldn't they do something?"

"Sit back and get ready for a history lesson."

"I already know all about NORAD."

"So you know that technology is a hell of a lot different now than when the complex was first built in the late 1950s."

"I've seen photographs of the early days."

"Those computers were the size of SUVs, even bigger. They took up whole rooms."

"It was a different world," she said. "Somebody like me wouldn't have fit in very well."

"NORAD headquarters was where they kept the most sophisticated electronic equipment. There's still a lot of top secret data and monitoring that goes on there, and Cheyenne Mountain is considered the best place to resist an attack by electromagnetic pulse. But

the computers inside the granite mountain are no longer impregnable. Hackers have found a way."

"Even when they get in, there are enough security
redundancies to stop tampering or launches." A smile
touched her lips. "You've told me this before."

Her memory gave reason for hope. More might slip
through the veil of amnesia. "You remember."

"Your voice," she said, "when you said words like
electromagnetic pulse, *EMP* and *impregnable*. I like
the way your mouth moved while you spoke."

He needed to start the relaxing techniques before
they got too far into watching each other's mouth.
"Close your eyes."

In a low, slow tone, he instructed her to relax her feet
and toes, then her legs, then her fingers and so on. He
kept his own eyes closed to avoid checking out each delicious body part. If he allowed himself to get aroused,
she'd hear the suppressed excitement in his voice and
get distracted. *Not yet.* He needed to concentrate on the
missing hours when she'd been abducted.

When her breathing reflected what he hoped was an
inner serenity, he said, "Open your eyes. Focus on the
flame of the candle."

Through half-lidded eyes, she followed his instructions. "Just so you know," she said, "I'm not asleep."

"It's okay. This isn't a magic show." He thought of
Nightshade dealing with bright-eyed, brave, energetic
Angelica. "Now I want you to slowly count backward
from five."

"Five…four…three…" She completed the sequence.

"Keep watching the candle," he said. "Last night, we
went to your parents' house in separate cars."

"Because you needed to stop off at FBI headquarters later, and I wanted to leave early to see Mom and Dad."

They never should have split up. Spence had been too casual, treating this assignment more like a vacation than a mission. She was right. They were dealing with nukes. He should have taken their actions more seriously. "Tell me about the weather while you were driving."

"It was a blue sky day until the sun dipped behind the Sangre de Cristo mountain range and the horizon turned to yellow and pink and orange. I was happy because this was my first field assignment…"

He'd known how proud she was to be out from behind her desk. Didn't quite understand the thrill, but he'd seen her excitement when she slipped her Glock into a holster under her blazer rather than carrying it in her purse.

She continued, "And I was eager to have my parents meet you. As soon as I walked in the door, Dad let me know he didn't like the idea of me being involved with another agent."

He'd sensed hostility from the general, who had gone to the trouble of looking him up on the internet. Spence's college degrees from second-rate institutions, paid for with football scholarships, made him proud. He'd achieved more than he'd ever expected. But her father pointed out that he wasn't exactly the product of an Ivy League education, wasn't good enough for his daughter.

This was a discussion for later. He moved her through the night. "When we left, I went first so I could check in with SSA Sheeran. You were going to follow."

"I stayed a bit longer than I planned to," she admitted. "Dad wanted to know why we weren't engaged."

Spence cursed himself. He should have given her that diamond he'd been carrying around for weeks. Oh, yeah, they definitely needed to talk when this was over. "And then you drove back to the hotel."

"In the parking lot…" Her sentence trailed off. Though she continued to stare at the candle, she blinked. "It happened almost exactly as I surmised. I was hit by a stun gun, then I was shoved into the trunk of a car and drugged."

She cringed, probably recalling the pain as she touched her hip where she had the bruise.

"In the trunk," he prompted, "could you see anything?"

"Too dark. And I was mostly unconscious. It was stinky, though. Exhaust fumes. And then… I woke up, sitting on a wood chair. My head jerked back."

"And you could see."

"I had on a black hood, but I could look out of the bottom. I had on a sweatshirt. My wrists were duct taped to the arms of the chair."

Her voice had dropped to a whisper as though fearful that someone might overhear. She darted a glance to the right and to the left. Her arms bent at the elbow, mimicking the position she'd described.

Her reaction was even better than he'd hoped. She appeared to be reliving the memory. He needed to choose his words carefully, to keep her in that time and place.

Gently, he asked, "Were you alone?"

"People were talking." Her head tilted back and she looked up. "The overhead lights were so bright that I could see them through the weave in the hood."

He offered a suggestion. "And they were still talking."

"Yes, and I tried to listen. They talked about a boss, someone who was older than them. They didn't mention names."

While he'd waited for her at the hotel, he'd gotten a text from her cell phone saying that she was spending the night at her parents' house because she and her mom had a lot to talk about.

Though he hadn't liked her plan, he decided to be understanding. The next morning, he had another text, telling him that she had an opportunity to go inside Cheyenne Mountain Complex with minimal supervision. A friend of her dad arranged it, and she wanted to take advantage.

When he tried to call her back, he was steamed, and she didn't answer. His instincts sensed something was wrong. He tried using the GPS tracking device he'd implanted in her arm but couldn't get a signal. If she'd been inside the mountain, that made sense. His GPS wouldn't work under tons of granite.

The next few hours crawled past. He vacillated between telling himself there was nothing to worry about and heart-stopping terror. Without alerting her mother to the possibility of kidnapping, he talked to her and found out that Angelica hadn't spent the night. She wasn't at headquarters. No one had a record of her being in Cheyenne Complex. Then he found her car in the hotel parking lot.

True panic set in. If the GPS tracker hadn't started beeping, giving him a signal to follow into the mountains, he might have gone berserk.

He returned to the exercise. "When they took off the hood, you saw your surroundings."

"Nothing special," she said. "A typical office with cubicles and computers, the room was similar to the setup at Peterson AFB."

"But not Peterson," he said.

"I couldn't see clearly, but no. Five men, they wore ski masks and nondescript clothes. Thin rubber gloves, purple. There were lights—bright like Maglites—aimed at me. One of them had an accent."

Five men? That must have been when Heller met up with Trevor and the hired thugs. "Describe the accent."

"He kept talking about Dallas. I'd guess he was Texan. I wish I could be more precise." Her eyebrows pulled down. "I tried to put together descriptions. A field agent should be able to remember details."

"You're doing fine," he assured her.

"They set a computer in front of me and told me to input the hacker codes I had already figured out. That wasn't going to happen. Nothing they could do would make me give up my secrets."

"Did they try?"

"They were all talk, and I had a plan. I started typing in codes for a program that I'd already rejected. But one of them knew computers and stopped me. I made a grab for his ski mask." She blinked several times. "I didn't get the mask off, but I recognized him. It was Lex Heller."

And he paid for his clumsiness with his life. "Did you say his name?"

"No."

"What did he do?"

"He yelled. After that, I don't remember much."

Her bravery touched him. The longer this exercise dragged on, the less he cared about the mission and the more he worried about her. Disregarding subtlety and guiding her along the path to remembrance, he took her hand.

"Did they hurt you?"

"I don't think so." She squeezed his fingers. Her touch was warm. "They asked if I wanted water or food. For a while, I was fastened to the arms of a chair but they used duct tape over the sweatshirt, nothing painful. On the other hand, they drugged me and took my memory."

"This is enough for tonight," he said. "I'm going to count backward from five and clap my hands."

"Don't bother," she said. "I'm not in a trance."

"Humor me. Five…four…three…"

"I overheard them say something about how it only takes one to show we mean business. Only one, one strike and we get top dollar for the other six."

He stopped counting. "A strike."

"And I know where they're going to attack."

Chapter Twelve

"Dallas," she said.

During the relaxation exercise, Angelica hadn't been hypnotized. Spence's voice soothed her, and he seemed to know all the right questions to prod her memory, but she hadn't succumbed to any kind of hocus-pocus spell. Conscious and aware of what she was saying, she'd been able to go deep and mine the memories from hidden corners of her brain. And she'd hit gold.

"It worked," Spence said.

"In a way," she conceded. "I remembered a bit more."

"You really hate to admit that I might be right."

He swooped, lifted her from the chaise and carried her to the bed. His caveman habit of picking her up was irritating but also sexy. In a primitive part of her psyche, she enjoyed his ability to dominate her with his greater size and strength. Never would she admit to such an old-fashioned attitude, but there it was.

His mesmerizing blue eyes raked over her face. When he was close like this, she didn't care about whether or not she could trust him or her dad's disapproval or the lack of an engagement proposal. He lay beside her. Her everything, he was all she wanted. She grabbed the front of his T-shirt and pulled him close.

"Dallas," he said. "I knew you had evidence buried in your subconscious. Our hacking threat just got specific."

With a groan, she ripped her gaze away from his handsome face, flopped back against the pillows and stared at the ceiling. "I suppose we have to deal with this."

"I need to get reassigned to the case."

Her lust would have to be put on hold. She was a field agent and needed to direct all her energy into their mission. Didn't seem fair but she'd have to wait to make love—until after they saved the world.

"We should hurry," she said. They'd already talked about the possibility of the Office1116 username in the emails pertaining to a date: eleven-sixteen. "The strike might be scheduled for the sixteenth, which is two days from today."

He tore open the sash on her robe and ripped the terry cloth open. Underneath, she still wore her blue-and-gray-striped nightgown, but that fabric was thin and clingy. When he lowered himself on top of her, she felt every hard ridge of his six-pack abs. His demanding kiss stole her breath away.

"I'll be back." He bolted across the room and grabbed his cell phone.

Though still dazed by their intense moment of contact, she managed to speak. "Wait! It's too late to call anybody on the East Coast."

"Protocol goes out the window when it comes to nukes."

With his cell phone at his ear, he left her alone on the king-size bed. Field agent protocol suggested that she make a few calls of her own. But she wasn't anxious to inform her supervisor that she'd been abducted, given amnesia and discovered a murder victim.

She threw off the covers and retrieved her personal laptop from her luggage. This machine wasn't powerful enough or well protected enough to dive into the dark web where she could research the codes from the emails: Y75110 and C4ICBM. From what she'd overheard while being held by the bad guys, she figured that something would be offered for sale, probably at a limited auction, probably after the strike on Dallas proved they had the capability to launch.

In the pocket of her robe, she found the FBI flash drive she'd gotten from Sheeran. An image of the redhaired SSA wearing a skintight, strapless gown tickled another memory. A photograph, where had she seen it? Angelica shoved those thoughts aside; she wasn't ready to go deep again.

Sprawled across the bed on her belly with the computer open in front of her, she plugged in the flash drive. The data displayed in a pattern of icons and files that she recognized as being similar to those used by Heller and his merry crew at Peterson AFB.

There was an array of maps, ranging from satellite photos to hand-drawn cartography. The area displayed was mostly Western United States and Canada, which made sense. NORAD was a joint operation between the two nations, designed to cover this part of the world with a protective net. Some of the markings on the maps indicated the facilities and silos where the weapons were kept.

Growing up near NORAD, she had a clearer understanding than most of the size and scope of this decades-old program. Numbers varied, depending on the source, but there were probably over five thousand active nuclear warheads and hundreds of launch missiles to send them on their way. Some had been decommissioned. Others updated.

A shudder went through her. She hated to imagine that someone had gotten control of these missiles and was able to launch at will. One strike could destroy Dallas, and the voices she'd overheard said there were six more. Seven missiles? No matter how far-fetched, that threat was enough to restart the Cold War.

In other files, there were memos from Peterson AFB, projections and lists of supplies. There were also transcripts of conversations regarding the NORAD hack, including a talk she'd had with Professor Fletcher. Seeing her words transcribed and documented was a little bit creepy. More worrisome was the fact that the FBI recorded a call with the professor. Were they monitoring him or keeping track of calls made on his phone? Their conversation never mentioned NORAD; they'd been discussing obscure cryptography software.

She homed in on the file labeled Office1116. Sources for the information were untraceable but she did learn a few interesting things. Lex Heller claimed to be her close friend, and he suspected her of holding out on information. He used the phrase "on account of the old man" a couple of times. As soon as she read the words, she heard them in her memory. References to the "old man." What did her father have to do with any of this?

The "old man" could also be the professor. She hated that Office1116 had anything at all to say about her and people she knew and loved. Professor Fletch wasn't a traitor and would never do anything to harm anyone else. Still, she reminded herself, the photo of the murder had been delivered to his doorstep.

Office1116 mentioned the three cities—Dallas, Seattle and Seoul—several times. There were mileage charts indicating how far these cities were from Colorado Springs and from other unnamed locations. She had the pieces to the puzzle but didn't know how it all fit together.

Sometimes, the solution to a problem required distance, similar to those artworks that looked like a bunch of dots when you were close and coalesced into recognizable forms when you stepped back. If she could print out the maps and equations, she might see the connections. Those types of graphics required different software than she had on her laptop.

She thought of Professor Fletch. He had exactly the type of computer she needed. Twice, he'd offered the use of his equipment, which she hoped was nothing more than goodwill on his part. She didn't want to think he was somehow involved and trying to send her a message.

She got out of bed, rotated her shoulders, stretched her arms and yawned. Considering all that she'd put her body through in the past few days, she wasn't feeling too much discomfort. Slowly, she paced across the carpet. The large bruise on her side was tender. Other than that, her aches and pains were minimal.

Through the half-opened door, she overheard her name. Talking into his phone, Spence said, "Agent Thorne has the expertise required for the job."

She appreciated his vote of confidence. Too bad she didn't share his enthusiasm for her ability to solve a complex problem.

."If we need help, we can use the local resources," Spence said. "This close to NORAD, you can't swing a cat without hitting a computer nerd."

When he ended the call, she slipped through the door and went to him. Her hands crept under his T-shirt and glided up his muscular torso and chest. "Are we on the case?"

"With the full support of Quantico," he said, raising his arms and pulling the shirt off over his head.

The light fur on his bare chest enticed her. She stroked with her palms while her fingers traced a path. The man was, as she had noticed so many times before, gorgeous.

"Did you hear what I said?" he asked. "I didn't mean to call you a nerd."

"I'm proudly nerd-like." Touching him made her pulse accelerate. Still, she tried to sound nonchalant. "But your metaphor should have been about a mouse, like a computer mouse. Don't say you can't swing a cat. You can't swing a mouse."

He placed his index finger across her lips. "No more talk."

She couldn't have agreed more. This time, she didn't allow herself to be slung over his shoulder like a piece of meat. Moving fast, she latched on to his hand and tugged him across the front room into the bedroom. Once there, she halted and they collapsed onto the bed wrapped in each other's arms.

Her need had never been greater. From the first moment she saw him, she had remembered that they were good in bed. Images of that past history replayed in her mind. Usually, they engaged in a reasonable amount of foreplay, gradually building to a climax.

Tonight was different.

Instead of a slow climb, she shot to the edge of the highest cliff. With her toes curled over the ledge, she stared into a thrilling abyss, ready to leap. Her breath came in ragged gasps. She arched her back, threw back her head and roared a feral cry of desperation and desire.

He lay on top of her and held her face in both of his huge hands, forcing her to meet his gaze.

"My sweet angel," he whispered. "I thought I'd lost you."

"No such luck."

"This isn't a joke." He kept her pinned. Though she bucked against him, he had her completely under his control. "If anything bad happened to you, I'd demand my vengeance."

"That's enough, Spence. I thought we were done talking."

"Whatever you want, angel."

He kissed her lightly. Too gentle, she wanted more. "Harder."

"Your lip is bleeding."

With the tip of her tongue, she tasted the blood. Her split lip from the escape through the snow hadn't altogether healed, not that she felt the pain. "It doesn't hurt."

"I'll find somewhere else to kiss."

He grabbed fistfuls of striped fabric and yanked her nightgown up and over her head. Stretched out on the sheets below him, she was naked, reveling in the subtle whisper of air across her skin.

His hands cupped her breasts, and his thumbs flicked the tight, rose-colored tips. When he ducked his head and suckled, an ever-expanding ripple of pleasure consumed her. Again, she cried out. Frantic and near climax, she wanted him inside her.

With her legs still spread, she sat up. Her fingers grappled with the waistband of his sweatpants. Through the fabric, she felt his thick, hard shaft.

He set her hands aside, rose from the bed and stripped. *Gorgeous!* Driven by uncontrollable forces, she wrestled her arms around him and dragged him onto the sheets, positioning herself to climb all over his muscular body. Her legs splayed across his lower abdomen, and she dragged herself lower until his erection eased between her thighs. At last, she joined herself with him. He filled her completely.

For a long moment, she didn't make a move. Nor did he. Their breathing synchronized. Their hearts beat as one.

Inside her, he twitched. That small movement was exciting, excruciating. *More, she wanted more.* Her muscles tensed as she gripped him.

"So sweet," he whispered as his arms encircled her.

When he flipped her onto her back and rose up above her, she knew foreplay was most definitely over. Starting fast, he plowed her thoroughly, and then he pulled out, slowly, almost to the tip, before plunging deeper. An orgasm rocked her from the inside out.

He didn't stop. While she was exploding beneath him, he kept going, pushing her to even greater heights. Finally, when she thought she couldn't take it anymore, he gave one final thrust. They finished together.

While her muscles fluttered and goose bumps marched up and down her bare thighs, her mind filled with visions of fireworks and starry nights. She wasn't sure how much she remembered, but this had to be the best sex ever.

Chapter Thirteen

Early that morning, they got on the road and headed up to the mountains. Spence almost kept driving when he recognized the shiny red pickup truck parked outside Pastor Clarence's cabin. "I don't suppose it's a coincidence that your dad is here."

"Afraid not," she said. "I called him this morning to tell him I couldn't go out to lunch, and I might have mentioned a visit to the pastor and Trudy."

Neither of those lovely people were the real reason Spence had returned to the cabin. Special Agent Trevor MacArthur was staying here with his aunt and uncle while his supervisors in Quantico figured out the next direction for his undercover work. While Trevor was here, Spence wanted him to show them the place where he and his three cronies met with Heller after he picked up Angelica. The location might trigger more memories from her.

So far, their best clues had come from the bits she recalled when she was being held captive, namely "a strike on Dallas in two days." When he'd warned his supervisors at Quantico, they set a lot of other investigative trails into motion. He and Angelica were to continue with what they'd started, and they'd be working alone unless they requested assistance.

SSA Sheeran and the other local agents could be used for backup and in specific situations. When Spence had talked to her on the phone this morning and informed her that her involvement wasn't needed, Sheeran accused him of not trusting her. And she was correct; he didn't trust anybody. The way he figured, the strike had to be an inside job. Personnel at Peterson AFB were compromised. The murder of Lex Heller was proof of that. The FBI field office was too close to the problem.

He parked on the road behind her father's truck. In the daylight with a blue sky overhead, the snow-covered cabin and rustic church were charming. The pastor and Trudy had carved out a pleasant life for themselves, except for her chronic illness.

Angelica let herself out of the SUV before he could come around to open her door. "It's as pretty as a postcard and a long way off the beaten path, but you'd never find Pastor Clarence's church unless you were looking for it."

"Your dad knew where it was."

"He knows everything," she said. "He might be retired, but he tries to run his mountain community the way he ran his command, with his sticky fingers in every pie."

Though she wasn't praising her father, Spence could see how much she loved the general. When she spoke of him, her eyes brightened and she couldn't help smiling.

Following her up the shoveled path to the front porch, Spence braced himself for a dose of her father's hostility. At their first meeting, the general had been mildly unpleasant, but now he knew his daughter was involved

in a dangerous investigation. Spence figured he'd be for-
tunate to escape with all his body parts still attached.

He placed his hand possessively on her shoulder.
Yesterday, she would have shrugged him off and called
him unprofessional. Today, she stepped into a closer
embrace and gazed up with warm, sexy eyes that set
off a chain reaction inside his gut. His hand slid down
her back and up under her parka to cup her jean-clad
bottom. He'd always been attracted to her, but not like
this. After last night, he was obsessed. Their lovemak-
ing had been more than satisfying.

General Peter Thorne flung open the door to confront
them. Though he wore a red-and-gray plaid sweater, his
posture was appropriate for a full-dress uniform. He
was a dignified man, a figure of authority. His hair was
thinning and pure white, but he made up for that lack
of hair with bushy black eyebrows. He barely glanced
at Spence, reserving all his attention for his daughter,
who greeted him with a hug and a kiss on the cheek.

Before he had a chance to read her the riot act, she
said, "Don't try to change my mind. This is my job. I
want you to respect that."

"You stumbled over a dead body," he said. "It's too
damn dangerous."

"My job," she repeated. "My decision."

Her statement was not unexpected, and her dad was
ready with a different solution. "At least let me assign
a couple of bodyguards to follow you around."

"Don't need them," she said as she tapped Spence
on the chest. "I've got him."

Trudy bustled up to join them. "Spence can handle
that job. I'll tell you, General Thorne, this young man

is very brave. He didn't back down a single inch when Angelica came after him with her violin bow."

Her dad hoisted his brows. "Dear woman, what are you talking about?"

"Let's chat over tea and cookies." She directed them to the very long table where she had arranged two plate-fuls of different cookies, orange juice and a tea service.

Angelica embraced Trudy and the pastor before moving on to the munchies. Spence didn't move fast enough to follow. Her dad steered him into a detour.

"You know I'm right," the general said in a low growl. "She shouldn't be doing this."

"Here's what I know." Spence matched his tone with a gravelly whisper of his own. "Angelica is smart, competent and trained as a field agent. She can find the answers. In so doing, she'll save countless lives."

"At what personal cost? I don't want her in danger."

"A few days ago, I slipped up." Spence didn't mention that the reason for Angelica being in danger was her desire to stay behind and make things right with her father. "I promise you, it won't happen again."

"If you fail—"

"If I can't keep her safe, I'll be dead." He'd gladly sacrifice himself for her, but that wasn't his preferred course of action. "And my funeral plan doesn't take effect for another sixty years."

He excused himself and found Pastor Clarence, who thanked him for getting the general to visit. The pastor's plans for Peter Thorne included a trip to a soup kitchen in Colorado Springs for a Thanksgiving feast and using his powerful basso to sing in Trudy's choir.

Spence interrupted, "Where's Trevor?"

"He's in the garage, warming up my car. He didn't

think it'd be wise to meet up with Angelica's dad. When you leave, pull into the church parking lot and wait for a minute. He'll drive past and honk, and then you follow him."

Spence could tell that the pastor enjoyed playing spy. "Should I honk back?"

"Probably not," he said. "We don't want to make too much noise. The general will catch on."

"How can I be sure it's Trevor?"

The pastor scratched his head. "I never thought of that."

"We'll take our chances."

He signaled to Angelica, and she quickly wrapped up with her dad and gave Trudy a pair of acoustic, sound-canceling headphones to listen to her music.

"I thought you might like these," Angelica said. "I had them in my luggage, and I have another pair back home in Virginia."

"Thank you, dear." Trudy popped the dark purple headphones over her gray hair and beamed a smile. "Do I look like a hip grandma?"

Angelica nodded. "The hippest."

After another few moments, they were out the door and into the SUV. Following instructions, Spence drove into the church parking lot, which had been cleared by a snowplow. He barely had time to turn the SUV around before he heard a car horn and saw a blue Volvo sedan, probably ten years old and equipped with all-wheel drive. With a crank of the wheel, he exited onto the road and fell in line behind Trevor.

"I've been thinking," she said, "how remarkable it was that you found me. Trevor never mentioned that he contacted you with the location of the van."

"He didn't." Spence had a bad feeling about where her line of reasoning might be leading.

"I could have been anywhere."

With a sense of impending trouble, he tried to divert her thinking. "The important thing is that I found you."

Undeterred, she continued, "There isn't much surveillance in the mountains, so I doubt you spotted the van on a camera feed. Even if you did, you wouldn't know I was inside unless Lex Heller passed on that information. But he didn't. What was it that pointed you in the right direction and led you to me?"

He said nothing. There were no words to make this right. The truth was indefensible.

"Aha!" she said. "Last night SSA Sheeran mentioned something about a chip. Would you care to explain?"

"Not really."

"Let me fill in the blank," she said. "You implanted a chip to enable GPS tracking in me…without my permission."

"For your protection."

"Before we left Quantico, you asked me if I minded having a chip implanted, and I said that I didn't want one. I refused. You did it, anyway. You chipped me like an implanted ID on a dog. Or a LoJack system on a car."

Her laser-edged glare seared off chunks of his flesh. He understood her outrage, but he wasn't going to apologize. The chip had worked exactly the way it was intended. The reason he'd been able to locate her in the sprawling mountain landscape was the tiny blip on a computer screen that marked her whereabouts.

"Here's what hurts," she said. "You never would have put in the chip if you trusted me. You figured I'd mess up, and you'd have to rescue me."

"I didn't see it that way."

"Answer me this," she challenged, "have you chipped any of your other partners? Or have you worn a GPS chip of your own?"

He could have gone through a complicated rationalization about how undercover agents can't have any implanted devices, but that didn't excuse him. All the justification in the world couldn't erase her logical conclusion that he didn't trust her.

Spence concentrated on the road. Trevor was leading them down from the secluded mountain area populated by a few cabins and many acres of National Forest. At the lower elevation, the packed snow on the road had melted in patches.

"I should have trusted you," he said.

"A tracking chip is something my father would do."

"I'm not like him." That was a comparison he could do without. "I wanted to keep you safe."

"You can't swaddle me in Bubble Wrap."

He didn't like to admit when he was wrong, but he wouldn't cling to a mistake. He hadn't given her enough credit, hadn't trusted her. "I'm sorry."

"Accepted."

He glanced at her stony profile. She'd forgiven him, but he was damn sure this was going to be one of those relationship issues she'd want to discuss. They'd disagreed about trust before. Angelica felt that trust came as an inseparable part of the love package, along with caring, respecting and sharing. On the other hand, he took a more pragmatic approach. Trust wasn't given but earned. If she wanted him to trust her as a field agent, she needed to step up her game.

At a crossroads, the Volvo turned into a parking lot

for a market, café, gas station and small motel. Spence followed in the SUV. The name of the motel appeared to be Hog Heaven and the sign was decorated with the neon outline of a pig with a curly tail. On the back side of the motel, Trevor parked, got out of the car and came toward them. He slapped Spence on the back and gave Angelica a hug.

Looking her over, he said, "Last time we met, you'd barely pulled yourself together. You clean up nice."

"So do you."

"Trudy's been stuffing me from morning to night." He gestured in the general direction of an abandoned porta potty that sat on one end of the building to a ramshackle shed on the other. "This is where we picked you up from Heller."

The asphalt parking lot stretched to the edge of a forested hillside. Dirty snow piled up in the shadow of the Dumpster. There was no one else in sight.

Spence shrugged. "Not exactly the type of place you'd want to store in your memory."

"There's something familiar. I'm not sure what it is." She hiked to the end of the parking lot and went past the porta potty, giving it a wide berth.

Spence turned to Trevor and asked, "Have you ever worn a GPS tracking implant?"

"Hell, no. I try to stay off the grid."

Spence felt the same way when he was working alone. "Suppose you had a partner."

"No chips," Trevor said. "I'd have to trust my partner to stay in touch."

And there was that word again. *Trust.* Spence shook his head and refocused on the task at hand. "When you and the three goons picked Angelica up, was she conscious?"

"Barely," he said. "Without letting the other idiots know, I took her vitals. Her breathing and pulse were regular. Her hands were cold."

He hated hearing about what she went through, even though she'd assured him that she wasn't badly mistreated. And he swore that he wouldn't leave her unguarded for the rest of the time they were in Colorado.

She came back around the building. "I remember the Hog Heaven sign but not from when Heller brought me here. This place is the turnoff that leads to Professor Fletcher's cabin."

The location was handy because they had plans to go to the cabin where the professor kept some unusual computers. But Spence didn't like having her old mentor connected in any way to the strike on Dallas. Good old Fletch made a good suspect because he knew computers, the photograph of the murdered Lex Heller had been delivered to his doorstep and Angelica had remembered references to "the old man," a description that suited the bearded professor.

After he thanked Trevor for his help, Spence drove around front and parked. Angelica had accepted his apology, but he felt the need for bonding and making things right between them. He arranged papers in a folder and handed it to her. "Get ready for some boring fieldwork."

"Doing what?"

"Questioning possible witnesses," he said. "We need to talk to the people in the motel, café and market. They might have noticed an important detail."

In the folder were ID photos of Lex Heller, Bo Lambert, Howie Dunne and the professor. Also, a photo of the van used to transport her. When Angelica paged through the assortment, she chuckled. "This is so old-school. I could call these pictures up on my computer tablet."

"Feel free," he said. "Is there anybody else you suspect? There are probably mug shots of the three thugs who were with Trevor. I don't like SA Ramirez. Add him to the lineup."

"And SSA Raquel Sheeran," she said as she flipped through identification programs. "She's got some of that evil dominatrix thing going on."

"Good call." He had no problem thinking of Sheeran as a woman in leather with a whip. "Add her and no more than two others."

"Because we don't want to overwhelm the witnesses," she said. Her mood improved significantly as she set up her array of photos and computer images. "Can I ask the questions?"

"Knock yourself out."

He followed her into the motel office, a worn-out room with a counter, a dead ficus and a sign-in book. None of the names in the book were their suspects, but he took a photo with his phone for possible evidentiary use.

She did all the talking, and she was good at it, hitting exactly the right note between authority and friendliness. Her natural poise kept these suspects on their toes as they went from the motel to the bar to the market. Spence was impressed that none of the men hit on her.

The kid with a military buzz cut who sat behind the cash register in the market identified the professor as someone who lived around here and sometimes came in to buy stuff. He got excited about Sheeran, not that he recognized her, but he sure did like those redheads.

Back in the SUV, they compared notes. None of these men had seen or heard anything unusual. Angelica had done a good job with the interviews, and he'd told her so. When he reached across the console and patted her shoulder, she shrugged him away. Now what had he done wrong? Dreading the answer, he asked, "Do we have a problem?"

"Looking at the photo of Raquel Sheeran, I remembered another picture." Her tone was frosty. "She's wearing a strapless formal gown covered with sequins. A man in a tuxedo stands beside her. That man is you."

Chapter Fourteen

"I'm not a jealous woman," Angelica said as she plugged Professor Fletcher's mountain address into the SUV's GPS. "Follow these directions. We'll be there in twenty minutes."

"We already talked about the picture of Sheeran and me." Spence drove from the parking lot onto a road she'd traveled many times before when visiting Fletch. "Right before we left Quantico."

She tapped her forehead to remind him. "Amnesia."

"The way your memory comes and goes can be real annoying."

"Do you think I'm faking it?"

"I didn't say that."

God, he made her furious. She would've slapped his face, but he hadn't shaved this morning and his firm jaw was covered with thick, blond stubble. If she touched him, she'd end up caressing him. He was too damn handsome.

"We don't have time for these spats," she said.

"Agreed."

Today was the fourteenth. The strike on Dallas would probably take place on the sixteenth. If the targeted time was the stroke of midnight, that was only thirty-eight hours from now. She needed to focus, but her memory couldn't immediately reboot after recalling the photo that was part of a larger picture of a formal event at the Kennedy Center. It was no big surprise that the photographer had taken several shots of shapely Raquel Sheeran with her mane of red hair. With Spence at her side, the combined magnificence was blinding.

Angelica wouldn't say that she was jealous of SSA Sheeran, aka Jessica Rabbit. Obviously, Spence was going to enjoy the view that Sheeran put on display. She didn't care that he'd escorted Sheeran to the event, but he'd told her that the photo was a fluke that happened to catch them in the same shot. He'd said they weren't together.

She exhaled an angry huff. "If you had just told me that you dated her before we met, I wouldn't care."

"You said we weren't going to...what did you call it?"

"Spat." Facing ninety degrees away from him, she stared out the front windshield. A narrow two-lane, winding road cut through a snowy forest of pine and conifer. In her peripheral vision, she noticed his large hand gripping the steering wheel, and she thought of how sensitive those paws had been last night when he stroked her inner thigh.

"We'll arrive at our destination soon," he said as he followed the GPS instruction to go right, then right again. "Do you need to call and let anybody know?"

"I talked to Fletch this morning. Your former girlfriend, SSA Sheeran, released him and the boys last night. Fletch was going to stay at his house in town and sleep late."

"She was never my girlfriend," he said.

"That's not what the gossip around the office says.

The way I heard it, you went out for three or four months."

"I'm going to say this again, for the last time. I was on assignment in Denver, which is where I met Sheeran. We went out to dinner a couple of times. She invited me to a ski weekend, where we spent the night in the same tiny cabin but not the same bed."

Others in his office had been quick to show her the photo in a back issue of an FBI publication and to tell her to watch out for Spence. "Were you at the party with her?"

"We came in a limo with four others. I wouldn't call it a date, but we left the event at the same time and rode back to the hotel together."

"And at the hotel?"

"We hugged," he said, "and went to bed in our separate rooms. In the spirit of full disclosure, I was dating another woman at the time."

Hooking up with two women at the same time sounded more like the image of Spence that provided the office with gossip. "If you're so innocent, why does everybody think you're a player?"

"I'm not." Before she could say anything else, he held up his hand for silence. "There's something else I want to tell you."

"Go ahead."

"I kissed SSA Sheeran. I didn't count how many times, but only twice with tongue. And I touched her breasts." He made a squeezing gesture with his hand, giving a clear indication of how he'd done a bit more than touch. "They're real and very impressive. But she isn't the right woman for me, and I didn't want to lead her on. She's a woman who takes revenge, and I didn't want to lose any of my favorite body parts."

"Why should I believe you?"

"Trust," he said, "is a two-way street."

She'd walked right into that one. He had every right to demand trust from her. If he told her he hadn't slept with the stunning redhead, she had to believe him. "Well played."

"I'm not trying to put one over," he said. "I meant what I said about Sheeran. She's a scary, high-maintenance woman."

Though familiar with the phrase, she asked, "What does high maintenance mean to you?"

"She demands all the attention, all the time. Her tastes are recklessly expensive. Everything has to be perfect. Did you notice that she had her FBI windbreaker tailored? She needs to be pampered. And the poor sucker who falls for her has to live up to her expectations."

"You've given this some thought," she said.

"I grew up poor. Working as a valet and a busboy, I had the chance to study these ladies. They aren't for me."

According to his story, he had still taken the opportunity to feel her impressive breasts. Angelica could hardly blame him.

On the left side of the road, she pointed toward a chestnut-brown house with a deck across the front and tall A-frame gables on either end of a garage. She'd always thought of the gables as peaked eyebrows and the garage as a mouth. The eccentric-looking home suited Professor Fletcher very well.

Tire tracks plowed through the snow on the driveway and disappeared into the garage, but nothing had been shoveled. The accumulation was five or six inches, deeper where the snow had drifted. Anxious to get started with the professor's computer programs, her hand was on the door handle when Spence parked on the road.

"You could drive a bit closer," she said.

He took his gun from the holster. "We'll proceed with caution. Tire tracks into the garage indicate that somebody is inside, and Fletch told you he wasn't coming up here."

Though she hadn't been planning to sneak up on the professor's house, she knew Spence was correct. This would be a short hike through the snow, which meant zipping her parka and pulling on a knit hat. With her gun drawn, she climbed out of the SUV and closed the car door as quietly as possible. She hoped, really hoped, they wouldn't find anything terrible inside.

She had no problem letting Spence take the lead. For a big man, he moved with incredible stealth through the ankle-deep snow. To reach the entrance, they had to climb a zigzag double staircase to the deck. The front door was in the center section between the peaked gables and above the garage.

Her hiking boots gave her good traction, but she slipped halfway up the second staircase. If she hadn't caught the banister, she'd have fallen. The gun fell from her hand.

She mouthed to Spence, "I'll get it."

Near the bottom of the lower staircase, she heard a noise. Someone was nearby. She froze in place.

"Hands up," a deep voice said. "Don't make me shoot."

"It's okay," she said. "I have permission to be here."

"You heard me," the voice said. "Just do it."

With a whoosh, Spence vaulted over the upper banister and landed in the snow beside the staircase—a dangerous move. He could have broken both legs, but seemed to be unharmed when he stood up straight and aimed his gun.

Until this moment, she hadn't completely forgiven him. But how could she stay angry at a man who naturally reacted like a superhero? He amazed her.

And Spence was definitely in charge. He snapped an order at the other man. "Put the gun down."

"No way am I going to shoot. I was joking around."

She turned. "Is that you, Dunne?"

"Now," Spence said. "Gun on the ground."

"Yeah, sure." He dropped the gun and took a step back. "We cool?"

Dunne and his man bun irritated her. He'd changed from his Hawaiian shirt to a dark green hoodie and an extra-long scarf that dangled almost to his knees. She scowled at him. "What are you doing here?"

"The professor wanted me to help you with his equipment. Some of the setups are weird."

Spence scooped up her gun and handed it to her. To Dunne, he said, "Take us inside. I have questions for you."

"More questions?" he groaned as he led them to the far side of the three-car garage where there was a regular, human-sized door. "At FBI headquarters, I must have talked nonstop for two hours. Big Red had one question after another."

Angelica had to ask. "Big Red?"

"You know who I'm talking about. Special Agent

Hottie. The legs on her are enough to make me confess to just about anything."

As Spence herded them through the side garage door that she hadn't known was there, he chided Dunne. "SSA Sheeran is a federal agent. She warrants respect."

Dunne chuckled to himself. "Hey, that wasn't an insult. I called her *Special Agent* Hottie, didn't I?"

Spence whipped out his cell phone. "I've got her on speed dial. Let's see if she finds your tone respectful."

"Please don't call her," Dunne said. "I'm sorry, really."

"Your sense of humor needs an adjustment. It's not funny to aim a gun at a friend or to call people names. Can you give me a 'yes, sir' on that?"

"Yes, sir."

She climbed the staircase from the basement level to the first floor. The living room furnishings were more appropriate for an office than a space for social occasions. There were desks and worktables and computers all over the place. When Fletch bought this house, he intended for it to be a hideaway where he could work uninterrupted on various projects. It hadn't quite turned out that way. His privacy was hindered by his bad habit of sharing the location with other professors and his students.

She walked through the kitchen and went past the round table where a box of chocolate-flavored breakfast cereal testified to the taste level of Dunne and his buddies. The most remarkable feature of the front room was a wall of windows overlooking a stunning view of the forest, rolling hills and the high peaks beyond.

Spence stepped up beside her. "I didn't realize we were on a cliff."

"This place is full of surprises," she said.

"If there's a way to cover those windows, we should use it. All that glass has to be letting in the cold."

"They're triple pane. Not bad as insulation."

"Also bulletproof," he said.

"Typical," she murmured. "You brought an innocent conversation around to danger."

"Bulletproof is a good thing. Does Fletch have a reason to be worried about assassination attempts?"

"I sincerely hope not."

How could she think of Fletch as a suspect? He was kind, sweet and would never hurt a flea. Surely, he wouldn't drop a nuke on a major city. But someone had plans for mass destruction, and that individual was someone she'd met.

She had to find this person or these people. But how? Her thoughts didn't naturally center on bullets and assassinations, and her brain still wasn't operating at full throttle. Maybe she wasn't cut out to be a field agent. If she'd been at her desk in Cyber Security headquarters, her stomach wouldn't feel like she'd been whirling in a centrifuge.

Spence whispered her name, and she looked up at him. "You're going to be okay," he assured her.

"What if I can't figure this out?"

"You'll get it. Your cyber buddies at NSA are working on this, too." He turned his head to look out at the view. "Inhale a deep breath. Take in the beauty. Trust yourself."

Sunlight glistened against the new snow. The sky above the peaks was a pure blue. She could feel herself calming down. "Fletch calls this house his crucible."

"Like the alchemy tool."

She reared back. "I didn't expect you to know that."

"I grew up poor, not uneducated."

"That's not what I meant. I just don't think of alchemy as the kind of thing a man like you would be interested in."

"It's not a favorite topic at tailgate parties," he admitted. "But I understand why your professor wanted a space where he could create."

"Do you ever have that urge?"

He nodded. "Maybe."

"Your undercover work is actually very creative. You might be a good actor."

"Or not." His grin was a bit self-conscious.

"Ready to get started?"

She pivoted and marched toward the kitchen, where Dunne was eating his chocolate cereal right out of the box. Needing to work with him rankled, but she'd do anything to save time.

"Show me a computer," she said, "where I can go deep."

"Are you talking about the dark web? Black hat operations? I didn't think you government types went in for that."

"Show me."

In a corner room with two windows and a colorful paisley, he showed her a bank of computers. There were three screens. The one in the middle was extra large.

"These babies suck up a lot of power," Dunne said. "When not in use, we turn them off. There are four linked consoles, and you have to turn them on in order from left to right."

He flicked the switches and little green lights came on. Though there wasn't a hum, she felt an energy surge.

"What about the screens?" she asked.

"They work the same way. Turn them on from left to right."

She sat in the swivel chair in front of the computers. Leaning forward, she turned on the screens. The two smaller displays came to life, showing pictures of mountain landscapes. The large center screen remained blank.

"What's wrong with it?" she asked.

"It's on." He pointed to the blinking light. "I don't know why it's taking so long to warm up."

A burst of red and yellow exploded across the screen, and then a Grim Reaper carrying a scythe appeared. From the eye sockets of the skull, squiggles crawled like snakes and formed two words in 24-point type: You're Dead.

Chapter Fifteen

Standing in the doorway across the room from the death screen, Spence watched Dunne's reaction. First, there was surprise and then a bright flicker in his eye. A muscle in Dunne's jaw twitched as though holding back a grin. Spence figured that Dunne hadn't expected a Grim Reaper but he wasn't scared by the skull or the threat.

Spence crossed the room to the swivel chair where Angelica sat with her fingers poised above the keyboard. He wanted that grotesque image to be far away from her.

"Turn it off," he growled.

"Not yet. I might be able to trace where it came from."

"I hate it."

"These graphics are nothing." She tilted her head to look up at him. "You don't play computer games, do you?"

Real life was scary enough without searching for additional on-screen thrills. "Can't say that I do."

"Well, some of the gaming images are horrendous. They'll give you nightmares."

She pounced on the keyboard. After a few strokes, the Grim Reaper faded to a box in the upper right corner while the rest of the screen filled with data streams.

Whenever he watched her doing her job, he was in awe. His angel was brilliant and beautiful.

His hands dropped to her shoulders, and he massaged. At the nape of her neck, he felt knots of tension and pressed hard against them until they released. She shrugged and gave a soft moan that reminded him of last night in bed.

Without looking up, she asked, "Do you think the threat is meant for Professor Fletch?"

"The computer belongs to him." Taking advantage of an opportunity to confront Dunne, he pointed a finger at the center of his skinny chest. "This could be a warning for you. Who did you tell that you were going to be here?"

"Nobody." He waved his hands as though he could divert Spence's intense scrutiny. "What about her? Somebody might want to hurt her."

"For your sake, I hope not."

Dunne shook his head. The hint of a smile was completely erased from his long, thin face. "What's that supposed to mean? For my sake?"

"Nobody knew we were going to be here but Fletcher. And he told you. That means either you or your mentor are responsible for the image on that screen."

"Not me. There wasn't time. I barely had a chance to change clothes before I left for the cabin, not enough time to set up complicated graphics."

Spence leaned toward Angelica, who was still tapping at the keyboard. "Is that true? Would it take a long time?"

"Maybe," she said as she shot a glance toward Spence. "I might have mentioned to my dad that we were coming here."

And Sheeran could have figured it out. It was unlikely that Dunne had anything to do with the death head. He knew Angelica would be here and had a grudging respect for her skills, but Spence didn't want to let him off the hook too easily. "You must have told somebody else."

"Nobody." He dug into his pocket, pulled out his cell phone and passed it to Spence. "See for yourself. I didn't call anybody."

"You could have used a burner phone."

"Think again," Dunne said. "I had nothing to do with the Reaper. If you want to know the truth, I'm worried that Fletch might be in danger."

Spence needed to develop a more precise psychology for Dunne—a profile. He was probably in his late twenties, a little younger than Spence but far more immature. Dunne dressed like a student. Yet, there was something about his clothes and his man bun that made Spence think of a disguise. Dunne was different from nerds like Lambert and Heller. He lacked their dedication and their innocence.

"Where do you work?" Spence asked.

"A coffee shop."

"Part-time?"

"That's right," Dunne snapped. "What is this? A job interview?"

A part-time job didn't earn enough money to pay rent. Spence drew the next logical conclusion. "Do you live with Fletch?"

"Congratulations, Secret Agent Man, you figured it out. Fletch is my boyfriend."

Angelica swiveled around in her chair and gave him a congratulatory thumbs-up. "I knew it. You're his type, slim and not too tall. I'll bet you have great hair when you take down that stupid bun."

"Should I say thank you?"

"If I were you," Spence said, "I'd take it. She's not big on compliments."

Behind Angelica, the Reaper image on the screen flashed in another explosion, and then faded into a tame, pleasant picture of a forest glen. The soft, bubbling sound of water rushing in a creek accompanied the image.

He was glad to see the threat disappear. "What happened?"

"It was on a timer," she said. "I went as far as I could in tracing. The best I can figure is that it originated at an internet coffee shop in Reykjavik."

Dunne chuckled. Spence was confused. "Explain."

"The programmer who sent the Reaper is good at covering his or her tracks. He or she made it appear as though the message came from an impossible location." She paused, thought for a moment, and then continued, "Actually, this individual is better than good. They're world-class."

"How do you know?"

"Because he or she is as computer savvy as I am. And I'm incredible." In her swivel chair, she spun in a one-eighty so she was facing the computer screen again. "If you gentlemen will excuse me, I have some web work to do."

Spence hustled Dunne from the room. In the kitchen, Dunne prepared a fresh pot of coffee while Spence rummaged through the fridge until he found the fixings for ham sandwiches. Still thinking about his profile for

Dunne, he couldn't decide if this guy was a suspect or a witness.

Dunne presented himself as a facilitator, willing to help when asked. The professor had sent him to open this cabin for them. Dunne had gone to pick up Lambert. He'd carried and displayed the computer image of Heller's murder.

While Spence spread mustard and mayo on slices of bread, he dissected that profile. Sometimes, a facilitator was a nice person who enjoyed helping others, people like the pastor and Trudy. Other times, facilitators were sociopaths who arranged situations to their benefit. He wouldn't be surprised to find that Dunne orchestrated the camera-under-the-door trip to the hotel that he, Lambert and Fletch had made, supposedly to meet with Angelica.

Ironically, it was Dunne who asked the next question. "How long have you and Angelica been dating?"

"Six months."

"Is it serious? Not that I care," he said, "but Fletch adores that girl, talks about her all the time. She was his smartest, most original, cleverest student."

"She likes him, too."

Impatient, he huffed. "So, is it serious?"

Spence knew better than to share personal information with a possible suspect. He and Dunne weren't buddies but adversaries. Instead of declaring his undying love or mentioning the engagement ring he'd been carrying around while waiting for the right moment, Spence gave a noncommittal shrug. "Why do you care? I thought you were gay."

"I go both ways." His upper lip curled in a sneer that he probably thought was derisive. "Don't get me wrong. I'm not conning Fletcher and I really care about him. He's the reason I'm concerned about her. I don't want to see him upset by having his sweetie pie angel end up dead."

Upset seemed like a mild description. "I'm guessing Fletch didn't feel too bad about Heller's murder."

"He was shocked. His first instinct when I showed him the computer image was to push it away."

Dunne sounded hurt, and Spence had to wonder why. "You didn't like that, the way he ignored the image."

"I had to make him look." He was vehement. "He needed to fix it, to make sense of it."

"Only Fletch could fix it."

"Damn right."

Spence set the plates with ham sandwiches in front of them on the center island. He needed to keep Dunne talking. "But Fletch didn't study the image, didn't go deep enough."

"That's her fault," he said. "Fletcher wanted to consult with Angelica. And—you won't believe this—he wanted to wait until morning."

"You needed to move a lot quicker than that," Spence said, keeping in mind that Dunne supposedly didn't know that the clock was ticking down the minutes to the strike on the sixteenth. "There's a deadline."

Dunne turned away. His mouth zipped into a straight line. Spence could almost see the walls Dunne was building to keep him from getting closer. Good, he'd hit a nerve.

From the guidelines he'd learned in FBI profiling, he had a fuller picture of Dunne. Not only was he emotionally immature but he was sexually confused and looking for a father figure like the professor. As a sociopath, Dunne lacked empathy. Everything was about him and satisfying his needs.

Spence had known sneaky kids like Dunne in foster care. They were fast talkers, friendly when they needed to be, but quick to throw you under the bus if it suited their needs.

Spence fed his ego. "You already figured it out, didn't you? You spotted the clue in that computer image. You're smarter than you look. You worked out the puzzle faster than the professor or Angelica."

"I haven't got a clue what you're talking about."

But he almost nodded in the affirmative. Spence pushed for more information. "There is a clue, isn't there?"

"How would I know?"

"Show me. You and I can go over the image together."

He could tell that Dunne was tempted. His fingers twitched, and he licked his lips, but he said, "I'm not an expert. I don't know what to look for. Besides, we don't have the computer with the image."

Actually, they did have that computer. Angelica had taken possession and hadn't turned it over to the FBI or to the computer nerds at Peterson AFB. Spence hesitated, not wanting to give Dunne too much information. "What can you tell me without the computer?"

"I suppose I don't need the image to give you the clue. Pay attention, you might learn something."

Spence nodded and said nothing, hoping that if Dunne kept talking, he'd eventually incriminate himself.

"You and Angelica found the body, right?"

Again, Spence nodded. He took a bite of his sandwich and chewed slowly. The ham was bland, nearly flavorless, but the mustard was spicy.

"Did you see any remote cameras in the room?" Dunne asked.

Another nod. "But none of them were hooked up."

"What if…" Dunne paused for dramatic effect. "What if there was a tiny, nearly microscopic camera on the wall behind Heller or in a heating grate or hidden on a bookshelf. Are you following me?"

"Keep going."

"The camera feed could have sent the photo to that computer," he said triumphantly. "Nobody had to be in the room to snap the photo. It was programmed."

"Angelica said the computer took that picture. It wasn't sent forward from anything else."

Dunne flapped his hand dismissively. "She's not infallible, you know. A remote camera feed makes more sense. I bet Heller set it up himself, to record visitors to his apartment."

If Heller had intended to make a record of other people, why would he point the camera at the back of his own head? That was some seriously flawed logic, but Spence didn't point it out. He wanted to keep Dunne engaged and talking. "You could very well be right. Heller must have had somebody working with him. And that person must have picked up the feed."

"Bo Lambert." Like any sociopath worthy of the profile, he was quick to dump the blame on some poor dope like Lambert. "The image of the murder showed up on a computer that belonged in Lambert's office."

"Which was also Heller's office."

"And didn't Lambert already admit that Heller offered him a job? Five thousand bucks for an afternoon?"

"Lambert said he turned down the assignment." Spence believed Lambert's confession that he'd almost gotten involved in Heller's weird scheme because of a long-ago crush on Angelica. Admitting his gullibility had to bring up painful memories.

"What if he was lying?"

It was time to call an end to this sparring match. Spence flipped the tables. "What about your alibi?"

Dunne stuffed his mouth with sandwich, maybe to keep from saying more that made him look worse. He choked out the words. "What about it?"

"The alibi went like this. You and Lambert and Fletch were together from when you and Lambert picked up the car until after dinner when Lambert found the computer."

"Another reason Lambert has to be the guilty one," Dunne said. "He found the computer."

"But he didn't commit the murder. We can't get around that alibi."

"Well, we weren't joined at the hip." Dunne thrust out his pelvis. "He could have slipped out. Wait, I remember that I took a little nap. That's when he did it. Maybe the camera feed was in his vehicle. And he had enough time to go back to Heller's apartment."

"How far is Heller's apartment from Fletcher's house?"

"I don't know. Maybe fifteen or twenty minutes away."

It was more like ten. Spence had clocked it this morning with Angelica before they headed to the mountains. Dunne had painted himself into a corner. He had time to sneak away from Fletcher's house and make a round trip to Heller's apartment and back.

In the worst-case scenario, Dunne shot his friend in the back of the head, picked up a computer and snapped a photo before he returned home.

Chapter Sixteen

Spence wasn't altogether sure what Angelica was doing in the corner office with the computers. Shortly after he and Dunne had finished their ham sandwiches and veiled accusations, she'd invited Dunne into her sanctum. She'd needed him to show her how to run the various printers, including an enlarger capable of creating documents that were three feet square. Then Dunne was out, Spence was in, and she asked him to shut the door.

The moment he turned and faced her, she was on him. Her arms twined around his neck. Her body aligned with his as she pressed him against the closed door. She kissed him carefully, still mindful of her split lip. Her tongue delicately explored his mouth, slid across his teeth, and then plunged deeper.

She pulled back. "You taste like mustard."

"Hungry?"

"Only for you."

He wrapped her in his arms and squeezed, crushing her slender body against his chest, stealing her breath, consuming her. He wrestled her feet off the floor, and she coiled her legs around him. He was hard as stone against her.

They shouldn't allow themselves to be distracted.

There was important work to be done. If they couldn't decipher the hack at NORAD, a major American city might be destroyed in a fatal strike. And yet, his every thought, every urge, led back to her. He wanted to be inside her, to stay with her for an hour or a day or maybe the rest of his natural life.

When he spoke, his strangled voice caught in his throat. He didn't sound like himself. "We don't have time."

"I know."

"Have you found anything?" he asked.

"I've got ideas."

"So do I."

He should be telling her that Dunne might be more involved than they'd thought and shouldn't be trusted. Instead, he settled her firmly against his erection. She rubbed herself up and down, creating a warm friction against him. The buttons on his jeans twisted between them. He wanted her to keep going, never to stop.

She threw back her head, and he nuzzled the slender column of her throat. A wild shudder went through her. Gasping, she slid down his body until her feet were firmly planted on the floor.

"I had to do that," she said.

"I'm glad to oblige." He would've been a lot happier if he'd gotten the same release that she achieved.

"Otherwise," she said, "I would have been too preoccupied thinking about you to concentrate on anything else."

Actually dizzy, he closed his eyes and leaned his back against the door. "How can I help?"

"Give me privacy. I need to pull things together."

He didn't want to go back to the other room with Dunne, especially not now when he was pretty sure the guy was a sociopath. "I'll just sit in the corner and be quiet."

"You make me crazy. You've got to go."

And so, he left.

THAT HAD BEEN two hours ago. During much of that time, he'd been on the phone with Quantico and the local FBI. Dunne had been granted entrance to her locked room, and she'd printed him a copy of the photograph of Heller, which he stuck under Spence's nose.

For a good twenty minutes, Spence studied the picture, noticing titles on books that were visible and squinting at the papers on Heller's desk. Among those papers was one with scribbles. Amid the scribbles was the code that was driving Spence crazy: Y75110.

The code had significance. It told him that Heller was connected to the hacking and the possible strikes. But Spence had already made that link when Trevor told him that Heller had been holding Angelica.

He stalked down the hallway to the corner bedroom. If he stood with his ear to the door, he could hear her plucking at the keys and printing and tearing papers. What the hell?

"Here comes trouble," Dunne announced from the front room. "It's Big Red."

"Sheeran?" Spence straightened his spine. "What's she doing here?"

"I don't know. She's coming up the stairs."

Spence rapped on the door. "Angelica, I need to interrupt."

She whipped the door open and stepped back to give him a full view of the corner office. Along one wall, she'd taped four huge, black-and-white maps of Western

United States. The eastern half of the country was on the opposite side. With markers, she'd put in dots of varying colors. The majority were red. The two windows were covered by transparencies that hung over the curtain rods. Thumbtacks fastened several smaller maps and coded charts to the wall in a pyramid pattern. Colored pieces of string attached some of the dots and codes. On a bulletin board, she'd tacked up copies of newspaper articles. It looked like the untidy nest of a giant bird.

"I'm not done," she said.

He shoved the door closed and locked it behind him. Until he could make sense of this chaos, he didn't intend to share with Sheeran. He turned to Angelica. "I'm going to need a little explanation."

"First, I need to tell you about my visit to the dark web." Her mouth twisted in disgust. "It's gross. Every perversion you can imagine has buyers and sellers."

"What did you find out about the hack?"

"I followed a couple of threads that tangled in and out and around. The hacker is offering an auction of six nukes and is demanding a multimillion-dollar payoff. The proof will be at Dallas on the sixteenth."

Somewhere in the back of his mind, he'd been hoping they were wrong. "Our theory is confirmed."

She nodded. "I sent the details and dark web links to my supervisor. Somebody from our office will pose as a buyer and go after the seller. It's the kind of operation they've done before."

"That's not going to help Dallas," he said.

"I'm afraid that's our problem."

He paced in a tight circle. The clutter prevented him from taking a regular-length stride. "Tell me about all this."

"Some of the maps are from the FBI flash drive. Others are from Peterson AFB."

As she explained, she brightened. Leaving the dark web behind, she enjoyed this part of the process—the puzzle solving. She continued, "I've been creating a timeline within each area that shows the original sites for missile silos and how they've changed over the years. New ones were added. Some were decommissioned."

"Why?"

She shrugged. "Why would I know how NORAD makes policy? The warheads taken off-line are aging and might need repairs."

"What I want to know," he said, "is why you set up this craft project with all the color coding?"

"One of the guiding concepts of cryptography is being able to look at a problem from a different perspective."

He was familiar with the idea. "Thinking outside the box."

She took his hand and dragged him into the center of the chaos. "Close your eyes and cover them with your hands."

He recalled last night when he'd guided her in a meditation exercise. This might be her version of the same thing. "They're covered."

"When I count to three, open them. See what object catches your focus."

She counted, and he peeked. His gaze went directly to the letter *C* on a map of the Western states. He moved closer to interpret the symbol, which appeared to be a designated sector in northern Colorado with two red-dot missile silos.

"Reminds me of C4ICBM," she said. "C4 might not mean explosives. Maybe it's a location."

From down the hall, he heard the husky rumble of SSA Sheeran calling his name. "I don't know why she's here," he said.

"Her reasons could be purely professional," she said with a tight-lipped smile. "Maybe she's got good news."

"Come with me."

"I'd rather stay here," she said. "I'm getting close. I can feel it."

She pushed him toward the door and closed it behind him. He heard the click as she engaged the lock.

STILL GAZING AT the door, Angelica closed her eyes, squinted hard and popped her eyelids open. She'd been hoping her intense concentration would make SSA Sheeran disappear, but that wasn't going to happen. She could hear the sexy tone of the redhead's voice in the hallway as she talked to Spence.

Shuffling through the mess of papers scattered on the floor, Angelica returned to her swivel chair behind the desk and typed a message to Bo Lambert. He'd been helping her find one of the first maps of the missile sites, circa 1955 when the Santa Claus tracking program started.

She knew the map existed because her dad showed it to her. Sixty years ago, when he was a kid and his father had been in the air force, they tracked Santa on a flight map. Every Christmas, her father repeated that tradition with his own children.

At the time, she hadn't been aware that the dots on the map represented missile silos that held nuclear warheads. Her dad certainly didn't tell her. But she was a curious kid and had figured it out.

Unlike the maps she'd taped to the wall, the early

versions couldn't be readily accessed. Those records
were on computers that weren't compatible with pres-
ent-day technology. To find them, Lambert had to make
a physical search in the archives at Peterson AFB.

Lambert emailed her back. He couldn't find the maps
she needed and suggested that those records might be filed
in the Cheyenne Mountain Complex. She needed to go
inside the Complex. But first, she'd call her dad. He was
the world's most organized person and could probably put
his hands on the family Christmas map in five minutes.

Again, she squeezed her eyes shut and popped them
open. The lines and contours on the maps blended like
an abstract painting. Thinking outside the box, she
played with the Y75110 code on the computer, breaking it apart to read: Y75-110 and Y7-5110. When she
squinted, the "5" looked like an *S*.

Before she pushed away from the desk, she went
through the shutting down sequence and made a call
to her dad. When she told him what she needed, he
responded—as she'd expected—that he knew exactly
where to find the Santa Claus tracking maps. She asked
him to meet her at Peterson AFB. If she found what she
was looking for, Angelica might need to borrow military equipment and personnel.

Down the hallway, she spotted SSA Sheeran leaning
against the center island in the kitchen and lecturing
about the murder of Lex Heller. Occasionally, Sheeran
referred to a computer tablet for the specifics.

"Cause of death is a .45 caliber bullet to the skull.
Gunshot residue indicates the barrel of the weapon was
close to the head when fired. No sign of a struggle.
There won't be an autopsy for the next four or five days,

longer if they send the body to the Colorado Bureau of Investigation in Denver."

"Why would they do that?" Spence asked.

"Who knows? It's not my jurisdiction. The local cops have got their reasons." She turned her head toward Angelica and tilted her sunglasses down to peek over the top of the lenses. "Good afternoon, Agent Thorne."

"Same to you." She nodded a hello, not offering to do another strength-sapping handshake. "I'm sorry to interrupt, but we need to go."

"Where are you headed?"

"Family business," she said. "We're going to catch up with my dad at Peterson."

"Great," Sheeran said. "I'll come with you. I've always wanted to meet General Thorne."

Angelica didn't believe that for one hot minute, and she didn't want to get stuck spending the rest of the day with the SSA. But they all were on the same team, and she couldn't refuse. "You can follow us."

She returned to the office to pick up her computer. While she was there, she figured that she might as well put together some of these maps. She took the maps of Western United States down from the wall and rolled them into a cylinder.

For one last time, she closed her eyes and popped them open. Her gaze landed on the code that had become so familiar to her: Y75110.

This time, for the first time, she saw it differently. They weren't numbers but letters. The "5" was an *S*. The first "1" was a capital *I*, and the second was an *L*. The code spelled a word: *SILO*. There were seven silos. The launch missiles and nuclear warheads inside the silos were the threat.

Chapter Seventeen

During the drive from Fletcher's cabin to Peterson AFB, Angelica reached across the console and held Spence's hand. She was cold, chilled to the bone with the fear of what might happen if she couldn't figure out how these missile silos were being manipulated. The warmth of his grasp reminded her that most of the world wasn't like the dark web. Most people weren't willing to launch a nuke and destroy an entire city, not even for a multi-million-dollar payoff.

At first, she'd been too tense to speak, but Spence wasn't going to let her sit in the passenger seat like a worried lump. He poked her with one question after another until he had the whole story.

"Seven missile silos," Spence said to summarize, "are going on sale to the highest bidder."

"Make that six," she corrected. "The nuclear warheads in one of them will have been used to wipe out Dallas."

"You're saying that these missile silos differ from all others in the system. They don't fall under NORAD's umbrella of protection with redundant computer programs and firewalls."

"Correct."

"Somehow," he said, "the bad guys have gotten control."

"Correct, again."

He glanced over at her. "You've got to breathe, angel."

"C-c-can't," she stammered. "Too scared."

"Me, too."

She gazed at his profile, still gorgeous. He didn't sound frightened. His hand wasn't shaking the way hers was. Though he might be quaking like an aspen under the surface, he appeared to have himself under control. It was an act he'd probably done many times on life-and-death assignments.

Though she lacked his years of experience, she had determination. She'd figure out how to eliminate the threat. She had to do it. The alternative was too terrible.

Spence had told her to breathe, and she concentrated on inhaling and exhaling deeply and slowly, trying to suppress her rising sense of panic. It was late afternoon on the fourteenth. The day was fading fast. Tomorrow there would only be one more day before the strike.

Approaching the base, they ran into heavy traffic. Even in a midsize city like Colorado Springs, rush hour was a factor. She glared at the "Kiss a Cowboy" bumper sticker on the truck in front of them. "Can't we go any faster?"

"We're making good time," he said. "We've already caught up to Sheeran and Dunne."

"She's supposed to be behind us. I told her to follow."

"Not her style," he said.

Sheeran and Dunne made an exceedingly odd couple. "Why did she bring him along?"

"I asked her to. It's one of those keep-your-enemies-close things. He needs monitoring. At best, Dunne's a sociopath. I don't want to contemplate the worst."

"He can't be totally worthless," she said. "Fletch likes him, and he's a good judge of character."

"Okay, but I'm warning you, as my partner, to be careful around Dunne."

"Another threat," she murmured through a clenched jaw. Danger seemed to be coming from every direction. "I wish I had more help."

"What about your team at NSA? Isn't there anything they can do?"

"They're doing as much as they can, prowling on the dark web, using undercover identities."

"Tell me how that works," he said. "How do you and your cyber buddies go undercover without leaving your desk?"

"It's similar to what you do." She gave his hand a squeeze. "We change our usernames and disguise our identifiable patterns."

"What kind of patterns?"

"Think of when you do undercover work," she said. "You might wear a different style of clothes, maybe dye your hair and put on an accent. You develop a new backstory. Right?"

"You got it."

"People have online personalities, too. Each person inputs data differently. Their language differs. Even the keystrokes are unique. When you go undercover in the cyber world, you have to conceal your computer personality."

"Have you ever been undercover?"

"Sure. My favorite fake identity spends a lot of time on porn sites, setting honey traps." As she grinned, she realized that talking to him was relaxing her. "My username for her is CherryPi, an oversexed math teacher who likes to see how things add up."

"Give me an example of how that works."

"Here's a story problem. If you have five men and four women, how can you put together three threesomes?"

"Not bad."

"I wanted something sexier but all the fun smutty names were already taken."

"I can't believe I didn't know this about you. CherryPi, huh?" He lifted her hand to his lips and brushed a kiss across the knuckles. "Are you good at talking dirty?"

"Only on the computer," she said. "So don't get your hopes up."

For a few miles, they were quiet, and she didn't mind. This wasn't the static, nervous emptiness she'd felt after she'd discovered the threat was real and she might be the only one who could stop it. Right now, the atmosphere was still, almost peaceful. She listened to the soft jazz he was streaming. Spence was skilled at all forms of relaxation. Being with him helped her mentally gather her resources and prepare for whatever might happen—even though she didn't completely trust him.

"Why did Sheeran come to Fletch's cabin?" she asked.

"Those words sound like trouble," he drawled. "I don't want to hear that you're thinking she was driven wild by unrequited lust and had to be in the same room with me."

"It never crossed my mind." Maybe the thought had occurred to her. But when he said the words out loud, they sounded completely ridiculous. "I've been emailing with the computer guy in their office, Agent Tapper, and he didn't mention Sheeran's visit."

"She's mad and doesn't want me to be the boss. Remember what I said about high maintenance?"

"Keep her away from me at Peterson."

"Why me?" He groaned. "I'd rather go head-to-head

with a drug cartel than attempt to manage a situation between two strong women."

"Am I that scary?"

"If you think I'm going to answer that question, you're dreaming."

Following the signs, he made a left and drove the SUV to the entry gates outside the base. SSA Sheeran had arrived before them, gained entrance and sat waiting in her vehicle on the other side of the gatehouse.

Angelica was ready to show ID, but the sentry at the gatehouse gave her a huge smile and raised the barrier without being asked. Had her father arranged this?

The sentry bounded up to her window. "It's been a while. How are you doing, Selena?"

That explained it. "Selena is my twin. I'm Angelica."

He made eye contact with Spence. "True story?"

"She's Angelica." He held up his shield. "We're FBI."

"Go on through," the sentry said. "Tell Selena that Garret Riley says hi."

Her twin sister made an impression wherever she went. This time, it was positive. A good omen, Angelica decided. She directed Spence through the base to a beige brick building next to a hangar. Her dad's red pickup was parked outside.

Angelica tucked the cylinder of maps under her arm and marched through the double doors. Spence, SSA Sheeran and Dunne came behind her, which made her feel as conspicuous as a drum majorette leading a parade. She'd rather slip in and out of the place where her dad had worked for years without being noticed. She was the quiet twin, the one who always did well and didn't expect to be noticed.

At the front desk, the gray-haired woman looked up

from her computer, studied Angelica and then beamed. "I thought I heard something about you being in town."

Rounding the desk, Angelica gave the ample Mrs. Dean a hug and inhaled the scent of snickerdoodle cookies that emanated from the brown cardigan she wore every day, no matter what the weather. "I thought you were going to retire."

"And leave my flyboys to fend for themselves?" she said with a chuckle.

Spence joined them and introduced himself, earning a pat on the cheek from Mrs. Dean. SSA Sheeran and Dunne weren't so polite.

"Your dad is waiting in the conference room." Mrs. Dean pointed down the corridor. "Unless you're fond of sludge, I advise against drinking the coffee he attempted to make."

On the table in the long room with a wall of windows facing a runway, her dad had already spread out his yellowed, worn, much-creased maps that looked ancient enough to belong to the Pirates of the Caribbean. With his hands clasped behind his back, General Peter Thorne paced in front of the table. His bushy eyebrows scowled at her. He gave Spence a nod and the same for Dunne. Raquel got a rise from the brows.

The SSA slipped off her sunglasses and held out her hand as she introduced herself and told him that she'd heard so much about him. Instead of her usual bone-crushing handshake, she grasped lightly and allowed her fingers to linger as she leaned closer to him. What was her angle? Knowing General Peter Thorne was a boost for anyone who had political aspirations. What was Sheeran trying to pull?

"It's always nice to hear compliments for my family. Who's been talking to you about my dad?" Angelica asked.

"Someone close to me," she said with a sexy toss of her red curls. "My papa served under General Thorne."

"You were an air force brat?"

"Just like you."

"Later, we'll talk." Angelica had neither time nor inclination to bond with Raquel Sheeran right now. They shared a background but not much else. At the table, she concentrated on the maps that showed a large swath of Colorado and Wyoming. She carefully smoothed a frayed corner where one of her brothers or her sister had drawn a picture of Santa in his sleigh.

She asked her dad, "Did you get these flight maps from Grandpa?"

"Sure did. He first showed them to me in 1959." He tossed a chipper little grin to SSA Sheeran. "My pop was an aviator, like me. I had hopes for my youngest boy going into the air force and making it three generations."

"I have my pilot's license," Angelica reminded him. "So does Selena. We're carrying on the family tradition."

"But flying isn't your livelihood."

"These maps," she said, "were they generated through aerial photography?"

He nodded. "They were used by NORAD. You see those blue circles? Those are missile silos. Santa wouldn't want to fly too close to those."

The map suited her needs perfectly. It was one of the oldest she'd seen that came from direct photography. With Spence's help, she compared the placement of the missiles on the Santa map and on a more recent rendition.

The scale didn't match, and the triangulation created a different slant. Also, the markings on the old maps were faded. This was a tedious exercise, and she was glad SSA Sheeran was keeping her dad occupied. Dunne stared out the window at a helo as the rotor started the swirl before liftoff.

She wasn't 100 percent sure what she was looking for on the maps, which made the finding more of a challenge. Finally, she looked up, met Spence's gaze. Quietly, she said, "It's not what you see, but what you don't."

"What's that mean?"

"A discrepancy." She pointed to similar areas on two different maps. "A missile silo that showed up on the older map was not on the newer."

"Are you sure?" he asked.

"Would you go to the front desk and get a magnifying glass from Mrs. Dean?"

When he strode from the room, her dad and SSA Sheeran huddled in closer. Though Angelica's hopes were soaring, she didn't want to say too much. After all, this was a top secret investigation.

Her dad glowered. "What's the big deal?"

"Until I'm sure, I can't talk about it."

"You can tell me," he said. "I have Level One Security clearance."

"We just want to help," Sheeran said.

There was value in having other people look for anomalies, and she trusted her dad. "I'm sorry, SSA Sheeran. I have to ask you to leave and take Dunne with you."

When the others were in the hall, she gestured for her dad to come closer. With her finger, she drew a circle around the missile silo on the older map and the same area on the newer. "Compare these two maps and tell me how they're different."

Even with her directions, it took a moment for him

to notice that the silo was not present on the more recent map.

"It didn't just vanish," her dad said. "Those silos are mostly underground and not meant to stand out, but they are solid installations."

"Maybe it was decommissioned," she said.

"That's how our nuclear treaty agreements are supposed to be going. We're supposed to take a bunch out of active deployment every year." He gave an uncharacteristic grin. "You know what they call those unactive warheads? Zombie nukes."

Angelica knew she'd have to do more research to figure out which silos had been decommissioned and which were under repair. Most of that work could be done on her computer.

Spence returned with the magnifying glass, and she used it to study the newer map where the silo should have been. A suspicious mound of dirt and rocks drew her attention. The top of the silo could easily be camouflaged.

She passed the magnifier to Spence. "What do you think?"

He scanned the area and concentrated on the same mound that she'd noticed. When he looked up, he shook his head. "I can't tell for sure."

"I know a way."

She took out her cell phone. Even after she moved back East, Angelica kept up her certification. She'd earned her pilot's license before she graduated from high school.

At a moment's notice, she could be ready for takeoff.

Chapter Eighteen

Spence jammed his long legs into the narrow space for the copilot's seat in the Piper Cub. He'd flown in small planes before, but nothing as tiny as this. If he stretched out his arms, he could touch both sides of the empennage at the same time. The interior cabin wasn't much bigger than a bathtub.

When Angelica suggested taking a plane to check out the missile silo, which was a little more than a hundred miles away, he'd envisioned a private jet and a possible opportunity to join the mile-high club. On their way across Peterson AFB to the hangars, they passed several sleek, good-looking aircrafts, and she'd teased him by telling him that she was qualified to fly this one or that one. Then they found the guy who'd taught her to fly, and he turned over the keys to the Piper. There was nothing luxurious about this single-propeller plane.

She finished her preflight check and climbed aboard. "With those heavy-duty tundra tires, we can land anywhere."

Though he was fairly certain he wouldn't like her answer, he asked, "When you say land anywhere, what does that mean?"

"When we hit the spot we're looking for on GPS,

we drop from the sky and come in for a landing on any flat space."

"Not an airfield?"

"Nothing to worry about, I've flown this little Piper all over the mountains for cross-country skiing and down to Albuquerque for the balloon races and up to Wyoming for the rodeo."

Still pondering the idea of dropping out of the sky, he asked, "Is this safe?"

"Sure." She fiddled with the dials on the console in front of her seat. He was tucked behind her, not so much a copilot as a no-pilot. She continued, "I'll get the GPS set for our missile silo coordinates and off we go. I'd like to get there before the sun goes down so we can make a good, thorough search."

She started the propeller, and he watched the blades slicing the air in front of the windshield. The noise was loud and irritating, reminding him of a lawn mower, and he was happy when she handed him a headset with a microphone attached. With the earphones in place, they could talk to each other.

"Can you hear me?" she asked.

"Loud and clear."

"Get ready for takeoff."

After a short, fast taxi down the runway, they were airborne. Though they were enclosed in the cabin, he sensed the wind rushing around them as they ascended. The elevation wasn't a problem for him. He liked heights and loved the way sunset gilded the edges of the clouds and the rim of the Sangre de Cristo mountain range. The sky took on that delicate rose color that could never really be described.

"There are no words," he said. "Flying into a sunset is pure magic."

"I'm glad you like it."

They bounced over the rough currents. His gut churned. He'd spoken too soon about the magic. If he hadn't been on the verge of throwing up, he would have asked her to turn back and let him out. A parachute was preferable to the jostling, not that there was any way he could leverage his big body to leap from this plane. He was stuck, trapped, uncomfortable and wondering how it was possible to feel claustrophobic while blasting through the sky like a cannonball.

This might be the perfect moment to talk to her about trust. He deserved relationship points for this plane ride. Literally, he had put his life in her hands with nothing more than a pilot's license and an assurance from a grizzled old man at Peterson AFB that she could soar like a hawk. Spence believed in Angelica so much that he'd volunteered for stomach-churning agony.

He seized control of himself. This was his meditation challenge, and he could breathe his way through the inner turmoil. He closed his eyes, concentrated. When he could look around again, he took in the positive beauty and dismissed the gut-wrenching discomfort.

He heard her voice in his ear. "How are you doing?"

"Good," he said, convincing himself. "When we land, what's the plan?"

"We need to search for the missile silo. It's possible that the map my dad has isn't accurate."

"It's a photograph," he said. "Taken in the late 1950s, obviously before Photoshop. And why would anybody add a missile silo to a picture?"

"I trust the map."

"It's possible that we'll search and find signs that the silo has been deactivated."

"Such a waste," she said. "I've heard that people are buying the old missile silos and renovating them into living spaces."

For him, it was hard to believe that anyone would voluntarily live underground without natural light. He shuddered. The Piper took a big bounce, and Spence did some controlled breathing.

He needed something to distract him. "Suppose we find the silo, what does it mean?"

"It's a physical indication of a problem in the computer system." Her shoulders shrugged. "In short, it's evidence. This missile silo was erased from the maps and the computer records. It's gone off-line, which means NORAD doesn't control the launch system."

"Let me see if I've got it," he said. "The bad guys who are selling these nukes on the dark web have control of weapons that supposedly don't exist."

"I need to verify with the computer records," she said, "but that's the basic plot."

Altering a computer program was something he could understand, but he was having a hard time with the concept of physically erasing the missile silos. "The military doesn't drop off these warheads and abandon them. There are launch crews who handle several installations. The way I understand it, these are the guys who make the final decision to push the button."

"They're called missileers," she said. "It's a specialized job in the air force."

The way she'd outlined the plot to steal seven nukes required a plan that was put into effect a long time ago.

"In the late fifties and early sixties, the perpetrators had to disguise the locations without anybody knowing."

"And change the computer programs," she said. "We're talking about primitive machines and software. That's what makes this plan nearly unstoppable. Even if we find the nukes, we have to figure out how the old computers worked."

"That's your department."

"Hold on to your seat," she said. "We're here."

She swooped from the sky and guided the Piper toward a gravel road that was barely visible in the dusk. Aiming for a road seemed more sensible than testing their luck on a field with splotches of snow.

Every muscle in his body tensed. He trusted her, believed in her and her abilities. He loved her. This wasn't the first time he'd thought those words or said them, but her amnesia had given him a restart. This time—when he told her—it might be the only time she remembered.

He wanted to make it special with a proposal of marriage and a diamond ring.

The tundra tires of the Piper made contact with the gravel road and they bounced several yards before coming to a complete stop. He couldn't wait to get out of the plane. When his feet hit the ground, his legs wobbled. He lurched forward, telling himself to shake it off. At the same time, his meditative side—the part of him that focused on breathing and sensitivity—was grateful beyond belief.

Both sides wanted her. He flung his arms around her shoulders. "You're amazing."

"Thanks." She snuggled against him. "Flying was never a big deal in my household."

They'd grown up in different worlds. He hadn't taken

a commercial flight until he left the foster care system for college. Sometimes, he thought her father was right, and he wasn't good enough for Angelica. The only way to find out was to ask her. After they completed this assignment, he'd propose. That seemed fair enough. All he needed to do before claiming her as his bride was to save the world.

She pointed to a stand of trees in the middle of an open field. "That's a landmark. The silo is near that."

"How near?"

"It's hard to tell from an aerial photo," she said.

"Does this land belong to anybody?"

"I don't know."

He figured it was a good sign that the field wasn't marked off by a barbed wire fence. The road she'd used to land was actually a long straight driveway leading to a ramshackle house that looked like it hadn't been inhabited in years. Colorado might pride itself on being the epicenter of new growth with a constant influx of new residents, but there were still desolate places like this relatively flat area.

He followed her as she trekked across the field. Though the land was cold and frozen, the weather system that brought the snow hadn't extended this far south. When they reached the trees, she made a left and followed the meanderings of a creek that was little more than a trickle.

His sense of direction was pretty good and he'd studied the contours of the land on the maps. He jumped the creek. "This way."

Approaching a rise in the land that marked the edge of a forest, he looked to the right. The last streaks of sunset were almost gone, and he pulled out a wide-beam flashlight.

She added a Maglite of her own. "It's going to be hard to find anything in the dark."

"A missile silo doesn't just disappear."

After all these years, tire tracks or indentations from heavy equipment would be long gone. Nature reclaimed objects that were left standing. Technology had been developed to x-ray the earth and see what was below the surface, but there wasn't time for that kind of search. By this time tomorrow, there would be only a few hours left before the deadline on the sixteenth.

She pointed her flashlight beam at a mound of earth that had looked suspicious on the aerial photography maps. "I think we should dig."

Easier said than done, the top layer of earth was frozen and they didn't have a real good idea what they were looking for. "Did you bring a shovel?"

"I'm sure there's something in the back of the plane."

The gallant thing to do would be to offer to search for it, but he had no desire to squeeze himself into the tiny Piper any sooner than he had to. Dropping to his knees beside the mound, he said, "You find the shovel. I'll start digging."

He pulled on his gloves, aimed the flashlight so he could see what he was doing and clawed into the frozen earth. His fingers barely made a dent. Without a shovel, this would be slow going. He contented himself with clearing the rocks and other debris.

She returned with the shovel—one of those flimsy collapsible tools that campers used. "Find anything?"

"No, but I agree with you. This is the most likely spot for the silo. I see subtle differences in the vegetation, and it makes me think this soil has been disturbed and then replaced."

"Would it still be different after so many years?"

"It might have been reopened more recently." The seeds to this crime were planted many years ago, but the current plot required awareness of the sites and the technology. "They needed to run checks on the missile and warheads inside."

She nodded. "How do you know so much about vegetation?"

"Searches for hidden graves. Some of the work at so-called body farms was pioneered in Colorado." Forensic anthropologists spent years deciphering their scientific studies of body decomposition and placement at different burial levels. "Not a fan."

"I've heard about the body farms. When I was in high school, a local aerial photographer found the hidden grave of a woman who had gone missing two years earlier. The earth was concave and the flowers different."

He took the shovel from her and stabbed into the mound. After the outer crust was broken, the dirt crumbled easily. If he'd been using a good shovel instead of this collapsible tool, he would have made faster progress, but the physical exercise satisfied his need to feel useful. She might be the brains in this partnership, but when it came to digging a hole, he was needed.

He plunged the blade of the shovel deep and heard a metallic clunk. Pulling back, he repeated the gesture. He had definitely hit something solid.

"I can't believe it," Angelica whispered. Her tone was reverent, as though singing in Trudy's choir. "This is it. We've found the silo."

"We'd better be sure."

He continued to dig, pulling up large chunks of earth. The clang of the metal shovel against the top of the missile silo echoed in the night. "New problem," he said. "What are we going to do with this? We can't just leave it here, exposed."

"And we don't know who we can trust at NORAD," she said. "Until we've found all seven installations, it's better to keep the traitors in the dark."

"Right," he said, still digging. "If we show our hand too soon, they might set off a nuke to prove that they can."

He'd uncovered enough of the round metal lid on a short concrete base to be satisfied that he'd found the silo. He threw down the shovel and stepped back. "I have people I can talk to at Quantico. We need to get experts out here to deactivate the warheads."

"Until someone else arrives, we'd better wait."

He slung his arm around her waist and pulled her close for a long, thorough kiss. He glanced toward the tiny airplane. If there had been more room, they could have gotten cozy in there. It might still work. He might be able to cram himself into the back. "Does it count for the mile-high club if the plane is on the ground?"

"Why would we try? When I went looking for the shovel, I found some lovely camping gear, including a tent and thermal sleeping bags that are probably good for subzero weather."

"That's what I love about Colorado. People here are ready to camp, 24/7."

"Not everybody is outdoorsy."

Growing up on the street, he was outside all the time, finding an escape from a usually overcrowded home.

He considered a vacant lot on the corner to be the great outdoors. But that wasn't his choice.

While he got busy on his cell phone, she set up a little nest using a tent, sleeping bags and a high-powered lantern. When she finished, she gave him a sexy wave, crawled into the tent and closed the flap.

His supervisory agent was enthusiastic about what they'd uncovered and understood the need for their investigation to be kept secret from everybody in Colorado. He promised to put things in motion and would call back with further questions and instructions.

Spence ended the call and approached the pup tent. He opened the flap. Inside, Angelica had zippered the thermal sleeping bags together and crawled inside.

"Don't make me wait any longer," she said.

"Or else?"

"I'll shred you like a cougar."

In the glow of the lantern, he saw that her arm was bare. Stretched out beside her, he pulled back the sleeping bag. Naked, she welcomed him with a teasing growl.

She was his favorite breed of wildlife.

Chapter Nineteen

Why hadn't they killed me? Angelica found herself asking that question over and over as she and Spence turned the missile silo over to a team of specialists. These missileers from the air force would disarm the ICBM's, deactivate the nukes and make the silo disappear again.

While she and Spence returned to Peterson AFB, the steady hum of the engine on the single-prop Piper relaxed her mind. Again, she considered the issue that Spence had raised early in their investigation. It made sense for the men who abducted her to kill her, to eliminate the threat. *Why am I still alive?*

She was exceedingly happy that they hadn't done the rational thing but couldn't help wondering why they dropped her off. According to Trevor, the thugs had been specifically instructed not to harm her.

After they landed, they came back to the hotel to catch some zees and regroup. Food was a priority. They'd ordered room service for another late-night meal. Sitting at the table in their hotel suite, she forked a bite of salad from the room service plate. She'd ordered blackened salmon, and it looked delicious. Spence ignored his healthy salad and gnawed on spare ribs. He'd been brilliant at the missile site. She'd come to expect his expertise in all things sensual, and he'd heated up their impromptu campsite in many amazing ways. But he'd also proved himself to be efficient and well-organized.

After he made a series of phone calls, it had taken less than two hours for the missileer experts to arrive. Under the supervision of an air force intelligence officer, they went right to work. Other teams were ready to roll as soon as they discovered the other sites.

Though she hoped the black hats would never know they'd been there, she realized that these were computer experts who would surely notice that one of their missiles had been deactivated. That was only one of many concerns.

"As soon as we're done eating," Spence said, "we'll get started on the other maps."

"Finding the other six won't be as hard as locating the first one." Other phone calls he'd made while they were waiting had recruited several unimpeachable researchers to compare the maps. She'd sent copies as soon as they landed at Peterson AFB. "You're really good at delegating."

"Call it a lazy man's skill. The more work other people take on, the less I have on my plate."

Lazy was the last word she'd use to describe him. With nothing but a cell phone, he'd mobilized a national research project that might prevent a nuclear strike. She checked the time on her cell phone. "Almost midnight."

"Tomorrow is the last day before the strike."

"What if they figure out what we're doing and make their move earlier?"

He cringed. "We have to hope and pray that they don't."

So much could go wrong. They might not find all the sites, even with teams of researchers. The deactivation of the nukes could be mishandled.

"We need to go to Cheyenne Mountain." The only surefire way to stop a launch was for her to reassert the computer protocols. "I need to tap into their computer system from the sixties."

"Can't you do it from a different machine?"

"The modern computers don't speak the same language as the early models."

And she didn't mind entering the Complex. Going inside was always exciting from a scientific standpoint even though the atmosphere made her nervous. The hollowed-out mountain had been constructed during a paranoid era to hold and preserve the nation's most dangerous secrets concerning military weaponry. It was a fortress, intimidating.

But she needed their old computers. If she could get them up and running, she could take the missiles offline herself. "The Complex is probably on high alert."

"Not because of us," he said. "I made it clear that none of this information was to be shared with the people who work at Peterson or Cheyenne Mountain or the local FBI."

"What about the missileers? Those men are air force."

"And we're holding them in safe houses and top secret locations until this is over." He chewed the last shred of rib meat from the bone. "You've barely touched your food."

"I'm worried," she admitted.

Why am I still alive? Lex Heller and the bad guys had gone to a great deal of trouble to abduct her, pick

her brain and give her amnesia. If they truly wanted
to keep their plans secret, why would they risk leaving her alive?

Someone was protecting her. The conclusion was inescapable. A person who cared about her had stepped in
and ordered that she be spared. She could only think of
two men who filled that bill: Professor Morris Fletcher,
her first mentor; and her dad.

There was more evidence against those two. While
abducted, she'd overheard someone refer repeatedly to
"the old man." Again, Fletch and her father fit the bill.
And, most damning of all, the long-ago hiding of the
missile silos had to be done by someone who worked
with NORAD and was active in the early sixties.

Elbow on the table, she rested her chin on her fist
and poked at her salmon with the other hand. "Who do
you think did this?"

"Dunne played a part. I'm sure about that."

"Why?"

"He shows sociopathic tendencies. I suspect he murdered Heller. His alibi is bogus. He was pushing the
computer photo of Heller's body, trying to convince
me it was *not* taken by the killer."

"He's innately creepy," she said. "I'll agree to that,
but I'm not sure he's a murderer."

"And I think he shot his friend and took the computer picture to use as a sort of trophy. When I inter-
viewed him, he was quick to throw Lambert under the
bus. Dunne is not a nice guy." He took a long drink of
water. "But he's definitely not a mastermind."

She agreed. "I want to find the person behind the
curtain, the instigator. Who set this operation in motion? Who's in control?"

He reached for her plate. "If you're not going to eat, I'll take your fries."

"Go ahead. I'm not hungry. You might as well take the salmon, too."

"Fish—" he pulled a face "—yuck."

"You sound like a kid."

"I swear I'm a grown man, fully grown." His eyelids lowered to half-mast, and there was something sexy about the way he looked at her. He stroked the dark blond stubble on his chin. "Do you want me to shave?"

"Leave the beard."

"It makes me outdoorsy." He patted his cheek. "Like the Colorado dudes you grew up with."

"I never knew anybody like you."

"Ditto."

Her finger stroked her lip, which was mostly healed. They'd been careful about kissing too hard, and she was ready for that caution to end. "Leave the beard. I'm curious to see what it feels like."

"Let me show you."

He rose from the table and took her hand in an absurdly courtly gesture. Now she had an appetite. She wanted him.

She stood, stepped into his embrace and went up on her tiptoes to rub her cheek against his stubble. The texture was interesting. Not exactly sandpaper, but it was a little prickly. "Doesn't feel like fur."

"Maybe if it was longer…"

"Up to you." She wasn't crazy about beards but didn't totally hate them. His seemed to grow fast.

He trailed the back of his hand along her throat. "Maybe my stubble would feel better in the hot tub."

"I'd feel better," she said. "Let's do it."

In a matter of moments, they had the water heated and the jets pulsing. The hot tub area was an addition to the hotel bathroom and had windows on two sides. They were up high enough so they could look down on the lights of Colorado Springs and still have full privacy. Spence hadn't bothered with a bathrobe. He shed his clothes and strolled around naked and confident. *Well, why wouldn't he be?*

She was more self-conscious. She tested the water with her toe, allowed the robe to slip from her shoulders and climbed in. As she lowered herself into the steaming, churning water, she felt his gaze resting upon her, studying her every move as though he'd never seen her before.

On the opposite side, he glided into the water. "How much do you remember about us?"

"I've been so busy trying to concentrate on the investigation that I haven't tried to put together a chronology."

"First date," he said.

"I know we started dating about six months ago after we worked together on an assignment. And I remember that we both hesitated because we thought it wasn't smart to date a person you worked with."

"We were never supposed to be on the same case," he said. "Never again."

"Oops."

He ducked his head under the water, bobbed to the surface and shook like a dog. "You already told me you remembered *Camelot.*"

The jets massaged her arms and shoulders. The bruise on her hip only ached a little bit. Another memory resonated in her mind. It was when he told her that he loved her for the first time. They'd just finished having sex, and the moment hadn't been terribly romantic. It took her a few days to respond. "Why are you asking about this?"

"If you've forgotten things about our relationship, it'll seem like the first time when I do them again."

"I can't believe this." She shook her head. "You want a do-over? A free pass?"

"I want to do this right." He scooted close to her and lifted her palms to his cheeks. "Touch the beard."

"You're right. It's much softer when we're wet."

"And it'll be even better when we kiss."

She joined her mouth with his and tasted his lips. Gently, his hands dived to stroke the most sensitive parts of her body. She returned the favor.

"I never forgot this," she whispered. "I remember the very good, exceptionally good sex."

She was happy to splash and grope and make love until they fell into bed exhausted. They needed the sleep. Tomorrow was the last day before the deadline.

Chapter Twenty

By seven o'clock the next morning, they were both up and dressed and steeped in information. At the table, Spence shuffled through their collection of maps, reading the location coordinates and talking to his Quantico SSA on the cell phone. He knew they were behind schedule and hoped their frantic efforts weren't futile. Last night, the researchers had only located three more of the off-line silos. Not good enough.

Three missiles were still unaccounted for. He recalled the words Angelica had spoken when he directed her through the guided meditation: *It only takes one.*

One nuclear strike would destroy a city, kill thousands and poison thousands more. The surrounding farmland and forests would take years to come back from the devastation. He and his supervisor had discussed the possible evacuation of Dallas, but Angelica talked him out of it, pointing out that the black hats could change their target.

She continued to pour over the maps, comparing them sector by sector. She'd gone from using her dad's map to another from a few years later. She'd alerted the researchers and sent them coded computerized messages indicating the new places to search.

"Wake up," his SSA barked. "You're fading out on me, buddy. I need you to be alert."

"Should I start rounding up suspects? Taking them into custody? I could use the local FBI."

"You told me you didn't trust the other feds in town. That's why I took Sheeran off the case."

"Right." He didn't trust anybody. Not the FBI or the air force or Angelica's dad. But he couldn't arrest them all.

"I sure as hell hope this investigation isn't based on some kind of lover's quarrel."

"With Sheeran? Hah! There's nothing between us. There never was."

"That's not how I heard it."

"You heard wrong."

"Come on, Spence, level with me. You're good at your job, but sometimes you get careless, especially when women are involved."

"Not this time," he said. "I've never been so cautious. Angelica turned my computer into an encoded device, which, as you well know, can be hacked, but it's harder. And I'm talking to you on a burner phone that can't be traced."

His years of undercover work had taught him to keep several alternate communications devices. When he ended his call, Spence was irritated. He was juggling as many balls as he could keep in the air and didn't need to be bothered with old gossip and innuendo.

He heard a rap on the hotel suite door. Looking through the peephole, he saw the great, big, redheaded problem glaring back at him. He whipped the door open.

"Not a good time, Sheeran."

"You can call me Raquel." She tried to enter, but he blocked her path. "We're friends, aren't we?"

"I'm busy."

"Too bad."

She jammed a straight arm against his chest and shoved. She dodged to the left, agile as a running back, but she was wearing her high-heeled boots. The only way he'd keep her out would be to tackle her, and that wasn't going to happen.

He stepped aside. "What do you want?"

"An honest update," she said. "There's something big happening, and I'm out of the loop."

"The decision was made at Quantico." Keeping her out was his idea, but he didn't actually issue the orders. "Take it up with them."

"This is my town, where I have my contacts and my snitches. I've got relationships with just about everybody."

"I'll bet you do."

"This isn't right. I should be in charge."

Angelica strolled into the room. After a night of tension and very little sleep, she should have been a wreck, but the color in her cheeks was high and her jaw thrust forward. She looked as formidable as her father, without the bushy eyebrows.

"Technically," she said, "I'm in charge. This isn't a matter of seniority but of expertise. Bottom line, it's a cyber crime. And I'm the expert."

"At least tell me the crime."

"You reported it," Angelica said. "The black hats are knocking on the door, hacking at NORAD and trying to steal our military secrets."

Spence was impressed by the way she danced at the

edge of the truth without actually betraying any information. He was more inclined to take physical action, picking up the SSA bodily and hurling her through the door.

Sheeran wasn't going anywhere. With an unwarranted sense of entitlement, she planted her bottom on the sofa. "I'm here to help. I'll do anything."

Angelica tested the offer. "Would you please make a fresh pot of coffee?"

Instead of flaring up, Sheeran went to the landline phone in the suite and called room service. In addition to coffee, she ordered breakfast.

He pulled Angelica into the bathroom and closed the door. "You've got to get rid of her. She's up to something."

"How do you know?"

"You're going to have to trust me," he said, "the same way I trusted you to fly that tin can through the night skies."

"You also said something about keeping your enemies close. We shouldn't tell Sheeran what we're really investigating, but she might be useful."

"The way a mongoose is useful to a cobra," he muttered.

She patted his cheek, which was clean-shaven again. He expected to be dealing with military personnel today, and they appreciated grooming. Following that line of thinking, he'd put on a button-down shirt with his jeans. A navy blazer would go over his shoulder holster.

Likewise, Angelica wore a fitted black pantsuit with sensible boots and a rose gold chain. She fiddled with the matching, engraved locket that dangled from the chain. "I spoke to Lambert, and he's arranged for us to get into the Cheyenne Mountain Complex this morning."

"We're not taking Sheeran there, are we?"

"Actually, I was thinking of inviting a few others. I'd like to have Fletch with me."

He shouldn't have to remind her that her former mentor was one of their suspects. "Why?"

"He knows more about the old computers than I do."

They were assembling a potentially combustible group, but she might be right about keeping a close watch on the enemy. If Spence was standing over them, none of these people could launch a missile.

THE DRIVE UP the side of Cheyenne Mountain to the North Portal entrance was winding and steep. After yesterday's blue skies, another cold front had moved in. It hadn't yet started snowing, but the wind battered their SUV, promising worse weather to come.

Spence drove the lead vehicle in their little caravan. He'd insisted on riding alone with Angelica so they'd have a chance to talk without being overheard. Holding in all the sensitive information while outsiders hovered wasn't easy. And the outsiders had multiplied.

Following them in another SUV, SSA Sheeran brought along her two coworkers, SA Ramirez and SA Tapper. Bringing up the rear was Dunne, Lambert and Professor Fletcher. It was a motley crew, held together by curiosity and mistrust.

With his hands-free phone, he'd spoken to his supervisor and discovered that not much had been accomplished. No other missiles had been discovered and deactivated. The total stood at four, which made it even more important for Angelica to figure out the computers and stop any attempt to launch.

Spence's supervisor had communicated with Angelica's bosses at Cyber Security, and her supervisor spoke to her. After he complimented her work, he issued an order.

"We have decided, in conjunction with the FBI, to stop investigating at six o'clock MST. At that time, you and Spence will step down."

Not what she wanted to hear. "Should we return to headquarters?"

"I'd like for you to stay on as an observer. The military will be called in and NORAD will go on high alert."

She swallowed hard, choking back her fear. This would be the moment when the fighter jets scrambled and other silos were opened and ready to strike back. "What if we need more time?"

"That's a risk we can't take. We need to be prepared for the assault."

Before he hung up, Angelica thanked him. "I appreciate that you let me contact Professor Fletcher as a consultant. I need his expert advice."

Her supervisor signed off with words of encouragement. Angelica had never heard this tough, taciturn federal agent sound so sincere. Nuclear threats had a way of bringing out the best in people. Or the worst.

She reached across the console and patted Spence's arm. "Did you get the word about pulling the plug on our investigation at six?"

"That only leaves us a few hours to find the people behind this scheme and to end it."

Tension squeezed her lungs. She was breathless. "Do you think we can do it?"

"We can do anything."

She appreciated his bravado. "On a totally different topic, I want to thank you. When the professor insisted that Dunne come along, you agreed."

"He's a loon."

"I don't know why the professor likes him."

"The first time I saw him today, Dunne told me that he was sure Lambert killed Heller. Apparently, Lambert confided to him that he'd left the professor's house to make a quick run to the store."

"Did he suggest a motive?" she asked. "Why would Lambert shoot his friend?"

"Professional jealousy."

"Of what? They both work in midlevel jobs at Peterson AFB." She held up her hand. "Wait! Let me guess, they were doing a computer start-up. It's the sad, well-worn story of Jobs and Wozniak at Apple."

"According to Dunne, they didn't aim that high," he said. "They're inventing the software for a game together."

"And why, according to him, did Lambert feel compelled to take a photo?"

"Dunne didn't have an answer for that one, but he tells the rest of the story convincingly. When sociopaths lie, they flesh out details, almost believing the lie really happened."

"How dangerous is he?"

"I don't think he'll try anything when he's surrounded by gun-toting air force personnel."

Dunne and Fletcher would be accompanied and supervised every step of the way. It required Level One clearance to enter the Complex. The FBI agents were another story. They could roam almost at will.

Approaching the three-story-tall Portal door, which stood at an elevation of about seven thousand feet, Spence marveled at the sheer size and scope of the engineering feat. He'd studied the blueprints for the impregnable bunker. The hollowed-out chambers covered about five acres. There were fifteen buildings and all were three stories tall. The reservoir, filled by a natural spring, was big enough for a rowboat.

Once inside, there was no immediate access to the outside world. Many of the office buildings had windows that displayed a camera feed of the parking lot or farther up the mountain. The ceilings in the main chamber reached high, and the light from the generators kept it from feeling like they were trapped inside a cave. He doubted his minor claustrophobia would bother him.

After they parked, their group clustered while air force guides dressed in camo and berets gave them the basic rules. *Don't touch anything. Don't go wandering off by yourself.*

They also confiscated all weapons and cell phones. Though he hated giving up his own guns, Spence was glad when SSA Sheeran and her two buddies were disarmed. Though he had nothing specific that pointed to their guilt, he didn't trust those three.

They were driven down the main tunnel to the entrance through the twenty-five-ton North blast door. Made of solid steel, the thick door stood open.

"The last time it was closed," the professor said, "was September 11. Our country never needed to use Cheyenne Mountain as a wartime bunker, but that's really what it is."

While Spence inspected the remarkable black door, Angelica asked her former mentor, "When was the first time you visited the Complex?"

"Dear me, it was so long ago. I don't remember the date, but Nixon was President. I was a student at University of Denver, and a bunch of us had a chance to take the tour. The Complex was remarkable. It influenced my decision to stick with computer technology."

On the other side of the blast door was a second protective door, similar to the first. As they proceeded down the corridor leading to the main chamber, Fletch continued to lecture. The man was a teacher, after all. He had a lot to say about the engineering and the excavation. When they came to the buildings, he got down on one knee to examine the hundreds of heavy-duty springs that made up the building's support system.

"These structures can't have basements," he said, "not without pile-driving through bedrock. And so, they used these springs, which serve the purpose of balancing the building in case of an earthquake or a slight shift."

Lambert had sidled up beside Spence. Quietly, he asked, "May I have a word?"

"Make it quick. Angelica might need your help in the computer area."

When they separated from the others, one of the guards stayed behind with them. Spence was glad to see the high level of vigilance.

"You've been talking to Dunne," Lambert said.

"Yes."

Lambert pushed his thick glasses up on his nose. "He's a liar, and he told me to lie about the alibi."

"After you left Heller's apartment, how long were you at the professor's house?"

"The whole time," he said, "But I wasn't with the other two. I was working on software for a gaming system."

"A project you shared with Heller."

"That's right." He stuck a plump finger under his glasses to wipe away a tear. "I don't think I can get it done without him. I'll try, but it was both of us. Sexy Lexy and Big Bo."

The racy characterization of these nerds amused Spence. He bit his lip to keep from smiling. "You were good friends."

"The best."

Dunne peeled off from the main group and charged toward them. Walking and talking at the same time, he said, "Don't listen to this pudgy weasel. He's jealous of me."

"Am not." Lambert stamped his sneaker on the floor. "You're a loser who works at a coffee shop. I'm a computer engineer."

Dunne waved to the professor. "Fletcher, did you hear what he said to me?"

The professor made a clumsy pivot and came back toward them, walking carefully. "Stop fighting, boys."

Angelica accompanied the older man, who clung to her arm as he shuffled along. Spence watched these separate, distinct persons as they arranged themselves in a circle. Dunne, the sociopath, waved his arms and made wild pronouncements about how Lambert was jealous and plotting. Lambert puffed out his chest and objected, although he was clearly intimidated by Dunne. The professor stroked his beard and mumbled in an attempt to make peace. Angelica didn't fit with the others. Though operating under a literal life-and-death situation, she kept her shoulders straight and her mouth shut.

Dunne blasted a final accusation at Lambert. "You think you're real clever with your new game, but the professor thinks it's boring and just like every other game."

"Is that true?" Lambert looked toward Fletch with pleading eyes. "You think I'm boring."

"He's not going to admit it because he's too polite, but I know the truth." Dunne sneered and said, "The old man doesn't like it."

As soon as he spoke, Angelica gasped loudly. When Spence turned and looked at her, he saw recognition in her eyes. She'd told him about hearing the very words that Dunne had spoken.

"It was you." She pointed at Dunne. "You were one of the people who abducted me."

Chapter Twenty-One

Those words about the old man were branded on Angelica's memory. Not even drugs and amnesia managed to erase them. Her first thought was that they were talking about her father, that somehow, he was involved in this treasonous plot. But Dunne had inadvertently named Professor Fletch as the old man who wanted to protect her. The facts didn't make sense. She couldn't believe he would perform such a traitorous act. Could he be the "old man," and still be innocent of the larger crimes?

Spence clamped his huge hand around Dunne's arm like an iron manacle. "You heard what she said. You were part of the group that kidnapped her."

Showing absolutely no remorse, he said, "Maybe I was."

Rather than locking Dunne up and throwing away the key, she watched as Spence tried not to be intimidating. He'd told her that the best way to manage a guy like Dunne was to sit back and let him talk. "Tell me about it."

"You should be thanking me." Dunne pointed at her. "I'm the one that told them not to hurt you. I protected you."

That was a screwy way of looking at kidnapping and

dosing her with drugs, but she didn't question his logic. There was something bigger at stake. He had information they needed. If he gave them names, they might be able to arrest the leaders and end the threat.

"I wasn't mistreated." She forced a smile. "And I thank you for the role you played in keeping me unharmed."

"It was all me. The other guys wanted to throw you off the edge of a mountain and see how high you'd bounce...except for the guy with the amnesia drugs. Oh, yeah, that was smart, really smart. We could let you go, and you couldn't rat us out."

"Why did you want to protect me?"

"Don't flatter yourself, babe. I don't have a crush on you." He scoffed at Lambert. "I'm not like him or this old man."

Fletch took Dunne's free hand and held it against his heart. His eyes were terribly sad. "I could have done more for you, Howie Dunne. You're not a bad man, I know you aren't."

"You're the only person who thinks that," he said. "That's why I couldn't let them kill her. If Angelica was hurt, I knew it would make you sad."

Fletch nodded. "You know me well."

"You're like a father, better than my father."

She would have been touched by this deep friendship if Dunne hadn't been so crazy. His emotions were askew, and his only truth was an admiration for Fletch.

Spence turned Dunne toward him. "Heller was there with you."

"Heller got me into this mess," Dunne said. "He was flashing around all this cash money, always hundreds. It started with easy stuff, dropping off a car or picking up a package. And I got paid a whole lot more than I ever made as a barista."

"What was the price for keeping an eye on Angelica?"

"A cool thousand."

The professor bowed his head. "If you wanted money, all you had to do was ask me."

"I like paying my own way."

She found his rationale totally unbelievable. He was equating his criminal endeavors with an honest day's work. "Did you have any idea what you were doing? Or the risk to other people? Did Heller bother to explain that he and his buddies wanted to nuke an entire city?"

"I found out," he said, "after the fact. They were talking about ICBMs and missile silos."

"And you knew it was wrong," Spence said. "Before that, right and wrong didn't mean very much."

"You're reading my mind." Dunne gave a short, mirthless laugh. "I went to Heller's house to tell him that I quit. No more of these jobs for me."

"And he told you that you couldn't leave," Spence said.

"So I shot him."

If she gave him the benefit of the doubt, his twisted morality made sense. He had committed murder, thinking he would stop a greater crime. More likely, he killed Heller because their partnership had become inconvenient.

"Were there others?" Spence asked. "Is there anyone else you can name?"

He shook his head. "Are they going to cut off my bun in prison?"

He'd be lucky if that was the only thing that got cut off, but she didn't say anything else.

Spence spoke to their guides for a moment. Then he returned to the group, still holding on to Dunne's arm. "I know Angelica's anxious to get started. Lambert and the professor will accompany her, and I'll catch up later."

"We'll go with Spence," SSA Sheeran said. "He might need our help interrogating this killer."

Angelica didn't gloat over Sheeran's failure as an interrogator. She'd had the first chance to question Dunne when she picked him up at the hotel that first night. Also, she'd spent significant time with him over the last few days. Was she keeping something a secret? What did she think she could do to get him talking?

She walked a few paces, flanked by Lambert and the professor. The old man's step slowed to a crawl, and she sent one of their escorts to find a wheelchair for him. They sat on a bench outside one of the buildings.

"It feels like we're waiting for a bus," she said as she took the professor's hand. "But this Complex is a bit small for mass transit."

Lambert piped up, "I've seen a couple of those little electric cars. Those could be taxis."

"Professor," she said, "I'm sorry about Dunne."

"The boy is sick, very sick. I thought I could save him and get him on the right track, but my help just wasn't enough." Inside his beard, he smiled sadly. "I try to heal all the young people I mentor."

"Not me," she said.

"Not you," Lambert echoed. "You're perfect."

But she hadn't been this confident when the professor took her under his wing. In addition to learning computers, they'd spent hours talking. Back in those days, she'd been so afraid of failing her father that she was almost paralyzed by that fear. Fletch helped her separate from him, and then she had learned to leave her mentor behind, too.

"You've changed," the professor said. "But you're still attracted to strong men, like Spence."

"Is he good for me?"

"You have to decide for yourself."

When he was seated in the wheelchair, they proceeded to the storage area for input data and computers. A regular business would have thrown all this outdated stuff away, but Cheyenne Mountain Complex was an air force installation, and the military never threw away anything.

"What are we looking for?" Lambert asked.

"Software that can be used to activate missiles from the late fifties or early sixties, and we need to find a computer that can process that software."

"A history project," he said brightly.

Fletcher gave them an idea of earmarks to look for while he searched for a machine that was still in working condition. The whole process gave her a greater appreciation for the early days of computers. Their functions might not have been as complex as current machines, but the innovation was stunning.

For over an hour, she and Lambert dug through a mountain of data. When they found promising software, they placed it on a table in front of Fletch. He did further study on several, but none got the thumbs-up.

She was glad to be busy. The activity kept her mind off the ticktock counting down to six o'clock, when the military would be put on high alert and the missile launch would be almost inevitable.

She placed a spreadsheet with dot matrix printing in front of the professor. "This looks like it has something to do with a launch. And it's dated 1959."

He tilted his head to see through his bifocals and slowly nodded. "You might have something significant here."

She sat beside him at the worktable as he plugged codes into the old computer console Lambert had uncovered. After only a few minutes, the printout came rolling out in the form of ticker tape.

"We're on the right track," the professor said.

She sent one of the guards to find Spence and bring him back here. He needed to know about the progress they'd made and to pass that information on to his boss. If other silos had been uncovered, they might be able to deactivate the launch from here. In the meantime, she and Lambert and the Professor continued to shift and adjust and input and print.

The guard returned and pulled her aside. "I can't find him."

"What about Sheeran and the other FBI agents?"

"Also missing."

The time was half past two. There was probably a reasonable explanation for Spence disappearing with Dunne, but she couldn't think of anything right now. She returned to the worktable, where the professor and Lambert were still trying to figure out what they had.

"Stay here," she said firmly. "Don't let anyone in unless they're with me."

She repeated those instructions to the guards. Then she was out of the computer storage building. Spence and the others were supposed to be in the communications command center, another three-story building with offices and video rooms. Running through the Complex without protection was foolish; she'd already been abducted once and didn't want it to happen again. At random, she approached two armed military police, who were dressed in green camouflage and held rifles. "Excuse me," she said. "I need your help."

The young men exchanged a glance. "Sorry, ma'am, we have an assignment and can't leave our post."

"My father is General Thorne." There were times when it was essential to pull rank. "Make the necessary call, get permission to leave your post and come with me."

After they spoke into a walkie-talkie for a moment, they faced her and saluted. "At your service, Special Agent Thorne."

"I'm looking for some FBI agents." She gave a description of the group. "They were supposed to be in this building, but I think I know a better way to search than running from place to place. Have you got security cameras?"

They escorted her to the area where several security screens covered the wall. Before she could even describe Spence and the others, the supervisor, a civilian, pulled up photos from the IDs they had handed over at the gate.

"Handy," she said. There wasn't an expectation of privacy in a supersecure location like this one. "Can you track these four?"

"Over what time period?"

"The past hour," she said.

She watched the screen that showed the entrance

to the communications building. They had entered together. There were a few images of them inside the building, but the interior surveillance wasn't as pervasive as the exterior.

"Over here." The supervisor pointed to a screen that showed water lapping against the walls of a cavern. "That's our reservoir. Nobody is supposed to be there without permission."

But there was a man, running. He wore a crazy Hawaiian shirt. It had to be Dunne. "When was this taken?"

"It's happening right now."

She turned to the air force guys she'd recruited at random. "Take me there."

"You might want to wait," the supervisor said.

Angelica turned her attention to the drama being played out on the surveillance screen. Dunne had jumped into a rowboat that was attached to a very short dock. He yanked the mooring loose, but before he could shove off, he froze.

Though there was no sound on the surveillance screen, she saw Dunne's mouth moving and imagined him shouting at someone who was unseen in this camera view. Dunne threw both hands over his head.

Before he could climb from the boat, he was shot in the chest. He crumpled onto the deck.

Chapter Twenty-Two

Spence had seen trouble coming, but he was unable to stop it. He rolled onto his side, propped himself up on his right elbow and pried open his eyelids. Blood soaked the shoulder of his sport jacket. He painfully twisted around, trying to apply pressure. If the knife had been a few inches lower, he would have had a punctured lung.

Where was he? The wall behind him was granite. He stared at the white, tightly coiled, heavy-duty springs that supported the weight of the building. How did he get here?

A wave of nausea swept over him. He closed his eyes and tried to remember what had happened.

He'd just finished his interview with Dunne when Sheeran joined him in the office he'd been using at the communication center. Both he and Dunne had gone silent when she entered. A sense of danger had pervaded the room. With the high heels on her boots clunking on the tile floor, she'd circled the desk.

Her attack had been fast and deadly. She yanked Dunne from his chair and held him in front of her with a sharp, thin blade aimed at his carotid artery.

"Do what I say, Spence. Or he dies."

"How did you get the knife past the metal detector?"

"It's high-grade plastic, sharp enough to slice through metal. I always carry an extra weapon in my boot."

Her instructions to him had been simple. She wanted him to use his handcuffs and fasten himself to the desk, stay in this office and let her get away.

"I don't have cuffs with me," he said. "What did you do with the other two agents?"

"They work for me." Her cool grin was pure evil. "Agent Tapper, my computer expert, will launch the strike against Dallas. Ramirez has international contacts."

"Ramirez," Dunne piped up. "I thought I recognized him. Was he running the kidnapping?"

"And not doing a very good job at it," she said. "He got nervous about killing Angelica, didn't want to be responsible for the murder of a federal agent."

Yet, he didn't seem to mind blowing up an entire city?

Spence hoped and prayed that the expert researchers had managed to find and deactivate the rest of the silos. There wasn't much time left, and he was pretty sure he wouldn't be able to stop this crazy witch. She was revealing details that she shouldn't tell, which meant that whether or not he had cuffs, she had to kill him.

"Why are you doing this?" he asked.

"It's my legacy. The millions I get from selling these warheads are my inheritance from my loving father, who never quite got his act together. Did I mention that he worked right here at Cheyenne Mountain Complex?"

"You said he served under General Thorne."

"And also right here. Last year, he died and told me what he'd done."

"Fifty years ago, your father took seven missile silos off-line," Spence said.

"I'm impressed," she said. "You and your little sweetie figured that out. What else do you know?"

"Here's what I don't understand," he said. "Why did you report the hack? Why call attention to it?"

"To cover my behind," she said. "Heller showed me the paperwork, and I soft-pedalled it. Everybody hacks everybody else, and nobody much cares. I mean, look at the FBI response to my report that there's evidence of hacking at NORAD. After a few, they send two agents pretending to be undercover. Pathetic."

Dunne wriggled in her arms, and she drew her blade across his cheek. Blood ran down his face. "If it weren't for this moron and his friend Heller stirring up trouble, I would have gotten away with this."

"Angelica found your advertising on the dark web."

"So I've heard." She sneered. "That was one of the secrets she blabbed when she was kidnapped and drugged. When it comes to computers, she's smart. Not so much when it comes to men. You're still commitment-phobic. Right, Spence?"

"There was never anything between you and me," he said.

"You wanted me." Her eyes flashed with anger. "I was smart enough to get out before it got too serious."

He stood and kicked back the desk chair behind him. "Do you really think you can blow up Dallas and walk away?"

"Sit down," she said.

He'd figured out his attack. If she was good with a knife, and he suspected she was, she could slice Dunne's carotid and still have time to throw the blade at him. He had to strike first, and there was a paperweight on the desk—a pretty glass ball with swirls inside. He'd throw the weight as a distraction, and then go after her.

He eased around the edge of the desk. Gradually, he was coming into range. "Have you gotten any bidders?"

"They're all waiting to see the first strike."

He considered for a moment. Then he played his last card. "You might want to reconsider."

"Why?"

"We've been tracking down your off-line silos and having them deactivated. Your legacy is already spent."

"You couldn't have done them all."

"We found one by Sterling and another near Grand Junction."

She seemed to be distracted. This was his moment. He flung the paperweight and scored a direct hit against her forehead. It wasn't hard enough to knock her out, but she loosened her grip on Dunne and lowered the knife. He jumped at her and knocked her knife hand out of the way. Dunne scrambled to his feet and rushed through the exit from the office.

Sheeran yelled to her cohorts in the hallway. "Stop him."

She hadn't dropped the knife. Flailing wildly, she lashed out and hit him below the left shoulder. The sharpened plastic plunged through flesh and sinew, but his arm still functioned.

He found the paperweight on the floor and used it again. This time, he aimed at her knife hand. With a yelp, she dropped her weapon and dashed out the door, which she locked behind her.

His shoulder should have hurt like hellfire. He was losing a lot of blood. But his adrenaline level was so high that he hardly felt the pain. He kicked at the door, which was, like everything else in the Complex, solid. Thinking there might be a key in the desk drawer, he yanked open the drawers.

No key, but he saw a little .21 caliber handgun in the upper right drawer. It would have been useful to have that earlier. He armed himself. The blood pouring from his wound made the floor slippery and he stumbled. His head whacked against the corner of the desk. His world went dark.

ANGELICA PACED IN the rear of the computer room while Professor Fletcher and Lambert worked to locate the silos and take the missiles off-line. Their work—combined with that of the other FBI researchers—had resulted in five sites being deactivated. Only two were left, barely enough to make the sale profitable, especially if one missile was used for the strike.

It made sense for the hacker to back down and cancel the auction. There was no reason to attack Dallas. Nothing important would be gained or lost. If they could contact the person in charge, they might be able to negotiate.

"I'm so close," Fletch said. "If I had the valid code, I could access the launch sequence and shut down the entire operation."

"What kind of code is it?" she asked. "Numbers? Letters? A binary sequence?"

"Not that complicated," he said. "Six or seven letters or numbers."

She tried to recall all the information she'd scanned and studied, hoping a password would become apparent. "Try Y75110 or Office1116. There was another one. Oh, C4ICBM."

Throwing out those codes indicated a deep level of desperation. She was beginning to lose hope, and she was scared. Spence had disappeared along with the other FBI agents, and an unidentified person had shot Dunne. Spence might be next. Or the killer might be coming for her and Fletch and Bo.

If Spence wasn't injured, she was sure he'd come for her. He'd sworn to protect her. She clenched her jaw. He should have been the one wearing the implanted GPS chip so she could always find him.

Two guards dressed in camo entered the room. "We have information, Agent Thorne."

Her heart plummeted. "Did you find Spence?"

"Not yet. We're still searching."

She pulled them aside, hoping to shield the professor and Lambert. "Tell me."

"Howard Dunne died on the way to the hospital."

Though she hadn't liked Dunne, a stab of remorse hit her in the gut. "Did he have last words?"

The guard nodded. "For the Professor."

From outside the building, she heard an alarm squawking and blaring so loudly that she automatically covered her ears with her hands. A voice on the public-address system told them that this "was not a drill." There were in the midst of a "Level Three threat."

She looked to the guards. "Level Three? What does that mean?"

"Prepare for nuclear attack."

They were too late. The strike was already underway. "What should we do? Is there a safe room?"

"Ma'am, this entire mountain is a safety bunker."

Professor Fletch joined them. He was beaming as he

shouted over the alarm. "I've got it. One of the codes you gave me busted through. C4ICBM is the answer."

"Can you shut down the launch?"

"I think so." He bobbed his head. "You don't look happy. What's gone wrong?"

There was no good way to deliver this news. "I hate to tell you this. Dunne was shot in the stomach. On the way to the hospital, he died."

The guard in camouflage spoke up. "His last words were for the medics to tell Fletch that he loved him."

The old man sank into the chair where he'd been working frantically, and he lowered his head. When she kissed his cheek, she tasted his salty tears.

"I'm sorry," she whispered.

"Go," he said.

"What?"

"I've heard your sigh and seen you pacing. You're worried about Spence. Lambert and I will disable the launch while you go find your man."

She didn't need to be told twice. Grabbing one of the armed guards, she dashed from the building.

SPENCE WOKE TO the sound of an alarm blasting and a voice on the PA system telling them about the threat. Special Agent Jay Ramirez knelt beside him, tugging at his arm.

"Wake up," Ramirez said. "Come on, man, we've got to get out of here."

"Stop pushing me," Spence growled. "We can't leave. Level Three means that Cheyenne Mountain is closed down with the blast doors shut tight. Nobody gets out."

When he tried to stand, the pounding in the back of

his skull was nearly as painful as the shoulder wound. Ramirez handed him a bottle of water.

"Drink it all," he said. "You're probably dehydrated."

"Did you drug me?"

"Hell, yes. Every time I tried to help, you'd take a swing at me. I gave you a sedative, and you're welcome."

"How did we get to this spot?"

"Your fault," he said. "Sheeran locked you in, and it took me a while to get the door open. When I did, you were gone. You'd climbed out of the second floor window. I figured it was a clever way to avoid all the cameras, and I followed."

"Why are you helping me?"

"When I found out what Sheeran was really doing, I had to stop her. I'm not officially undercover, but I kind of am."

"I'll vouch for you."

"I was hoping you'd say that." He urged Spence forward. "We should go to Command Central where they have the big screens. We can watch the fireworks. And you can get somebody to patch up that shoulder."

"What fireworks?"

"You don't think these technology geniuses are going to let Sheeran nuke Dallas, do you? There's got to be a counter strike. When those missiles start flying, I want to watch."

"We have to stop her," Spence said. "Where is she?"

"I'm not sure, but she's going to need an old-fashioned computer system for Tapper to make the launch. Where would she find equipment like that?"

"The computer storage area." He glugged the rest of the water. Adrenaline pulsed through his veins. "Angelica is in that building."

When he stumbled around the corner of the three-story building, he saw empty streets as the alarm continued to split the air. Everyone had a specific job in case of a threat. He needed to be with her. Never should have left her alone. Why didn't he learn after the first abduction? He had to protect her. She was his world, the only woman he ever truly loved.

With Ramirez jogging at his side, Spence headed toward the computer storage building. He held his left arm stiffly, trying to keep from jostling the wound. With his right hand, he felt the .21 caliber handgun that he'd taken from the desk drawer. He hoped he wouldn't have to use it. The military could take care of Sheeran and Tapper.

The door to the computer building flew open, and Angelica came out. She dashed toward him with her arms wide-open, but she didn't grab him when she got close.

"You're hurt."

He truly didn't feel it. "We've got to hide."

"We can't leave the professor in there unguarded."

"Get him." They could all go at the same time.

"Not yet," she said. "He's almost done."

He allowed her to drag him into the computer room on the first floor. A couple of guards in green camo helped him to a chair in the back of the room. He didn't ask to be fussed over but didn't object when they dressed his wound.

The alarm went silent, finally. He shook his head, trying to clear it. Again, it felt like he went unconscious. When he looked up, there was his sweet angel sitting beside him.

The door behind her opened, and Sheeran marched

in. She had her knife in one hand and a gun in the other. "If anybody moves, I start shooting."

One of the guards reached for his weapon and she fired a bullet into his Kevlar vest, knocking him backward.

Her demands were ferocious. "Whatever the hell you're doing in here to shut down my computer, stop it. Now."

"You're too late," Angelica said. "It's over."

Spence could see Sheeran's intention as she lifted her gun. He was quicker. With a flip of his wrist, he drew his weapon and fired twice. He hit her in the arm and in the leg. The .21 wasn't a powerful weapon, but it was enough to stop her.

As soon as she went down, the guards took her into custody. Then, they went upstairs to pick up Special Agent Tapper.

Ramirez was the only man left standing. And he had a hell of a lot of explaining to do.

With the threat ended, Angelica directed Spence down a hallway to a small, quiet office. She made him sit.

"We did it," she said.

"Your first field assignment was a success."

She filled him in on how she and Fletch had broken the codes. He told her about Sheeran and her father's strange legacy.

"Dunne was murdered," she said.

"That poor fool," Spence said with a shake of his head. "He actually was trying to turn his life around. The reason he took the photo of Heller was so he could show it to the professor and have him figure out the danger."

"Dunne didn't want a strike on Dallas?"

"He said he wasn't a monster. And he knew that killing all those people would be wrong. I misjudged him."

They sat quietly for a moment, contemplating what had happened and what might have been.

"I messed a lot of things up on this assignment," he said. "Can I still get a do-over?"

"That depends on what you want to do."

"The first time I told you I loved you, it wasn't very romantic. So I wanted to do this right."

Gently, she wrapped her arms around him. "I love you back."

"You're getting blood all over your clothes," he said.

"I don't care." She kissed his forehead, then his chin. "Tell me again."

"I'll go one better." He took a small velvet box from his pocket and opened the lid. "Marry me, Angelica."

Without hesitation, she accepted.

"Is your dad going to be okay with this?"

"It's not his decision."

"And do you trust me?"

She stared at the diamond glittering on her finger. "Without trust, there can't be love."

He couldn't agree more.

* * * * *

Look for these previous books by USA TODAY
Bestselling Author Cassie Miles:

MOUNTAIN BODYGUARD
MOUNTAIN SHELTER
MOUNTAIN BLIZZARD

Available now from Mills & Boon Intrigue!

MILLS & BOON®

INTRIGUE
Romantic Suspense

A SEDUCTIVE COMBINATION OF DANGER AND DESIRE

A sneak peek at next month's titles...

In stores from 7th September 2017:

- **Rough Rider** – B.J. Daniels *and*
  Pine Lake – Amanda Stevens
- **Point Blank SEAL** – Carol Ericson *and*
  Texas Showdown – Barb Han
- **Mr Serious** – Danica Winters *and*
  Stone Cold Christmas Ranger – Nicole Helm

Romantic Suspense

- **Mission: Colton Justice** – Jennifer Morey
- **The Agent's Covert Affair** – Karen Anders

Just can't wait?
Buy our books online before they hit the shops!
www.millsandboon.co.uk

Also available as eBooks.

MILLS & BOON®

Why shop at millsandboon.co.uk?

Each year, thousands of romance readers
find their perfect read at millsandboon.co.uk.
That's because we're passionate about
bringing you the very best romantic fiction.
Here are some of the advantages of
shopping at www.millsandboon.co.uk:

* **Get new books first**—you'll be able to buy
  your favourite books one month before they
  hit the shops

* **Get exclusive discounts**—you'll also be
  able to buy our specially created monthly
  collections, with up to 50% off the RRP

* **Find your favourite authors**—latest news,
  interviews and new releases for all your
  favourite authors and series on our website,
  plus ideas for what to try next

* **Join in**—once you've bought your favourite
  books, don't forget to register with us to rate,
  review and join in the discussions

Visit **www.millsandboon.co.uk**
for all this and more today!

Join Britain's BIGGEST Romance Book Club

- **EXCLUSIVE offers every month**
- **FREE delivery direct to your door**
- **NEVER MISS a title**
- **EARN Bonus Book points**

Call Customer Services
0844 844 1358*

or visit
millsandboon.co.uk/subscriptions

* This call will cost you 7 pence per minute plus your
phone company's price per minute access charge.